the two of us

Books by Victoria Bylin

Until I Found You

Together With You

Someone Like You

The Two of Us

the two of us

Victoria Bylin

BETHANYHOUSE
a division of Baker Publishing Group
Minneapolis, Minnesota

Published by Bethany House Publishers
11400 Hampshire Avenue South
Bloomington, Minnesota 55438
www.bethanyhouse.com

Bethany House Publishers is a division of
Baker Publishing Group, Grand Rapids, Michigan

Printed in the United States of America

Library of Congress Cataloging-in-Publication Data

Names: Bylin, Victoria, author.
Title: The two of us / Victoria Bylin.
Description: Minneapolis, Minnesota : Bethany House, a division of Baker Publishing Group, [2017]
Identifiers: LCCN 2016059756| ISBN 9780764230431 (hardcover) | ISBN 9780764217388 (softcover)
Subjects: LCSH: Man-woman relationships—Fiction. | Weddings—Fiction. | GSAFD: Christian fiction. | Love stories.
Classification: LCC PS3602.Y56 T96 2017 | DDC 813/.6—dc23
LC record available at https://lccn.loc.gov/2016059756

This is a work of fiction. Names, characters, incidents, and dialogues are products of the author's imagination and are not to be construed as real. Any resemblance to actual events or persons, living or dead, is entirely coincidental.

Cover design by Kathleen Lynch/Black Kat Design

Author is represented by the Steele-Perkins Literary Agency

17 18 19 20 21 22 23 7 6 5 4 3 2 1

To Alan F. Scheibel
A fallen soldier in the war against Alzheimer's disease

And to the army that fought at his side
Dorothy Scheibel
Mike Scheibel
Peggy Scheibel
Patti Scheibel
Kathy Neal

The staff at Homestead Nursing Center

God sets the lonely in families, he leads out the prisoners with singing; but the rebellious live in a sun-scorched land.

—Psalm 68:6

chapter 1

Mia Robinson couldn't take her eyes off the man in a cowboy hat working a claw-machine game, the kind where a child—or a boyfriend or father—put in a dollar and tried to grab a toy in thirty seconds or less.

The machine was about fifteen feet from her in a coffee shop across from the Las Vegas hotel she had checked into late last night. The breakfast crowd was gone and the lunch crowd was just beginning to arrive on a Thursday that promised to swelter in the June heat.

The angle of her booth, a small one for just two people, gave her a clear view of the cowboy's profile. Tall and lean, dressed in Wrangler jeans and a black T-shirt that hugged his biceps, he worked the levers with the skill of a fighter pilot. His long legs ended in worn boots, a tan Stetson crowned his head, and dark scruff lined his jaw. His beard scruff matched the brown of the shaggy hair showing just below the hat. She guessed him to be in his early thirties, confident, and stubborn.

No one ever really grabbed the toy, did they? The thrill was in the chase, the gamble, the chance of beating the odds.

Mia settled back against the brown vinyl booth and stifled a yawn. As tired as she'd been after a full day of work and a late flight, she had tossed and turned while rehearsing what she planned to say to her sister. Technically Mia couldn't stop Lucy from marrying Sam Waters at the Happy Daze Wedding Chapel that afternoon. Lucy was almost nineteen and pregnant, but in Mia's opinion, getting married so young wouldn't solve the problem. It would only add another layer of difficulty.

Fighting another jaw-cracking yawn, she focused back on the man at the claw machine. With his hands loose on the controls, he swung the claw to the right and dropped the metal tongs into the pile of stuffed animals. To her amazement, he lifted out a white duck, swung it to the side, and deposited it in a metal chute. She expected him to take the toy to his table and give it to a child or girlfriend, or maybe just leave with it, but he put more money in the machine and went back to work.

Maybe he had two kids.

Glad for the distraction, she watched him work while she ate her omelet. Without missing a beat, he snagged an elephant, a giraffe, and a turtle. By the time she pushed her plate away, he had won several more toys. Mesmerized, she sipped a third cup of coffee while he liberated a brown hen with a floppy red comb.

Mr. Claw Machine didn't miss a single time. How many hours had he practiced? Probably thousands. Some men never grew up, and apparently he was one of them.

Mia's phone vibrated with a message. Hoping it was Lucy, she rummaged through the gum wrappers and receipts in her sack of a purse until her fingers curled around her phone. When she swiped the screen, instead of Lucy's smiling face, she saw the professional logo for Women's Health Associates, the medical office where she worked as a nurse practitioner.

The text read *Ann B in L&D.*

L&D stood for *Labor and Delivery*, and Ann B—they never used last names because of HIPAA privacy laws—was one of

Mia's patients. Mia didn't deliver babies. Not yet. That fell to Dr. Karen Moore. But Mia was interested in midwifery and had planned to be present for the potentially complicated delivery.

Sighing, she texted back, *Wish I could be there. Am out of town.*

"I will not resent Lucy," Mia murmured as she put the phone back with the gum wrappers. She loved her sister fiercely, and sometimes love required sacrifice. But she had to admit to being disappointed.

Sighing, she glanced at her watch. Three hours until the wedding. Rather than pace in her room, she signaled the waitress for more coffee and settled her eyes on Mr. Claw Machine as he scooped the stuffed animals off the bench.

When he made a clicking sound with his tongue, a big dog with golden fur lumbered to its feet and gave a shake to straighten the red vest it wore, displaying the words *Service Dog*. A row of skulls-and-crossbones lined the hem, but whatever diabolical message the skulls implied was negated by the fact that the bones were shaped like dog biscuits.

Mr. Claw Machine had a sense of humor. Great shoulders too. And arms long enough to cradle an entire menagerie of stuffed animals. When he turned, his light-colored eyes met her gaze across the aisle. She told herself to look away, but the toys in his arms tugged a smile out of her. His mouth formed a smile in return, his lips a soft contrast to the bony contours of his high cheekbones and straight nose, both ruddy from hours in the sun.

Arms bulging with toys, Mr. Claw Machine strode with his dog to the back of the coffee shop. Too curious to be polite, Mia craned her neck and watched as he went from table to table, giving toys to children and chatting with their parents. He didn't allow anyone to pet the dog, but at his command, the dog sat and offered handshakes.

He was headed her way with three toys and two tables between them. At a booth with a mom and a little girl, he gave the child a pink elephant. Next he handed a giraffe to an elderly woman seated with her husband. With one animal left, he looked Mia full in the face.

What she saw stole her breath far more than his good looks. Behind the tan and the laugh lines, his expression betrayed a weariness that made him seem older than she had guessed him to be. She knew that look well. People wore it in the days after major surgery, when they were in pain and muddled with anesthesia, making jokes and insisting they were fine when they weren't fine at all.

Their gazes danced in the way of curious strangers, a man and a woman who noticed each other and felt the mysterious searching of a human heart. Dishes clattered. A child laughed. Another one cried. Life exploded all around them in colors and sounds as ordinary and spectacular as a sunset.

Look away, Mia told herself. She unconsciously covered her bare ring finger. She'd been hurt enough by two broken engagements, one years ago in college and the other recent and still painful to the touch. No way would she risk her heart only to be dumped again.

She had prayed long and hard after the last breakup. Without a husband or children, she was free to go wherever God called her. It was time to make a change, so last week she had applied for a job with Mission Medical, an international aid organization that provided medical care in Third World countries. If she beat out the stiff competition, she'd be based in Dallas but would travel the world, working to set up clinics for women and children. She'd be out of the country for six months at a time, maybe longer.

But what did she do about Lucy and the unplanned pregnancy? Her sweet, head-in-the-clouds sister needed her too.

Mr. Claw Machine approached Mia's table. "Good morning."

"Good morning."

He held out the last stuffed animal. "This one must be for you."

The brown hen. It figured. With her thirtieth birthday on the horizon, Mia felt like a carton of eggs with a best-by date that was still reasonable but a lot closer than the dates on all the other cartons. Anyone who checked the dates left the old carton and picked up a newer one. That was what Brad had done when he dumped her last month for that MRI tech.

She didn't think her life ended at the age of thirty. Far from it. Professionally, she was just getting started. But personally, she was worried. If she wanted to get married and have children, now was the time. Some women had no problem conceiving as late as their mid-forties, but others did. Hormone treatments and IVF worked sometimes, but not always. Working for an OB-GYN, Mia saw the struggle more often than most people, and she was acutely aware of the risks—even a little paranoid, maybe.

The fat hen dangled in front of her face, its stick-on eyes going in two directions, the red comb flopping, and the orange beak as crooked as a beckoning finger. Mia's gaze rose to the man's face. The pain she'd glimpsed earlier was gone now, or at least buried behind a self-deprecating smile.

"Thank you." She took the gift from his hand. "I've always wanted a brown hen."

His brows collided. "Really?"

"No." She laughed. "But this one is charming."

Instead of moving on, he studied her face as if he recognized her. That happened occasionally. Patients came and went in the big hospital where she had worked before joining Women's Health Associates. But Denver was seven hundred miles away, and she was certain she'd never seen this man before. She would have remembered his eyes. They were the color of a grassy meadow on a spring day, fringed with dark lashes, and as piercing as needles pricking skin.

Some people looked away as the needle did its job. Others watched with calm intensity. Mia was a watcher.

So was Mr. Claw Machine, it seemed, until he focused on the dog at his feet. "Pirate."

The dog locked eyes with him.

"Say hi to the lady."

Pirate raised a paw and gave her a slobbery smile.

Mia gripped the dog's paw. "It's nice to meet you, Pirate." The dog looked so intelligent that she half expected him to answer back in full sentences. "I wish I had some bacon for you."

"So does Pirate," the man replied. "But he's working right now."

"I see the vest." Mr. Claw Machine had brought up the dog, so Mia felt comfortable asking questions. "What breed is he?"

"Mostly golden retriever, maybe some shepherd. Strays often make the best hearing dogs."

Her eyes flicked to the side of Mr. Claw Machine's head. Now that she was looking, she could see a small in-ear device. The way he had studied her face earlier took on new significance. He didn't seem to be reading her lips, but she imagined it helped to watch people form words.

Behind him, an elderly woman was coming down the aisle with a walker. Pirate nudged him, and he turned. When he spotted the woman, he started to say good-bye to Mia. At the same moment, a waitress arrived with an armload of plates for the family seated across the aisle. Another family bailed out of the corner booth and crowded the aisle even more.

"Look, Mommy! A dog!"

A little girl charged toward Pirate. Her mom clasped a firm hand on her shoulder, but the woman with the walker kept coming, and the waitress played musical plates with meals for three kids. The aisle was completely blocked.

"Excuse me!" The woman with the walker squeezed closer to the tables. "Excuse me, please!" Judging by the pinched look on her face, she was headed to the bathroom and in a hurry—the kind that led to a person falling.

With nowhere to go, Mr. Claw Machine indicated the empty seat across from Mia. "May I? Just until the crowd clears."

"Of course."

He signaled Pirate to slip under the table. As the dog squeezed against her feet, the man folded his lean body into the booth. It was too small for his long legs and wide shoulders. Too small for all three of them, but especially too small for Pirate, who hit the table with his head, tilted it, and sent the contents of Mia's water glass straight into her lap.

●●●

Jake Tanner hadn't planned to say more than a few words to the woman seated across from him. He certainly hadn't planned to sit down with her. As for the spilled water, that was what happened when Pirate decided it was time to climb into Jake's lap.

It wasn't a casual decision on the dog's part. He'd been trained to be Jake's hearing dog, but their bond went deeper. If Jake seemed nervous or on edge, Pirate stuck to him like glue. Women didn't make Jake nervous in the least, but apparently this one set off that inner twang, because Pirate was poking Jake in the belly with his nose.

While reassuring Pirate with a word and a scratch, Jake looked sheepishly at the woman. "Sorry about that."

"No harm done." She blotted her lap with a napkin. "It's just water, and there wasn't much of it."

"Still—"

"It's no problem at all." Her tone told him she meant it. "I'm a nurse. Water is nothing compared to the stuff I've dealt with."

Jake believed her. Thanks to the bomb blast that ended his career with the Denver Police Department, he had spent more time in hospitals than he cared to remember.

When Nurse Girl tipped her head, the motion reminded him of the sparrows that perched on the deck of his parents' home an hour west of Colorado Springs. Her hair, medium brown with blond highlights, also brought to mind those ordinary birds, which up close weren't ordinary at all.

Her blue eyes were riveted to his, studying him, waiting for him to say something.

Recovering, he asked an easy question. "Where are you from?"

"Denver."

"Small world. I used to live there."

Her eyes lit up. "That's a coincidence. Then again, it's a big city. Did you move from there to here?" She fluttered her hand to indicate Las Vegas.

"No. I still live in Colorado. Echo Falls, to be precise."

"I've heard of it. It's a tourist town, isn't it?"

"Mostly."

"What do you do?" she asked politely.

Three years ago he would have told her he was a police officer. Two years ago he would have said he *used to be* a police officer. Now he skipped the glory days. "My dad owns a vending-machine business. I help him run it."

She stroked the hen perched on the seat next to her. "That explains why you're so good at the claw machine. You've been practicing."

"All my life. My dad has a barn full of old games."

Hotels and bowling alleys no longer wanted Pac-Man, Donkey Kong, and old-style pinball, but they were perfect for the camp Jake wanted to start for kids who had lost a parent in the line of duty. Kids like Sam Waters, the son of Jake's partner, Connie Waters, who had been killed in the bomb blast that left Jake partially deaf. Starting the camp meant everything to him. Unfortunately, a local opposition group called Stop the Camp, or STC for short, was battling tooth and nail to stop him.

Pirate pressed against Jake's knee. The aisle was clear now, and if he was going to get a haircut before the wedding, he needed to leave. He wouldn't have chosen a hasty marriage for Sam or any young couple, but he was certain that under the circumstances, Connie would have supported her son's decision to take responsibility and marry Lucy Robinson.

Taking responsibility was Connie's strength, and Jake had admired her for it, though the commitment she demanded from *him* would haunt him forever. Lying prone with her head in a puddle of blood, smoke thick in the ringing silence, she had mouthed, *Help Sam*.

Deafened by the explosion, Jake had spoken a reply he couldn't hear. *I will, Connie. I promise.*

She had died minutes later, and Jake and Sam had become a family born of that promise. Sam, eighteen at the time, had returned to college and his ROTC scholarship. Without other family, he called and texted Jake a lot. They were brothers, friends, and a little bit father and son.

Nurse Girl didn't seem to be in a hurry, so Jake risked a question. "What brings you to Vegas?"

"A wedding."

"Me too." Not surprising. Weddings were a dime a dozen in Las Vegas.

"Weddings aren't my favorite thing." She placed her napkin on the table, revealing her bare ring finger as she let out a sigh. "I especially don't like weddings that are spur-of-the-moment. The one I'm going to today . . ." She shook her head. "I'm worried sick."

"Why?"

"My sister's a little crazy."

"Or in love."

"Or both." Her mouth settled into a worried line. "She's a wonderful person, but I'm afraid she's being impulsive. She has a tendency to act first and think later."

"What about the guy?"

"I haven't met him, but so far I'm not impressed. A quickie Vegas wedding isn't the way to start a life together."

Jake thought of last night's dinner with Sam and Lucy. Sam was only twenty-one, but he'd grown up fast when his mother died, and his faith had grown too. Jake was determined to support the young couple a thousand percent. Too bad Nurse Girl didn't have that same peace of mind.

"Maybe it'll work out," he said.

"I hope so."

He heard what she didn't say. "But?"

"But I doubt it." She rolled her eyes in a cute way that seemed to make fun of herself. "Sorry for the gloom and doom. I'm not usually a pessimist."

Neither was Jake. "You're worried."

"Yes." Nurse Girl sipped her coffee. When she looked at him, her blue eyes were calm again. "Who's getting married in your life?"

"A friend." That was the easiest way to explain his relationship with Sam. "I'm the best man. It's a happy day for them."

"I wish them all the best." Envy whispered in her voice, but he didn't hear even a trace of bitterness. She glanced at her watch, a practical style she probably wore on the job. "I need to leave."

"Me too." Jake rubbed his jaw. The ceremony wasn't for two hours, but he wanted a haircut and a straight-razor shave, like a slick detective in an old Hollywood movie. Las Vegas brought out his inner Robert De Niro, the part of him that enjoyed gangster movies like *Casino* and *Heat*. The good guys won, but at a tremendous cost.

At his urging, Pirate wiggled out from under the table. Nurse Girl left a generous tip, picked up the check, and tucked the brown hen under her arm.

They paused in the aisle, standing face-to-face with Jake looking down and Nurse Girl looking up. Her head would have fit nicely against his shoulder. She was pretty in an outdoorsy way with a trim figure, tanned skin, and that sun-streaked hair, but what most stood out to Jake were her eyes. They were the color of the pool at the base of Echo Falls, and they invited a person to dive right in.

They walked together to the register. She paid, and they left through the double doors.

"Thanks for the hen," she said.

"My pleasure."

He tipped his hat, and they went their separate ways. Ten paces later, Jake turned and looked back. So did Nurse Girl. The desert sun blazed straight above, rendering her almost shadowless on the white concrete. She seemed terribly alone in the harsh light. And definitely flustered to be caught looking back at him.

"Tomorrow," he called to her, raising his voice over the traffic noise. "Pirate and I will be here for breakfast at eight o'clock. Why don't you join us?"

He approached her, reaching into his shirt pocket as he walked. When he reached her, he handed her two business cards. One for Tanner Vending with his name on it, and the second from Love-A-Dog Rescue. The dog rescue was his mom's mission in life.

"My name is Jake Tanner."

Nurse Girl read both cards, smiled at the cartoon on the dog rescue card, but didn't say yes or no to breakfast. Neither did she give him her name. Smart woman. What happened in

Vegas stayed in Vegas, unless a story about a missing woman ended up on CNN.

When she peered at him with those jump-in-the-water eyes, he saw the smoke and flames of a battle he knew well. To leap or retreat? To plunge ahead with the courage of a soldier, or to hold back with the wisdom of a judge?

"It's your choice," he said, meaning it. "Either way, it's been a pleasure."

"For me too." A smile tugged at her lips, but she didn't say anything else.

Jake replied with a dip of his chin, then turned and headed for the barbershop. At the entrance, he ran his hand along his bristled jaw, anticipating a close shave and maybe breakfast with Nurse Girl. His heart gave a strong beat of anticipation—something he hadn't felt in a while—and it wasn't because of the shave.

chapter 2

Meet a stranger for breakfast? No way. But as Mia rode the mirrored elevator to her room on the fourteenth floor of the Las Palmas Hotel, she hugged the stuffed hen to her chest. Someone like Lucy might have thrown caution to the wind and enjoyed a flirtation, but Mia was far more reserved.

Even so, she was tempted. Mr. Claw Machine had impressed her with his stuffed animals, easy manner, and good looks, but there was no point in starting a relationship doomed to end. Her first interview with Mission Medical was scheduled for Monday afternoon via Skype. With a little luck, she'd make it through the lengthy interview process, move to Dallas in January, and travel overseas soon after that.

But what did she do about Lucy and her newborn baby? *Impulsive* described Lucy to a *T*. But so did words like *fun*, *generous*, and *caring*. Feed a stray cat? Of course. Bring it inside their crackerbox apartment? Definitely. Oh, it has fleas. Oops.

Oops should have been Lucy's middle name.

With a nostalgic smile on her lips, Mia set her purse and the hen on a small table in the corner of her room. She loved Lucy with her whole heart. Maybe too much, because she couldn't imagine joining Mission Medical and leaving Lucy alone to cope with the demands of an infant. As for Sam Waters, Mia wasn't impressed. Birth control, anyone?

But who was Mia to judge? She said no to sex before marriage for herself, but she'd be the first to admit to being tempted, especially when Brad had teased her about being as old-fashioned as a black-and-white television.

Her phone rang with the tone assigned to Lucy. They were in the same hotel, but Mia didn't know Lucy's room number. Hoping to see her sister before the misguided ceremony, she snatched the device to her ear. "Lucy! How are you?"

"I'm wonderful! Can you believe it, Mia? I'm getting married. It doesn't seem real."

"It's a big decision. I'd really like to talk before—"

"No."

"But—"

"I said no."

"Lucy, I—"

"Mia, don't. You're not like me at all. You're like your dad. Mom used to say that."

"I remember."

"And I'm like *her*." Defiance shot across the phone. "I miss her, Mia. Especially today."

Mia squeezed her eyes shut. Cancer. Years of it. Just the three of them, because Mia's father, a soldier, died in a car accident when she was nine, and Lucy's father, a man their mother never married, had slipped out of their lives before Lucy was born.

"I miss her too," Mia murmured.

Lucy's voice wobbled over the phone. "Promise me something, okay?"

"What is it?"

"That you won't ruin today. Please?"

"Of course I won't. But—"

"See? That's what I mean."

Mia pinched the bridge of her nose. "I'm sorry, Lucy. Really, I am. It's just that I worry about you."

"I know you do, but I wish you'd stop. I love you, Mia. We're sisters forever. I want you at the wedding, but I don't want to argue, okay?"

Neither did Mia, but how did she hold back when every fiber of her being believed Lucy was about to make a truly serious mistake?

With her throat aching, Mia stared at the stuffed hen roosting on the table, its eyes going in two directions. *Why did the chicken cross the road?* It wasn't just to get to the other side. The hen was going back to rescue her chicks. For better or worse, Lucy was Mia's chick. From the moment their mother placed baby Lucy in Mia's arms, Mia had felt a bone-deep responsibility for her tiny, wailing, helpless little sister.

With razor clarity, last Tuesday's phone call played through her mind.

"Mia, I'm pregnant." Lucy had taken a breath. "Sam and I are getting married on Thursday."

"Oh, Lucy. No."

"Yes. In Las Vegas. I know how disappointed you are, but there's more. I'm quitting school."

Disappointment hadn't begun to describe the churning in Mia's gut. How could Lucy throw away an education and the security of a solid career? Her grades weren't the best, but she had survived her freshman year and made friends. She had also met Sam Waters, fallen in love, and melted into a puddle of hormones.

Mia was all for melting. She'd done some melting herself and knew the joy of being in love. It was the puddle part that upset her. Whether it was a puddle of hormones or a puddle of tears, Mia mopped up the mess.

That phone call had ended with Mia quizzing Lucy about

the pregnancy, learning she was eight weeks along, and biting her tongue as she wrote down the name of a Las Vegas hotel and the address of a wedding chapel. Mia had cancelled her patients for Thursday and Friday, booked a flight to Las Vegas, and begged God to stop Lucy from ruining her life.

Now here they were. Sisters as different as granite and wind. One secure and steady, the other as unpredictable as a butterfly. One plain and practical, the other so beautiful she turned heads everywhere she went.

Lucy breathed into the phone. "Mia?"

"Yes?"

"Be happy for me, okay?"

"I am." A white lie, but only someone truly wicked would tarnish her sister's wedding day. "As your maid of honor, I should be with you. Do you want help getting dressed?"

"No. I can manage." Lucy described the little white dress she'd bought at Walmart. "It's beautiful and perfect. I love it."

Mia wasn't ready to let her baby sister go. "Did you invite any friends?"

"No. Just Sam's best man."

No doubt a fellow ROTC student, probably a skinny kid with a crew cut and gangly arms. Maybe acne. Good grief, Mia felt old today. And alone. Why did turning thirty bother her so much, especially when her birthday was still two months away?

She hooked a strand of hair behind her ear. "Just one more question. How are you feeling? Has the morning sickness kicked in yet?"

"Ugh. Big time."

"Try sour things." Mia made a mental note to buy Lucy some Lemonhead candies. She'd heard from a patient that they worked wonders.

"I will."

"And Lucy?"

"Yes?"

"I really do want what's best for you." With that final declaration, Mia uttered a soft good-bye, ended the call, and plugged in her phone. Keeping her smartphone charged was one of her obsessions, along with being on time and flossing her teeth.

Just as she set her phone on the table, it vibrated to signal a text. When she swiped the screen, she saw what used to be her favorite picture in the world. *Brad* . . . She needed to delete him from her phone, or at least change the photo of him to one that didn't open old wounds. Swallowing hard, she read the text.

Would like to meet for coffee tomorrow. Have some news. Don't want you to hear it through the rumor mill.

"Oh no," she mumbled. "Really, Brad? So soon?"

She knew what was coming. He'd been dating that MRI tech for three months now, and she'd seen them huddled together at the Starbucks close to the medical building where they all worked.

She texted back. *Can't. Am in Las Vegas.* Maybe he'd think she was having fun, something he'd told her she wasn't very good at.

He texted back just one word. *Oh.*

One confusing word. That was all. She didn't like his staccato texts, but that was how Brad sent messages. Once the conversation started, he typed a few words at a time and hit send, over and over.

He texted back. *Can't call right now.*

Mia sighed. "I didn't ask you to."

Talk tonight?

"Why?" she said to his picture. "What's the point?" She texted back. *Just tell me now. I think I know.*

She expected a quick reply, but the wait stretched into a full minute. Finally a word bubble popped onto the screen.

You're an amazing woman, Mia. Things didn't work out for

us, but you'll always be someone I admire. You know Nikki. She and I are officially engaged. I didn't mean to do this by text. Sorry.

Mia wasn't angry with Brad about the breakup. He'd been honest with her, even gentle, which somehow made everything worse. He'd stopped loving her but couldn't say why, leaving her to wonder where she had failed. Was it her personality? Or maybe he'd lost interest because she wouldn't sleep with him before the wedding. Mia valued her purity, but sometimes, like when Brad walked away, she wondered what she was missing and if she really was too rigid, like he said.

A dull ache ballooned against her lungs, stealing her breath as she texted back. *Be happy. I mean it.*

"That's it." She tapped the screen, pulled up Brad's contact info, and changed the photograph to a faceless icon.

The A/C groaned and throbbed in her ears. The lifeless television pitied her from its place on the wall. And the stuffed hen stared at her with its crossed eyes.

"Pathetic," Mia muttered to the hen. "That's what I am. Pathetic."

She hated that feeling. *Hated it.* She didn't have time for self-pity. She was a woman of action, right? She was brave. Stalwart. She had earned a Bachelor of Science in Nursing and a master's degree, and she had raised Lucy at the same time.

Mia was strong and steady. But she also tired of being a boulder and wanted, maybe, for just one morning, to be a butterfly. Before she could talk herself out of what she was about to do, she snapped a picture of the hen and texted it to Jake Tanner.

See you at breakfast. My name is Mia.

●●●

Dressed in his black suit pants and starched white shirt, Jake made the first loop of a Windsor knot in his burgundy tie. He was almost finished when Pirate nudged him in the thigh. When Jake looked down, the dog trotted back to the nightstand, where Jake's phone flashed with a message or call. He would have heard it, but he'd forgotten to reset the volume after leaving the coffee shop.

"Thanks, partner. I'll get it in a minute."

Pirate sat by the nightstand, his plume of a tail thumping as Jake cinched the knot against his Adam's apple. The call was probably from Sam, maybe to remind him to bring the wedding rings. Nervous but confident, Sam had left the room he was sharing with Jake ten minutes ago to pick up Lucy and drive to the wedding chapel. Jake would join them there, and so would Lucy's older sister, a woman Sam hadn't yet met.

Pirate waited by the phone until Jake lifted it and saw his mother's caller ID. The picture of Claire Tanner, taken before her Alzheimer's diagnosis, yanked his heart out of his chest. She was in stage four now, approaching stage five—still herself but not always.

Jake would have done anything to save her this grief, but Alzheimer's disease was unstoppable. All he could do was support her, love her, and back up his dad in her daily care, a task that exhausted them both. Jake's younger sister and older brother both lived out of state and had families and busy lives. They called often, but there was nothing they could do to help right now except pray.

Had Claire meant to call, or was this one of her famous "moops" dials? *Moops* stood for *Mom* and *oops*. Even before the Alzheimer's diagnosis, she'd been clumsy with her phone, though the joke no longer struck Jake as funny.

Steeling himself for a conversation that would be confusing at best, he called her back. After four rings, the call went to voice mail. Knowing she couldn't remember how to retrieve a message, Jake hung up and called his dad.

Frank Tanner picked up immediately. "I thought you were in Vegas."

"I am." He told his dad about the missed call from his mom. "I'm just checking to be sure she's all right."

"Crud."

"What?"

"I'm in the Springs. We were a day late on restocking the machines at the Mountain View." A five-star hotel and a big account for Tanner Vending.

Jake usually handled the restocking, but between Sam's wedding and a meeting with an attorney about establishing nonprofit status for the camp, he'd let the vending machines slide. "Is Mom home alone?"

"She's at Barb's house." Her best friend and another retired teacher.

"She's probably fine," Jake said, "but I'd like to be sure."

"Me too. I'll call Barb."

"Let me know, okay?" With Alzheimer's, some days were better than others, but in Jake's opinion, they were at the point where his mother couldn't safely be left alone. He started to pace. "We need help, Dad."

"I know, son. But who?" Frank heaved a soul-deep sigh. "There's no one in Echo Falls. And besides, your mom won't like it."

"Sometimes there's no choice."

"I'd like to hold out until an apartment opens up at Westridge."

Westridge Acres was a multi-tiered senior living community with a special memory neighborhood. Frank and Claire were on the waiting list for an apartment. The plan was to move while Claire had some small capacity to adapt, and for Jake to turn the house and ranch into a summer camp. Unfortunately the waiting list for Westridge was a mile long.

So far Jake and his dad had managed to meet Claire's needs, but it was only a matter of time before her needs outpaced their ability to care for her. They needed help, but Jake decided not to push the issue over the phone. "Shoot me a text when you find her, okay?"

"Sure thing." Frank ended the call.

Still holding the phone, Jake dropped down onto the bed opposite the one where Pirate was taking a nap. He couldn't imagine his life without his dog. They had met when Jake went home to Echo Falls to recover from his injuries. Pirate, one of his mother's rescue dogs, had taken to Jake immediately, and Jake's audiologist had suggested training him to be a hearing dog.

They were a perfect match. When Pirate wasn't working, he was an ordinary dog and Jake's best friend. He was also a glutton for treats and clumsy, like when he knocked water in Nurse Girl's lap.

Jake's phone vibrated in his hand. Pirate jumped off the bed but sat when Jake signaled him to stay. Expecting good news from his dad, he opened the text and came face-to-face with the goofy hen he'd given to Nurse Girl. Below were the words, *See you at breakfast. My name is Mia.*

"Well, what do you know?" Jake ruffled his dog's fur, smiling at the pleasant surprise. "Breakfast is on."

Pirate tilted his head, listening to Jake's tone even if he didn't understand the words.

Jake envied him. Pirate was in his prime, undamaged, and content to take life a moment at a time. When he sensed danger, it was real, and when he didn't, he slept like a log.

Unlike his dog, Jake slept lightly, worried, and lived with hearing loss. He was also alive, set on starting the camp to honor Connie Waters, and determined to be the best son he could be. Jake had a lot to live for—and a lot to give. He just wished he didn't feel so dead inside. Since the blast, his emotions had been flattened, a word used by the department psychologist who had guided him through his recovery.

His gaze went back to the hen on his phone. "Mia," he said out loud. "Pretty name."

Pirate, his tongue lolling, cocked his head as if he were asking Jake what he planned to do next.

That was easy. Jake liked everything he knew about Mia. Granted, it wasn't much, but she'd sparked his interest enough to inspire that impromptu breakfast invitation.

He replied to her text, finished dressing, and put the service vest on Pirate. After pocketing the wedding rings, his wallet, and his phone, he headed to the hotel parking lot, where he'd left his crew cab truck.

With Pirate in the back seat, Jake drove to the Happy Daze Wedding Chapel, parked in the back lot, and walked around to the front. In the midst of the Las Vegas glitz, the white clapboard chapel exuded a naïve charm. The interior was just as old-fashioned, even rustic, with water splashing over a fake rock waterfall. There wasn't a gift shop, slot machine, or Elvis impersonator in sight.

"Jake!"

Turning, he saw Sam striding toward him. Nerves were to be expected, but Sam was as white as a wedding dress.

Jake's brows snapped together. "What's up?"

"It's Lucy." Sam didn't speak again until he reached Jake's side, and then he spoke barely loudly enough for Jake to hear. "She's spotting."

Jake wasn't sure he'd heard right. "Spotting?"

"Yes. Bleeding." Sam dragged his coat sleeve over his brow. "You know what that means, right?"

"Of course." A possible miscarriage. Jake felt sick for both Sam and Lucy. "How bad is it?"

"It's not much," Sam said, "but she's scared, and she wants

to talk to her sister. She's a nurse, and she knows about this stuff. I'm going back to be with Lucy. Would you wait here and tell Mia we're in the bride's room?"

"*Mia?*" Jake had heard the name as plain as day. He just couldn't believe it.

"Mia," Sam repeated with a little more volume. "Lucy says she's average height and has brown hair."

And blue eyes the color of a mountain lake in the sun. Considering her reaction to today's wedding, Jake's different opinion, and especially tomorrow's date for breakfast, their next meeting promised to be anything but dull.

chapter 3

Mia climbed out of the taxi, paid the driver, and paused to take in the Happy Daze Wedding Chapel. The wooden building looked like it had been lifted off the set of *Little House on the Prairie* and dropped in Las Vegas by a Kansas tornado. When "Somewhere Over the Rainbow" floated into her mind, she wondered who was crazier—Lucy for going through with a hasty marriage, or Mia for finding the chapel sweetly romantic.

She'd read about Happy Daze and been surprised to see how many old-time Hollywood stars had eloped here. The stories were charming, but the passion and excitement made her head spin. Spontaneity? Not her style, something Brad had criticized. *You overplan everything, Mia*. Quite a comment, coming from a man whose kitchen was as neat as a surgical tray.

But tomorrow would be different. She was having breakfast with a handsome stranger who had passed the Google test. Love-A-Dog Rescue really existed, and so did Tanner Vending. Jake Tanner had a Facebook account, but it was set to private, just like her own.

Right on time, Mia walked through the chapel door. Unsure of where to go, she glanced at the empty reception desk.

"Mia?"

The familiar voice shocked her. She had heard it two hours ago, though with less urgency. Turning, she saw Pirate, but the man in a black suit didn't look at all like Jake Tanner. The beard scruff had been scraped away to reveal a strong jaw, well-shaped lips, and a faint scar on his left cheek. His dark hair was shorter now, buzzed up the sides but longer on top, cut with military precision.

No cowboy hat. No snug black T-shirt. No armload of stuffed animals. But this man was undoubtedly Jake Tanner.

Mia's jaw dropped.

His didn't. Without a trace of surprise, he approached with Pirate trotting at his side. "Small world, huh?"

"Yes, but—"

"Lucy's having a problem. Sam asked me to meet you."

The puzzle pieces snapped together with disturbing clarity. Jake was Sam's best man. He and Mia were here for same wedding, and they disagreed rather strongly about the wisdom of it. But this wasn't the time to debate. The grim look on his face shoved everything except Lucy to the back of Mia's mind. "What's wrong?"

"She's spotting."

Mia winced. A few drops of blood could mean nothing. Or they could mean everything. The ramifications of such a loss slapped her in the face. If Lucy lost the baby, there would be no need to rush into marriage, but her sister's heart would shatter into a thousand pieces.

Swallowing a lump, Mia peered into Jake's eyes. "Where is she?"

"In the bridal room." He motioned her toward a wide hallway with an arched ceiling. It led to a rectangular waiting area with two sofas, the entrance to the chapel, and another hall with a flowery sign that said *Brides Only.*

Jake stopped in the lobby, leaving Mia to take the last ten

steps to the bridal room alone. Her purse, heavy on her shoulder, held everything from Kleenex to a Swiss Army knife. She could fix almost anything with the contents of her purse, but she couldn't stop nature from taking its course.

She tapped on the door and cracked it open. "Lucy?"

"Mia! Come in."

The lush green carpet muting her steps, Mia stepped into a square room with mirrors on three walls. Lucy, wearing the little white dress from Walmart, was lying on a pink satin couch with her head in Sam's lap, her knees bent, and her face stained with tears. Her blue eyes looked at Mia through her ruined makeup, but what hit Mia hardest was their mother's floating heart necklace dangling from Lucy's neck. For a blink, Mia forgot everything except the sweet little girl who brought home a bird with a broken wing because she thought her big sister could fix it.

Mia hurried to Lucy's side and reached for her hand. "Oh, honey, I'm so sorry you're going through this."

"I'm so scared." Lucy's voice came out in a whisper.

Sam started to ease Lucy's head out of his lap so he could stand, but Mia shook her head. "Please. Don't get up." She offered her hand. "I'm Mia."

"Sam Waters." He looked her square in the eye. "I love your sister, Mia. We want this baby."

Lucy sniffed back a fresh flood of tears. "We do."

"Of course you do." But wanting a baby and caring for one were two different things. Lucy was practically a child herself. As for Sam, Mia was both impressed by his demeanor and irked by the circumstances. But that conversation needed to wait, so she pushed it out of her mind and perched on the couch next to Lucy. "Let's start with some facts. Bleeding is fairly common in the first few months of a pregnancy. How heavy is it?"

Lucy described the bleeding as light and pinkish, not dark and red.

"That's good. Any cramps?"

"Some." A whimper squeaked from Lucy's throat. "What if they get worse? What if—"

Sam snatched his phone out of his coat. "We can't take chances. I'm calling 911."

"Sam, no!" Lucy almost laughed. "Mia knows about these things."

"I do," Mia assured him. "And we have to be realistic. If Lucy is miscarrying, there's nothing anyone can do."

Anguish burned in his dark eyes. Any doubts Mia had about Sam's commitment, even the secret belief he'd be relieved by a miscarriage, disappeared when he let out a shuddering breath. "So what do we do?"

Hoping to offset their fear, Mia kept her voice light as she stood. "How about a trip to the ER for an ultrasound?"

Sam jumped on the idea. "That sounds good."

Lucy swung her legs to the side and sat up straight, inhaling to steady herself against the emotions crashing on her face. Sam stood and held out his hand. Staring into his eyes, Lucy squeezed his fingers so hard her knuckles turned white. "We're not getting married today, are we?"

Sam dropped back down and held her tight. "Not today, Pudge. But we're still getting married. I promise."

Pudge? Mia's lips twitched. Only a woman in love would grin at that nickname, and Lucy was smiling through her tears.

"I won't be pudgy if I lose the baby."

"But you'll still be Lucy." Sam cupped her chin and kissed her. "That's more than enough for me."

Mia pivoted to avoid seeing Lucy cradled in Sam's arms, but the mirrored walls captured the kiss and reflected it all around the room. Her breath locked in her chest, leaving her starved for air like an asthma patient. Brad had never looked at her that way, nor had her ex-fiancé in college or the youth pastor she dated while working on her master's degree.

By the same measure, Mia hadn't looked at *them* the way Lucy looked at Sam. She was drowning in him, soaking in the strength of his embrace, and holding him so tight her arms quivered.

Maybe Mia hadn't loved Brad after all. Maybe that was why he'd found her lacking. Or maybe she was too rigid, like he said. Too quick to follow rules that begged to be broken, especially when she was almost thirty and as old-fashioned as that black-and-white television.

Get a grip. This wasn't the time to think about herself. But as she headed for the door, she thought of Jake Tanner waiting outside the room. Something had sparked between them, something strong enough to make her send that impulsive text. But they were no longer strangers flirting over coffee. That kind of behavior wasn't like her at all, and she needed to be sure Jake Tanner knew it.

Pasting on the calm expression she had practiced in nursing school, Mia went to speak with him.

●●●

When the door to the bridal room opened, Jake shot to his feet. With Pirate poised at his side, he tried to gauge Mia's expression as she walked toward him. He couldn't read her at all.

"How's Lucy?" he asked.

"Scared. So is Sam." She pulled her phone out of her giant purse. "The spotting is light, but we should still get an ultrasound. I need to find an ER."

"Here." Jake held up his phone to show a hospital four miles away. He'd Googled it while waiting for them. He'd also received a text from his dad saying his mother was fine and that he'd call Jake later.

Mia's brows lifted with surprise. "Thank you. That's perfect."

"Just common sense." Being a cop, even an ex-cop, paid off in the experience department.

The door opened again, and Sam and Lucy walked out arm in arm. The poor girl looked awful, especially compared to the way she had glowed at dinner last night when Jake first met her. He had taken the couple to a steakhouse to celebrate and discovered that Lucy was sweet, funny, and not a fan of bloody steaks. She was perfect for Sam, who tended to be formal and reserved.

Lucy already felt like a kid sister, so Jake tapped her on the arm. "How're you doing?"

"We'll see." She tried to smile. "It's all so—oh no." Every speck of color drained from her face. Swaying, she leaned hard against Sam.

Sam, almost as ashen as Lucy, tightened his arm around her waist. "Pudge! What's wrong?"

"I'm . . . I'm lightheaded."

Sam and Jake both snatched up their phones to call 911, but Mia told them to wait. Jake lowered his hand. Sam didn't.

Mia studied Lucy with a professional eye. "Any pain?"

"No."

"Did you eat breakfast this morning?"

"No. I was too sick."

"How about lunch?"

"No." Lucy's voice quavered. "I . . . I forgot."

"Oh, honey." Mia dug in her purse again. This time she produced a box of Tropicana orange juice and a bag of rainbow Goldfish crackers. "You know you get hypoglycemic if you don't eat."

Lucy winced. "You're right. I know."

"Hypo-what?" Sam asked.

"Glycemic," Mia explained. "Low blood sugar. It runs in the family. If we don't eat right, we get the wobbles."

Sam snatched the juice box from Mia, stabbed the straw into place, and wedged the box into Lucy's hand. "Drink it. Now."

While she chugged the juice, Mia opened the crackers. Lucy ate a few, but she was still as white as her dress.

Jake watched, tense and ready to do something—anything—to help. Standing around didn't suit him at all.

Apparently it didn't suit Sam either, because he placed one arm behind Lucy's knees, the other around her shoulders, and swept her off her feet. "I'm carrying you to the car."

"I'm too heavy!"

"You're as light as a feather." He grinned at his own lie, took three steps, then turned back to Jake, his face tight with confusion. Sam rarely acted without a battle plan. His hesitation now showed how upset he was.

"The hospital," he asked. "Where is it?"

"Four miles from here," Jake replied. "It's called Desert Central. I texted you the link."

"Thanks, Jake. You're the best."

He shook his head, silently denying the praise. "Go. We'll meet you there."

"One more thing," Sam said. "Would you tell Mrs. Carson what's going on? She's the chapel wedding coordinator."

"Sure thing," Jake replied.

Sam strode down the hall to the back entrance, leaving Jake with Mia at his side, the wedding bands in his pocket, and the weight of questions only God could answer—and would answer in His own good time.

Mia let out a slow breath. "So no wedding today."

"No." Jake knew how she felt about the subject, but he saw only worry on her face. "Let's wrap things up with Mrs. Carson, then I'll drive you to the hospital."

"Thanks. I took a cab here."

"I saw."

"Oh, that's right." She paused. "This is awkward, isn't it?"

Not to Jake. "We might have different opinions about Sam and Lucy, but we both want what's best for them."

"Yes, we do." She clutched her bulky purse to her side. "But I was talking about breakfast tomorrow. I'm a little embarrassed about sending that picture."

"Don't be."

"But—"

Pirate nudged Jake's knee. He turned and saw a trim, middle-aged woman in a business suit and a frilly blouse. A name tag identified her as Mrs. Carson, Chapel Director.

Her eyes darted between Jake and Mia. "Are you here for the Robinson-Waters wedding?"

"Yes," Mia replied, "but Lucy's having a health issue. They're on their way to the ER and have to cancel today's ceremony."

Mrs. Carson touched a hand to her frilly blouse. "I am so sorry."

"Thank you." Mia paused. "We're leaving for the hospital now. Is there anything we need to take care of? Any expenses?"

"Nothing," she said. "Mr. Waters paid in full. I wish I could offer a refund, but—"

Jake broke in. "We don't expect one."

He ran a business and knew the drill, though he toyed with the idea of paying the bill himself. It was what Connie would have done, but Sam had a lot of pride. He and Jake butted heads all the time about picking up restaurant tabs. He wouldn't appreciate the interference.

Mia reached in her purse and pulled out her wallet. "Sam and Lucy have enough to worry about. I'd like to pay for today. Could you transfer the cost to my Visa?"

Jake winced on Sam's behalf.

Mrs. Carson shook her head. "I can't do that without Mr. Waters's permission, but come with me. I have something for Lucy."

With Pirate at his side, Jake walked a step behind Mia and Mrs. Carson to the gift shop, where Mrs. Carson retrieved a pretty bridal bouquet from a refrigerated display case. She handed it to Mia with the reverence due a bride. "Take these to Lucy."

Mia took the flowers in both hands, raised them to her nose, and sniffed. When her eyelids drifted shut, Jake wondered what—or who—she was seeing. Her eyes opened again, revealing those blue depths that reminded him of sky and water.

Her mouth formed a tight smile, the kind that came with effort rather than enthusiasm. "The flowers are gorgeous. I'm sure Lucy will enjoy them."

Jake hoped so. No matter what happened today, the young couple had decisions to make. Being in love wasn't always easy, and looking at Mia's misty expression now, she no doubt agreed with him.

●●●

Mia held the bouquet at her waist with both hands, her fingers tight on the wrapped stems as she walked with Jake and Pirate to the back exit. Pictures of her own canceled wedding flashed in her mind, but there was no other way to comfortably hold the arrangement of roses, orchids, and delicately scented freesia.

With each step the flowers weighed a little more, especially when she and Jake exited into the heat smothering the asphalt parking lot. The sun beat down on her head, stole her breath, and turned her arms into noodles. When they arrived at his truck, a dark blue pickup with a crew cab, he lifted the blooms with one hand, his fingers brushing hers.

"I'll put this in the back." He opened the door, set the flowers on a shady part of the seat, and signaled Pirate to hop in. Next he offered Mia a hand up to the passenger seat. Hampered by high-heeled sandals, she gratefully gripped his fingers and climbed inside.

Behind her, Pirate panted like a steam engine. The dog needed water. She reached into her purse for the bottle she always carried and rummaged for the plastic sandwich container from yesterday's lunch at work.

She was about to open the bottle when Jake slid into the driver's seat. His gaze slid to the pink sandwich holder, then to her face. His brow quirked with a question, but instead of asking what she was doing, he turned on the truck and the A/C, then opened the center console and took out a collapsible rubber bowl and a quart-size bottle of water that put her pint-size bottle to shame.

"Excuse me a minute," he said. "Pirate needs a drink."

"I was thinking the same thing."

"He'll just be a minute." Twisting around to the back seat, Jake set the bowl on the floor mat opposite the flowers. "There you go, partner."

While Pirate lapped the water, Jake glanced again at Mia's sandwich holder. "You're prepared for anything."

"I try."

"So do I."

"But life happens, doesn't it?" She glanced at the clock on the dash. "One minute things are normal, and the next"—she gave a helpless shrug—"they're not."

Jake reached for Pirate's bowl and dumped the dregs in the parking lot, saying nothing. Had he heard her? She wasn't sure and decided not to press when he put on a pair of Ray-Bans and steered out onto the busy street. Mia didn't mind silence. As long as Jake was comfortable with it, so was she.

But then he surprised her by clearing his throat. "This isn't the day Sam and Lucy planned, is it?"

"No. Then again, they didn't really *plan* anything."

"You mean the baby."

"Exactly."

When he didn't reply, Mia assumed he agreed with her. "I hope the baby's okay, but delaying the wedding isn't a bad thing. It'll give them time to think about what they're doing."

"True."

"I hate to see Lucy drop out of school."

Jake nudged the sunglasses higher on his nose. "Maybe she'll go back to college later."

"I doubt it."

"You never know."

"I suppose it's possible, but I know my sister. Lucy doesn't like school."

"It's not for everyone."

"No. But we all have bills to pay." Mia didn't mean to sound bitter, but she knew what it was like to count quarters and dimes to buy groceries. "What if this marriage doesn't last? How will she support herself?"

Jake gave her a sidewise glance. "I say we give them a chance. Sam's a good kid. He loves her."

Love. Mia wanted to believe it was enough, but couldn't. Love didn't pay the rent or buy diapers. It didn't save a mother from cancer or a father from dying in a car accident.

She pushed those thoughts out of her mind until Jake turned onto a street lined with apartment buildings sporting cracked stucco and burglar bars. It was the kind of neighborhood Mia had grown up in. She'd never told anyone, but her mother once shoplifted baby formula for Lucy. Humiliated, Mia never again set foot in that grocery store.

A sign with a blue *H* along with an arrow pointing straight hung from a traffic signal. Jake steered the truck into the left lane. "I took Sam and Lucy to dinner last night. We talked quite a bit about the future. Sam has a good plan."

"Lucy doesn't know what *plan* means."

"Sam does."

"But Lucy is still impulsive. She doesn't think ahead. Like today—forgetting to eat lunch. I know it's her wedding day, but that's all the more reason to plan against a drop in blood sugar."

"A baby changes people. She'll learn."

"I hope so." But questions swirled in Mia's mind. "Where are they going to live?"

"You don't know?"

"Lucy doesn't always confide in me." The confession weighed like a rock in Mia's stomach. She wanted to support Lucy in every possible way, but Lucy rarely asked for advice, probably because she didn't want to hear what Mia would say. "I learned about the pregnancy on Tuesday. We didn't talk about anything except the wedding."

"Then let me fill you in." Jake made a right turn. "Lucy's going to work part-time at whatever retail job she can get until the baby comes, and they'll live in Sam's apartment."

"Can they afford the rent?"

"Easily."

"How?"

"Sam's a senior on a full ROTC scholarship. He receives a stipend, plus he has a monthly income from a trust fund set up with his mother's life insurance. He won't control the money until he's twenty-five, but they won't starve."

"I see." Mia was almost impressed. "That doesn't change the fact that Lucy is only eighteen. And Sam's, what, twenty-one?"

"Twenty-one going on thirty." Jake kept his eyes on the traffic.

"His mother was my partner in the Denver PD. I've known Sam since he was thirteen."

"Denver PD?" She had assumed he stocked vending machines for a living. All work was noble in Mia's opinion, but policemen made sacrifices few people understood.

"I'm retired now." He indicated his ear. "Disability."

Still surprised, she took in the hard set of his jaw. She was too polite to ask him what happened, but her nursing instincts kicked in. That wounded look in his eyes, the one she'd seen in the coffee shop, made more sense now. She also knew from Lucy that Sam's mother had died in the line of duty. A chill prickled up her spine, leaving her both curious and aching.

Jake cleared his throat, maybe to change the subject. "Sam has been through a lot. He's a responsible kid."

"Responsible?"

"Yes."

Mia bristled. "Excuse me for being blunt, but Mr. Responsible got my eighteen-year-old sister pregnant."

Silence ballooned between them, thickening with every breath. She'd offended him, but she believed in facing facts.

Stone-faced, Jake let out a sigh. "You win, Mia. Sam's responsible *most* of the time. He's human, and he messed up here. He'd be the first person to admit it. Now he's trying to do what's right."

"This isn't 1850, or even 1950. They don't have to get married."

"No, they don't. But they're in love, and they want to build a life together. What's wrong with that?"

After two broken engagements, Mia didn't believe in easy promises. "There's a lot wrong with it."

"Like what?"

"Almost everything." Someone needed to be realistic, and as usual, the job fell to her. "For one thing, like I said before, I hate the idea of Lucy dropping out of school. She'll be career-challenged the rest of her life and dependent on Sam. What if he leaves her?"

Jake said nothing.

"A woman needs to be able to support herself. What if something happens to Sam, like a war injury or a car accident? Or cancer or—"

"I get it, Mia."

"But—"

"I get it." His fingers clenched the steering wheel, turning bone-white as he veered into an empty strip mall. There was no shade, just a row of desiccated queen palms, cracked asphalt, and the sun glaring off the windshields of two parked cars. The instant the truck stopped, Pirate tried to crawl between the seats and into Jake's lap.

Jake flung his sunglasses on the dash, then wrapped the dog's big head in an awkward hug. "Relax, buddy. We're fine."

Pirate wagged his tail but didn't back down. Jake rubbed the dog's ears, crooned to him, then gave a hand signal Pirate instantly obeyed by returning to the back seat. Jake's green eyes, the only color in his pale face, met hers. "Sorry."

Nothing made sense to Mia. Not the sudden stop, not the dog's reaction, and especially not the mix of fire and ice in Jake's stare. She fought to collect her thoughts. "What—what just happened?"

"You struck a nerve with the 'anything can happen' argument."

His hearing aids . . . the service dog . . . his partner's death. Something terrible had ravaged his life. "Jake, I'm so sorry. That was insensitive of me."

"Don't worry about it."

"There's no excuse." She flattened her palm against the top of her chest. "I'm not usually this . . . this volatile. I'm just so worried about Lucy."

"Forget it. I overreacted." He reached back and gave Pirate another scratch. "I lost my partner and a lot of my hearing when some nutjob booby-trapped a building. You might remember it."

"I do." The whole city had buzzed with the crime. Lucy had told her only that Sam's mother died in the line of duty. "I'm truly sorry for what you went through, and for bringing it up."

"It's life. Most of the time I'm done with it."

"PTSD?"

"Some, but it's mild compared to what some people face." He put the truck back in gear. "Let's get to the hospital."

Mia wanted to say more, but a good nurse knew when to mind her own business. This was one of those times, though she couldn't help but worry about the lifeless look in his eyes. They reminded her of green Depression glass from the 1930s, the kind etched with fragile designs that captured what little beauty the world held at that time.

She raised her hand to touch Jake's arm but stopped herself. She didn't have the right to comfort him with a touch, nor did she want to stir up dangerous feelings. Next week she'd begin the Mission Medical application process. With a little luck, it would be the start of a new adventure, one that wouldn't break her heart.

chapter 4

As soon as Lucy checked in at the hospital registration desk, a woman in scrubs led her to a curtained cubicle in the ER. Sam stayed at her side, holding her hand. She knew Mia would want to be with her, but Lucy was glad to be alone with Sam. This was their problem, and they needed to handle it together.

The ER wasn't busy, so things moved fast. A nurse took Lucy's blood pressure and temperature; a physician's assistant asked her the same questions Mia had asked; and she was taken to the ultrasound room, where a technician made small talk that gave no hint of the test results.

Now back in the cubicle, dressed and sitting in a chair, Lucy gnawed her lower lip while Sam sat next to her, nervously jiggling his leg. His fidgeting drove her a little crazy, especially with her own fears rattling in her head. If she lost the baby, what would they do? Lucy ached to talk about it, but Sam would tell her to trust God and wait for the facts. That was fine for Sam, but Lucy's faith wasn't that strong. Sometimes she wondered if she had any faith at all, though she had never shared her doubts with Sam.

The curtain rings rattled on the rod, and a woman in a white coat greeted Lucy with a smile. "I'm Dr. Gordon."

Sam shot to his feet. "How's the baby?"

Lucy stayed seated, but her hand flew to her belly. Would God listen if she prayed? She had done some stupid things in her life, normal things like trying cigarettes and drinking in high school. She had shoplifted just once on a dare and felt terrible.

Sleeping with Sam could be counted as a mistake too. A sin. But the baby wasn't a mistake. Lucy loved this child with her whole heart.

Dr. Gordon took a Polaroid off her clipboard and handed it to Lucy. "Right now, the baby's fine. You're about nine weeks along, and we detected a strong heartbeat."

Relief washed through every inch of her body, leaving her limp as she laughed and cried at the same time. With tears blurring her vision, she drank in the shape of a head and a curved spine.

Sam rested a hand on her shoulder. "There he is—" His voice cracked. "He looks like a lima bean."

"Beanie Boy," Lucy said. "Or Beanie Girl." She couldn't stop smiling, but her heart remained in her throat. Sam gave her shoulder a squeeze, then focused on Dr. Gordon. "What about the bleeding? Do you know what caused it?"

"We can't be certain, especially this early, but it looks like a low-lying placenta." The doctor pointed to a curve on the photograph. "Can you see that?"

"Not really," Lucy admitted.

Dr. Gordon pointed again. "That's the placenta. We expect it to move up in the course of the pregnancy. If it doesn't, you'll need careful monitoring and a C-section. Right now, as a precaution, I'm putting you on pelvic rest."

"Is that bed rest?" Lucy liked to sleep in as much as anyone, but she far preferred to be busy.

"No," Dr. Gordon answered. "It means no heavy lifting.

Nothing strenuous. And no sexual activity. Do you have an obstetrician back in Colorado?"

"Sort of," Lucy replied. "My first appointment is in two weeks."

"Good. You'll be around twelve weeks at that point. The OB will probably do another ultrasound. Until then, I suggest you play it safe."

"Absolutely." Sam lowered his hand and stepped back. "We'll follow the instructions to the letter."

Lucy would do anything to protect the baby, but no real honeymoon? She reached for Sam's hand, but he was too far away.

Dr. Gordon excused herself, leaving them alone with the Polaroid, their fears, and Sam standing with his shoulders squared.

Lucy blew out a slow breath. "I've never been so scared in my life."

"Me either." He remained two steps away while he studied her face. "Luce, I have to say this."

"What?"

"Maybe this happened for a reason. To make us think about how important this commitment is. If you're at all unsure about getting married—if you want to wait—"

"Do you?" she asked, frightened.

"No!" With one long stride, he spanned the gap between them, then dropped to one knee the way he had a week after the pregnancy test. At first he'd been shocked by the news. They had used precautions. Well, most of the time. There had been a few nights when they got carried away and weren't prepared, because Sam felt guilty and wanted to put the brakes on that part of their relationship. The brakes went out rather easily on that slippery slope.

He held her hand in both of his. Someday she'd have an

engagement ring, but today her finger was bare. They needed baby things far more than Lucy needed a diamond.

Sam stared into her eyes, his gaze battle-hard yet tender. "I was ready to marry you an hour ago. And I'm ready now."

"I'm ready too," she said. "But this *is* fast. We could just live together for a while."

Lucy had already moved some of her stuff out of her dorm room and into his apartment. She needed to be out by Monday afternoon, and they had planned to finish moving on Sunday. But now she couldn't lift the boxes, and she had nowhere to go except to Sam's apartment or back home with Mia.

"No way do I want to just live together," Sam said.

"But—"

"Come on, Pudge." He squeezed her hand. "We've been over that. If my mom were alive, she'd kill me."

"Because of your own father." Lucy knew the story well. When Connie Waters caught her husband having an affair with a neighbor, she had moved out with four-year-old Sam, built a career for herself with the Denver PD, and taught her son to be a man of his word no matter the cost.

"I won't play house with you," Sam said. "You deserve better than that."

Did she? With a sister as accomplished as Mia, Lucy felt too small to matter to anyone, but she loved Sam for believing in her. "I love you so much."

"I love you too. I say we get married tomorrow at the county clerk's office. I know you wanted a real wedding, but—"

"Yes, but I want you more."

A grin stretched across his face, making his cheeks even fuller as he pushed to his feet. "Ten years from now, we'll renew our vows. By then you'll have a honkin' diamond on your finger."

"And two more kids."

"Or three."

"Or—"

Groaning, he rolled his eyes. "Don't you dare say four."

Lucy hugged him hard. She really did want a wedding, just a small one with pictures and pretty flowers, but she'd give up anything for Sam and the baby. "Tomorrow sounds good. But I have to warn you, Mia won't like it."

"It's not her wedding."

"No. But I hate the thought of telling her. You don't know how she is. She'll make a case like an attorney. When we argue, she makes me crazy. I get all confused and she wins."

Sam took out his phone. "What's her number?"

"What are you doing?"

"Calling her."

"Why?"

He gave her his most patient look. "I want your sister to be happy, but I won't let her interfere with *us*. By the time I finish talking to her, she'll like me or she won't. The bottom line is respect. I'm going to give it to her, and I expect it in return."

"Are you going to say all that on the phone?" Mia wouldn't like that. She believed in face-to-face conversations.

"Definitely not."

"Then when?"

"Later. First she needs to know that you and the baby are fine. Then I'll ask her to meet me for coffee. That's when I'll tell her we're getting married tomorrow at the county clerk's office. She can stay for the ceremony, or she can fly home. Her feelings matter, but I won't let her push you—or me—around."

No wonder Lucy loved Sam. He was the strongest person she'd ever known. Even stronger than Mia.

●●●

Mia was with Jake in the hospital waiting room when Sam called to tell them about Lucy and the baby. She sagged with relief at the good news, especially about the baby's strong heartbeat, but frowned when Sam ducked her request to speak to Lucy. Instead he asked Mia to meet him alone at the hotel Starbucks. At Jake's suggestion, the invitation turned into dinner for the three of them at the Safari Café, a poolside restaurant decorated like a tropical rainforest.

At precisely six o'clock, Mia arrived at the restaurant and walked into a jungle of mechanical toucans, fake trees, and blasts of electronic thunder. A man-made stream gurgled over black lava rocks, and somewhere in the back of the dining room, an elephant trumpeted. The atmosphere struck her as a little too "Me Tarzan, You Jane," but Sam's invitation impressed her. He was protecting Lucy, which was admirable. But he was also in Mia's way, which wasn't.

As for Jake, she wasn't sure why he had invited himself, though he hinted about an idea she might like. She was about to approach the hostess when she spotted him standing off to the side. Dressed in dark khakis and a polo shirt the color of pine needles, he greeted her with a wave. Pirate was nowhere in sight.

Mia hesitated. With their attention on the possible miscarriage, she hadn't officially canceled breakfast with him. She hated loose ends and was eager to say something, but she didn't want to taint the conversation with Sam. The breakfast problem would have to wait.

She approached Jake with a friendly smile. "Hi."

"Hi," he said back.

"I don't see Pirate."

"He's a little too big for a crowded restaurant. I left him snoozing in the room."

"I thought you took him everywhere."

"Not necessarily. I use him mostly when I'm alone to alert me to sounds I miss without the hearing aids, things like a knock on the door."

Mia remembered the episode in the truck. She still felt bad about her remark. "He's also a friend."

"And a bit of a mind reader." Jake indicated the crowded restaurant. "Let's sit. Sam came early and saved a table."

More high marks to Sam. He had planned ahead and made it easy for her to find him. When Mia reached the table, a square one with a view of the pool, he stood and offered his hand.

"Mia," he said graciously, "thank you for coming."

"Thank you for inviting me."

Jake pulled out her chair, then took the seat opposite her that gave him a view of both the pool and the bustling restaurant. Sam sat next to him, his back to the glass wall.

Her gaze flicked between their faces. They didn't look anything alike. Jake's face was lean, hard, and difficult to read. Sam's face was round and expressive. With his muscular arms, square jaw, and buzz cut, he belonged on a US Army recruiting poster.

Mia set her purse at her feet. "How's Lucy?" It still rankled her to be kept away from her sister, especially with her symptoms.

"She's doing a lot better." Sam gave Mia all the details of the hospital visit and answered her questions with the kind of precision she appreciated and rarely got from Lucy. The bleeding was lighter now, and the cramping had stopped. He and Lucy had stopped at a Subway on the way back, and she had devoured a six-inch turkey sandwich on wheat bread, a big chocolate chip cookie, and two cartons of milk.

With every word out of his mouth, Sam impressed Mia more. After a waitress took their drink orders, he reached into his shirt pocket. "How would you like to see the first picture of your niece or nephew?"

"I'd love it!" Mia pinched the white edge of the Polaroid and studied it through the damp sheen in her eyes. She saw ultrasound pictures all the time, but this one came alive in her mind. She imagined the little legs kicking against Lucy's belly, the fingers clenched in a fist, and the baby's thumb in its mouth.

A lump scraped against her vocal cords, roughening her voice as she handed the photo back to Sam. "She's lovely."

"Or *he*." Sam grinned. "We'll be thrilled either way."

"So will I." Mia smiled, but in her mind she heard the tick of her own biological clock and the soft tread of her approaching birthday. She was done with dating and might never have kids of her own, but she was going to be a fabulous aunt.

The waitress returned with their beverages, whipped out her notepad, and took their orders. Mia went with the Jungle Salad. Jake ordered a bacon cheeseburger with coleslaw, and Sam ordered the half-pound Elephant Burger, an extra side of fries, a quesadilla, and a glass of milk.

"Good grief!" Mia laughed out loud when the waitress left. "Does Lucy know how much you eat?"

Sam answered with a grin. "I might order dessert too. But I'll get that to go so I can share it with her."

Jake shook his head. "Your mom used to complain that you drank a gallon of milk a day."

"I did. But only during football season."

"Your friendship," Mia remarked. "Jake told me he worked with your mother. I just want to say that I'm sorry for your loss."

"Thank you." Sam gave the kind of gracious nod Mia would have offered. "She was a remarkable woman. Did Jake tell you she was his training officer?"

"No, he didn't mention that."

Jake grumbled under his breath. "You are *not* going to tell stories on me."

"Sure I am." Sam winked at Mia. "If my mom were here, she'd tell you Jake was a snot-nosed rookie—"

"Thanks a lot," Jake complained.

"—with a mile-wide ego. She'd also tell you he was the best cop she ever worked with."

Mia turned her attention fully to Jake. "Somehow I'm not surprised."

She expected a smile or a light remark, but his brows collided in a scowl aimed at no one except perhaps himself. "I wasn't the best when we walked into that building. If I could do it over again—"

Sam cut him off. "I know that. And *you* know that *I* know it. So stop the whining, all right? My mom would be the first to tell you to—"

"Get over it," they said in unison.

Emotion deepened the lines fanning from Jake's eyes. When he swung his gaze to the window, Mia gave him his privacy and turned back to Sam. They chatted about the baby until a waitress arrived with their plates.

Sam offered a short blessing, and they began the meal. When Mia cut into the perfectly grilled chicken on top of her salad, she thought of the time thirteen-year-old Lucy had surprised her with spaghetti for dinner. Not the most skilled cook, Lucy didn't fully drain the pasta before she added the jar of sauce. They had christened the dish "spaghetti soup" and laughed for a week.

Smiling at the memory, Mia looked at Sam. "You do know Lucy can't cook, right?"

"She makes great spaghetti soup."

Mia almost dropped her knife. "She told you about that?"

"She cooked it for me one night." Sam took a bite of his massive cheeseburger, chewed twice, and swallowed. "It's a lot better than most MREs."

Jake must have seen her confusion, because he translated. "Army talk for Meals Ready to Eat."

"I won't tell you some of the other names for them." Sam cut his cheesy quesadilla with one quick slice of his knife. "My CO says MREs are great training for marriage. I'll eat whatever's in front of me."

"I hope you don't starve to death," Mia said between bites of her salad.

"I won't."

Confidence. She had it too, but hers was hard-earned and tested. She wasn't so sure about Sam's. Cockiness and confidence looked a lot alike, especially in handsome young men who wore uniforms.

The three of them bantered through the meal, trading stories and getting to know each other. Mia enjoyed every minute, especially the good-natured ribbing between the men.

When they were nearly finished eating, Sam cleared his throat. "Before we go any further, I'd like to make a few things clear."

"Please. Go ahead." Mia welcomed honesty.

"I love your sister, Mia. I can take good care of her."

"You mean financially," she replied.

"Yes. I'm in my last year of a full-ride ROTC scholarship. I'll graduate in June with an engineering degree, hopefully summa cum laude, then I'll begin a six-year stint as an army officer. The next year will be a challenge with the baby, but I have a secure future."

"Yes, you do," she agreed. "But life doesn't come with guarantees. Feelings can change. In fact, they *will* change. You and Lucy are both young, especially Lucy. She's only eighteen."

"Almost nineteen." Sam paused to let the fact stand. "I won't sit here and tell you Lucy and I love each other as if that's reason enough to get married right now. The baby pushed up our timetable, but the real foundation here is that Lucy and I have our faith. We're not perfect, but we're committed to making this marriage last a lifetime. With God in the middle, I believe we can do it."

Mia had spouted similar words when she was engaged to Brad, and they had come back to haunt her. Now she leaned on God alone, not other people. "That's admirable, Sam. It's just that . . ." The words trailed to nothing, mostly because Mia didn't want to explain herself. "Let's just say life is full of surprises."

"It is," he agreed. "There's one more thing you should know. It might be a surprise, or it might not."

"The trust fund," she said for him.

"Yes." His face softened in a way Mia recognized from her own reflection in the mirror, when she thought of her parents. Grief and love did a complicated dance, and Sam knew that rhythm. "I'd give just about anything to have my mom instead of that money, but I won't lie. Having money in the bank makes life easier."

Did Sam know how poor she and Lucy had been while Mia finished school? Her own mother hadn't left a dime. No life insurance. No house with a little equity. Nothing except some treasures like the floating heart around Lucy's neck and the Swiss army knife that had belonged to Mia's father.

Earlier, in Jake's truck, she had wondered if love was enough to sustain two human beings through a lifetime of trouble, joy, and the doldrums in between. Now she wondered if love and money together were enough to compensate for Lucy's youth and inexperience.

Mia had to admit, Sam was wise beyond his years, someone she would call an old soul. He really could provide for Lucy financially. He was also a man of faith. Christians weren't perfect by any means, but his faith meant he'd do his best to make this marriage work. And if the marriage worked, Lucy wouldn't need Mia to mop up her spills. Mia would be free to take the job with Mission Medical and make a change of her own.

She gave Sam a softer smile. "You've almost persuaded me."

"Good," he said. "Because we're getting married tomorrow at the courthouse."

"Tomorrow?" Mia threw back her shoulders. "I thought you'd wait at least a few weeks. Why the rush? This is—"

Jake drummed his fingers on the tabletop. "This is where I come in."

chapter 5

Jake wasn't at all surprised by Sam and Lucy's decision to get married tomorrow. Back in Colorado, when Sam first told Jake about the wedding, Jake had put the kid through the third degree. He'd come away from that talk convinced Sam was marrying Lucy because he loved her, not out of obligation. The two of them were alike in important ways and opposites in others. A good balance, Jake believed.

Even so, he had pushed Sam to think long-term again last night. They were sharing a room in an effort to preserve a bit of wedding tradition, and Jake had been man-to-man blunt.

"I wouldn't be your friend if I didn't throw out some other options. You don't have to marry Lucy to take responsibility for the baby."

"You don't get it, Jake."

"Get what?"

"I love her. I want *to marry her. I've prayed long and hard. I know we're young, but a hundred years ago getting married at this age would have been typical."*

"It's not now."

"Maybe it should be," Sam tossed back. "I'm a Christian. I want to live my faith. But I'm human too, and marriage is

God's plan for sex. Why should Lucy and I wait to get married until she's . . . what? Twenty-one? Until she graduates college? Who made the new rules, anyway?"

"Beats me," Jake admitted.

"Lucy and I want to build a life together—not two lives we have to merge in three or four years. It's true we're individuals, but we're also a couple and committed to each other. We're not waiting," Sam had finished. "There's just no good reason."

There wasn't a thing Jake could say to that. He respected Sam's logic, and abstinence struck him as unrealistic when men and women waited until their late twenties or thirties to get married. And where did that lead for some people? Pregnancy scares. A lack of commitment. Broken hearts. Jake had been part of that culture until he met Connie. More of a lioness than a mother bear, she had taught him as much about life as she had about police procedure.

Jake held back a lonely sigh. His own love life was in the tank, a fact he couldn't seem to change. He envied Sam falling so deeply in love with Lucy. But he was also a realist, and he hoped Sam, Lucy, and Mia would like the idea that hit when his father called back to say he'd found Claire with Barb. They'd been in the kennel feeding the rescue dogs.

Mia and Sam were both focused on him now, Mia with wariness and Sam with trust. The trust bothered him, because Sam's pride was about to take a hit. But Mia's wariness bothered him even more. Unless Jake's instincts were as bad as his hearing, she didn't trust easily, a sign that life, or maybe some fool, had kicked her to the curb.

Determined to put her at ease, he put an extra measure of goodwill in his voice. "I have a suggestion."

"What is it?" Mia sounded desperate.

"Sam knows about my mother. Her name is Claire. She has Alzheimer's disease."

Mia visibly winced. "I am so sorry."

"Thank you. She's in the middle stages. My parents are on a waiting list for a senior community with a memory care neighborhood, but there's a long wait. Unfortunately, we've reached the point where she shouldn't be left alone."

Jake paused to let the details sink in, but Sam forged ahead. "What are you getting at?"

"A solution to your problem and mine," Jake replied. "I'd like to invite Lucy to move in with my parents and help with Claire. You two can get married tomorrow or in two months, it doesn't matter to me. But this way Lucy will have a place to live, Claire will have a companion, and you can go off to LDAC knowing she's not alone."

"LDAC?" Mia asked. "What's that?"

"An ROTC thing," Sam answered. "Leadership Development and Assessment Course. I'll be gone for four weeks in July."

Her eyebrows lifted. "With the spotting—"

"I know." Sam dragged a hand over the back of his neck. "If this turns into a bigger problem, I don't want her living alone."

Neither did Jake. Retired or not, he was a cop at heart and lived to protect people. "It's a big house. She can have that back bedroom on the first floor. In fact, after you're married, you can both live there as long as you'd like."

Mia interrupted. "What about medical care? How far is Echo Falls from Colorado Springs?"

"It's about an hour," Jake replied. "Some people commute every day."

Her brows furrowed. "That's farther from a hospital than I'd like. Is there a doctor in town?"

"For now, yes. Dr. Collins is retiring at the end of August. He's hoping to find someone to take over the practice."

She gave a small shake of her head. "That's tough in the current business climate. I wish him luck."

So did Jake. His plan for the camp was to host groups of boys, six at a time, for a one-week stay that would include hiking, sports, handling power tools, car repair, and just hanging out at night. Someone was bound to need stitches at some point. That was just how boys were.

Mia folded her napkin into a neat rectangle and set it on the table. "Jake's idea sounds really good. As much as I'd like Lucy to stay with me in Denver, she'd be alone all day. This way, she'll have company. But I'm worried about her helping Claire. Alzheimer's disease is demanding at best."

"And torturous at its worst," Jake added. "My mother is still herself and fairly lucid, but she repeats and gets confused. Some days are better than others." And some days were awful.

Jake and Mia both turned to Sam, who was already shaking his head. "We'd like to help with Claire. You know that. But Luce and I are getting married tomorrow. That's not negotiable."

"Sam?" Mia spoke quietly, but she also sounded like she meant business.

"What is it?"

"Maybe you should ask Lucy what she'd like to do. She's a romantic, and canceling today's ceremony was a disappointment. If you wait just a little while, you could plan another wedding. I think she'd like that."

When Sam didn't speak, Jake decided to sweeten the deal. "How about getting married at the house? Invite some friends. Have a cake and toss the bouquet."

"That reminds me." Mia turned to Sam. "Mrs. Carson gave us the bridal bouquet. It's in my room. I can bring it to Lucy whenever you'd like."

"Thanks." Sam reached for his phone. "I'll call her now, but I'm pretty sure I know what she'll say. We don't want to put off getting married."

While Sam called Lucy, Jake traded a glance with Mia. When she mouthed *Thank you*, he answered with a nod.

He and Mia listened as Sam asked Lucy how she was feeling. Her cheery voice echoed loudly enough for them to hear, and Mia smiled slightly. When Lucy paused to breathe, Sam relayed Jake's offer. "We don't have to decide right now, but we do have to decide when to get married. What do you think? City hall tomorrow or Echo Falls whenever we want?"

Sam's brows shot to his hairline. "You do? Echo Falls?" Looking at Jake and Mia, he raised a hand palm up as if to say, *I don't believe this.* "Sure, Pudge. I'm fine with waiting a week. Let me tell Jake and Mia, and I'll call you back."

Looking sheepish, Sam set down his phone. "That shows what I know. Lucy loves the idea of getting married in Echo Falls, but we still want to do it fast. How about the weekend after this one? That'll give us a week to plan something."

"Perfect," Jake said.

"I'd have preferred a month," Mia admitted, "but a week is better than tomorrow morning. What did she say about taking care of Claire?"

"She said yes right away, but you know how she is."

"Impulsive."

"And eager to help," Sam added. "Lucy has a good heart."

"Yes, she does." Love and pride rang in Mia's voice. Misty-eyed, she reached in her purse for a tissue. In Jake's opinion, Lucy wasn't the only sister with a good heart.

After she dabbed her eyes, Mia took Sam's hand in hers and squeezed. "Lucy is blessed to have you in her life, and so am I. I always wanted a little brother."

"You've got one," Sam declared. "I won't let Lucy down. Or the baby."

Jake hoped not, but he'd once been as naïve as Sam. People stumbled, sometimes on their own good intentions.

The waitress arrived with the bill and handed it to Sam. Jake didn't bother with their usual check-snatching game. Tonight's victory belonged to Sam, who signed the receipt, excused himself, and stood. "I'm going up to see Lucy. But, Mia?"

"Yes?"

"Would you stay with her tonight? She told me to ask you. She'd like it, and so would I."

"I'll bring the flowers."

Standing, Mia hugged Sam long and hard. Jake rose from his chair and clapped Sam on the back. Connie would have been proud tonight.

As soon as Sam left, Mia turned to Jake. She seemed unsure about what to do next, whether to sit down or to leave. With his breakfast invitation hanging between them, he indicated her chair. "How about coffee?"

She hesitated just long enough to remind him of that moment outside the coffee shop, when she had turned back and met his gaze. The look in her eyes had been a mix of turmoil and sweetness, and she wore the same look now.

After a breath, she slid back onto her chair. "Coffee would be nice."

While he signaled the waitress and ordered, Mia pulled a notepad and pen out of her purse. "What you're doing for Lucy and Sam is really nice. Can I get the address where she'll be living?"

"1817 Tanner Road."

"Your parents own the whole street?"

"It's a small ranch and horse property, but they stopped keeping horses a few years ago. My dad and I run the vending machine business. Love-A-Dog Rescue was my mom's passion. We're set up for twenty dogs, but we're down to five. When they're adopted, we won't take on any more."

"Lucy loves dogs."

"How about you?" The question popped out of his mouth. There was no reason to ask, except that he wanted to know. How a person felt about dogs said a lot about their nature.

Her mouth twisted into a sweet little smile. "If you mean dogs like Pirate, definitely. But if you mean a dog like the flea-bitten stray Lucy brought home that ate the couch? Not so much."

"The couch, huh?"

"Just two cushions and a throw pillow." Mia shook her head. "I'm glad the owner showed up, because neither of us could bear to take it to the shelter. If Lucy's physically able, she'll love working with the dogs."

"I'm grateful for anything she can do. We really do need her help."

Mia opened her mouth to say something but closed it. The silence thickened until they spoke at the same time.

"About breakfast—"

Judging by the dire tone of her voice, she was about to cancel on him, which struck him as wise. That flirtation in the coffee shop had been between strangers who could walk away and not think twice about each other. He and Mia weren't strangers anymore, and their friendship was potentially complicated.

"You go first," he offered.

"No, you. Please."

Jake had no problem speaking his mind. "As much as I'd enjoy having breakfast with you tomorrow, I think it would be smart to stick to being friends."

"Because of Lucy and Sam."

"Yes."

She let out a slow breath. "I feel the same way. Thank you. You just saved me from a somewhat embarrassing speech. That picture I sent of the hen—I don't usually do things like that."

"Like what?"

"Have breakfast with a stranger."

"Me either." Funny how things worked out. She didn't move to leave, so he said, "So you live in Denver. What part?"

The question opened a floodgate, and they talked for an hour about easy things like Echo Falls and the craziness of Las Vegas. He told her about his plans for the camp, including how hard it was to find a name for it. "Unofficially I call it Camp Connie, but that won't fly with teenage boys."

"No. But you'll come up something, I'm sure."

"What about you?" Jake asked. "You have a great career that's going strong."

"I do, but I'm hoping to make a big change." She met his gaze with a look so full of purpose he could imagine her doing anything from scaling Mount Everest to becoming an astronaut. "Have you heard of Mission Medical? They send medical teams overseas. I'm applying for a permanent position in their women and children's division. They're based in Dallas, but I could be assigned to work anywhere in the world."

"You'd be great at it."

"I hope so, but the application process is long—not to mention highly competitive. If God opens the door, it'll border on a miracle."

"Get ready. I happen to believe in miracles." For one thing, he'd survived a tragedy. For another, neither Sam nor the department blamed him for what happened, though Jake still carried the weight of that mistake.

He wondered why Mia wanted to join Mission Medical so passionately, but the question struck him as too personal. Instead he focused on the logistics. "Where do you think they would send you?"

"It could be anywhere. Bangladesh. South America. Even West Africa."

Home of Ebola, terrorist groups, and a dozen other high-risk situations. Jake couldn't bear the thought of Mia on the frontlines in the war against disease and violence. Waves of hot and cold shot through his body, a reminder of the days immediately after the bomb blast. If Pirate had been there, he would have crawled into Jake's lap and licked his face.

As Jake fought off the panicky feeling, a familiar numbness settled into his bones. He welcomed the respite, but good feelings faded away along with the bad ones.

Mia must have seen his expression because she tipped her head in that curious way of hers. Jake didn't try to explain. He merely smiled back, glad that he'd see her again at the wedding in Echo Falls, maybe dance with her, and definitely be her friend.

chapter 6

After three cups of coffee with Jake, Mia delivered the wedding bouquet to Lucy and spent the night with her. The caffeine kept her awake, and she and Lucy talked until after midnight about everything from the wedding to babies to men. When Lucy told her more about Jake and how he wanted to honor Connie's memory with the camp, they agreed on three things. Brad was a jerk; Sam was a prince; and Jake was a hero.

On Friday afternoon, while waiting for her flight back to Denver, Mia Googled news stories on the blast and gleaned the details. The decision to go into the abandoned building had been Jake's. The bomb blew out the inside walls, but the building didn't crumble. Injured himself, he had carried Connie to the curb before he collapsed.

According to Lucy, Jake rarely talked about that awful day, and neither did Sam. Sam knew Jake didn't walk on water, but he thought he came close.

Mia was at peace with the wedding plans, but when her plane landed at DIA, her heart slowed to an aching crawl. She didn't miss Brad at all, especially after the good time she'd had with Jake, but she missed being in love.

On the other hand, she didn't miss it enough to risk another broken heart. Applying to Mission Medical, moving to Dallas, and traveling around the world was far safer for her peace of mind than falling in love again. If God opened the door to Mission Medical, Mia intended to charge through it.

Saturday afternoon, Lucy called to say she had met Claire and they hit it off. Lucy was moving in with the Tanners the next day, and Sam had gotten out of the lease for the apartment they planned to rent. Instead he would live in Echo Falls and commute to school when the semester started.

"Life is good," Lucy told Mia. "I just hope your dreams come true too."

"So do I," she replied, thinking of Mission Medical.

On Monday morning, the day of her Skype interview, she saw patients in Dr. Moore's office as usual. The day was crazy busy, but fifteen minutes before the interview was scheduled to start at one o'clock, Mia managed to close the door to her office. After shoving the clutter out of view, she tested Skype, put on fresh lipstick, and hoped her teddy bear scrubs made her look caring and not silly.

With her heart thumping, she put her life in God's hands with a silent prayer. *I want your will, Lord. Not mine. If you're calling me to go overseas, kick the door open wide. I'll do my best, but the results are up to you. Always.*

As she breathed an "Amen," the Skype sound twanged, and a photograph of a woman named Sheryl Hastings appeared on the screen. Her braided hair was pulled back into a professional bun, and her ebony skin glowed against a coral top.

Mia accepted the call and greeted Sheryl with a friendly smile. "Good afternoon."

"Good afternoon, Mia, I'm Sheryl Hastings. It's a pleasure to meet you."

"Likewise."

Sheryl handled the webcam awkwardness like a pro. "As you know, this interview is the first step in a long process. If you make it past today's screening, we'll conduct a background check and you'll move on to a panel interview in Dallas. The final step is a team-building exercise with other applicants."

"I read about the process on the website." She had also read dozens of blogs and social media posts by both applicants and professionals on-site. The team-building exercise worried her, because participants were sworn to secrecy. No one would say exactly what it involved, and Mia liked to be prepared.

"So—" Sheryl looked down at her notes. "Let's get started. Tell me about yourself."

"I'm twenty-nine, single, and currently see patients as a nurse practitioner in a women's health practice. I'm also a volunteer coordinator with the free Sunday clinic run by my church. We see patients of all ages with a wide variety of health problems."

Sound natural. Not like you rehearsed in front of mirror. Which she had.

Over the next ten minutes, she shared all the details of her life—her background, why she chose nursing, what a typical day was like in Dr. Moore's office.

"You're a busy lady," Sheryl remarked.

"I really do love my work." Mia hoped she didn't sound too goody-two-shoes.

"What did you do prior to joining this practice?"

"I worked on a med-surg floor at Denver Community Hospital. As much as I enjoyed it, I wanted more independence. I earned my master's degree and trained with Dr. Moore. She kept me on when I finished school."

"Have you ever lived outside of the United States?"

"I spent eight weeks in Haiti, working as an administrative assistant on a vaccination project. It was a grad school internship." Fortunately the family of Lucy's best friend had invited Lucy to live with them for the summer.

"So you learned something of the logistical problems we face."

"Yes."

Sheryl made another note. "Have you traveled to any other foreign countries?"

"No. That's it." Mia knew her eight weeks of experience on foreign soil was the bare minimum Mission Medical required. Most applicants had far more, but she hoped her domestic charity work would make up for what she lacked.

"How about within the United States?" Sheryl asked. "Have you lived anywhere other than Denver?"

"No. This is my home."

"So you've never lived anywhere else?"

"No." That made three *No*'s in a row. With her stomach sinking, Mia searched for something to show off her adaptability, but all she could think of was the time she tried calamari and gagged on it. Not impressive.

But she had another story to tell and other strengths. "While my college friends traveled and gained new experiences, I stayed in Denver to raise my sister. Our mother passed away when I was twenty and Lucy was barely ten. It was tough, but we made it. I'm proud of that."

"That's admirable."

"I'm just glad we were able to stay together. God opened a lot of doors in those years."

"Like what?"

This wasn't the direction Mia expected. "When I needed a job that would let me stay in school and be home for Lucy, I found one doing home-based medical billing. My old Corolla held together for twenty years, and Lucy"—Mia's biggest challenge of all—"well, she's full of surprises, but she's also a very special person."

"How so?"

"She's outgoing, friendly, and generous to a fault."

"What about you, Mia? How are you special?"

"Me?"

Sheryl smiled. "That question isn't on the official list, but I like to ask it."

"I'm not special at all." Mia didn't like how that sounded, as if she were trying too hard to be humble. "Let me put it this way instead. We all have gifts. Mine are organization, a love of people, and a passion for healing."

Sheryl made another note, then paused for several seconds. Finally, with a carefully blank expression, she thanked Mia for her time. "I think that's all I need."

"Wait. Please." The interview was too short. Sheryl should have asked Mia if she was interested in specific countries and about her ideas for the clinics. Mia leaned forward in her chair, her fingers tight on the armrest. "I'd like to add something."

"All right."

"I want this position. I know I'm short on foreign experience, but I'm eager to serve. When I set my mind to do something, I finish it. I won't let you down."

Sheryl stared at Mia through the screen. "I appreciate your candor, Mia. In return, I'll be honest with you. Going overseas requires a high degree of adaptability. The living conditions won't be what you're accustomed to. Have you ever gone a week without a hot shower?"

"No," she admitted. Even in Haiti, the accommodations during the internship had been comfortable.

"Have you eaten strange foods?"

Mia winced. "Just sushi from King Soopers. That doesn't count, does it?"

"No, it doesn't. I'm sorry, Mia, but we don't want to invest in an applicant who isn't able to adapt."

"No, of course not. But I *can* adapt. If you'll give me a chance, I'll add to my experience." Her mind flashed to the Safari Café and Jake mentioning Dr. Collins and his plan to retire. "In fact, I can take a step today. There's a clinic in a mountain community that needs someone fast. I'll apply for the job."

"What would you do there?"

"General practice."

"Hmmm."

"I'll prove to you I'm adaptable."

"You're certainly determined." Sheryl paused, her expression neutral as she considered Mia's plea. "Moving to a small town isn't at all equivalent to what you'd experience in a Third World country, but your willingness to make a big change shows a high degree of flexibility. That's important."

Mia swallowed hard and prayed. *Please, God. I need a break here.*

Looking down, Sheryl skimmed her notes. "Your volunteer work is a plus, and your letters of recommendation are outstanding. You have excellent skills, and there's no doubt you're dedicated."

Mia didn't breathe until Sheryl peered back through the screen.

"All right," the interviewer finally said. "Let's continue. *If* Mission Medical accepts your application, which countries most interest you?"

Air rushed into Mia's lungs. Her hope would live at least a few more days. "I'll go anywhere. West Africa. Bangladesh. Wherever the need is greatest."

"Foreign languages?"

"I'm studying French online."

Sheryl made another note, asked Mia a few more questions, and wrapped up the interview. "That's all I need. Do you have any other questions for me?"

"Not at this time. I've done a lot of research. It would be an honor to be part of your organization."

"You'll hear from us by the end of the week. If you make the cut, the next interview will be in Dallas sometime this summer." Sheryl offered a small smile. "They'll want to hear about that change you're making and why."

"Yes. Thank you."

"And, Mia? One more thing."

She waited.

"I want to personally thank you for your time and interest in Mission Medical. This world is a soul-wearying place. We need people like you. We need them everywhere—both here and abroad." With those final words, Sheryl's image faded from the computer screen.

Mia slumped back in her chair. Interviews exhausted her, but she didn't have a minute to spare if she was going to prove her adaptability. She Googled "Dr. Collins Echo Falls," picked up the phone, and called his office. A young-sounding receptionist answered on the third ring.

"Echo Falls Primary Care. This is Kelsey. May I help you?"

Mia introduced herself and explained that she had heard through a friend about Dr. Collins's plan to retire. "I'd be interested in filling in on a temporary basis."

"Really?"

"Yes. I can email my CV right now." Her curriculum vitae was three pages long and included her education, work experience, and her contributions to three research articles.

"Can you fax it?" the receptionist asked.

"Sure." A fax? Dr. Collins and his practice weren't exactly on the cutting edge.

Another phone rang in the background. "Oh. Wait. May I put you on hold?"

"Of course." Mia glanced at the computer clock. She had a dozen things to do before starting up with patients, but this was important to her. She tapped her foot against the desk, chewed her lip, then heard a click and a male voice.

"Ms. Robinson? This is Dr. Collins."

She bolted upright. "Yes. Hello, Doctor."

"Kelsey tells me you're interested in working for me."

"I am. Very much."

"Tell me about yourself."

For the second time in an hour, Mia rattled off her qualifications and experience. With Sheryl, she had let her personality show. With old-school Dr. Collins, she kept her tone formal. He grunted a few times, and asked about her preceptorship and how long she'd been licensed.

When she finished answering, he barked a question. "Can you be here on Wednesday at three o'clock for an interview?"

"That's perfect." Wednesday afternoon was Mia's time to catch up on paperwork. With a little rescheduling, she could drive up for the interview and stay through Saturday for Lucy's wedding.

"Fine. Fax your CV and references."

The phone clunked in her ear, leaving Mia with her heart racing as she printed out her CV, wrote a short cover letter, and faxed the package to Echo Falls Primary Care. If she and Dr. Collins reached an arrangement, she would need to give Dr. Moore two weeks' notice, find a place to live in Echo Falls, and clean out her apartment.

Mia glanced at the clock, then at the pile of phone messages on her desk. She didn't have time to call Lucy, but she did it anyway.

Her sister answered on the second ring, cheerful as always. "Hey. What's up?"

"How would you feel if I took a job in Echo Falls?"

"Really? I'd *love* it."

"It would be temporary, but I'm desperate." Mia told Lucy about the interview, the need to prove her adaptability, and her call to Dr. Collins. "The interview is Wednesday."

"That's great! I'll tell Jake and his dad that you're getting here early. The house is huge. They won't mind at all."

"No, don't. I'll stay at a motel." Mia didn't want to impose on the Tanners, but mostly she liked her privacy. At times she craved it. But what did that say about her adaptability? "On second thought, that would be nice. But only if it's okay with the Tanners."

"They'll be glad to have you, especially Claire."

"Are you sure?"

"Positive. She used to do a lot of entertaining. In fact, she's teaching me how to cook. It's funny how her hands sometimes know what her brain can't remember."

"Just let me know what they say."

"I will."

Mia glanced again at the clock. Her first patient was probably waiting in the exam room. "Gotta run—"

"Bye!"

"Bye!"

That was how they ended most of their calls, sometimes in midsentence, because when Mia said she needed to go, she meant it. She did a quick skim of the phone messages to check for emergencies, saw nothing that couldn't wait for her next break, and hurried out of her office.

In the hallway, she glimpsed herself in a mirror. The teddy bear scrubs wouldn't cut it for an interview with old-school Dr. Collins. She wanted something new, maybe a business suit in a cheerful color instead of the gray and beige she usually favored. She also wanted a fabulous new dress for Lucy's wedding.

Jake Tanner had nothing to do with that desire. Not a thing. But it wasn't lost on her that she'd be seeing a lot of him if she moved to Echo Falls.

chapter 7

Jake walked with his mom into the Echo Falls Emporium, a combination market, deli, and variety store with a hundred-year-old history. He wrangled a cart from a row of them and gave it to his mom.

"I just love that girl," Claire said for the fourth time.

She meant Lucy. Last Saturday, when Sam brought Lucy to the house for the first time, the poor girl dashed to the bathroom and threw up. Whatever resentment Claire felt about needing help vanished the minute she saw Lucy's stricken face. A mother at heart, she took Lucy under her wing, and they bonded over crackers and dill pickles.

Now they planned to make the wedding cake together. Jake smiled at the thought, but he hoped they remembered to put in the sugar. Mia was right about Lucy being a little scatter-brained, and his mother's memory was at the cat-and-mouse stage, where thoughts emerged and vanished before she could wrap her mind around them.

Claire pushed the small cart down the baking aisle, her gaze intense as she studied the boxes and jars, cans and bags, a million colors and shapes, and a thousand words in a hundred different styles of print. Every few steps she stopped and studied her list, until she reached a row of small orange boxes.

"Baking soda," she said as she lifted the Arm & Hammer brand.

"That's it." Jake used the same stuff to clean battery terminals.

She checked the item off her list, said the words out loud a second time, then read the next item. "Baking powder." Her brows furrowed. "What's the difference? I used to know that."

Jake didn't have a clue, but he snagged a can off the shelf. "I don't know, but here it is."

A sigh whispered from his mother's lips, one that echoed the constant ache in Jake's own soul. Every day she lost a little more of her old self, and the downhill slide seemed to be picking up.

They made their way to the bags of flour. White or wheat. Bleached or unbleached. All-purpose or special for cakes. Gold Medal, Pillsbury, or the bargain store brand? His mother clutched his arm. Thinking she was confused and maybe frightened, he put his hand over hers.

As he turned to say he'd handle the flour crisis, she waved to Kelsey Baxter at the far end of the aisle.

Jake liked Kelsey. The office manager for Echo Falls Primary Care was cute with brown eyes and bouncy hair, and she supported Camp Connie. They had dated a few times—a couple of lunches and a singles gathering at church. He had tried hard to feel more for her than he did, but he couldn't seem to warm up to anything about her. Not her looks. Not her outgoing personality. Nothing. Friendship was the best he could do. To his consternation, Kelsey's feelings weren't so mild. She lit up like Christmas whenever she saw him. Like now.

"Claire! Jake!" She hurried toward them, a red plastic basket dangling from the crook of her elbow.

Jake greeted her with a nod. "Hello, Kelsey."

She gave Claire a quick hug. "Did you two hear the big news?"

His thoughts went to Camp Connie and the battle for the zoning change. "What's up?"

"Dr. Collins found someone interested in taking over his practice. She's coming this afternoon for an interview."

Jake knew all about it. "Mia Robinson, right?"

Surprised, Kelsey drew back. "This *is* a small town. How did you hear?"

"Mia is Lucy's sister," Claire explained. "And Lucy is . . . Lucy is living with us."

"Who's Lucy?" Kelsey turned to Jake.

"Sam's fiancée."

"Got it." Kelsey shifted the basket to her other arm. "I wondered how a stranger heard about Dr. Collins. That phone call came out of the blue."

Not to Jake. Lucy couldn't stop talking about how great it would be to have Mia in Echo Falls, and Jake couldn't stop thinking the same thing. Mia and Las Vegas popped into his mind about ten times a day. He'd learned a lot about her over those three cups of coffee, and he'd been impressed with her compassion, personal drive, and slightly goofy sense of humor. When they parted at the elevator, she'd thanked him again for the stuffed hen and dubbed it Henrietta.

He'd been tempted to quiz Lucy about her sister, but that seemed nosy. Besides, knowing Lucy like he did now, she'd see right through him and play matchmaker. Next to *Frozen*, the Disney movie about two very different sisters, *Beauty and the Beast* was her favorite. She and Claire watched one movie or the other almost every day.

Kelsey glanced at the bags and boxes in the shopping cart. "It looks like you're baking a cake."

"For . . ." Claire's voice trailed off. "What's her name again?"

"Lucy," Jake replied.

"Lucy," Claire repeated. "She's engaged to Sam."

Kelsey's smile froze in that helpless way of someone who didn't know what to say when an Alzheimer's patient repeated something. She glanced at Jake, compassion bright in her eyes, then tried again with Claire. "Jake told me about Lucy already."

"Oh, that's right." Claire fluttered her hand. "And her sister is coming to visit. What's her name?"

"Mia."

"Mia," Claire said firmly. "She's Lucy's sister. And Lucy's engaged to Sam. We're making a cake."

Small talk exhausted Claire as much as giving a speech to a crowd. Knowing she was near her limit, Jake put his hand on her back but spoke to Kelsey. "We need to finish shopping."

"Of course," Kelsey said. "But there's one more thing I need to tell you."

"Sure. What is it?"

"The Stop the Camp group is picking up steam. They're holding a rally."

Jake stifled a groan. "A rally? When?"

"In about a month." She reached into her purse, a much smaller one than the sack Mia carried, and handed him a piece of paper the color of an orange traffic cone. "This is the flyer they asked us to put up in the office. You know how Dr. Collins feels about politics. He said no."

"I don't like politics either," Jake muttered. "I just want to start a camp for some hurting kids."

Four months ago the idea had seemed simple. With his parents relocating to Westridge, Jake was destined to be the sole occupant of a six-bedroom house on a property with three outbuildings. It was ideal for a youth camp, but he needed a zoning change much like the one other homeowners routinely obtained to start bed-and-breakfasts.

No big deal, right? But he'd been wrong. His plan had stirred up a volcano of local resentment because of a five-year-old tragedy. Arson, committed by a teenage boy living at a rehab facility. The six fires, set in the dry month of August, had terrified the entire community. Four of the incidents had been dumpster fires, small and quickly contained, but the fifth was set at a vacant cabin. It had burned down the garage and nearly spread to a stand of piñon pines.

The sixth fire destroyed the home of long-time resident Bill Hatcher. A widower in his late sixties, Bill had fled from the burning house, fallen down concrete steps, and dragged himself away in spite of a shattered tibia. Now he used a cane and lived with constant pain. The fire had destroyed every photograph of his late wife, the watercolors she had painted, and everything else she loved, including their elderly cat.

Jake, a victim of a crime himself, understood Bill's loss in his own marrow. The circumstances were both sad and tragic. But a camp for sons of fallen heroes was light-years removed from the group home that had closed in the aftermath of the fires.

To Jake's consternation, some people didn't see the difference. In all good conscience, they believed they were protecting their town, their property, and their families. Others opposed the camp for less noble reasons. Unfortunately, drama and gossip were favorite pastimes in Echo Falls. *Stirring the pot,* as Frank called it. Either way, opposition to Camp Connie was growing, and the group was organized enough to raise money and choose Bill Hatcher as chairman.

Jake took the flyer from Kelsey and saw a photograph of the Hatcher home engulfed in flames. Jaw tight, he read the group's call to action.

Keep City Problems in the City
By William T. Hatcher, Chairman
Stop the Camp Committee

I know from personal experience that a youth camp is a Trojan horse for crime—everything from shoplifting to acts as heinous as arson. If you're willing to fight to preserve our safe and quiet way of life, please join the Stop the Camp Committee at a rally . . .

"This is ridiculous." His fingers itched to ball up the flyer, but instead he folded it into fourths. "Hatcher's playing on fears that aren't realistic. People need facts."

"They won't get them from Bill." Kelsey sighed. "You two need to debate."

"I offered when the Stop the Camp group first formed, but I didn't get an answer." Jake jammed the flyer in his back pocket. "I'll ask again. Or better yet, I'll call Marc Scott." The Chamber of Commerce president. "He's leaning in our direction because it'll bring in business from the visiting families. Maybe he can persuade Bill to turn the rally into something more civilized."

"That's a *great* idea! If anyone can do it, you can. Jake, you're brilliant!" Kelsey had a tendency to gush over him, a habit that rubbed him the wrong way. He didn't deserve the praise, didn't want it, and felt like an imposter in the face of her hero worship.

"Thanks for the info," he said, almost monotone. "I'll let you know what Marc says."

"I'll help in any way I can. But you know that." She waited a moment, maybe hoping he'd invite her to the house to talk some more.

No way could he give that invitation. Kelsey, a junkie when it came to local politics, could have told him where town leaders stood on the issue of the camp, but he needed to be careful of her feelings.

Claire broke the silence. "Lucy's getting married. We're baking a cake."

The movie *Groundhog Day* used to be one of his favorites. Now he couldn't stand to watch Bill Murray live the same day over and over, much like Claire did. Jake nodded a quick goodbye to Kelsey.

Smiling her sympathy, she murmured, "See you later."

He indicated Claire should push the cart, something that gave her a sense of security, and they went back to grocery shopping. They were in the soft-drink aisle when Jake thought of Mia again. She'd be at the house for four days, and he wanted her to feel welcome. He shot a quick text to Lucy. *What does Mia like to drink? How about snacks?*

She answered with *That yucky soda water (lemon/lime), green apples, mini carrots, whole grain bagels (yuck). She likes Skittles too, but don't tell her I told you.* She finished with a row of smiley faces.

Jake smiled too. "Come on, Mom. Let's check out the candy aisle."

"Candy?"

"Lucy says Mia likes Skittles."

"Mia?"

"Lucy's sister."

Claire lit up. "Oh, that's right. Lucy's getting married."

With her hands knotted on the cart, his mother steered down an aisle filled with M&M's and gummy bears, twelve kinds of Life Savers, peppermints, licorice, chocolate in bags and bars, not to mention SweeTarts, Nerds, and movie-size boxes of everything from Milk Duds to Junior Mints.

Claire stopped abruptly, her eyes suddenly dull with confusion. Jake guided her to the Skittles and put a couple of the original red bags in the cart. With Claire, it paid to keep things simple.

But what about Jake? He used to relish a challenge, the more complex the better. What had happened to the man determined to make detective before he turned thirty-five? The man who solved problems with logic, chased down trouble, and tackled it head on? Aside from the Stop the Camp fight, Jake's biggest problem now was what to eat for breakfast. Or maybe it was the dead weight in his chest when he went to bed alone and woke up alone. He hadn't felt really alive since the tragedy.

Did he want to be a bachelor the rest of his life? No wife. No kids. A monk, essentially.

No, he did not.

He was tired of being alone. Tired enough to toss four more bags of Skittles into the cart, each one a different color with a different assortment of flavors. He hoped he had found Mia's favorite.

●●●

On Wednesday afternoon, Mia walked out of Echo Falls Primary Care in a daze. Dr. Collins had skimmed her CV, agreed to her salary request, and asked when she could start. With a new RV in the driveway, he and his wife were eager to live their retirement dream while they still enjoyed good health.

In Colorado, a nurse practitioner could prescribe, diagnose, and treat without physician oversight, so once she started work, Dr. Collins was free to travel. They agreed on a start date in two weeks. Since she was possibly leaving in six months, he wanted to keep the practice up for sale. Mia was fine with that. Considering it hadn't sold in a year, she believed the job was secure.

"Thank you, God," she said out loud as she turned left on Tanner Road. She could hardly believe it. When it came to her love life, God moved with glacial slowness. But when it came to her career, He moved fast, opening doors the instant she knocked.

Mia made a mental list of things to do. Calling Dr. Moore and finding a place to live in Echo Falls took top priority. Maybe she'd ask Jake to help her find a little house to rent. Or maybe not. She liked him a lot, too much for a woman hoping to leave the country in six months. Staying just friends was both smart and wise, especially with his strong ties to Sam.

With her adrenaline still rushing, Mia drove a half mile down Tanner Road and parked in front of the house Lucy had described as a castle made of wood. The description fit the multistoried, haphazard layout that suggested rooms had been added in different decades. A wide deck with several wooden steps leading up to it reminded Mia of a moat with a lowered drawbridge.

She expected Lucy to greet her, but it was Jake who came down the steps. Pirate trotted at his side, a four-legged squire to his master, but Jake didn't resemble a medieval knight in the least. Dressed in Wrangler jeans and work boots, he was the spitting image of Mr. Claw Machine, except for the cowboy hat. When her heart gave a happy bounce, Mia realized she needed to be careful. The man she had considered a handsome stranger was now a handsome friend.

Pirate wasn't wearing his red vest, so when he and Jake reached Mia's Toyota 4Runner, she greeted him with a friendly scratch to his neck before she looked up at Jake.

His mouth hooked into a grin. "He's glad to see you. So am I. How did the interview go?"

"Great." Her mind stuck like glue on Jake being glad to see her. The feeling was entirely mutual. "I start in two weeks, or sooner if I can make arrangements with Dr. Moore."

"Congratulations."

"Thank you. I'm happy about it."

He hauled her suitcase and a garment bag to the house, and she carried her purse and computer. When they reached the front door, slightly ajar, he nudged it wide with his elbow and moved to the side to give her access. "The stairs are to the right."

The interior of the house stole Mia's breath. A glass wall faced the higher elevations of the Rocky Mountains behind the house, and a massive brick fireplace promised heat on a cold night. Two big couches made a V in front of the hearth, and a triangular table displayed a scattering of papers, magazines, and a laptop. She guessed Jake had been working on something.

Feeling both awkward and impressed by the house, she retreated to the safety of good manners. "Thanks for inviting me to stay the extra nights. Four days is a long time for a house guest."

"Not for my parents. They love company, especially my mom."

As they climbed the stairs, Mia slowed to take in a gallery of family photographs that spanned at least four generations. She tried to spot Jake, but with so many pictures, it was like playing *Where's Waldo?* until her eyes fastened onto a family portrait taken about ten years ago. It showed Jake and his siblings—a brother and a sister—and Frank and Claire. The Tanner house was a real home, the kind Mia once dreamed of having for herself.

Jake guided her to a corner room with a twin bed with a lacy comforter, matching curtains, and a pile of throw pillows. Pastel prints of Monet's *Water Lilies* graced the walls, and a bookcase held an assortment of paperbacks, including a copy of *Anne of Green Gables,* Mia's favorite book ever.

"This is lovely," she said.

"It was my sister's room." Jake indicated the Monet posters as he hung her garment bag in the closet. "She's an artsy type. Lives in Chicago now."

"Older or younger?"

"Younger by two years. I have an older brother too. He lives in LA with his wife and two kids."

"It's nice to have siblings."

"It is." He set down her suitcase. "It's tough for them being away with my mom's health problems, but we keep in touch. I'm glad I'm around."

"I'm sure they are too."

He paused. "You and Lucy—"

"We're half sisters. Different fathers." Mia set the computer bag on the desk. "I hope she's not driving you too crazy."

"Not at all. She's great with Claire, and my dad appreciates the help. She's down at the kennel with my mom. Why don't you put on something casual? I'll take you to see her."

"Sounds good."

"I'll meet you downstairs."

He disappeared down the hall, leaving Mia to close the door with a soft click. She traded her business suit for jeans and a short-sleeved plaid top, gave her hair a quick fluff, then dabbed on lipstick and walked down the stairs. She spotted Jake on the couch, hunched forward with his attention on the laptop. He didn't hear her approach, and Pirate wasn't with hm.

Mia cleared her throat. He still didn't hear, so she raised her voice. "Jake?"

Startled, he jumped to his feet. "I didn't hear you." He stuck his finger in his ear and wiggled the hearing aid. "It's time for a battery change. I'll be right back."

He went into another room, maybe the kitchen. Mia walked to the wall of windows and looked up at the mountains. In a year they'd still be there, essentially unchanged. Mia, on the other hand, would be far away. She'd also have a brand-new niece or nephew. Her sole regret concerning Mission Medical was missing out on being the world's best aunt.

When Pirate's toenails clicked on the wood floor, she turned and saw Jake in the doorway, his shoulders slightly bent and his hand to his ear as he adjusted the hearing aid.

Satisfied, he gave her a nod. "That's better. Let's find Lucy."

He lifted his Stetson from a hook by the door, put it on, and called Pirate. The three of them left the house, crossed a wide yard, and approached the outbuildings. While they walked, Jake shared the history of the ranch. Founded by his great-great-grandfather in the 1890s, it had been home to cattle and a way station on the old Ute trail. In the 1930s, a new generation of Tanners added cabins and turned the property into a hotel to serve the growing populations of Colorado Springs and Denver.

When their success ebbed in the 1970s, Jake's grandparents knocked down the cabins and sold off most of the land. His father started Tanner Vending to make a living, met Claire on a blind date, and married her.

"They don't want to leave," Jake said as they neared the first outbuilding, "but they can't stay here forever."

"Not without a lot of help." Mia ached for the entire family. She'd cared for Alzheimer's patients on the med-surg floor. Frustration and pity went hand in hand. "She seems young for Alzheimer's."

"She is. She's only sixty-six."

"So it's early onset."

"Yes, but she doesn't have the genetic type. Even so, the disease scares my brother, sister, and me to death."

"I can imagine." Because of her mom, cancer scared Mia the same way. "How is your dad doing health-wise?"

"Just fine. He loves this place, but he's seventy-one and not getting any younger."

"So it's all on your shoulders. The house. The business. *And* starting the camp."

"Don't forget the dogs. And this." He pushed open the door to an old barn and flipped a light switch. "Welcome to the Tanner Pinball Museum."

Mia caught her breath at the sight of at least fifty pinball machines, all dark except for two games near the door. The tall back of the one called Pop & Go showed cartoon weasels in top hats bopping each other with bowling pins. The other was called Clown Car.

She gave Jake a sly look. "I bet there's a claw machine in here somewhere."

"Over there." He pointed to a big machine on the far side of the barn. "I practiced a lot as a kid."

"And you haven't lost the knack."

"Actually I did lose it." Peering out from under the hat, he shifted his attention back to the pinball games. "I spent a lot of time out here while I was recovering—both with the claw machine and playing pinball. There's something satisfying about whacking a little silver ball, and I could hear the noise without my hearing aids."

Mia touched his arm. She couldn't help it.

He gave a shrug, but his tone carried an edge. "The idea for Camp Connie was born out here."

"How?"

"When Sam came to visit, we spent hours playing different games. We also worked on his car, hiked to the top of Echo Falls, and shot the rapids farther down the canyon. He said it helped him to just hang out. We decided together to start Camp Connie."

"It's a worthy cause. But it's also a lot of work."

"Some," he said. "But I have the time. The vending business takes up maybe four days a week between driving the routes, stocking machines, ordering, and making repairs. My dad and I work together on it, but the camp is all mine. Right now I'm working on a business plan, researching insurance, and getting ready for a fight over the zoning change we need."

"A fight?" Mia couldn't believe it. Over a camp for kids who had lost a parent? "I can't imagine why anyone would be against it."

"There's some history here." Jake told her about the arson from five years ago, Bill Hatcher's loss, and the formation of the Stop the Camp group.

She was about to ask more about the zoning battle when a chorus of barking cut her off. She raised her voice. "That must be the kennel."

His mouth quirked up in the half smile she'd come to recognize. "Good work, detective."

Mia laughed. "Hey, I'm a nurse. I notice things."

"So do I."

"Oh yeah? Like what?"

Pausing, he studied her face with an intensity that stole her breath. "You're five foot six, about one hundred and twenty pounds, blue eyes, brown hair. No visible scars. And you smile like the *Mona Lisa* when you're nervous."

Awareness rippled from her toes to the nape of her neck, an exquisite tingling that defied her common sense. Jake was the kind of man she admired—one who paid attention to detail and saw past the masks people wore. If she wasn't careful, he'd see past hers.

She covered her nerves with a laugh. "The *Mona Lisa*? Thanks. I think."

"It's a compliment," he said, still studying her. "I pay attention too. It's a habit from being a cop."

"You must miss it."

"Yeah. I do. But it's over now." He indicated the dark barn. "A hundred years ago, a place like this would have been filled with livestock. Now it serves another purpose. We can adapt and move on, or live in the past. I adapted."

"I'm adapting too," Mia murmured. "Both by moving here and applying to Mission Medical."

He gave her a curious look, but she didn't want to say more about her reasons for making a big change.

The silence thickened until he aimed his chin toward the door. "Let's check out the dogs."

They walked side by side to a building with white siding and a low roof. The interior was warm, well lit, and separated into about twenty dog-sized cubicles. Flaps on the wall allowed the dogs to go outside. The spaces were empty except for one, where a little white dog sat huddled in the corner.

"She looks lonely," Mia said to Jake.

"She is."

"What's her name?"

"Officially it's Peggy McFuzz, but she goes by Fuzzball, Fuzzy, or Miss McFuzz if she's being a princess."

"That's adorable." Mia clicked her tongue to get the dog's attention. Fuzzy's ears perked up, but she stayed in her safe place. "Did you name her?"

"No. She came to us with a history. Her owner passed away unexpectedly. The family felt bad about it, but no one could keep her."

Mia's throat swelled with a familiar lump. If she hadn't managed to raise Lucy, her sister would have gone into foster care, a little like Peggy McFuzz. "Is she eating?"

"Not a lot."

"The poor thing."

"We might move her into the house. Or better yet, how would you like a dog?"

"Oh no. I couldn't." Mia backed away. Growing up, she had wanted a roly-poly puppy as much as any little girl, but her mom couldn't manage one. "I'm leaving in six months, remember?"

"Just checking," he said with a smile. "Peggy McFuzz has the power to melt hearts."

So did Jake, but Mia was dead set on never melting again, even if he did look ridiculously handsome with that cowboy hat riding low on his brow.

He opened the back door, and she stepped into a large fenced play area for the dogs. Claire and Lucy stood about twenty feet away in the shade of an oak, throwing tennis balls and mangled frisbees to four dogs of various breeds and sizes. Pirate let out a bark and wagged his tail.

"Go for it." Grinning, Jake gave the dog a hand signal.

When Pirate galloped into the fray, Lucy spotted Mia, squealed happily, and ran to her.

"Thumb's up!" Mia called, making the gesture. "I took the job."

Lucy pulled her into a hug and squeezed so tightly that Mia could barely breathe. If there was anything better than hugging hard, she didn't know what it was.

"This is terrific! I can hardly believe it!" Lucy leaned back and dabbed at her eyes. "I'm so happy I'm crying. Do you have a tissue?"

"You know I do." Mia pulled one from her pocket. "With the wedding, I brought ten boxes."

"Ten?" Lucy gaped at her.

"Not really." Mia grinned at her own joke. "Just three."

She caught Jake smiling at her. Since when was Kleenex funny? Or maybe he thought *she* was funny. Brad had never laughed at her lame jokes, and she rather enjoyed making Jake smile.

Claire stood next to him. With the two of them side by side, the family resemblance was undeniable, except Jake's hair was pure coffee brown, and Claire's short style was threaded with gray. Their eyes matched as well, but Claire wore red-framed glasses.

Mia held out her hand for a friendly shake. "I'm Mia. It's nice to meet you, Claire."

"Mia," Claire repeated. "Yes."

"Thank you for taking care of my sister."

"We love Lucy."

"She's pretty special." Mia winked at her. "At least when she's not driving me crazy."

Lucy giggled. "I don't drive *you* crazy. *You* drive *me* crazy!"

Claire laughed with them, then clasped her hands over her chest. "Lucy's getting married. Did you know that?"

Jake started to say something, maybe to cover his mom's social clumsiness, but Mia stopped him. There was no reason to make excuses for Claire.

Mia spoke to her directly. "Yes, I did know."

Claire seemed pleased. "We're baking a cake."

"What fun!" Go slow, Mia reminded herself. Express one thought at a time, because that was all Claire could process. "Do you like to bake?"

"I love it."

"Do you like to make cakes?"

"Oh, yes." Claire beamed at the attention.

Lucy turned to Jake. "We need to round up the dogs, then we can all go to the house for dinner. It's in the Crock-Pot."

Jake looked as hungry as Sam at the Safari Café. "What are we having?"

"Your mom's beef stroganoff," Lucy said with pride. "I just need to boil the noodles."

"Don't forget to drain the water," Mia warned, "or we'll have—"

"Stroganoff soup!" Lucy declared.

Claire seemed confused, but she laughed. "*And* we're having Skittles for dessert. Jake bought them for Lucy's sister."

Skittles? Really? Lucy must have blabbed to him, but for once Mia didn't mind. She was sweetly charmed by Jake's thoughtfulness.

His face wasn't exactly red, but he'd been caught off guard. "Uh, Mom?"

"What?" Claire said.

"That was a secret." Turning to Mia, he gave a sly wink. "Someone told me you have a closet addiction."

"I do."

Claire shrugged. "Well, it's not a secret now. I have Alzheimer's, you know. I say what I shouldn't and forget what I should."

Jake laid an arm across his mother's thin shoulders and gave her a squeeze. "You're also the best mom in the world."

Claire rested her head on his shoulder, tears welling until she blinked them back. Someday she wouldn't know him, but at this moment, they were mother and son in the best possible way.

Lucy clasped Mia's hand and held tight, a reminder that they too were family.

Jake's deep voice broke the silence. "Why don't you ladies go back to the house? I'll round up the dogs. When Dad and Sam get home, we can eat some of that stroganoff soup."

"And Skittles," Mia added to tease him. "I'll fight you for the red ones. They're my favorite"

Jake grinned at her. "Mine too. How about we share them?"

"I'll share too," Claire chimed in. "Did you know Lucy's getting married?"

"She sure is," Mia replied.

Lucy winked at Jake. "Don't tell Mia, but I opened the bag and ate all the red ones."

"You did not!" Mia scolded.

"Oh yes, I did! The baby wanted them."

They all laughed as they headed toward the house, especially Claire, even though she didn't really understand the joke. Sometimes love needed to be put into words. Other times words got in the way, and a touch or a hug, or just belonging, said more than enough. For Mia, this was one of those times.

chapter 8

Jake enjoyed himself more in the next three days than he had since he left Denver. Between Lucy's giggling, Sam's classic case of nerves, and Mia's enthusiasm about moving to Echo Falls, he'd been pulled out of the serious business of starting Camp Connie and caught up in the exuberance of a wedding.

On Thursday, he helped Mia find a rental house close to her new office. The house was old, but he approved of the extra insulation and double-pane windows. As for the door locks, he planned to replace them personally. With a rental property, you never knew who had keys.

On Friday morning, he taste-tested a sample of the wedding cake. When he declared it perfect, Claire and Lucy traded high fives. And on Friday night, while Mia hung out with Lucy, Jake played pinball with Sam, assuring him Connie was watching from heaven and that his mom would be proud of him.

Saturday dawned bright and clear, a perfect day for a summer wedding. Jake and his dad put out chairs, arranged tables, and hung battery-operated lanterns from the eaves and in the nearby trees. Mia came outside to offer advice on the arrangement, then slipped back into the house to help Lucy dress for the twilight ceremony.

As best man, Jake's first responsibility was to Sam, but he couldn't stop himself from worrying a little about Mia. They were both a lot older than the college kids invited to the wedding, and he knew how *he* felt—like an old guy with hearing aids and a trick knee. Someone who didn't fit in. No way did he want Mia to feel left out. They were in this together, and he intended to make the night fun for her.

At precisely six o'clock, or 1800 military time, the twenty-two folding chairs were filled with guests. Sam and Lucy stood in front of ROTC Chaplain Reginald Grant, and Jake and Mia were in their positions as best man and maid of honor.

"Ladies and gentlemen!" Chaplain Grant's voice boomed as if he were addressing a full battalion. Forget mild-mannered Father Mulcahy of *M*A*S*H* fame. Chaplain Grant was taller than Jake, hard-muscled, bald, and wore a fruit salad of ribbons and metals on his chest.

"We're here today to honor Sam Waters, Lucy Robinson, and the commitment they're about to make to each other. I've known Sam for three years, and I've recently gotten to know Lucy. It's an honor to officiate their wedding."

Jake's gaze strayed to Mia. She was utterly captivating in a strapless, peach-colored dress that shimmered in the last rays of the sun. The silk brought out coppery highlights in her hair, and so did the peach-colored flowers in her bridesmaid bouquet. She also held Lucy's bridal bouquet for the second time since Jake had met her.

Was she always the bridesmaid and never the bride? Always the woman who worked behind the scenes? It seemed like it.

Chaplain Grant broke into his thoughts. "Today's ceremony will unite Sam and Lucy as husband and wife. But there's a little more to it. As you all know, they're going to be parents in about six months. A family . . ." His voice trailed off, inviting every guest to think about what family meant to him or her.

"Family," he repeated more firmly. "Science defines it in terms of blood and DNA, but our hearts understand family through shared experiences. Memories. A tender touch in a crisis. Or that trip to the principal's office when a teenager makes gunpowder in the chemistry lab—by accident, of course."

Laughter rippled out from the crowd, mostly from the guys.

The chaplain's eyes twinkled. "DNA determines that first physical link, but love alone holds a family together. A woman's love for a man who has promised to honor, love, and protect her until death parts them. And a man's love for that brave woman who vows to stand by him through thick and thin. But there's a problem here."

No kidding. *To honor and protect* . . . Jake lived by those words, but what did a man do when he failed to live up to them? Connie should have been here today, seated in the front row with a handful of tissues, crying happy tears.

"We're imperfect human beings," Grant continued. "We're destined to fail. The only love that never fails is God's love. His love for his children—*us*—is boundless, battle-tested, and bold. It's trustworthy, tried, and true. That kind of love requires action." He paused. "Don't worry, I'm done with the *A* words, but I want to be brutally clear on my next point."

He waited until even the squirrels in the trees seemed to snap to attention.

"Love is a choice. It's keeping promises when they're tough to keep. It's staying when you want to leave. And it's seeing the other person through the same forgiving lens through which God sees us all. Marriage is a conscious act. A decision. And that's the step Sam and Lucy are taking today."

The chaplain ended with a crisp nod, then focused on Sam with his hawkish eyes. "Are you ready, son?"

"Yes, sir!" Sam's voice came out way too loud.

Fresh echoes of laughter mixed with the slight breeze. Jake

glanced at Mia, expecting to see a smile, but she was biting her lip, maybe to hold back tears. Her bare ring finger flashed through his mind, and he recalled the way she had stoically held Lucy's first bouquet. He'd bet his hearing aids some fool had broken her heart, and he didn't like the thought at all. In fact, he wanted to deck the jerk who had hurt her.

Where had that thought come from? No mystery there. Mia was lovely and sweet, good-natured, and just plain sexy in that short dress and those spiky heels. Call it chemistry. Call it electricity. Call it nature or animal instinct. Whatever *it* was, it roared and thumped in his chest, until his gaze landed on the empty chair in the front row where Sam had laid a white rose to remember his mom.

Vicious buzzing erupted in Jake's ears, and Connie's ashen face shimmered in front of his eyes. Without Pirate, he was on his own against the pictures snapping through his mind. Connie prone on the concrete floor. Blood on the side of her head. The lack of all sound, even his own voice trying to rouse her. The buzz in his ears morphed into jackhammering that matched the panicked beat of his heart.

Lord, help. I'm losing it here. Desperate for a steady breath, he focused on Sam and Lucy to ground himself. Out of the corner of his eye, he noticed Mia watching him.

Her brows lifted. *Are you okay?*

How did she know? Did his weakness show, or was she an exceptional nurse, the kind who interpreted faces and body language as plainly as words? Either way, a silent bond formed between them. Steadier, Jake drew in a lungful of cool air. The jackhammering in his ears eased to a manageable buzz, and he replied to Mia with a crisp nod.

To his relief, she answered with a calm dip of her chin. He hated it when people overreacted to him overreacting.

When the chuckling at Sam's overly loud voice faded, the

chaplain cleared his throat. "Repeat after me. 'I, Samuel Jason Waters, take you, Lucy Anne Robinson, to be my wedded wife.'"

Sam repeated the age-old words and the ones that followed. For better, for worse. For richer, for poorer. In sickness and in health until death parted them. Lucy went next. Where Sam's voice boomed like a cannon, hers warbled like a wren singing its heart out.

The chaplain cued Jake for the ring. When Sam reached for it, Jake pressed the gold band into his palm. They traded a strong look, then Sam turned back to his bride.

"Now, Sam," Grant continued, "repeat after me. 'With this ring, I thee wed.'"

Speaking in a slow, calm voice, Sam recited the vows and slipped the ring onto Lucy's finger—no small feat, considering she was bouncing on her toes.

"Lucy," the chaplain said, "it's your turn."

Teary-eyed, Mia held out the ring with a steady hand. Instead of taking it, Lucy pulled her sister into a hug so long and tight, even Jake choked up. When they broke apart, Mia was a watery mess and Lucy was the steady one. Ring in hand, she spoke her vows to Sam, her eyes glued to his and her voice cracking.

Chaplain Grant raised his arms. "In the name of the Father, the Son, and the Holy Spirit, I pronounce you husband and wife. Sam, you may now kiss your bride."

And he did. Thoroughly.

For Jake, time froze into snapshots of Sam drawing Lucy close, the kiss, the tangle of their arms, her white dress and Sam's black suit. And finally, a picture of Mia in shades of peach and gold with two bouquets trembling in her hands.

When Sam finally ended the kiss, Mia gave Lucy back her bouquet. As the couple walked down the tiny aisle, Jake approached Mia with his hand extended. Her trembling fingers found his, and she squeezed, smiling through her tears.

"Can you believe this?" She gave a tiny sniff. "I'm a mess, and I don't have a tissue."

"Here." Jake pulled a handkerchief out of his pocket. He didn't usually carry one, but a best man needed to be prepared, so he had borrowed it from his dad.

Smiling her appreciation, Mia blotted the moisture from her cheeks. "Thank you, Jake."

It felt good to ride to the rescue again, even if it was just with a handkerchief for a teary woman.

●●●

An hour later, after a buffet dinner served on the deck, Mia joined Frank and Claire at one of the tables pushed to the side to make room for dancing. Jake was plugging speakers into an iPad, and Sam and Lucy were holding hands and talking with friends, waiting for the music and their first dance. Mia, relaxed now that the ceremony was over, sipped a glass of the lime soda water she liked.

Claire was in especially good spirits tonight. Instead of being overwhelmed by the crowd, she thrived on the snippets of conversation that matched her attention span. Relaxed and at ease with Frank at her side, she turned to Mia with a sparkle in her eyes. "You should be next."

Not again. How many times had a well-meaning soul teased her about marriage? Too many. Mia feigned ignorance. "For what?"

"To get married."

"I don't think so, Claire."

For once, it didn't hurt to say those words. Yesterday she had received a congratulatory email from Mission Medical and a request to schedule a panel interview the week of August sixteenth. The timing worked perfectly, another gift from God. By then, she'd have stories to tell about adapting to her new life in Echo Falls.

Claire nudged her again. "Don't give up hope, Mia. It's worth waiting for the right man." When she patted Frank's knee, he covered her hand with his larger one. "I can't imagine my life without Frank. Especially now, though why he puts up with me—"

He kissed her cheek. "You know why."

Love. The kind that lasted. Mia glanced down at Frank's hand on Claire's, his knuckles swollen with arthritis and age spots dotting his skin. She thought of the pictures in the stairwell, especially the wedding picture of Claire and Frank gazing into each other's eyes. Mia ached for them and the challenge of Alzheimer's, but she envied their strong marriage.

The first notes of a popular love song trickled out of the speakers. The crowd pulled back to make room for the bride and groom's first dance. Sam took Lucy's hand in his, and they swayed together in the way of people who didn't really know how to dance.

Claire let out a sigh. "I remember my own wedding like it was yesterday. I just wish I could remember what I did ten minutes ago."

Frank looped an arm around her shoulders. "I've got it covered, honey. Ten minutes ago, you were sitting here with me, and you'll be with me ten months from now. Even ten years. You know that."

A warm glow settled in Mia's chest. No wonder Frank and Claire had been married so long. Frank truly loved his wife and knew what commitment meant.

When the music faded to a whisper, Sam and Lucy invited their friends to join them. Someone turned up the volume on a Maroon 5 song, and the party took off.

Grinning, Frank stood and offered his hand to Claire. "What do you say? Shall we show these kids how it's done?"

Claire laughed. "I don't know this song at all, but I say yes!"

Arm in arm, they hit the dance floor as if they were in their twenties again.

Mia sat alone, her toes tapping on the wood and her heart full of relief, because she really didn't like to dance, as well as sadness, because she wasn't dancing. She supposed it was Jake's duty to ask her, but she hoped he didn't. In fact, this was a good time to restock the big ice chest holding soft drinks.

She took two steps before he caught up to her.

"Mia?" He stood with his hand extended and one brow lifted slightly above the other. "Shall we?"

"Dance?"

A grin split his face. "You really are a detective."

She laughed, both at herself and at Jake. "What can I say? The music was a clue."

"Music?" He tapped his hearing aid. "What music?"

"You mean—"

"I'm playing with you," he said. "I hear the song just fine. What do you say? Just one dance."

Mia hesitated. "I don't know—"

"I have to warn you," he said, glum-faced, "I dance like a circus bear."

Before she thought too much about it, she took his hand. "Now *that* I have to see."

As they reached the edge of the crowd, the music changed from the quirky beat of Maroon 5 to the strains of Coldplay and "A Sky Full of Stars." Mia's breath snagged at the back of her throat. She loved this song and Lucy knew it. But Lucy didn't know Mia had planned it for her own first dance with Brad.

Well, not anymore. But she still loved the song.

Jake put his hand on her back, took her in his arms, and glided into the music with a grace she didn't expect.

"You lied," she said over the lyrics.

"About what?"

"Dancing like a circus bear."

A sly grin curled his lips. "Yeah, I know. But I wanted you to say yes."

And she had. But now what did she do? She didn't want a romance with Jake or any man. On the other hand, why not dance for the joy of it? For once in her life, she had nothing to lose or gain by accepting a man's invitation. She and Jake were just friends, and they both wanted to stay behind that line.

She gave a light laugh, looked into his eyes, and let the song carry her. The music soared higher with every beat, taking her with it. When Jake spun her around, she ended the twirl with a silly little curtsy. He grinned, and so did she.

They were good together, she realized. But not as good as Frank and Claire, who were pulling off a foxtrot worthy of *Dancing with the Stars*.

Mia leaned into Jake. "Those two can dance!"

"It's good to see." He spun her around again, then pulled her closer than before, but not too close, while he watched his parents with a sad smile. Aching for them all, Mia stepped even closer to him.

The music faded into the final piano notes, and they stood together, breathing in unison, until the next song began with a slow, haunting rhythm.

"One more?" He lifted a brow.

"I'd like that."

An hour later, when the playlist wound down, Jake and Mia gave their toasts as best man and maid of honor; the cake was served; and Lucy prepared to toss her bouquet. Claire urged Mia to join the game, but Mia stayed behind with Jake and his parents. Teasing and laughter filled the air, and when Lucy's best friend caught the flowers, Mia clapped wildly.

She didn't want the night to end. Apparently neither did Jake, because after Sam and Lucy left for a night at a honeymoon cottage, they cleaned up the deck and kitchen together, then relaxed on the sofa and indulged in leftover wedding cake. With Pirate curled at Jake's side, they talked until after midnight.

Jake brought up that moment during the ceremony when she'd noticed he was emotionally rattled. "Sometimes memories strike like a snake in the grass."

"What did it?" she asked, absently stroking Pirate's thick coat.

"That white rose on the empty chair."

"It was a lovely gesture," she said. "And utterly devastating."

Jake stretched one long leg. "I'd give anything to hit rewind and not go into that building, but we can't change the past. In a perfect world, no one would die, at least not tragically. But that's out of our hands. Only God knows what the future holds or why the past is what it is. Without my faith, I'd be lost."

"Me too," she said. "Sometimes we just have to move on and do something completely new."

"That's what Camp Connie is about."

"And why I decided to apply for the job with Mission Medical."

"It's a good cause." He studied her for a moment, his expression relaxed but still piercing. "Can I ask you something a little more personal?"

"Sure." Why not? After all, they were just friends. Good friends, now.

"Why the big change?"

"This." She waggled her ring finger. "A broken engagement. Actually the second one, though the first disaster is ancient history. Even so, I needed to jump-start my life, so I did. Getting the coordinator job is a long shot, but I'd love to do that kind of work. There's a plastic surgeon who specializes in correcting facial abnormalities in children. That's the kind of difference I want to make."

"You glow when you talk about it."

"I do?"

"Like the stars in the sky," he said, quoting the song.

Silence settled over them, drifting down like a soft blanket. Mia gave in to the first yawn, Pirate gave the second, and Jake yawned last.

Tired, relaxed, and happy, she and Jake stood and faced each other. He didn't try to kiss her good-night, and that was good. On the other hand, she fell asleep dreaming of that sky full of stars and wondering about all the things she had missed in her life, particularly the one thing she was saving for the husband she'd probably never have.

●●●

When Sam stepped out of the bathroom of their honeymoon cottage, a tiny log house with skylights that let in the silvery glow of the moon, Lucy saw his pajamas and grinned. The bottoms were black and white plaid, and the T-shirt top said, *I Heart My Awesome Wife*. Her pajamas matched his, except they were pink and her shirt said *I Heart my Awesome Husband*.

She hugged her knees to her chest. "This was the best day of my life."

"Mine too."

"But it's going to be the worst night ever." The spotting had stopped, but she was on pelvic rest until she saw her OB next week. Lucy understood the biology of pregnancy and the laws of chance, but she couldn't help wondering why this had happened to them. Was God angry with her? Punishing her because she and Sam had sinned?

Sam took her hand and kissed it. "You have to laugh at the irony. We couldn't keep our hands off each other, and now I'm afraid to be in the same room with you."

"It *is* ironic, isn't it?"

"Very."

"Sam?" Her voice came out in a peep.

He dropped onto the edge of the bed and took her icy hand in his warm one. "What is it, Pudge? What's wrong?"

"I don't know exactly." Or maybe she did, but she was afraid to voice her fears. Would Sam be disappointed in her? She was a Christian, but her faith didn't measure up to his.

"Give it a shot."

"All right. The spotting and all. The fact we can't make love on our wedding night. Do you think God is punishing us?"

"No way!" He covered the top of her hand with his other one, making a protective shell. "He loves us, Lucy. And He loves the baby."

"But we messed up."

He scooted back an inch. "I don't want to make light of sleeping together before getting married, but a mistake doesn't make God love us any less. It means we're human and need a Savior. You know that, right?"

"Well, yes. It's just . . ." She shook her head. "I don't know what I mean."

Yes, she did. She was afraid she couldn't measure up to other people. Couldn't be like Mia. Couldn't be the good wife Sam deserved and the strong one he needed to succeed in his career. She was afraid that God didn't really love her, because while Mia was busy saving the world, Lucy could only make people smile.

Sam was one of those people, and making love made him smile more than just about anything. Without that mysterious connection, she worried they'd fight and he'd get tired of her. She didn't bother to voice her fears. He'd make promises, but would he be able to keep them? Considering he had broken the one he made to himself and to God to stay pure, she didn't know what to think.

He leaned in for a kiss, then trailed a finger down her cheek. "We're going to be fine, Pudge. You know I love you."

"Yes."

"And I love Beanie Baby."

Her hand went to her tummy. No bump yet, but she wasn't her skinny self either.

Sam gave her a last squeeze and let her go. "Let's stop talking about what's not happening tonight and do something else."

"Like what?"

He pushed off the bed, went to his duffel, and came back with their computer tablets. "How about Googling baby names?"

"Oh, I'd like that!" She thought constantly about the baby's gender. A boy with Sam's good looks, or a little girl she understood? Lucy hoped for a girl, but Sam would love a boy.

They Googled names for girls first and made a list of possibilities. Lucy thought Elizabeth was pretty, and Sam liked Anastasia, which she didn't like at all. Using Constance as a middle name was a strong possibility, since they both agreed his mother would want a little girl to have her own first name.

The list for a boy started with Noah and ended with Igor, because by midnight they were slaphappy.

After setting the tablets aside, Sam turned out the light and spooned her in his arms. He kissed her neck, then whispered, "I love you, Pudge. I always will."

"I love you too," she crooned back.

In just minutes he was snoring in her ear, but Lucy lay awake under the stars shining through the skylights, her hormones pinging and her soul aching. Closing her eyes, she prayed silently to the God who scared her to death.

Help me, Lord. Please. I don't know why Sam loves me, and I don't know how to be a good wife and mother. I forget to eat, and I lose things, and—and—I'm in so far over my head it isn't funny. Amen. By the way, I'm Lucy . . . Lucy Waters now, not crazy Lucy Robinson. I hope Sam's right about you loving us, because I'm so scared I can hardly breathe.

She whispered, "Amen," felt Sam stir against her, and tried not to cry.

chapter

9

Mia returned to Denver on Sunday morning, went to work on Monday, and was thrilled when Dr. Moore cut her loose with just a week's notice and her heartfelt support.

"Get on with your life, Mia," she said. "You've needed a change for a while."

"Thank you. It's true." A weight lifted as Mia admitted to the fact that her life had become stagnant. She supposed friends sometimes saw things in her she couldn't see for herself.

Over the next five days, she walked around in a cloud of heady excitement. For a woman who liked having a daily routine, making a big change was both scary and invigorating. She finished packing up her apartment, took Jake up on his offer to help her move into her new house, and on Saturday morning left Denver with her 4Runner crammed to the roof with boxes and clothes.

With her heart light, she took the Echo Falls exit from the four-lane highway, crossed a high bridge, and drove another thirty miles along the river. Running fast and high with the last of the spring runoff, it splashed over scattered granite boulders glistening in the sun. Far in the distance, she saw the top half of the double-decker waterfall that gave the town its name.

Echo Falls, so named because the bottom waterfall echoed the top one, was a popular spot for hikers. Maybe someday she'd make the climb to see it in person. Or maybe not. Pictures on the town's website showed a steep, slippery trail. The last thing Mia needed right now was a twisted ankle.

A sign welcomed her to the town of Echo Falls, Population 5,025. She turned left on Main Street and saw the Brownie Emporium, a storefront restaurant with a sign that advertised breakfast, lunch, and dinner. She supposed it was the Echo Falls version of the Cheesecake Factory and decided to grab lunch before she met Jake at the house.

With her stomach growling, she parked in an angled space a few shops away, climbed out of her car, and paused to take in her new stomping ground. The row of storefronts, all restored and painted bright colors, belonged in another era. Mia felt as if she'd stepped back in time until she reached Blackstone Apothecary, where an orange poster covered the bottom corner of a display window. Heavy black letters tossed down a gauntlet.

Stop the Invasion!
Keep Crime Out of Our Town

With her heart heavy, she skimmed the poster's dire predictions about crime and violence. The wording struck her as extreme, but the photograph of the burning house was a stark reminder of human brutality. Sometimes she thought the whole world suffered from PTSD on some level.

She was still reading the details when the glass door to the restaurant opened and a tall man with a stocky build, deep-set eyes, and close-cropped white hair stepped onto the sidewalk. Her attention dipped to the aluminum cane clutched in his gnarled hand. A future patient? It seemed possible. Echo Falls was a small, friendly town, so she returned his gaze with a polite smile.

"Good afternoon," he said, approaching her. "I see you're interested in my poster."

Uh-oh. No way did Mia want to talk about Camp Connie. "It caught my eye, but I'm only here temporarily."

The man shifted more of his weight to the cane. "I'm Bill Hatcher, Chairman of the Stop the Camp Committee."

"Oh—" A second too late, she schooled her features into another polite smile. "I'm Mia Robinson. I'm taking over for Dr. Collins."

Mr. Hatcher's eyes narrowed. "I heard about you. You're a friend of Jake Tanner's."

"Yes, I am." Mia wasn't surprised by his knowledge. Dr. Collins had told his frequent flyers to expect her, and news traveled fast in a small town, complete with gossipy details like how she had heard about the position.

Mr. Hatcher's nose flared. "I presume you're on his side in this mess."

"I'm not on anyone's side." At least not publicly. Mia thought it was both unprofessional and unwise to mix medicine and politics. She didn't want to alienate patients with her opinions, and she didn't want to dodge debates in the office. She had shared her intention to remain publicly neutral with Jake over the wedding cake, and he wholeheartedly agreed.

Hatcher stood straighter, glaring down at her. "You're a doctor, right?"

"A nurse practitioner."

"Close enough. You have training, so you know something about teenagers and mental illness."

"Yes, I do. But it's not my specialty."

"But you've seen the news." His face wrinkled into a scowl. "This crazy world is full of sociopaths. Kids who don't know right from wrong. Kids who don't respect the law or other people's property. That camp is a Trojan horse—"

"Mr. Hatcher, please. Let's not argue."

Ignoring her request, he ranted on about the camp and teenagers in general.

Mia sealed her lips, allowing him to blow off steam. After listening for another minute, she broke in as gently as she could. "I need to go now."

"Fine! Ignore the problem." He stabbed his cane at the poster. "But *my house* burned to the ground in that fire. My twelve-year-old cat died. I lost every photograph of my deceased wife, the quilts she made—"

Mia's hand flew to her chest. "I am so sorry."

"*Sorry?*" Hatcher snarled at her. " Do you think that changes anything?"

"No, but I wish it could."

He jabbed the cane crookedly down on the sidewalk, lost his balance, and lurched forward, swearing at himself as he tumbled into her. Mia grabbed his elbow to steady him, but he was a large man, and they both nearly fell.

"Hey!" Jake's voice bellowed from ten feet away. "Back off, Hatcher. *Now.*" He strode forward with his jaw tight and a glint in his eyes. Pirate, ears pricked and tail high, matched his pace.

"It's okay," Mia called to Jake. "Mr. Hatcher's cane slipped. That's all."

Jake halted a step away and looked her up and down. "You're not hurt?"

"No. Definitely not." Except her knees were wobbly, a sign of low blood sugar, no doubt exacerbated by her pounding heart.

Jake acknowledged her with a nod, then squared off with Mr. Hatcher. "Is there a problem here, Bill? Because I'm the one you should be talking to."

Mr. Hatcher sneered at him. "You know the problem, Tanner. You're bringing in a bad element."

"I'm doing no such thing."

"Oh yes, you are!"

Jake's voice dropped to a growl. "Let's keep this civil, Bill. You and I can disagree without shouting at each other or involving innocent bystanders like Ms. Robinson."

Mia opened her mouth, intending to be a peacemaker, but Mr. Hatcher spoke first, glaring at her. "There's no such thing as an *innocent* bystander in a democracy. Every citizen is called to participate."

"I agree," Jake replied. "But there are rules of engagement. I already offered to debate you. Why not take me up on it at the rally you're holding? We'll go head-to-head, with Marc Scott as moderator."

A confident gleam burned in the older man's eyes. "All right. We'll do that."

Jake held out his hand. "So is it a deal?"

"Agreed. But get ready, Tanner. I'm going to prove you wrong on every front."

"You're welcome to try."

Hatcher gripped Jake's hand and shook. Eyes locked, neither man let go for a solid three seconds. Mia didn't know who loosened his fingers first, but she didn't think it was Hatcher. He shifted his cane to his right hand, mumbled an apology for stumbling into her, then headed to a white pickup truck. An orange sticker with a stylized flame and the words *Stop the Camp* glared a warning from the rear window.

His eyes glued to Hatcher's back, Jake ran a hand over Pirate's head. "The sticker is new. We'll probably see a lot of them."

Mia's stomach rumbled loudly enough for Pirate to turn and look at her.

So did Jake, who didn't bother to hide an amused smile. "Even *I* heard that. How about lunch?"

"That sounds good. I'm starved."

He paused to study her face. "You look a little shaky. Did Hatcher do that to you?"

"Not at all. It's low blood sugar. I was on my way to grab a sandwich when he saw me looking at the poster. As soon as I eat, I'll be fine."

"Then let's go." He rested a protective hand on the small of her back and steered her toward the café. "Lunch is on me, and we're getting it right now."

●●●

Jake didn't expect Mia to faint, but as they walked with Pirate toward the café entrance, he kept his hand in place just to be sure. Hatcher had no business pressuring her, especially when she was staying neutral—rightly so, in Jake's opinion.

He held the door, ushered her inside with Pirate leading, and suggested a table in the back where the dog could stretch out and Jake wouldn't have to work to hear over the buzz of the lunch crowd. An old friend from high school waved, but most of the people were strangers visiting Echo Falls for the weekend.

He and Mia ordered sandwiches and iced tea at the counter, then went to a table where he could sit with his back to the wall like he preferred. Mia added real sugar to her tea, took several swallows, then eased back in her chair. "That tastes good."

"I hope Hatcher didn't upset you too much."

"Not at all." She swirled the tea with her straw. "I actually feel sorry for him."

Jake admired Mia's compassion, but Hatcher could be a bully when it came to stopping Camp Connie. "Losing his home was a tragedy. That's undeniable. But the Stop the Camp group isn't looking at the facts."

"No. It's emotional for people like Bill."

"Very much so." For Jake too.

Mia took another long sip. "Living with the memories must be hard for him. Does he have any family?"

"Just a daughter. I think she's in Miami."

"I wonder why he didn't move to be closer to her."

"His business," Jake replied. "He owns Precision Pumping and Backhoe. He's been in Echo Falls as long as I can remember."

Mia wrinkled her nose. "Pumping, as in—"

"Septic tanks."

"Ewww."

Jake grinned. "It's a dirty job, but—"

"Somebody has to do it," she finished. "Kind of like nursing at times."

"Or being a cop." Both noble professions that took a toll but made the world a safer place.

They chatted casually until the waitress brought their order. When she left, they both bit into their sandwiches. Mia chewed thoughtfully, then dabbed at her lips. "I can see why people enjoy living here. Echo Falls is a nice little town."

"It was nicer before the Stop the Camp group started."

Jake's gaze skimmed to the window, where yet another orange poster announced the rally. The ugly things were everywhere, but he had friends too—including Mia. While she ate, he stole glances at her face. She seemed steadier now, and he couldn't help but notice the pretty glow of her skin, the way she sipped her tea, the bread crumb on the corner of her mouth.

She swallowed a bite of her turkey sandwich. "Hatcher sure is serious about opposing the camp."

"Irrational is more like it."

"Or dedicated."

"Irrational," Jake repeated. "I plan to bring up small groups of kids for a week at a time. We'll do some camping, hike, learn basic life skills, and play pinball. Those things helped Sam after Connie died, and they can help other kids in his shoes."

"I can see the benefits. But I wonder . . ." Lips sealed, she shook her head. "I almost forgot. I'm staying neutral."

Her questioning didn't sit well at all. "You're also a friend and someone I respect. What's bothering you?"

She wrinkled her nose in that cute way that signaled he wasn't going to like what she had to say. "I hate to see the town ripped apart."

"Me too."

"All the time and money. The ill will." She shuddered. "It seems like such a waste."

"I couldn't agree more." Jake ate another bite of his BLT. "I have big plans for the camp. First-class camping equipment, a couple of old sports cars to work on, kayaks for rafting. I have plenty of time on my hands, but no way am I spending a dime on bumper stickers."

"How are you funding it?" Mia asked.

"Donations. Plus I have some savings. There's no mortgage on the house, so I can take out a loan for capital improvements. This isn't a full-time, year-round operation, so the overhead isn't impossible. Plus I'll keep the vending business going."

Looking down, Mia continued to eat her meal. Jake did the same, though he barely tasted the food. Her opinion mattered to him. So what *wasn't* she saying? Rather than pry it out of her, he slipped Pirate a piece of bacon. When the dog finished wolfing it down, Mia smiled but remained quiet.

Silence didn't bother Jake at all, but dangling questions stirred up his cop instincts. Leaning back, he decided to do a little prying after all. "So what are you thinking?"

"More about Bill Hatcher."

Not what Jake had hoped to hear. "What about him?"

"It's not easy to get over a trauma like he experienced. You know that better than most people."

He appreciated her directness, if not the reminder. "We all have stories to tell." Jake didn't consider himself unique in any way. Soldiers coming home from Iraq and Afghanistan, some with horrific injuries, endured far greater challenges than his.

"Yes, we do," Mia agreed. "And we all react differently. Is there any way you could put Bill at ease?"

"Believe me, I've tried."

He told her about the first newspaper notice regarding the zoning change, and how Hatcher called him on his parents' house phone, irate but civil enough for Jake to invite him to lunch. "I tried to explain the plan to him—the activities, the calendar schedule, even the security system I'll need to install for insurance purposes. Nothing appeased him."

"He's pretty hardcore," Mia agreed. "And you can't move the camp." Her voice rose on the last word.

Was she asking him a question or agreeing with him? Jake couldn't tell, but her ambivalence was an answer in itself. Mia doubted his choices, his dream, the cause that kept him from sliding back into dark places. "Move the camp? Absolutely not. This is my home too."

"Yes. Of course." She seemed more supportive now. "I just wish there was another way. Judging by the number of posters, he has a lot of support."

"So do I."

"I'm sure you do. It's just—" She made that wrinkle-nosed rabbit face again. "I worry about you."

No man wanted a woman to worry about him. It implied he might fail. "Me?"

"Just a tiny bit." She made a pinching motion with her thumb and forefinger. "You've put so much of yourself into starting the camp, and you're in for a fight."

"The camp is worth it." The effort gave him a purpose, something to do with his time, an identity other than a retired, disabled, has-been cop. "Some things in life are worth fighting for. This is one of them."

"But at what cost?"

"We'll see. With a little luck, the hostility will blow over."

Mia stayed silent, either out of respect for Sam's loss, or because she didn't want to argue anymore.

Jake wasn't ready to let the debate go. "You know what it's like to lose a parent. If you weren't around, who would have taught Lucy to drive, or helped her open a bank account? No one. And that's what a lot of boys experience when they lose a parent. Take Sam." Jake's pulse picked up. "When the transmission started slipping in his old Mustang, he didn't know enough to check the fluid. He kept driving and destroyed the transmission."

Mia winced. "Ouch."

"He could afford to buy something new with his mom's insurance money, but not all kids are that fortunate. The purpose of Camp Connie is to give teenage boys hands-on experience with real life. We're going to have car clinics, driving lessons if I can swing the insurance, power-tool projects, and maybe shooting classes, but that's another insurance nightmare."

"You're fighting a lot of battles."

"Yes, I am. It's worth it."

She smiled that *Mona Lisa* smile he couldn't read. "I think it's an excellent plan, Jake. I just wonder—" She shook her head. "Never mind."

"Tell me."

"I was going to say it's a lot to take on, especially with insurance and liability issues. But then I felt like a hypocrite for questioning you. Big plans take big faith. Those are the best kind."

"Like working for Mission Medical."

"Exactly."

She set her napkin on the table. "I really do hope the camp is a success. But I can't help but worry. I know how it feels to have something taken away." She waggled her bare ring finger.

"Sorry for the pain," he said, meaning it and not at the same time. "But you lucked out. I don't care if those guys were doctors, lawyers, or brain surgeons. They weren't good enough for you, Mia. Not by a long shot."

"That's not how it felt at the time."

But what he said was true. In Jake's opinion, Mia's gifts were extraordinary. The better he knew her, the more he admired her intelligence and compassion. She brought light into a dark room, quiet into a noisy day, and a soft touch to a hard, cynical world. She deserved better than a broken heart.

Jake reached across the table and squeezed her hand. "Trust me, Mia. Those two fiancés? They were morons."

"That's sweet of you."

"You don't believe me?"

"You're being nice, but there are two sides to every story. I figure I—never mind." Withdrawing her hand, she rolled her eyes to the ceiling. "Here I go again." She made air quotes. "'Woman dumped by fiancé for younger woman.' I'm so tired of being a cliché."

"You are not a cliché."

"I feel like one."

"Well, don't." He'd been down this road with his sister when a boyfriend broke her teenage heart. "I'm going to tell you what I told my kid sister."

"What's that?"

"Stay brave and remember who you are by the love and grace of God. Then tell me where the jerk lives so I can punch him in the nose."

Mia's eyes glistened in the light. "Does your sister know how lucky she is to have a big brother like you?"

"I tell her every time I see her."

"I bet you do!" Mia's grin was genuine now. "And I bet you chased off a lot of boys when she was in high school."

"Just a few."

He wanted to chase them away from Mia too. And the impulse wasn't the least bit brotherly. But was that wise? She planned to leave in six months. Then again, why not enjoy themselves while she was here? Nothing over the top, just time together. A deeper friendship. A kiss or two to help her forget that rotten ex-fiancé.

His blood heated with the thrill of the chase, something it hadn't done since the bomb blast, and he savored the sensation of coming back to life. It had been a long time since he'd planned a date with an eye on romance, but he was sure he hadn't lost the knack. A dozen ideas popped into his head. Dinner in the Springs, or at Andy's Barbecue Shack on the river. A trip to Pikes Peak. A hike to the top of Echo Falls.

Any of the above.

All of the above.

But right now, the first step was helping Mia move into her house. He glanced at her clean plate. "Are you ready?"

"Yes, I am."

They walked out of the café with Pirate leading the way, Jake's hand firmly on Mia's back, and smiles on both their faces.

chapter 10

On Monday morning Mia dressed carefully for her first day as the new primary care provider for Echo Falls. She twisted her hair into a French knot, applied her makeup with extra care, then opened the closet in her new bedroom.

Brown pants or charcoal? A beige top or something colorful? Instead of choosing, she trailed her hand along the peach silk of the dress she wore to Lucy's wedding. She couldn't help but think about Jake. Yesterday after church, he had taken her for a long drive around the community. Seeing the historic houses and old shops delighted her, but the number of orange signs left them both dismayed.

As she chose gray slacks and a pink top, she recalled his passion for Camp Connie. Jake wasn't like other men she had known. Instead of obsessing over sports cars like Brad, he put other people first. So did Frank, and that family DNA lived and breathed in Jake. The Tanner men were exceptional. So exceptional, Mia could almost believe in love again.

Almost . . . She stopped with her hand on her lab coat. There was nothing *almost* about falling in love, and nothing *almost* about a broken heart. That first breakup in college, when she discovered her fiancé with her roommate, had shattered her confidence in men. Brad, on the other hand, had shattered her confidence in herself. But that was all in the past. She had moved on to a new phase of her life.

At peace again, she slipped into her lab coat, put her stethoscope in her purse, and drove the six blocks to her new office. Today's plan called for her to shadow Dr. Collins and establish her authority with both patients and Kelsey Baxter, the office manager.

As she pulled into the parking lot, she took in the butter-yellow Victorian house with a long wheelchair ramp. With her purse on her shoulder, she climbed the front steps and walked into the waiting room.

A glass window rattled on its metal track as it slid open. Kelsey, leaning forward from a desk chair, greeted her with a smile. "Mia, welcome!"

"Thank you."

Kelsey indicated the door to the exam area. "Come on back. Dr. Collins won't be here for another hour. That's when we start patients."

As Mia turned the knob, she mentally shifted her demeanor from employee to boss, specifically Kelsey's boss. That was a new role for Mia, and she made a mental check mark on her list of new experiences to share at the Mission Medical interview next month.

When she stepped into the office area, she glanced at the labeled cupboards, neat countertops, and the stack of clipboards loaded with registration forms. Kelsey was just as squared away in a red polo shirt with the EFPC logo.

"You're organized," Mia said with a smile. "So am I."

"Good." Kelsey gave her an easy grin in return. "How about a quick tour?"

"Perfect."

"And a cup of coffee. We'll start in the kitchen."

Coffee in hand, they chatted while Kelsey showed Mia the

exam rooms, a storage closet, and a cabinet with prescription samples. Mia had been out of primary care for a while, but she had studied up and felt prepared.

When they returned to the front office, Kelsey handed her a printed schedule, then glanced at the clock. "Mrs. Hargrove is our nine o'clock. She'll be five minutes late."

"You know the patients."

"Pretty much."

"That's a big help." Mia sat in a chair at a side desk. "How long have you worked for Dr. Collins?"

"Five years. I started part-time as a senior in high school. Now"—she spun the chair a half turn—"I'm what Dr. Collins calls the office brain. I know the patients, the insurance issues, all the stuff that isn't written down but should be."

"'Office brain' is a perfect description." Every business needed someone like Kelsey. "I hope you're not planning to look for another job."

"Oh no! I love Echo Falls." Kelsey crossed her legs with a little kick, but a sigh whispered from her lips. "The only problem is dating."

This subject was too personal for the tone Mia hoped to set. On the other hand, Dr. Moore was a friend and mentor to her entire staff. Mia wanted to be that kind of leader. "What's the problem with dating?"

"Are you interested in anyone?"

What an odd question. And it was definitely too personal. All business now, Mia hoped her answer would end the conversation. "I'm leaving in six months. Dating is off the radar."

"Good. I was worried."

"About what?"

"You and Jake." A cloud passed over Kelsey's heart-shaped face. "It's none of my business, but he and I have gone out a few times. I like him a lot."

Mia blinked away her surprise. She didn't think for a second Jake and Kelsey were still involved. She knew him better than that, but questions fluttered through her mind. How close had they been? How long had they been apart? And why had they stopped seeing each other?

Mia wasn't nosy by nature, but she wanted to know what was going on. "Are you still dating?"

"No. Not at all. I just wish . . ." Her voice trailed off.

The last thing Mia wanted was tension with her new office manager, especially over a man she considered a friend. "Jake's a great guy. I hope things work out for you."

"You do?"

"Yes, I do." Mia tossed her Styrofoam cup in the trash. "Just to be clear, Jake and I are friends. With Lucy taking care of Claire, we see a lot of each other. He's like a brother to me. Like tonight, I'm having dinner at the house. No big deal."

It really wasn't. Lucy was learning to cook, and she had invited Mia to dinner with a text. *We'll celebrate your first day, plus I need victims for my lasagna!*

Jake would be among the victims. Mia gave in to a wave of sweet anticipation, but when she glanced at Kelsey, a love-sick puppy destined to suffer disappointment, she saw herself—the old Mia who had suffered through two broken engagements. Being rejected hurt, but life went on if a person held tight to God and found a new purpose.

Shrugging off the past, she adjusted her lab coat with a hunch of her shoulders. "I'm dead serious about landing the job with Mission Medical. Romance is the last thing I want or need in my life right now."

Kelsey tried not to smile. "Really?"

Mia held up both hands, palms out. "I've been down Heartbreak Road before. I'm done."

"Oh, Mia. I'm sorry."

"Don't be. I have a great career, a wonderful sister, and I'm excited at the prospect of joining Mission Medical. In fact, I'm happier than I've ever been."

Kelsey studied her with wide eyes. "I really admire you."

Mia didn't know what to say. While she appreciated the compliment, she couldn't help but envy Kelsey and her innocent hope. The girl wore her heart on her sleeve the way Mia once had.

The door to the waiting room opened, and Mrs. Hargrove walked in, five minutes late just like Kelsey had predicted. While Mia reviewed the notes in the e-file, Kelsey checked the patient in. Dr. Collins arrived through a back door, and Mia started her first day at Echo Falls Primary Care.

●●●

"You're going to be around for dinner, aren't you?" Claire said to Jake for the fifth time that hour.

"Sure," he said again. "I'll be here."

They were together in the kitchen, lasagna scenting the air with garlic and Jake on "mom" duty. His dad would arrive home soon, and so would Sam. Lucy was lying down for a few minutes after her hard work, both cooking and keeping an eye on Claire, who was having a rough day, the kind where she fidgeted with everything from the mail on the counter to the spoons in the drawer. Jake had stopped trying to help her find what she wanted and was leafing through a camping equipment catalog.

His mom turned from the silverware drawer. "You're going to be around for dinner, aren't you?"

"Yeah, Mom. I'm staying."

Jake could only imagine what went on in her head. His own frustration seemed small by comparison, and he was looking forward to tonight. Mia would arrive any minute. The little celebration was Lucy's idea and perfect for Jake's next move on the romance front. Tonight after dinner, he intended to walk her to her car. A kiss? A dinner invitation? Hopefully both.

"Jake?" His mom looked at him as if he'd just walked into the room. "You're going to be around for dinner, aren't you?"

"I sure am." *Lord, give me patience.*

Pirate popped up from his spot on the floor, nosed Jake's thigh, and headed for the front door, his signal that someone had knocked.

Mia? Probably. Before the hearing loss, Jake would have known by the rhythm of her knock or the tap of her steps on the wooden stairs. He missed that ability, but his other senses compensated. When he opened the door, he saw her in vivid detail, especially the fresh pink lipstick that matched a bouquet of flowers in her hand. The scent tickled his nose—or was Mia wearing perfume?

She held out the flowers. "These are for Claire."

"Not for me?"

She rolled her eyes. "I wish I had a snappy comeback, but I don't."

"You don't need one." He liked her sense of humor just the way it was. "Come on in. You can give the flowers to my mom. How did your first day go?"

"Good." She set her purse on the sofa and followed him toward the kitchen, still holding the bouquet. "Dr. Collins couldn't have been nicer, and Kelsey's terrific."

"She's a nice girl."

"Pretty too."

Was that a hint in Mia's voice, or were his hearing aids playing tricks on him? The last thing he needed was Mia playing matchmaker.

At the door to the kitchen, he started to make a joke about Cupid needing to get a life, but his gaze shot to the gas stove. A blue flame rose from the front burner, on full blast without a pot on it—and a forgotten dish towel so close the edges were smoldering.

Claire, oblivious, was rattling spoons in the silverware drawer.

"Mom!" Jake charged forward, threw the smoking towel in the sink, and cranked off the burner.

Pictures flashed in his mind. The blast blowing a hole in the wall of that abandoned building. Connie flying backward and landing like a rag doll. A wall of heat. Billows of smoke and dust. His chest constricted as if he were breathing that polluted air, then his vision tunneled until Pirate pushed against his leg. *Breathe deep,* he told himself. *It's just a memory.*

But that open flame was in the here and now. He'd left his mom alone for less than two minutes, and she'd nearly burned down the house.

Mia rested her hand on his biceps. Saying nothing, she stroked lightly, a nurse offering comfort to someone in pain, or maybe a woman offering comfort to a man. The first thought embarrassed him. The second one grounded him back in the moment.

Claire turned to him. "What's wrong?"

Mia, still holding the flowers, answered for him. "The burner was on."

"Oh—" Panicking, Claire spun to the stove, then faced Jake with a belligerent scowl. "It's not on."

"It was."

"But it's not on now."

Let it go, Jake told himself. Claire couldn't put the pieces together, and he couldn't do it for her.

The back door opened and Frank walked in. He started to greet them with his typical hearty hello, saw the standoff by the stove, and frowned instead. "What's wrong?"

Calmer now, Jake kept his voice level. "I left to open the front door for Mia. When we came back, the burner was on high and a towel was about to catch fire."

Frank grimaced in a way Jake saw often these days. "Take a break, son." He put an arm around his wife's waist. "Your mom and I will finish whatever she's doing."

"We're celebrating Mia's first day on the job," Claire piped up. "She's Lucy's sister."

Repeat. Rewind. Repeat. Jake felt like a man swimming in glue.

"That's right," Mia told his mom. "I'm Lucy's sister and I brought flowers."

"Oh!" Claire lit up. "I love flowers!"

Frank reached for the bouquet. "Thank you, Mia. I'll help Claire put these in water. Why don't you and Jake relax in the living room?"

Jake knew his father wasn't a saint, but he came close. "Thanks, Dad."

Relieved, Jake guided Mia to the couch facing the big windows. Pirate dropped down on the floor and put his head on Jake's boot, while Mia leaned back into the couch and let out a slow breath.

"That was unnerving," she said.

"And predictable. My dad took the knobs off the stove a month ago so this sort of thing couldn't happen. But today Mom and Lucy were cooking. I didn't give the stove a thought when I left her alone. That's one of the worst things about this disease. Sometimes life seems normal when it isn't."

Mia touched his foot with hers. "I'm just so sorry for you. Your dad too. This isn't pity. It's—"

"Compassion," he said, looking at her. "I know that. So does my dad."

A sweet light spilled from Mia's eyes. "He's a good man, isn't he?"

"The best. But he'd tell you he's as human as anyone." No doubt about it, but Jake saw no reason to bring up mistakes from the past. "What keeps him strong right now is his faith. And that's tested every day."

"I can't imagine seeing someone you love fade like that."

"It's rough."

"And just now with the stove—" Mia glanced back at the kitchen. "I hate to think about what could have happened."

"A fire," he said, tasting bile. "Or she could have picked up the dish towel and been seriously burned." And it would have been his fault. Sick to his stomach, he turned his gaze to the window and stared blindly at the sky.

"But it didn't happen, did it?" Mia shifted closer to him on the couch. When he didn't turn, she cupped his jaw with her hand, forcing him to stare into her eyes. Her pupils dilated in the dusky light, and her lips parted. Silent and still, she appeared to be searching for words.

Jake didn't need them. Her expression told him everything he needed to know. A first kiss dangled between them, but he wasn't about to take it with his parents ten feet away. Instead, he put his hand over hers, lowered his head, and brushed his lips against her palm.

Slowly, as if she couldn't decide what to do, she slid her hand off his jaw, looked down at her lap, then met his gaze with a look he couldn't decipher.

"We're all safe now," she said.

"Yes, we are." Safe in body, though not in the tender places of their hearts.

"It's time to get back to normal."

"And that is?"

"Being friends." She scooted back six inches, crossed her legs, and laced her hands over her knees. Something in the hall caught her attention, and she turned.

Jake looked over his shoulder and glimpsed Lucy. When Mia faced him again, she added, "Normal means enjoying a family dinner." Winking at him, she raised her voice. "Unless Lucy gives us all food poisoning."

"I heard that!" Lucy called from the hall.

Jake didn't mind the interruption at all. He'd given Mia something to think about, and unless he had misjudged the longing in her eyes, they weren't going to be just friends too much longer.

●●●

Mia jumped off the couch and walked with deliberate calm into the kitchen. Frank and Claire were preparing a salad, and Sam was putting on oven mitts in order to carry the lasagna into the dining room. Desperate for something to erase the kiss lingering on her palm, Mia searched the counter for bread to slice or napkins to put out. But Lucy, for once, had everything under control.

Mia didn't. If Jake had made the first move, she would have kissed him. What kind of stupidity was that? And now she was battling tears and didn't know why. Stuffing back the rush of emotion, she turned to her sister. "What can I do to help?"

"How about lighting the candles?"

The last thing Mia needed right now was to sit next to Jake with candlelight flickering on his handsome face.

He came up behind her and laid a hand on her shoulder. "I'll do it." After fetching the matches from a high shelf, he walked back through the doorway.

Sam followed with the lasagna, and they all migrated to the dining room, which was lit by two circles of votive candles. The flowers Mia had brought sat on the hutch, loosely arranged in a crystal vase.

Lucy swept her arm to indicate the table. "Isn't this fabulous? Claire and I made the lasagna from her mother's recipe. We even made our own garlic butter for the bread."

"Two loaves," Jake remarked. "I take it that's one for Sam and one for the rest of us?"

Grinning, Sam gave a thumbs-up. "You guessed it, bro. But cut me some slack, okay? I'm working my tail off these days."

Mia laughed with everyone else, but her entire body tensed as Jake pulled out her chair, just like Frank and Sam were doing for their wives. "Thank you," she murmured without looking at him.

When everyone was settled with Frank at the head of the table, Claire opposite him, and Sam and Lucy across from Jake and Mia, Frank held out his hands. "Let's say grace."

They all joined hands in a circle that put Mia between Jake and his father.

Frank cleared his throat. "Father God, we thank you for the food we're about to eat and the loving hands that prepared it. Thank you for Lucy, Lord. You know what a blessing she is to Claire and me. We thank you for Sam, serving his country. And we thank you for Mia, her nursing skills, and the courage to take on new challenges. Thank you for Jake and his vision for Camp Connie. And finally, Lord, thank you for my wife, a woman we all love, respect, and admire. Amen."

Frank's prayer soaked into Mia's soul, reminding her of God's love and her new call to join Mission Medical. So what if Jake had kissed her palm? It was just a moment, one of those times when a person reacted without thinking. Nothing between them needed to change.

Lucy served the lasagna, which Frank and Jake both declared perfect. An hour after Claire nearly burned down the house, the six of them were stuffed with good food and trading stories about their days.

"So you like it here," Frank said to Mia.

"I do. Very much. Primary care is a nice change from women's health."

"We're sure glad to have you." His eyes drifted to Claire.

"Going all the way to the Springs for a routine doctor visit isn't easy for some of us."

"Definitely not," Sam said through a yawn. "I make that drive five days a week."

Lucy gave him a soulful look, then rested her hand on her tummy. "The baby and I sure appreciate it."

Mia gave silent thanks that Lucy was past the twelve-week mark. She'd had the second ultrasound, and while the baby's heartbeat remained strong, the spotting was intermittent. Her doctor, playing it safe, had kept her on pelvic rest.

When the newlyweds started to make eyes at each other, Jake turned to Mia. "So you've officially met Kelsey."

Mia was glad Jake brought her up. "Yes. I like her a lot."

Lucy caught Mia's gaze and winked. *Not good*. Lucy got a thrill out of tossing verbal firecrackers and watching people gawk when they went off.

"So, Jake," Lucy said, "you know Kelsey, right?"

"Yes, I do."

"She's cute, isn't she?"

Jake said nothing, but Mia caught Lucy's drift and played along. "She's also smart and has a terrific sense of humor. She's great with people too."

"She's also single." Lucy gave Mia another wink. "Seriously, Jake, you should ask her out."

"Ask who?" Frowning, he tapped his hearing aid.

Lucy and Mia answered in unison, their voices loud and clear. "Kelsey!"

Jake tapped his ear again. "Did you say Mia? That's a great idea."

With the candles burning in two bright circles, he turned his head to the side, revealing both the mischievous quirk of his lips and the sincerity in his eyes. The scoundrel had heard every word.

Trying to play it cool, Mia raised her hands palm out. "Forget it. I'm leaving town, remember?"

Lucy patted her tummy. "You could change your mind. Beanie Baby and I would love that."

"So would we," Frank said for himself and Claire, who was overwhelmed and quiet tonight. "But let's leave that for another day. What do you say, guys? Shall we do the dishes?"

Sam nodded, but when he yawned, Frank waved him off. "Sam, you're dismissed. Get some sleep."

"I'll help," Claire said.

"Me too," Mia offered.

Lucy and Sam voiced their thanks and excused themselves. To Mia's consternation, Frank turned to Jake. "This is Mia's time to celebrate. Your mom and I can handle the dishes. It's a nice night. Why don't you two take a walk?"

Thanks a lot, Frank. No way did Mia want to be alone with Jake in the moonlight. Standing, she pasted on a smile. "Would it be terrible of me if I bailed out now?"

Jake gave her a look that said he knew exactly what she was doing. "Not at all. I'll walk you to your car."

So she wasn't getting away as easily as she'd hoped. She hugged Frank and Claire good-bye, hurried through the living room to snag her purse, and walked to her car with Jake striding to catch up with her.

"Mia, wait."

She stopped at the car door, keys in hand. "I really am tired, and I have another long day tomorrow. I need to go home. You know how it is. I just—"

"What's wrong?"

"Nothing." *Liar.*

He looked into her eyes, searching for answers and raising questions at the same time, until she took a step back.

"All right. If you really want to know, I feel like an idiot for what happened on the couch. I shouldn't have touched you at all. And then—" The memory of her palm on his jaw zinged through her. All she could do was mumble under her breath. "I am so sorry."

A grin split his face. "I'm not."

"Jake, no. I can't—we can't—"

"How do you know?"

"I just do—It's—I—" Sighing, she sealed her lips. Why couldn't she think on her feet?

He stayed at her side, the moon gleaming down on them. "I want to thank you, Mia."

"For what?"

"I haven't felt what I'm feeling now in a long time, and God knows I tried to feel it."

"With Kelsey?"

"Yes, but there's nothing there. No chemistry. No sparks. None of this." He trailed his thumb down her cheek.

Desire shimmered down to her toes, then up to the nape of her neck, swirling until goose bumps made her sway.

He lowered his hand but kept her pinned in place with his eyes. "I mean it, Mia. I feel like I'm waking up from a deep sleep, even a coma."

"That's good." She meant it. "If I've helped you at all, I'm glad."

He waited, giving her time to say more, then he bent and kissed her cheek. Mia's eyes drifted shut, but she still saw a sky full of stars and Jake's handsome face. Trembling with questions she was afraid to ask, and even more afraid to answer, she slipped into her car and drove away.

Sparks, even small ones, were dangerous things. Before she trusted any man with her heart, she needed to believe he wouldn't rip it out of her chest. With Jake, she could almost believe it, and that thought scared her most of all.

chapter 11

Over the next ten days, Jake prepared carefully for the Stop the Camp debate. If he won over the town's support, obtaining the zoning change would be a breeze. On the other hand, if Hatcher bulldozed him, Jake would be forced to make a choice: Spend money and time on politicking, or trust God to open the door for the zoning change. Or give up the camp, which wasn't an option.

He wasn't going to give up on Mia either. She was avoiding him, but he didn't mind the lull. Like apples on a tree, their feelings needed time to ripen. Just as important, he didn't want Mia anywhere near the Camp Connie controversy.

On Friday evening, when Jake strode into the crowded community center, he was prepared, confident, and determined to deliver a knockout punch. Pirate, his vest on display, walked at his side as they approached the front of the room, where Hatcher and Marc Scott were waiting.

The men greeted each other in curt tones, then Marc pulled a quarter out of his pocket. "You two know the format. Ten-minute opening statements, questions from the floor, then you'll each have five minutes to close. We'll flip a coin to see who goes first. Any questions?"

"Not from me," Bill replied

Jake shook his head. "No. I'm set."

Marc tossed the quarter into the air. Jake called heads and lost. Hatcher chose to go second and close, the same choice Jake would have made.

The men shook hands, and Jake stepped with Pirate to one of the three wooden podiums positioned six feet apart. He signaled Pirate to lie down, then surveyed the room. Judging by the sea of orange T-shirts and signs, Jake and his supporters were outnumbered two to one.

Frank, Sam, and Lucy sat directly in front of Jake, two rows back from the front. Kelsey and her mother were present, along with some people from church and a few old friends. Claire was home with her friend Barb, no doubt watching old episodes of *The Mary Tyler Moore Show*, her latest obsession. Jake didn't see Mia and was relieved.

Marc, standing at the center podium, tapped the microphone, then called for order.

Instead of quieting down, someone on Hatcher's side started a rhythmic clap, and the crowd erupted in a chant.

"Stop. The. Camp."

"Stop. The. Camp."

Jake's hearing aids amplified the noise and dulled it at the same time, almost like listening underwater.

Marc banged a gavel. "Ladies and gentlemen!"

The chant continued for two more rounds before Hatcher raised his arm to call for silence and the crowd obeyed.

Bending slightly, Marc spoke into the microphone. "Thank you for coming tonight. If there's one thing we can all agree on, it's that Echo Falls is our home. We're here to listen to both sides of the debate about a proposed youth camp. As many of you know, Jake Tanner has requested a zoning change. An organization called Stop the Camp has formally protested that request."

Applause broke out. Not a surprise, though Jake had hoped for less of it.

Marc waited for quiet. "Bill Hatcher, chairman of Stop the Camp, won the coin toss and opted to go second. As agreed upon, Jake and Bill will each make a short opening statement, then we'll take questions from the floor." Marc turned to Jake. "Mr. Tanner, are you ready?"

"Very much so." Jake opened his mouth to tell a joke, something light to capture the crowd's attention. But before the first word left his tongue, the door to the auditorium swung open, and Mia walked in.

He forgot the joke. He forgot everything except Bill Hatcher cornering her in front of the Brownie Emporium. He didn't want her here, but in some place deep and low, he took pride in her respect for him.

Gripping the podium, he stood tall, squared his shoulders, and skipped the joke.

"Why a camp for kids who have lost a parent in the line of duty?" he said in a booming voice. "Why a camp for teenage boys, named after Connie Marie Waters? The story behind this effort isn't easy for me to tell. Some of you know I was an officer with the Denver PD for seven years. Connie was my training officer and an extraordinary woman. She died three years ago in the bomb blast in Denver that made national news."

Connie, forgive me. We should have waited to go inside, but I was too eager. I thought— It didn't matter what he'd thought. She was gone.

He focused hard on the faces peering up at him. "Sergeant Waters met me at a call to check out suspicious activity in an abandoned building. I went in first. She followed, watching my back. The call turned out to be a setup by a man with a grudge against the police."

No one twitched a muscle. Even the men and women in orange T-shirts listened respectfully.

"Connie left behind a teenage son. His name is Sam, and he's here with us tonight. You'll hear from him later, but first let me tell you how the idea for the camp was born."

Jake told the rest of the story: his hearing loss and other injuries, Connie's request that he help Sam grow into a good man, and finally, how they'd been doing routine maintenance on Sam's car when the idea hit.

"Hey, Jake?"

"Yeah?"

Oil dripped over Sam's thumb as he held the filter. "Can I bring a friend up here next week? His car's falling apart. Maybe you could show him a few things."

"That's how it started," Jake told the crowd. "That friend of Sam's didn't have anyone to teach him basic car care, how to use power tools, or how to change out a bad light switch. At this camp, I plan to teach those skills in an environment that encourages community service and personal responsibility. Add in hiking, fishing, and kayaking down the Echo River, and you have my vision."

Hoping for applause, he waited. When it didn't come, he knew he needed to play tough. Shoving aside his notes containing facts and figures about delinquency, he took aim at the heart of Hatcher's reasoning.

"Ladies and gentlemen, I've known Bill Hatcher my entire life. He's a good man. I respect him. But he's wrong about a youth camp bringing crime to Echo Falls. He'll tell you the boys who visit will bring in drugs and commit acts of vandalism, but that isn't true. And it's not true for one reason."

Jake stared hard at a man in an orange T-shirt, a science teacher at the high school. "As much as we don't want to admit it, drugs and crime are already here."

Murmuring rumbled in the back of the room, and someone rammed an orange sign into the air.

Jake ignored it.

"Youth everywhere are at risk, even in Echo Falls. Teenage boys crave excitement and thrive on adventure. Those traits need to be shaped in healthy ways so that kids grow into responsible adults. Adults who pay taxes, raise families, hold jobs, and make this world a better place.

"The boys I hope to bring to this camp have lost a parent to violence. They aren't violent kids. They're the victims of it." He held up his stack of notes. "I have a bunch of facts and figures about delinquency, but you won't be impressed by them. Frankly, I'm not either. We can't fix this entire broken world, but we can help one boy at a time."

He scanned the crowd with a confident gaze. "Thank you for coming tonight, and I hope you'll support our effort."

A smattering of applause broke out, mostly from his side of the room.

Marc Scott cleared his throat. "And now we'll hear from Mr. Hatcher."

Hatcher, leaning on the podium instead of his cane, studied the crowd for ten seconds, then huffed into the microphone. "Let's skip the formalities. You all know me."

"You bet we do!" a man shouted.

"And you know what happened five years ago. A teenage boy set my house on fire. I will not allow that kind of violence back into our community. Not even a man as heroic as Jake Tanner can change my mind."

Hatcher lowered his voice, causing people to lean forward in their seats. "Sometimes good intentions are misguided, even foolish. I'm no fool"—his voice boomed now—"but I'm afraid Jake Tanner is!"

Thunderous applause echoed off the brick walls. Chanting

erupted again. Jake's ears started to buzz, but Pirate didn't budge. Inwardly Jake remained confident and calm, until Mia stood up from her seat in the back row and made her way to an empty chair behind Lucy.

Jake stifled a groan. Tonight he had wanted to protect Mia, not persuade her to step forward. Would folks hassle her at the clinic? She couldn't possibly know how poisonous local politics could be, but with the declaration she'd just made, she was going to find out.

It was up to Jake to protect her. He just hoped he could do a better job for Mia than he'd done for Connie.

●●●

Mia didn't care who saw her walk forward to join the Tanner family. Determined to support Jake, she slid into the seat behind Lucy and tapped her shoulder.

"Hey there," Lucy whispered. "I'm glad you came."

"Me too."

"Jake needs all the help he can get." Lucy turned back around, leaving Mia to watch Jake standing tall while Hatcher hurled insults. She had come tonight because she knew from the gossip bouncing around town and in her own waiting room that Jake was in for a rough time.

For the next thirty minutes, she listened to questions that revealed everything from legitimate concern to ignorance to irrational fears. When a woman declared that kids with ADHD or autism all caused trouble, Mia nearly leapt out of her seat.

The questions Jake received generally came from the business community. How many kids did he plan to host each summer? Would some of the families rent cabins while the camp was in session? How much construction did he plan at the Tanner ranch?

Every time Jake answered a question, Mia wanted to cheer. At the same time, she cringed at the bitterness coming from others. By the time Marc Scott signaled the last question, Mia knew only one thing with certainty. She was far too invested in this decision for a woman leaving town in six months.

"Jake," Marc said, "you have three minutes to wrap up."

"Thank you, Marc. I'm going to turn the microphone over to Sam Waters, Connie's son, and the inspiration for this project."

Mia hadn't noticed before, but Sam was in his formal ROTC uniform. He traded places with Jake and Pirate, cleared his throat, and thanked Jake for allowing him to speak. Now seated in the front row with Pirate, Jake answered with a silent nod, and Sam began.

"Ladies and gentlemen, I'm here tonight to persuade you to support a cause that honors my mother by helping the sons of fallen heroes—like her. When you're a teenager, losing a parent is about the worst thing that can happen. Your entire world spins out of control, and the person who knows you inside and out is gone.

"I wouldn't be wrapping up a college degree and wearing this uniform if it weren't for Jake. In short, he taught me how to be a man. Those lessons changed my life, and I want other kids to have that opportunity. Thank you."

Lucy clapped so hard her chair shook. Mia clapped just as hard, but her thoughts were with Jake.

After a nod from the moderator, Bill Hatcher, his face etched with rage, leaned over the microphone. "That's all very nice. I appreciate our young soldier. I think we all do. But look at him!" He jabbed a finger at Sam. "Do you think he's typical of the messed-up kids Tanner wants to bring up here? I don't.

"I have one goal, folks. I don't want anyone—and that includes Jake Tanner and his family—to be the victim of a crime, especially one that could have been prevented. Especially a crime as horrific as arson. If we open our town to this camp, we will all be in danger.

"Trust me, folks. That risk is not worth taking. If Jake knew how it felt to see his home burn to the ground, he'd agree with me. Thank you all for coming tonight. I trust you'll join me at the County Commissioners' meeting on October tenth. Together we can put a stop to this nonsense."

The crowd on Hatcher's side erupted in a cacophony of clapping, shouting, stomping, and chanting.

"Stop. The. Camp."

"Stop. The. Camp."

The noise slapped at Mia's ears. She could only imagine what it sounded like to Jake. Finally, when Hatcher left the podium, the outburst faded to a roaring conversation.

Mia slipped out of her empty row, hugged Sam, said hello to Frank, then moved toward Jake to offer congratulations on a job well done. Before she reached him, a small crowd hemmed him in. A couple of men slapped him on the back; a few others shook his hand. Mia waited with Lucy, who looked adorable in a new pink maternity top.

Jake glanced in her direction a couple of times, but she couldn't read his expression. Did he appreciate her support, or was he worried because she had publicly taken his side? Either way, she wasn't the least bit sorry she had moved up to the front.

When Lucy joined Sam, Mia glanced again at Jake and saw him talking to Kelsey and a woman she guessed to be Kelsey's mother. Knowing how Kelsey felt about Jake, Mia stayed where she was, close enough to hear without being involved.

"You were great!" Kelsey said to him.

Jake shoved his hands in his trouser pockets and focused on Kelsey's face, maybe to read her lips. "Thanks. I appreciate your support."

"Of course!" Kelsey laid her hand on his arm, her face full of concern. "I can't believe the awful things Hatcher said."

Jake eased back from Kelsey's touch, glanced at Mia, and called for her to join them. She didn't want to get caught in something personal, but she couldn't leave without speaking to him.

She greeted Kelsey's mom first, told her what a great job her daughter did, then turned to Jake. "You and Sam were terrific. I think you even changed a few minds."

Jake's mouth pulled into a frown. "Maybe. But I'm starting to hate the color orange."

"Me too!" Kelsey stepped closer to his side, as if she belonged there.

Jake eased back again, subtly but with enough intent that Mia wondered how Kelsey could miss his signals. On the other hand, what signals had Mia missed with Brad? When it came to romance, she no longer trusted her instincts.

"Hey, everyone." Jake raised his voice to include Frank, Sam, and Lucy. "How about coffee? I'm buying."

"Sure." Kelsey smiled up at him, her cheeks glowing pink. "We can plot out what to do next."

Mia heard the *we* and felt sorry for them both, but not sorry enough to get in the middle.

Ignoring Kelsey, Jake turned to Frank. "How about it, Dad? You can take Mom a white chocolate brownie."

Frank shook his head. "I need to get home. You can bring it for her. In fact, get a dozen. I'll hide them for later."

Sam looped an arm around Lucy's expanding waist. "Count me out. I have to pack for LDAC, and Lucy and the baby need their sleep."

Mia wasn't about to be a fifth wheel. "Sorry. I need to work on my Mission Medical interview." A lame excuse. Kelsey and Jake both knew she was fully prepared.

"Are you sure?" Kelsey asked, obviously not meaning it.

"Positive." Mia looked up at Jake, saw the tight line of his mouth, and knew how badly he wanted to discourage Kelsey without hurting her feelings.

Their group headed for the exit. Frank, Sam, and Lucy made it out the door, but a woman stopped Jake with a question. A small crowd of supporters gathered, blocking his path. Kelsey stayed at his side, but Mia slipped away.

As she turned to wave good-bye, Kelsey mouthed, "Thank you!"

Mia drove home feeling both lonely and relieved. Coffee still sounded good, so she made a cup of decaf, took it to the couch, and dropped down in front of the cold fireplace and a mantel lined with photographs, including a new one of Lucy and Sam taken at the wedding.

What had the chaplain said about marriage? Something about imperfect human beings and God's love being boundless, battle-tested, and bold. Mia sipped her decaf, pondering the lonely beat of her own heart. As a little girl, she had felt loved by God and trusted Him easily. God never let her down, but people did. They disappeared from her life the way her father had, suddenly and without a good-bye. Or like her mother, who had said good-bye a hundred times before she slipped away.

And what about the good-byes that cut like a knife? The college fiancé who had cheated on her. And Brad, who left her because she wasn't enough. Not young enough. Not fun enough. Not pretty enough. And maybe because she hadn't been willing to sleep with him before the wedding.

If she had, would they still be together? Maybe, but it didn't matter. Mia was proud of her choices, but sitting alone on her sagging couch, staring at a cold fireplace and Lucy's wedding picture, she couldn't help but wonder what she was missing and might miss the rest of her life.

Sighing, she curled her feet under her thighs. She might never have a husband, but her faith was strong enough to take her on a new adventure. Her partner in life was God. How could she complain about that?

The King of kings was on her side.

The Prince of Peace would fight for her.

Drawing strength from her faith, she used her phone to visit the Mission Medical website. Clicking through the links to their various programs, she imagined herself organizing vaccinations in Ghana and caring for orphans in Bangladesh.

She was reading an inspiring blog by Dr. John Benton, the plastic surgeon who operated on kids with cleft palates, when a text message alert popped onto the screen. She saw Kelsey's ID and read, *Thanks for ditching tonight. Coffee was nice.* ☺☺☺

Mia read the message twice, couldn't think of a thing to say, and decided to deal with Kelsey and her crush in the morning. Two seconds later, her phone hummed again, this time with a message from Jake. *Thanks for coming tonight. Just hope you don't pay for it.*

A warm glow lit her up on the inside. She shot back a reply. *I'll be fine. You're doing something good. Proud to know you!*

He replied immediately. *Likewise.* She thought he was done, but a second text popped up on the screen. *Missed you at coffee.*

"I missed being there," she said to no one. Then she sent back *Ha! I'm not getting in Kelsey's way!*

Just a few seconds passed before Jake answered. *I wish you would.*

Mia's fingers froze on the phone. "I wish I could, but—" Instead she texted, *She likes you a lot. Too much, huh?*

No kidding. There was a pause, then a second word bubble appeared. *Sleep well, detective.*

Somehow the nickname felt like a kiss. Was she crazy for not exploring the delicate feelings fighting their way to the surface? What was the harm in testing the waters with a real date? She didn't have the answer to that question, except that she was either crazy or a coward.

Crazy? No. She was too careful to act foolishly.

A coward? No. She was wise to be cautious.

Another word struck, and it resonated down to her marrow. *Committed*. The word fit her to a *T*. She had made a commitment to serve God through Mission Medical, and if they offered her the job, she would keep that promise. How could she not? God had cracked open the door with the job in Echo Falls, and He had opened it even wider when she made the cut for panel interviews.

For better or worse, Mia was determined to honor God. Human beings might let her down, but her heavenly Father never would. "It's you and me, Lord," she said out loud. "I won't let you down either."

chapter 12

Jake hated politics, but he cared about Camp Connie enough to walk up and down Main Street with an armload of flyers and Pirate at his side as a goodwill ambassador. He intended to drop in on stores ranging from the dry cleaners to the lumberyard and to ask to leave a stack of flyers for customers to pick up if they wanted.

No ugly orange posters.

No drama.

The flyers were Kelsey's idea, and she had pulled them together with pictures from Jake's phone. Instead of a burning house, the flyer displayed pictures of Sam and his friends. Underneath were five bullet points that promoted the benefits of the camp to local businesses.

Jake appreciated Kelsey's help, but he wished she'd give up on him. Mia wasn't helping either. That coffee invitation had been for her, a bridge between her reluctance and a real date with just the two of them. As much as he wanted to ask her out, it wouldn't happen until she indicated she might say yes. And that wouldn't happen tonight, because Jake was driving Sam into the Springs to catch a flight to Louisville for LDAC training at Fort Knox.

He had just three hours to hand out his flyers, so he picked up his pace.

The owner of the hardware store was neutral on the camp but glad to help Jake out.

Alice at the Brownie Emporium told him to pin them to the bulletin board. She liked the idea of more business, but she didn't want the mess made by teenagers.

The real estate office was his next stop. Without exception, the four realtors loved the idea. They wanted to sell and rent houses, so the more people who knew about Echo Falls, the better.

Jake headed to Blackstone Apothecary next. Charles Blackstone, a pharmacist for forty years, was on Hatcher's side, but he was also a fair man. Jake rounded the corner into the parking lot and saw a pile of shattered glass below a gaping display window. Charles, dressed in a white coat that matched his hair and trim moustache, wielded a broom with enough force to send particles of glass into the air.

From what Jake could see, the window had been broken from the outside, with most of the glass falling inward. He approached Charles but stayed several feet back to protect Pirate's paws.

"Looks like a break-in," Jake said.

The pharmacist stopped sweeping but kept one hand on the broom, holding it like a flag planted in sand. "It happened last night."

"That stinks."

"You bet it does." Charles aimed his chin at the broken window. "Good thing I put in that silent alarm. Deputy Ross roared up and caught them red-handed."

"Who?" Jake asked, not wanting to hear what he already suspected.

"A couple of teenage boys up here for the weekend." Charles raised a brow at him. "They came in yesterday with one of their moms to pick up suntan lotion. They seemed like nice kids."

Hint, hint. Jake ignored the inference. "That's a tough break. Crime happens everywhere. Even here."

A snort huffed through the pharmacist's nose. "Sure it does. But we don't have to invite more of it. That's why I'm siding with Bill. You need to read the Letters to the Editor in tomorrow's *Echo Falls Gazette.* We filled four pages."

Just what Echo Falls didn't need. More vitriol. More fear. The scathing comments rankled Jake down to his boots. He itched to fight for his cause, but not with Charles. The pharmacist was a family friend.

Jake indicated the broom. "Want some help sweeping up?"

Blackstone shook his head. "No, thanks. But, Jake?"

"Yeah?"

"I went to high school with your dad, and I've known your mom since they moved up here as newlyweds. Her illness is tragic. So is what happened to you. You're a good man."

Jake waited for the *but.*

"But I don't want a bunch of kids coming and going in this town. You can talk all you want about supervision and moral duty and making a difference, but all it takes is one bad apple, and you have a tragedy like what happened to Bill. I know the logic, the big talk, the Christian thing to do. I also know that a couple of idiot kids busted my window because they wanted to steal cash or drugs, or just make trouble. They succeeded too. I have a mess on my hands and an insurance claim to file. Those two brats just gave me a month of headaches."

There wasn't much Jake could say, especially with the shards of glass sparkling in the sun.

"So do us all a favor. Rethink this camp of yours."

If only he could. . . . Jake wanted peace of mind, not more trouble. Somehow the camp meant to honor his partner and friend was destroying his hometown. Connie would have been deeply troubled by the fighting, maybe enough to back down. But how could pulling the plug on Camp Connie be the right thing to do? If Jake didn't fight for kids in need of leadership, who would?

"I can't do that," he said to Charles.

"You *could*. You just don't want to."

He met the older man's gaze with a firm one of his own. "You have a point. But I'm committed to this project. I have good reasons."

"Yes, you do. I just hope the town doesn't blow apart."

"So do I."

The pharmacist went back to sweeping glass. Jake turned to leave, but Pirate nosed him and he turned back, catching Charles's voice.

"Jake? One more thing."

He waited.

"If your home or business had been vandalized, I bet you'd think twice about starting this camp."

"That's a valid point." Jake didn't add that his whole life had been vandalized by the bombing suspect. "But I have an equally valid point. If you knew what his mother's death did to Sam, you might change your mind too."

Charles merely grunted, then went back to sweeping.

Jake walked away with Pirate at his side and the flyers in hand. He felt sorry for Charles. Bill Hatcher too. But to honor Connie, Jake would fight for the camp until the final vote by the Board of County Commissioners.

But at what cost? With Mia's voice in his ear, he went back to distributing flyers.

●●●

"I wish I didn't have to go," Sam said to Lucy as he slung his empty duffel bag onto the bed.

"Me too." A month without Sam? She didn't know how she'd survive.

They were in their room in the back of the Tanner house, savoring a few minutes alone before Jake drove Sam to the airport. *I will not cry,* she told herself, *at least not until after we say good-bye*. If she was going to be the wife of an Army officer, she needed to be strong for both Sam and the baby.

Sam lifted a stack of white T-shirts out of the dresser and began to refold them. Lucy did their laundry, but she couldn't make creases the way Sam did.

He glanced at her tummy while he worked. "How's Beanie Baby today?"

At sixteen weeks, the lima bean was now the size of an apple. Unfortunately, Lucy was still spotting and still on pelvic rest. Sam was great about it, but Lucy felt terrible. It was awfully hard to feel like a good wife when you couldn't make love to your husband.

Aside from the spotting, Lucy was in what Mia called the sweet spot of pregnancy, those middle weeks between morning sickness and feeling like a whale. When Sam returned, they would go together for the standard twenty-week ultrasound, an anatomy scan that would tell them the baby's gender and give an update on the placement of the placenta.

She laid her hand on the baby bump. "He's doing great. I just wish he'd kick so you could feel it too."

"I'll feel it when I get back. By then he—"

"Or she."

"—will be kicking like a soccer player."

Lucy tried to pull off a smile, but her lips squished into a trembling line. Turning away, she pushed off the bed and pulled Sam's socks out of his drawer. He folded them into neat little balls.

"You're good at that," she said with a sigh.

"It's just practice."

"I don't think so." Some people cut straight lines with scissors, and others, like Lucy, just couldn't do it. "I could practice all day, and you'd still end up with sock-puppet zombies."

Sam flashed a smile, the one that made her melt. "I happen to like sock-puppet zombies." He picked up one of the messy pairs and pretended to stalk her with it.

Giggling, she grabbed a pair out of the drawer and battled back. Somehow the socks ended up on the floor, and she ended up in her husband's arms, kissing him as if he were leaving for a year rather than a month.

The kiss both shattered her resolve and strengthened it. Easing back, she dared to look into his eyes. "I want to be a good wife."

"You are."

"I just wish—" *Wish you were staying home.* "I'm going to cry when you leave, but I refuse to start now."

"Ah, Pudge." He held her even tighter. "It's not that long. We can do this."

"Yes," she whispered. "But I'm going to miss you terribly. I get so scared sometimes. Mia's here, and I love Frank and Claire, but it's not the same."

"We'll talk every night. I promise." He pressed his lips to her temple, holding tight until she couldn't feel the difference between his flesh and hers. Breathing deep, he placed his hand on her tummy.

Move, Beanie Baby! Move! Maybe, if Sam felt their baby kick, she could believe God was looking out for them all. Sam believed in her, but he didn't know how badly she struggled to believe in herself, and how weak her faith in God really was.

Come on, Beanie Baby. Please.

Nothing. Not even a flutter. Sam breathed a sigh, and they eased out of each other's arms. He resumed packing, and Lucy sat on the bed until he zipped the duffel shut and faced her. This was the last time they'd be alone for over four weeks.

Chin raised, she offered a wobbly smile. "You stay safe, Soldier Boy. I love you."

"I love you too."

He kissed her again to prove it. Long and slow, hard and demanding. Everything a kiss between a husband and wife could be. She clung to his shoulders, kissed him back, and wished again the baby would kick so they could share that moment.

Sam kissed her again and again, until the clock ran out on them. "I have to go now."

Her throat slammed shut. She would not cry. *She wouldn't.* He slung the duffel over his shoulder and strode out of the bedroom. Lucy followed him down the narrow hall and through the front door. In the yard she saw Jake waiting by his truck.

Sam stopped on the deck, cupped her jaw, and kissed her one last time. "I'm proud of you, Luce."

"No. I'm proud of you!"

He stroked her cheek with his thumb, hiked the duffel on his shoulder, then marched down the steps. Jake opened the door to the crew cab, Sam slung the bag inside, and the men climbed in the front. As Jake backed away, Sam held his arm out the window in a final salute.

Lucy blew him a kiss, smiled hard, and rested a protective hand on the baby. And then it happened. Beanie Baby kicked so hard Lucy lost her breath.

"Sam!" she shouted. But the truck was a hundred yards away.

Lucy knotted her fists. *Why, God? Just five minutes.* Was He punishing her? Sam would say no, but he didn't know how far away Lucy felt from God. No matter how hard she tried, she couldn't shake the feeling of not being good enough. Or at least not as good as Mia.

Tears flooded her eyes. *Lord, I can't do this. I can't! I need Sam.* But he wasn't here.

Mia was here, but Lucy didn't want to lean on her sister. She wanted to be her own strong person, and she especially wanted Sam and Mia to be proud of her. All her life Lucy had leaned on other people. For the next four weeks, she was on her own.

"It's you and me, God," she murmured as she walked back into the house. "I hope you're listening, because the baby and I need all the help we can get."

chapter 13

The days passed quickly for Mia. She saw patients at a pace that seemed leisurely after Dr. Moore's hectic practice, and she spent a lot of time at the Tanner house with Lucy. She and Jake saw each other often, but Mia made it a point to avoid being alone with him.

Before she knew it, late July turned into mid-August. The interview in Dallas—and her thirtieth birthday—were next week. Lucy was nineteen weeks along and keeping busy with Claire. Sam would be home in less than two weeks, and Jake was juggling Tanner Vending, Claire's needs, and politicking for Camp Connie.

It was a beautiful Saturday afternoon, and Mia was headed to the Tanner house for a surprise activity Lucy refused to reveal. Driving with the window down, she relaxed with the knowledge that Jake and Frank wouldn't be home. They were servicing accounts in the Springs, then stopping by Westridge Acres to check Claire's status on the waiting list. A phone call would have sufficed for most people, but Frank, admittedly old-fashioned, preferred to do business face-to-face.

As Mia pulled into the driveway, the rescue dogs barked a greeting from the kennel. Later she'd visit Peggy McFuzz, but Lucy and Claire were waiting with that surprise activity. A cookie bake-off? A walk in the woods to collect pine cones? Or maybe she'd pass out coloring books and new boxes of crayons, the big ones with sixty-four colors. Coloring was one of Claire's favorite pastimes now.

Mia enjoyed coloring with her, but she disliked surprises, even small ones. Lucy, however, delighted in them. Not knowing what to expect, Mia climbed out of her car and slung her purse over her shoulder.

Lucy waved to her from the porch. "Oh, good! You're here. We can get started."

"On what, exactly?"

"You'll see."

Mia walked up the wide steps and gave Lucy a hug. "How's my niece or nephew?"

"Great. That blog I follow says he's about the size of banana now."

Mia grinned as they stepped into the living room. "That's wonderful. And how are you?"

"I'm—wait here, okay?"

"Sure."

While Mia waited by the couch, Lucy stole a peek at Claire in the kitchen. "Just had to check," she explained in a low voice. "I don't want Claire to hear anything negative about the pregnancy. It confuses her."

"Negative?" Mia's stomach dropped to the floor. "Tell me."

"No cramps or anything. I feel great. But I wish the spotting would stop."

"Is it any worse?"

"No. It's the same. Maybe lighter. But I've been reading more about placenta previa. I'm scared I'll need a C-section."

Mia let out the breath she'd been holding. "You might, but there's still time for the placenta to move up. You'll know more after the next ultrasound."

"Two weeks," Lucy said with a sigh. "I don't know how much more of this I can take."

"What's the matter, Luce? Is it Sam being gone?"

"A little."

"The pregnancy?"

She tried to smile. "That's a lot of it."

"And what about Claire?" The repetition unique to Alzheimer's made Mia want to hide in a closet. "If taking care of her is too much for you—"

"Oh, no! I love Claire." Lucy took another glance into the kitchen. "Sometimes, when she has a good day, we talk about when her kids were babies. She has some great stories. I get tired of hearing the same ones over and over, but that's okay. It's all she has right now."

Mia's heart swelled with pride in her sister for her compassion, and pain for Claire because she needed it so badly. And a little shame for herself, because for all her training, she couldn't do what her baby sister did every day.

Lucy glanced sheepishly at her feet. "Do you want to hear something I never thought I'd say?"

"Tell me."

"I'm really good at taking care of Claire. At first I didn't understand, so I started reading blogs, medical articles, and message boards for caretakers. It fills the evenings with Sam away, but mostly I did it for Claire. Do you remember how I wanted to be a preschool teacher?"

One of Lucy's many goals, along with trying out for a reality show and starting a jewelry business. "You were pretty serious about it."

"Being with Claire at this stage isn't all that different. We color together and play simple games. It's kind of great, actually. She's losing language, but we still talk, usually about the past. Did you know she was an elementary school teacher?"

"No, I didn't."

"She loves to watch the birds that come to the feeders. She's really special, Mia. Come with me." Lucy motioned her forward. "I'll show you what we're doing today."

Claire called from the kitchen. "Lucy?"

"Here I am."

Lucy went straight to Claire and admired the picture she had colored, leaving Mia to survey the most recent changes to the kitchen. In addition to the knobs missing from the stove, Post-it Notes with words like *Plates* and *Cups* clung to every cabinet. A pocket-size photo album called *My Family* sat on the table, and a dry erase board by the refrigerator announced the important details of the day.

Today is Saturday
Mia is coming over
Mia is Lucy's sister

The changes were simple yet brilliant, and they were all Lucy's doing. Mia spun toward her. "I am so proud of you!"

"You are?"

"Yes, I am." Lucy didn't need a college degree to meet Claire's needs. She just needed love, and Lucy's heart brimmed with it in ways Mia envied.

She turned her attention to Claire, now coloring a different picture in the My Little Pony coloring book. Her colors of choice were pink, purple, and blue, perfect for a carousel horse if not reality.

"Hi, Claire," Mia said.

Startled, Claire glanced at the white board first. "Mia!"

"How are you today?"

"I'm just fine."

Mia and Claire shared a long hug. Even with Alzheimer's

disease, or maybe because of it, Claire gave the best hugs. As they separated, sunlight streamed through the window, throwing shadows on a table covered with a plastic cloth. Markers, glue, and an open tackle box full of sparkly doodads sat in the middle.

"What's all this?" Mia asked.

"It's for the surprise." Lucy stepped into the laundry room and came back with a big white box, the kind that held copy paper, and set it in front of Claire. "Would you open it for us?"

Surprisingly serious, Claire raised the lid, saw the contents, and lifted out a small wooden house with a sloped roof, a round hole, and a feeding tray. "Birdhouses!"

"For chickadees," Lucy said. "We're going to decorate them."

Claire lit up. "I love chickadees."

Mia didn't usually enjoy crafts, but who could resist brand-new markers and sparkly doodads?

The three of them sat around the table, went to work with the markers, and glued on trinkets, oohing and ahhing over every bit of beauty. When they finished an hour later, Lucy lined up the houses in a row, put out a plate of cookies, and they talked about nothing but the birdhouses. Of the three of them, Claire's was the most flamboyant, with purple and yellow stripes; Mia's house was the most natural, with green sides, a brown roof, and gold stars; and Lucy's house, colored red, white, and blue, belonged in a Fourth of July parade.

"I miss Sam," she said quietly.

Claire's eyes brightened like the sun pressing against fog, lightening it but not removing the mist entirely. "I know you do, honey. I miss Frank all the time."

"He'll be home soon," Mia offered.

"Will he?" Claire blinked back a sheen of tears. "Someday I won't know him."

Lucy gripped Claire's hand in both of hers. "He loves you,

Claire. You might forget his name, even who he is, but he will always love you. So will Jake. I love you too."

"I'm such a burden!" The cry burst from Claire's throat, and she hunched forward, sobbing so hard her shoulders shook.

Lucy came around the table and pulled Claire into a hug, her face pinched to fight tears of her own. With her own eyes moist, Mia snatched a packet of tissues out of her purse. After several seconds, Lucy straightened. Mia took a tissue for herself, then offered them to Claire and Lucy.

"Okay, ladies," Lucy said in a voice close to steady. "We're going to play a game."

Fresh confusion washed over Claire's face, as if she couldn't remember why she was crying. "I like games!"

Lucy snapped her tissue like a magician. "On the count of three, we blow our noses. Whoever honks the loudest wins."

Claire laughed, then honked before Lucy even started to count.

"Claire wins!" Lucy declared. "She gets to pick what we do next."

A pleased expression crossed the older woman's face. Who didn't like to be in charge now and then, especially a former teacher? Thinking hard, Claire tapped her chin with her index finger until her gaze landed on the coloring books.

"It's coloring time," she announced like the teacher she'd once been. "You girls pick your favorites, okay?"

Lucy picked the *Frozen* coloring book, and Mia went for an adult book full of geometric shapes. They were deep into the project when one of the rescue dogs barked in the distance. The others joined in a raucous chorus that didn't let up.

Mia and Lucy ignored the noise, but Claire leapt to her feet. "The dogs—I forgot to feed them."

"They're fine," Lucy replied. "They probably heard a squirrel."

"No—" The barking intensified into a warning, maybe panic. Claire headed for the door. "Something's wrong."

Lucy laid a hand on her arm to stop her. "You stay with Mia, okay? I'll check."

"No way." Mia was already on her feet. "You're pregnant. Stay here with Claire."

Lucy smiled her thanks. "It's probably nothing. You know how the dogs—" She stopped in midsentence and sniffed. "What's that smell?"

Mia smelled it too. "Smoke!" Dashing through the living room, she shouted over her shoulder, "Call 911!"

She flung open the front door, saw smoke pluming from the far side of the kennel, and charged across the yard. Because of the angle, she couldn't tell if the building was on fire, or if the flames were coming from the woodpile behind it. Either way, she needed to get the dogs out of the kennel before the fire spread. She knew better than to run into a burning building, but a quick assessment of the smoke told her the fire was small, even containable if she could work the fire extinguisher mounted by the door.

As she rounded the corner of the building, she saw the door gaping wide. It should have been closed, so who had left it open? With no time to think, she filed the thought away as she stopped at the threshold, breathing heavily as she took in the sight of a glowing electric heater too close to a box of rags, now on fire and sending fingers of flame up the back wall. Instead of fleeing to the yard through the flaps in the back of their kennels, the frightened dogs were huddled in corners or barking crazily.

Mia yanked on the fire extinguisher. Once. Twice. But a clamp held it tight, and she couldn't break the grip. Instead she snatched a towel off a hook by the sink, pressed it to her nose, and opened the first stall door.

The boxer named Shadow charged past her. The second and third dogs followed his lead. Chico, a feisty Chihuahua, snarled and bared his teeth. Mia ignored the growl, picked him up, and tossed him squirming and yapping out the door.

Only Peggy McFuzz remained. The smallest and most vulnerable, she occupied the stall closest to the back wall. The smoke was thicker now, more pungent and swirling. Coughing in spite of the towel pressed to her nose, Mia approached, expecting to see Miss McFuzz cowering in a corner, but the little dog was nowhere in sight, and the gate to her stall was open at least six inches.

Had she fled or hidden? Flames licked higher on the wall. Smoke stung Mia's eyes, blurring her vision with murky tears.

"Fuzzy?" Her voice shook in spite of her effort to stay calm. "Come on out, honey."

Off to the right, a tremulous whine pierced the whip and crackle of the fire. Mia whirled, straining to see through the smoke. "Fuzzy!"

She heard another whine, more of a whimper, but she couldn't locate the dog. Any second the flames would reach the ceiling. She called Fuzzy again. Each time the dog yapped in terror, until finally Mia realized Miss McFuzz was in a corner much closer to the flames than Mia wanted to be, hiding behind tools and a metal ladder leaning against the side wall.

Mia knew the rules. Get out of a burning building. Don't go after a pet. Leave it all to the professionals. But she was already inside, and Peggy McFuzz would burn alive if Mia didn't take a chance.

chapter 14

Jake glanced at the clock on the dash of his truck. With a little luck, Mia would still be at the house when he, Pirate, and his dad pulled into the driveway. They were returning earlier than expected, so maybe he'd see her before she dashed off. After the visit to Westridge, he needed a little TLC himself. His parents were still number 5 on the waiting list. Not good news with his mom losing more of herself every day.

Frank yawned in the passenger seat, blind to the beautiful drive he'd made a million times, often with his wife at his side. Jake couldn't begin to fathom his dad's heartache. Nor could he imagine his dad without his mom, but that day would come. Feeling melancholy, he followed the river, driving slower than usual because of a broken vending machine strapped to the bed of his pickup.

They were about three miles from home when a plume of smoke caught his eye. "Do you see that?"

Frank strained against his seatbelt for a better look. "Either some crazy fool is burning trash in August, or something's on fire. I don't like it."

"Me either."

The smoke thickened in front of their eyes. Dark and dirty,

the boiling column was close to Tanner property. Way too close. Jake stomped on the gas in spite of the vending machine. It lurched, but the truck hugged the asphalt. Behind him, Pirate sat up and whined. The truck ate up the miles, but not fast enough for Jake's peace of mind. He took the final curve at maximum speed, squealed into the long driveway, and knew with utter certainty a building on his family's property was ablaze.

He floored the gas pedal, not caring about the gravel spitting beneath the tires. A hundred feet away, flames shot to the sky from the back of the kennel. At the end of the driveway, he slammed on the brakes and leaped out of the truck.

"Get Pirate," Jake called to his dad. "Put him on his leash, or he'll follow me."

"Will do, son."

Lucy and his mom were on the porch. Mia's car sat off to the side, but there was no other sign of her.

Shouting and bouncing on her feet, Lucy pointed at the fire. Jake couldn't make out the exact words, but he heard Mia's name and realized with a sickening chill that she was trying to save the dogs.

Crazy woman! He charged full speed toward the burning building, blocking memories of Connie as he ran. He couldn't hear a thing except his own breathing, but his vision stayed sharp. Halting briefly at the door, he peered through the acrid smoke. There was Mia, close to the flames, shoving aside tools before dropping to a crouch. Jake yanked the extinguisher out of the clamp, charged forward, and sprayed down the wall closest to her.

"Mia! Get out *now*." He'd drag her out by her hair if he had to. He'd do anything to keep her safe.

"I almost have her—"

"Get out!"

"It's Fuzzy. She's hiding." Mia flung a shovel out of the way. "I can see her."

The flames danced to the side and shot back up the wall. White paint bubbled in front of his eyes, and the putrid air assaulted his lungs. The back door to the kennel was fully engulfed. He sprayed foam until the extinguisher gave out. Dropping it, he turned to Mia just as she stood up with Miss McFuzz clutched in her arms.

He grabbed her by the elbow, covered his mouth with his sleeve, and half dragged her past the stalls and out the main door. Eyes stinging and lungs on fire, they sped into the yard. At a safe distance, they both stumbled to their knees, hunched over, and coughed up smoke.

Safe . . . Mia was safe. But Jake felt no relief, only a numb awareness of the low-pitched siren of a fire truck pulling into the driveway. Two men in turnout gear jumped off the sides, the captain barked orders, and the firefighters unwound the hose.

Jake staggered upright, offered his hand to Mia, and helped her to her feet, the dog still clutched against her chest. When she rested her head on his shoulder, he drew her close and pressed his cheek against hers. She reeked of smoke, a smell that would haunt his dreams forever, but her body remained perfectly still. Not a shiver. Not a tremble. He knew how adrenaline worked. In about five minutes, she'd be a mess.

Lucy ran up to them with Claire, Frank, and Pirate flanking her, and let out a shriek. "Mia! Are you *nuts*?" She yanked Mia from his arms and tried to hug her.

While Frank and Jake traded a look, Pirate plastered himself against Jake's side, refusing to budge until Jake reassured him.

"I'm fine. Here." Mia shoved Peggy McFuzz into her sister's arms. "Take Fuzzy inside."

Lucy gaped at her. "Come with me. You need water or—or—oxygen or something." She spun around, searching until she spotted the fire captain. "We need an ambulance!"

Jake interrupted. "Lucy, stop."

If his words reached her ears, they didn't reach her brain. "I can't believe this. Mia could have died. The house could have caught fire—"

"Stop," Mia murmured. "Please."

"But—"

Pulling Mia back against his side, Jake stepped in. "Lucy, take Pirate and Miss McFuzz into the house. Take Claire too." It was an order. A polite one, but still an order.

Lucy chomped hard on her lower lip, looked at Mia, then back at Jake. "All right. But—but you take care of her, okay?"

"I will. I promise."

After a shaky sigh, Lucy headed for the house with the dogs and Claire. With Mia safe and still holding herself together, Jake surveyed the action in the yard. The fire crew was dousing the last of the flames, and Frank had rounded up the rescue dogs. Everyone could manage without him while he took care of Mia.

He nudged her toward the barn with the pinball machines. "Come with me."

"But the fire—"

"Is being handled."

"The dogs—"

"My father knows what to do."

"Lucy—Claire—"

"Everyone's fine, Mia." *Except you*. "I want to talk to you for a minute."

Before she could protest again, he led her into the barn. The only light streamed from a window high in the front wall. After the heat and brightness of the fire, the chilly darkness soothed his skin and eyes. Leaving the door wide, he guided Mia into the shadows.

She turned to him, stunned and glaring. "Why are we here? What is it? I don't—"

"Go ahead," he told her. "Cry."

"What?"

"Cry. I know you want to."

"I—I—" Blinking hard, she pressed the back of her hand to her mouth, collected herself, then spoke with a warble. "There are things to do. I can't cry now. I just—" *Can't.* She ducked to hide her face, hunching forward as her body succumbed to a violet shudder.

Jake clasped her shoulder with one hand and tipped her face up with the other. She blinked furiously, but tears spilled down her cheeks in crooked streams. In the next breath she slumped into his arms. "I was—I was . . ."

"Scared."

"Yes."

"But you didn't think about it then."

"No."

He held her even tighter, kissed her temple. "You did what you thought needed to be done."

"You understand."

"All too well."

Trembling now, she clenched the front of his shirt in her fists and buried her face in the crook of his neck, sobbing.

He pressed his lips to her smoky hair, then to her temple. When she whimpered, he kissed the salty tears on her cheek. Savoring the ability to be strong for her, he dropped soft kisses on her face, the corners of her mouth, until his lips completely covered hers. When she kissed him back, he enjoyed every taste, every sweet tremble, until her body stiffened and she leaned back.

Her hands still clung to his shoulders, but she looked down, hiding her face from his gaze. A squeak pushed out of her throat. Pulling back even more, she covered her cheeks with both hands, then looked up with her red-rimmed eyes. "What—what just happened?"

Jake knew exactly what had happened. They'd been hurled from the safety of friendship to the brink of being in love. Knowing Mia, she'd retreat with the full force of her will, so he offered the simplest answer he could. "We kissed."

She gaped at him. "Good work, detective. But that's not what I meant. *Why* did that happen?"

Because I'm falling in love with you. The words dangled in his mind like a sun spinner, glinting in the direct light but fading at the next turn. Was he ready to fall in love? The answer was yes. But could he give Mia what she needed? And what about Mission Medical and her plans for the future?

Her eyes pleaded for an answer, so he told her the truth as he knew it. "The fire made you stare death in the face. It affected me too. That kiss was us fighting back."

"Is that all?"

"No."

"Then what?" Her voice cracked on the last word. "I can't do this, Jake. I fly to Dallas next week for the panel interview. If I get the job, I'll leave Echo Falls permanently. I've made a commitment to God and myself. Being anything more than friends would be too . . . too much."

Too dangerous. Too intense. Too real. The problem was obvious to him. While Jake thrived on a challenge, Mia needed an escape valve.

He laid a hand on her arm. "Right now, the fire chief needs to talk to you, so here's the plan." Mia liked plans, and so did Jake. "You go to Dallas and kick butt on that interview. When you get back, we'll talk about what just happened."

"That sounds good." Her voice came out steadier. "But, Jake, there's something I have to say."

"I'm listening."

She took his hands in both of hers. Squeezing hard, she raised her face to his. "Walking into that fire couldn't have been easy for you. Thank you for riding to my rescue."

"No white horses, please." He was an ordinary man, not a mythical knight in shining armor who never fell off his horse.

"I know." Her mouth settled into a gentle curve. "You were doing what had to be done. But I still appreciate it. I was so focused on Peggy McFuzz that I lost track of the flames. If you hadn't pulled the extinguisher—"

"I'm just glad you're safe." He wanted to forget the what-ifs, so he let go of her hands and motioned to the door. "Let's talk to the fire crew."

When they emerged from the barn, Jake squinted against the sun. The fire was out except for a few embers. Two fire fighters were hosing down hotspots, while Frank and the captain, a man named Wayne O'Keefe, waited by the truck. Deputy Brian Ross, also responding to the 911 call, was with them, his black-and-white cruiser parked to the side.

Captain O'Keefe made sure Jake and Mia were both unharmed, then he focused on Mia. "What can you tell us, Ms. Robinson?"

She described hearing the dogs, running into the kennel, and seeing the space heater next to a flaming box of rags. Jake and his dad traded a sad look. The evidence pointed to Claire and an Alzheimer's mistake.

"Frank!"

They all turned to the house and saw Claire hurrying down the steps with Lucy behind her.

"Frank!" she shouted again. "The dogs are loose! We need to find the dogs."

"It's handled," he called to her.

"The dogs are out!"

"No, honey. They're in the garage."

"There was a fire," Claire said in the same tone. "The dogs are out. We need to find the dogs."

Lucy caught up to Claire and hooked an arm around her waist. "The dogs are safe. Let's go look at them."

Claire blinked, but her confusion didn't clear. She looked at Lucy as if she were a stranger, then at Jake. "There was a fire—"

Jake hated Alzheimer's. *Hated it.* He hated fire, fear, and everything in between. Tonight he planned to murder a punching bag.

When Lucy and Claire were out of earshot, Captain O'Keefe and Deputy Ross both turned to Frank. The fire captain took charge. "Do you think Claire got mixed up and turned on the heater?"

"I'm sure of it." He looked ten years older than he had an hour ago. "While you and your crew were putting out the fire, I asked Lucy if Claire had been alone at all." He focused on Mia. "In no way does this reflect poorly on Lucy. We all know what it's like to watch out for Claire."

Jake reached for Mia's hand but focused on Frank. "What happened?"

"Shortly before Mia arrived, Lucy needed to use the bathroom, so she sat Claire in front of the television. When she came out, Claire was in the kitchen."

"Lucy must have been in the bathroom awhile," Deputy Ross remarked.

"It doesn't matter," Frank said. "Lucy does a great job. When she came out, the back door was open but the screen door was closed. Claire was safe, so she didn't think anything more of it."

Wayne looked as troubled as Frank. "I'm sure you're taking steps to protect her as well as yourselves."

"Every single day." Frank nodded to include Jake. "We stopped at Westridge this morning. There are only four people ahead of us on the waiting list, but it could be weeks or even months before there's an opening."

Deputy Ross paused in a respectful silence, then took out a notepad and clicked a ballpoint pen. "You'll need a police report for the insurance claim."

Jake dreaded the hassle, but his father disliked paperwork even more than he did. "Dad, I can handle this. Why don't you check on Mom?"

"Thanks. She's going to need some extra attention."

As Frank left, Captain O'Keefe glanced at the two fire fighters stringing yellow hazard tape around the smoldering ruins of the kennel. Jake recognized Tom Olander, a guy he knew from high school, and Kevin Romano, a new recruit and a gym addict with cut muscles and a low sports car doomed to get stuck in the snow.

The fire captain excused himself to assist his men, leaving Jake and Mia with Deputy Ross.

"Just a few more questions for Mia," the deputy said.

When she raised her chin and nodded, almost childlike with her eyes wide and serious, Jake rested his hand on her back. Claire wasn't the only woman who needed a little extra TLC today. So did Mia, and Jake was both honored and determined to be the man to give it to her.

chapter 15

When Mia walked into the office on Monday morning, Kelsey welcomed her with a grin and a phone message from Carl Dixon, the editor of the *Echo Falls Gazette*. Carl wanted to interview Mia about the fire for Friday's front page.

Some people thrived on attention, but Mia didn't enjoy the spotlight at all. Yesterday at church, Lucy had bragged to everyone about Mia and Jake saving the dogs. The hugs and questions exhausted her, and deep down she felt undeserving of the praise. She might have saved the dogs, but Jake had saved her. Only he knew that she'd fallen apart in the aftermath of the fire.

And only Mia knew that she'd fallen apart after that kiss.

That night, she had hugged Henrietta while pondering the emotions coursing through her. Her feelings were like the Echo River at flood stage, eroding some shores and building up others. Like Jake had said, she would give Mission Medical her best shot. But could she do that when her heart was torn between her feelings for him and keeping her promise to God?

Kelsey dropped back into her seat at the computer. "I hope you don't mind. You had a cancellation at eleven, so I told Carl to come then."

"That's fine," Mia replied, though she would have preferred catching up on the day's notes.

"I feel awful for the Tanners."

"So do I." Especially for Claire. With the kennel destroyed, Jake and Frank had called Love-A-Dog Rescue headquarters and asked them to pick up all the dogs except Peggy McFuzz. They were keeping Fuzzy for Claire, who had never been without a dog in her life. The two of them needed each other.

As Mia reached for her printed schedule, Kelsey turned back to a form on the computer screen. "I'm updating some credentialing info for the practice. When's your birthday?"

"It's next week." Mia gave the date and year.

Kelsey grinned. "So it's the big 3–0."

"That's right."

Kelsey stared at her. "Wow."

Trying to joke, Mia made air quotes. "Is that 'wow, you look great,' or 'wow, you're ancient'?"

"Wow, as in you're eight years older than me."

Mia forced a laugh. "That's awfully close to 'wow, you're ancient.'"

"At thirty? No. But . . ." Kelsey stopped and gave a shrug instead. "I don't have a career like you do. Mostly I want a family of my own. Kids. A dog. Even PTA meetings." She shook her head. "I wish Jake felt like I do. But he's just so broken."

Mia bristled. "Broken?"

"Yes. On the inside. He doesn't seem to feel much of anything, except when he talks about Camp Connie."

Or when he kisses me. Those precious seconds were burned into Mia's mind along with the memory of Jake saying he felt alive again—thanks to her. The effects of their kiss shimmered through her again. As many times as she had kissed her fiancé in college and later Brad, she'd never experienced the oneness she felt with Jake. She had surrendered fully to that kiss, savored it, until she realized she was melting just like Lucy. If Mia melted into a puddle, who would mop up? Could she trust Jake to be the strong man she wanted to love forever? Maybe she wanted too much from any man. Only God could love her perfectly.

"Mia?"

"Sorry. I got distracted." She snatched the printed schedule off the counter. "You were talking about Jake. It's tough. I know how it feels to be disappointed."

"I do care about him," Kelsey insisted. "I'm just tired of hoping he'll wake up and things will be different."

"It sounds like you're giving up on him."

"I probably should, but I just . . ." Kelsey shook her head.

Jake would be relieved if Kelsey backed down, but her wistfulness touched Mia to the core. "I went through two broken engagements. It was awful, but I learned something important."

"What?"

"I can be perfectly happy as a single woman. My life has meaning apart from any relationship, including a romantic one. What matters more than anything is loving God and loving people. If Mission Medical offers me the job—"

"Oh, they will," Kelsey interrupted. "You're great with people, and you're smart too."

Mia appreciated her enthusiasm, even if it was naïve. "I hope so, but there are no guarantees."

"No, but you have what it takes. Me?" Kelsey pointed at her chest. "I'd be scared to death."

"I am," Mia admitted. "But God has a plan for my life. And He has a plan for yours too."

"Do you really think so?"

"Yes, I do." Mia held up the schedule. "Now, if you'll excuse me, I need to get ready for patients."

Kelsey swiveled her chair to face the computer. Mia walked down the hall to her office, where she pulled up the week's calendar on her laptop. The trip to Dallas was blocked out in blue, from Thursday afternoon when she'd fly to Dallas, through Saturday, when she'd return on an afternoon flight. Rather than ask Lucy or Jake to drive her, she planned to take her own car and park in the long-term lot.

The fact that Saturday was her birthday struck Mia as fitting. A new decade for a new phase of life appealed to her, but she had no desire to celebrate this particular birthday. With a little luck, Lucy would overlook it, and Mia would come home from the interview with news that she'd been bumped to the next step.

The thought should have thrilled her. Instead, as she freshened her lipstick, she recalled Jake's searing kiss and wondered if she'd ever again feel as confident about her choices as she had sounded to Kelsey.

●●●

Sam had promised to call Lucy every night, but it didn't happen. Like the supportive wife she yearned to be, she accepted the disappointment and stayed strong, but today had been awful. She needed to hear his voice, so she texted him to please call if he could.

Now she was alone in their too-quiet room on a moonless Monday night. A single lamp lit her side of the bed, and her Bible was open to Proverbs 31. No way could she live up to that ideal woman, a fact she shared with God as if He were in the room with her. He didn't talk back, of course, but praying helped.

Five minutes before ten o'clock, when a sergeant would call for lights-out, her phone played Sam's ringtone.

"Sam!"

"Hey, Pudge. What's the matter?"

"Everything!" He already knew about the fire and how she'd

left Claire alone for five minutes. "Claire can't stop saying, 'There was a fire,' and a man from Love-A-Dog Rescue took all the dogs except Peggy McFuzz. The poor thing is terrified and won't come out from behind the couch."

"It's tough for everyone."

"I feel so guilty. I shouldn't have left Claire alone."

"Look, it's a big house. You can't be everywhere at once."

"I know. It's just—"

"You're human." He lowered his voice. "And you're pregnant. If this is too much for you, we'll make a change."

"No. I'm fine." Lucy laid a hand on the hard curve of her belly. The baby kicked often and was as long as a carrot now. "I'm just so sorry about what happened."

"Don't be." His voice came out sharp. "You needed to use the bathroom, right?"

"Yes. And I saw some blood." She'd been so scared that she'd stayed in there longer than usual, terrified the spotting would get worse and praying it wouldn't.

"Don't you dare blame yourself." Sam sounded more like a drill sergeant than her husband. "Did Jake or Frank say something to bring this on? I swear I'll—"

"No! Not at all. Frank told me not to worry about it, and Jake took Claire for a brownie when the rescue people picked up the dogs. He told me twice I'm doing a great job, and I should remember the birdhouses and not the fire."

"He's right."

"I guess. I just wish it hadn't happened."

"Well, it did." His voice deepened, taking on a bluntness she didn't like. "And now you have to move on. You can't fix it, Luce. Give it to God. Bad things don't make sense. But He knows about them, and He loves us."

Lucy wished she could believe the way Sam did, but how could God love her when she made mistakes like leaving Claire alone? Mia would never have made the same decision. Lucy was sure of it.

Sam's weary voice whispered in her ear. "I don't know why bad things happen—things like a hard pregnancy or my mom dying. I don't know why Claire plugged in the heater. I just know God sees it all. Good and bad. He knows."

"You're talking to yourself, aren't you?" LDAC was even harder for him than it was for her.

"Yeah, I guess I am." Fresh strength hardened his voice. "It's tough, but I was born for this kind of stuff."

"I'm super proud of you. You know that." Last week he'd received his third evaluation and was leading his entire platoon. "I just miss you so much."

"Same here." His deep voice whispered over the phone. "It won't be long now."

"Just five days. August twenty-first, to be precise. Oh!" Lucy slapped her hand to her forehead. "That's Mia's birthday! I almost forgot." She usually gave her sister a funny card and a little gift, but a decade change called for something big. "I have an idea. What do you think about giving Mia a surprise party?"

"Does she like surprises?"

Lucy hummed into the phone. Personally, she loved surprises, except the kind that involved pregnancy tests. Mia was different. "She doesn't like bad surprises, but good ones? I don't think she's had many of those."

"I'm fine with it," Sam said. "But you don't have much time to plan a party."

She also needed to be with Claire and couldn't do a lot of running around. "Do you think Jake would help?"

Sam snorted into the phone. "The way he looks at your sister? Oh yeah, he'll help."

"You should have seen them after the fire. He couldn't take his eyes off her. But you know what's really crazy?"

"What?"

"Mia let him help her. She's usually stubborn about things like that. She's different with Jake."

"He's different with her too." The last words stretched like old elastic, a sign he was yawning. "I'm beat, Luce. You get some rest, okay?"

"I love you." She blew a lonely kiss.

"I love you too. Tell Beanie Boy that Daddy says hi."

"Or Beanie Girl. Sam?"

"Yeah?"

She heard chimes in the background, the signal for lights out. The barracks would have plunged into darkness. "I miss you."

"I miss you too. I wish—"

A voice bellowed, "*Waters!*"

"Bye, Pudge."

"Bye—" she said to empty air.

Tears welled as the phone died in her hand. She tossed it on the bed, sighed, then ambled to the open window and stared up at the inky sky. "God? Are you there?"

The stars twinkled a reply, but they were millions of miles away.

"It's me, Lucy. I just want to say thank you for Sam. And for Mia. And for saving the dogs." Her heart swelled all the way into her throat. How could the Creator of the Universe be listening to her?

"I feel so small right now." Like a single tiny star. To her eyes, the stars were mere pinpricks of light, but she knew from her freshman astronomy class that they were really huge balls of fire and gas, complex and a trillion miles away. Who but God could create such a thing? Who but God could knit a child in its mother's womb?

Lucy's breath caught in her throat. "Help me, Lord, to know who you are. I don't know what else to say, so I'll sign off now. Amen."

She stood at the window a moment longer, letting her mind slide down from the sky and back to the lonely bedroom. Knowing she couldn't sleep, she decided to talk to Jake about Mia's party. He was a bit of a night owl, so she walked out to his office in the barn. Like she expected, she found him working on his laptop.

She tapped on the doorframe. "Knock, knock."

"Who's there?" He swiveled his desk chair, smiling at his own lame joke.

"Lucy."

"Lucy who?"

"Lucy who's going to plan a surprise party for Mia. Will you help?"

●●●

Mia didn't strike Jake as the kind of person who liked surprises. In fact, he was fairly sure she wouldn't care for a room full of people shouting *Surprise!* any more than he would, which was not at all. But what did he know? Lucy was her sister. Maybe Mia had a secret wish for that kind of attention.

He shut down the letter to the editor he'd been writing, a response to the latest barrage from the Stop the Camp group, then indicated the extra chair. "I'm in. What do you have in mind?"

Lucy sat, folded her hands in her disappearing lap, and hiccupped. "Oops. That happens a lot these days."

Pregnancy was a mystery to Jake—a glorious one but also mildly terrifying. Back in the police academy, he'd undergone first aid training, including a crash course in childbirth. His fellow officers mostly felt like he did—he'd rather face a 9mm Glock than a woman in labor.

With Sam gone, Jake felt especially protective of Lucy. The party plans could wait a moment. "How are you feeling?"

"Okay."

"Just okay?" He lifted his brows. "If you need anything at all, tell me. I'm serious, Luce."

"I feel fine." She hiccupped again. "I just miss Sam. I thought working on a party for Mia would be a good distraction."

"Any ideas?"

"I want to go all out. Something big and fun. What do you think of an 'over the hill' theme?"

"Uh—" No. Just no.

"Never mind." Lucy pursed her lips. "That's for forty." She thought a moment, then lit up from the inside. "I know!"

"What?"

"How about an old-fashioned birthday party? The kind with silly games and a piñata? We could have it here, or . . . wait! I have a better idea."

Jake's head was spinning.

"Maybe we could use the back room at Castro's Cocina." The best Mexican restaurant in town. "She loves the food, and it'll be an even bigger surprise. We can celebrate her birthday *and* the interview in Dallas."

Jake had been thinking about that interview too. "When will she know if she made the cut?"

"I don't know, but it doesn't matter. Mia always comes out on top."

So did Jake—or at least he used to.

"I'll die of shock if she doesn't get the job. I'm going to miss her when she leaves." Lucy paused, watching him with a twinkle in her eyes.

Jake recognized that Cupid look but ignored it. "Who do you plan to invite?"

"Everyone." Lucy picked up a pen and pad of Post-its. Jake offered her paper from the printer, but she shook her head. "This is fine."

They made a list of guests that included people from church, Kelsey and her mom, friends Mia had made in the business community, and the crew at the fire station. The firefighters, including Kevin Romano, were Lucy's idea. Jake was less enthusiastic about them. She also insisted on organizing games, including pin the tail on the donkey and musical chairs. "The sillier, the better. We want Mia to have *fun*."

Lucy filled a dozen squares with crooked notes. Jake couldn't help but marvel at the differences between the sisters. Mia would have whipped out a legal pad and made a three-tier outline.

When they finished, Lucy gathered the notes in a haphazard collage and stood. "This is going to be great. I'll send emails and text messages tomorrow."

"Do you have all the contact info?"

"Pretty much. I'll use the church directory plus the Chamber website. If I need anything, I'll ask you or Kelsey."

"Perfect."

"Just one more thing," she said. "How are we going to get Mia to the restaurant? I don't want her to catch on."

Jake thought a moment. "How about if I offer to drive her to the airport and pick her up? Then I'll find a reason to stop at Castro's."

"What if she says no? She usually leaves her car in the long-term lot."

"I'll handle it." If necessary, he'd make up a story about being in the Springs anyway, or maybe he'd warn her about car burglars. Break-ins didn't happen often, but why take the chance?

When Lucy left, Jake turned back to the computer and his letter to the editor. He read two lines before he closed the document and Googled Mission Medical instead. For the next half hour, he read every word about how the organization cared for people all over the world.

Mia's future was in God's hands, not Jake's. But all he could think about was how perfect she felt in his arms, how good it felt to be more than her friend, and how much he wanted her to stay in Echo Falls.

chapter 16

Calm and confident, Mia rode the elevator from her room on the nineteenth floor of the Preston Hotel in Dallas to the conference area reserved by Mission Medical. She was among two hundred applicants being interviewed by seven different panels.

Most of the people were applying for temporary field assignments lasting six to nine months. Mia was part of a smaller group, about twenty or so, applying for a permanent position as a clinic coordinator. Tonight she'd attend a presentation about the organization's different programs, and tomorrow she would fly home, pretend it wasn't her birthday, and meet Jake at the airport.

Don't think about him, she told herself. Since that kiss in the barn, she'd felt like a pinball in one those old machines. Every time the ball bounced off a plastic post, the post lit up and went *ding-ding-ding! You win!* The problem was, she couldn't have it all, and she no longer knew what she wanted or where God was leading her. She loved her work in Echo Falls, and she loved being close to Lucy and part of the Tanner circle. She couldn't imagine leaving them. Or Jake. On the other hand, she was about to walk through a door she believed God had swung wide.

As much as Mia wanted to do well today, she wanted one thing even more, and that was clarity.

Pushing her worries aside, she rounded the corner to the interview area, marked by a row of poster-sized photographs of children helped by Mission Medical facilities. After five minutes, a check-in clerk led her to a conference room arranged with four overstuffed chairs around a low square table. Three of the chairs were occupied by two men and a woman, each wearing a conference badge.

As Mia entered the heavily air-conditioned room, the men stood and smiled warmly. She immediately recognized Dr. Leonard Winkler, the founder of Mission Medical. White-haired and sporting a trim moustache, he bore the marks of time in a tropical environment, including a deep tan and patches of smooth skin indicative of skin cancer surgery.

He offered Mia his hand. "Ms. Robinson. It's a pleasure to meet you. Thank you for traveling to Dallas."

She returned his handshake with a firm grip of her own. "It's a pleasure to be here, sir. Mission Medical does excellent work."

"Only because of people like yourself as well as my two colleagues here." He turned to the other man. "This is Dr. John Benton. He specializes in the repair of cleft palate and facial abnormalities."

"Dr. Benton—" What a thrill! Mia avidly followed the blog he wrote about his work in West Africa. The photographs taken of children before and after their surgeries touched her deeply. His work truly saved the lives of children who would otherwise be outcasts.

Because of the blog, she felt as if she knew him. He was taller than Dr. Winkler and leaner, with dark blond hair, and wore a Hawaiian shirt as blue as his eyes. Known for his sincerity and deep compassion, he was one of Mia's inspirations for applying to Mission Medical.

He gripped her hand with both of his. “May we call you Mia?”

“Of course. Yes. Please do.” If she wasn’t careful, she’d start to gush. “I read your blog. It’s an honor to meet you.”

He shrugged off the compliment. “I like kids.”

Dr. Winkler indicated the woman who had remained seated. A redhead with beautiful skin, maybe in her fifties, sat with her legs crossed and a notepad in her lap. “This is Sally Richmond. She’s part of our HR department.”

The women traded greetings, Mia sat, and Dr. Winkler relaxed back in his chair. “Tell us about yourself, Mia.”

She gave a short list of her qualifications, how she raised Lucy while studying nursing, then summarized her strengths. “I’m organized, adaptable, and passionate about my work. Joining Mission Medical would allow me to use my skills to truly make a difference”—she made eye contact with Dr. Benton—“in countries with some of the greatest needs on the planet.”

Dr. Winkler laced his fingers over his chest. “You can make a difference in America too.”

“Yes, sir.”

“We see from your CV that you were a coordinator for the Sunday Hope Clinic in Denver.”

“Yes. I supervised one of the weekly clinics.” She emphasized *supervised*. “My job involved scheduling staff, training volunteers, and referring patients for follow-up. It was more administrative than direct patient care, but I still loved it.”

“We’re looking for those skills,” Dr. Winkler remarked. “Tell us about the biggest challenge you faced personally.”

The question surprised her. She had prepared remarks about the problems the clinic faced, but the panel wanted more than a professional opinion. They wanted to see into her heart. “I couldn’t do enough.” That was all she said. Judging by their nods, that was all she needed to say.

Dr. Winkler cleared his throat. "I think we all feel the same way. Let's move on. You recently made a change from women's health to primary care."

"And from Denver to Echo Falls." She wanted to emphasize change on a personal level. "I moved from the city where I've lived my entire life to a small mountain town."

"What motivated you?" Dr. Winkler asked.

"During the Skype interview for this position, I realized I needed to show I could be adaptable or you wouldn't even consider me. When I learned the only physician in Echo Falls was about to close his practice, I saw a chance to help a community and broaden my experience at the same time."

Both Dr. Benton and Sally glanced down at copies of her CV. Sally spoke first. "You've been overseas just once."

"Yes. To Haiti for an internship."

"What did you do?" she asked.

"The clinic vaccinated children against a variety of diseases. As a student, I looked after the nonmedical supplies, helped calm the children, and generally made myself useful." The memory warmed her from head to toe. "We made a difference that summer."

Dr. Benton stretched a long leg. "I like you, Mia."

"Thank you."

"I think you have what it takes." He tossed his notepad on the table. "Do you like kids?"

"I love kids."

Dr. Benton's mouth curved into the half smile she recognized from photographs on his blog. "So do I. My group will be the first to include the new clinic model you'd be organizing if you take this job. I want you on my team."

Her jaw dropped. "Really? That would be—"

Dr. Winkler broke in. "Now hold on, John. As usual, you're ten steps ahead of the rest of us."

"Sorry, Leo." But he didn't look at all apologetic, especially when he smiled fully at Mia.

Dr. Benton might not care about the hiring protocol, but Mia did. She focused on Dr. Winkler, who seemed more amused than annoyed by his colleague's interruption.

"John is jumping the gun," Dr. Winkler said, "but I like what I'm hearing too. I'm especially pleased that you left a comfortable position in an established practice to meet a need in a small community."

"I'm the one who benefitted the most." Mia meant it. "The past two months have opened my eyes to all sorts of things."

"Like what?" Sally asked.

Falling in love again . . . A man named Jake Tanner . . . The seesaw of her emotions tipped, and she landed hard. If she joined Mission Medical, she would live in Dallas and travel the world. She'd be hundreds, if not thousands, of miles from Jake. Skype was great for keeping in touch, but you couldn't kiss a man through a screen. You couldn't rub the tension out of his shoulders, or trade a bite of a meal, or even gaze at the same stars in the night sky.

And what about Lucy, Sam, and the baby? Mia could see the baby smile and hear gurgles of laughter through her phone, but she couldn't kiss the top of the baby's head, change a diaper, or rock the teething child in her arms.

Mia's patients worried her too. Without a buyer, Dr. Collins would close the doors on the clinic. Kelsey would be out of a job, and patients like Mrs. Hargrove would have to drive an hour one-way for routine care.

"Mia?" Sally prompted.

"Yes. Let's see." She could barely recall the question. Something about her eyes being opened. *Think, Mia. Refocus. You can do this.* She didn't dare talk about her personal turmoil, so she focused on the people who had touched her the deepest. Jake topped that list.

"Probably the biggest lesson I've learned in Echo Falls is that one person can make a difference. A friend of mine is starting a camp for teenage boys who have lost a parent in the line of duty. It's a great cause, but there's some local opposition."

Dr. Benton grunted. "Politics. I hate it."

So does Jake. Without knowing it, he had come to her rescue. "My friend dislikes it too. But he's committed. I admire him tremendously. He retired from the Denver Police Department because of a duty-related injury. Instead of being bitter, he's taken a tragedy and turned it into the motivation to help others."

"That's admirable," Sally said. "We don't all recover from trauma. It changes us in some deep, intrinsic way."

"And trauma and tragedy hit us all." Mia paused. "My parents both died too soon. As hard as it was, that loss made my faith stronger."

"How?" Dr. Winkler asked.

"I had to take care of my sister." Now Mia was on familiar ground. "I was twenty when my mom passed away. Lucy was barely ten. I had a choice: take care of her, or let her go into foster care." Mia would never forget those frightening days after her mom's passing, being alone in their apartment and telling Lucy not to be afraid.

"I was terrified," she admitted now. "I used to say to Lucy, 'It's you, me, and God.' And it was. Somehow we made it, and here I am."

Dr. Winkler gave a respectful pause. Dr. Benton nodded, and Sally just smiled until Dr. Winkler cleared his throat. "One more question, Mia. If we don't accept your application, what will you do?"

"Exactly what I'm doing now." The ease of her answer surprised her. "I'm very happy in Echo Falls."

"Thank you, Mia." Dr. Winkler stood, and everyone else followed suit. "You'll hear from us in a few weeks."

She shook Sally's hand, then turned to Dr. Benton. He squeezed her fingers, leaned in a bit, and whispered, "You nailed it."

"I hope so," she murmured.

As she exited the conference room, the photographs of children called to her heart, and she shivered with the hope the panel would move her to the next step. What a terrific opportunity! And to think God had opened this door.

But how could she bear to leave Echo Falls?

This minute, still high on adrenaline, she missed Jake so much her knees wobbled. Plunging her hand into her purse, she rummaged for her phone. When she turned it on, a text from him popped up on the screen. *You'll do great. Praying for you.*

She could hardly wait to see him. Was that an answer to her prayer for clarity? On the other hand, she was terrified of the risk to her heart.

A female voice came from off to the side. "Mia?"

Startled, she turned and saw Sheryl from the Skype interview. Mia reached out to shake her hand, but Sheryl hugged her instead.

"So tell me—how did the interview go?"

"Good. Maybe even great." A genuine smile split Mia's face. "I'm kind of in shock."

"Dr. Benton, right?"

"Yes."

"He's a good man. I knew you were scheduled now, so I came to say hello."

"I appreciate it."

"Coffee?"

As much as Mia wanted to chat, she wanted to hear Jake's voice even more. "I wish I could, but I need to make a phone call."

"I'll walk you to the elevator."

She and Sheryl fell into step, passing the posters as Sheryl asked her more about the interview. When Mia told her about Dr. Benton wanting her on his team, Sheryl stopped dead in her tracks. "Girl, you better get ready for some big changes."

"Really?"

"It's not for me to say. You know that. But John Benton is a legend around here. If I were you, I'd get ready for the next step. It's a big one."

"You're talking about the team-building exercise."

"Also known as 'the scare the daylights out of you' exercise."

"The *what*?"

Sheryl repeated herself, emphasizing *daylights*. "It's designed to test both your personal fortitude and your ability to work with other people."

They were in front of the elevators now. One of them was open and waiting, but Mia ignored it. "I know about the team-building exercise, but the 'scare' part is new to me."

"That's because the candidates all take an oath to keep their stories to themselves. No blogging, Twitter, Instagram, or Facebook posts, because surprise is part of the plan."

"But you just told me—"

"Yes, I did," Sheryl said with a hint of glee. "You see, I'm part of the plan. The team building can be anything from extreme camping to something tamer—whatever Dr. Winkler cooks up for your group. Either way, now you have something to think about."

"You mean worry about!" Mia tried to laugh off her concern, but she didn't deal well with the mysterious and unknown. "Any hints about what this experience might involve?"

"Two years ago a group went skydiving."

Mia gaped at her. "You have *got* to be kidding."

"I'm dead serious. And I'm relieved to say they all lived through it."

When Mia sputtered, Sheryl broke out laughing. "The skydiving part is true, but in fairness, the five people in that group all had military experience."

"Well, I don't!" Mia thought a quick prayer. *Okay, God. That's a deal-breaker. I'm not jumping out of a plane.* "What else have they done?"

"One of the crazier things was stock car racing."

Maybe she could handle that, but only with a helmet, a safety harness, and a flame-retardant suit. "Did anyone crash?"

"No, but the final race was sure exciting."

"I can imagine."

"Dr. Winkler plans the challenges himself. Frankly, the ones I told you about were extreme even for him. The exercises typically involve camping with next to nothing, or your group could be given something entirely different, maybe even low-key. The idea is to take you out of your comfort zone, whatever that is."

Another elevator dinged. As people spilled out, Mia gave Sheryl a quick hug. "I better run, but thanks for the warning. I think."

Sheryl laughed. "You'll do fine. Just let God be your guide."

"Amen to that."

Mia meant it. God had never let her down, and she was sure He wouldn't start now. She just needed the courage to grow in her faith and do whatever He asked of her . . . except skydiving. If Mission Medical asked her to jump out of plane, she'd politely decline.

Alone in the elevator, she shot to the nineteenth floor without stopping. Her pulse sped up with the ride, and when the doors opened, she had her card key in hand. The instant she walked into her room, she tossed her purse on the bed and called Jake.

●●●

Shirtless, sweating, and frustrated, Jake raised the splitting maul high over his head and brought it down on a round of pine. Chilly evenings were a few months away, but the wood needed time to dry out. If the coming winter was typical, the Tanner clan would burn through four cords.

He did his best thinking when he broke a sweat. With Mia and the interview heavy on his mind, he welcomed the physical exertion. Today's interview mattered to her, which meant it mattered to *them*. He wanted her to do well, but he also wanted her to stay in Echo Falls.

He raised the ax again, aimed the blade, and let it fall into the wedge of pine. The two halves shot in opposite directions and landed ten feet apart.

"Nice cut," his dad said from behind him.

"One cord down. Three to go."

Frank picked up the piece at his feet and added it to the growing pile that would need to be stacked. More work for Jake's muscles while he tried to keep his mind busy. Knowing his father was here for a reason, he wedged the ax blade into the stump, then wiped his face with his shirt, which was hanging on a nearby fence.

"So what's up?" Jake asked.

"I just got back from town. You need to know that I had a run-in with Hatcher."

Jake muttered under his breath. "He needs to leave you out of this. What happened?"

"Your mom and I were at the Brownie Emporium. Bill was politicking as usual. You know your mother. She may be losing her memory, but she's a mother bear when it comes to her cubs."

Jake hadn't been a cub for a long time. Now it was his job to protect his mom. "Do I need to tell Hatcher to his face to leave you out of this?"

"No. I handled it." Frank propped a boot on the chopping stump. "He didn't see us in the corner booth, so he was talking about you personally, not just the camp. Your mom and I both heard him say he hoped the kennel fire taught you a lesson. Your mom stood up like she was going to give him a piece of her mind, but then she just sat back down and started to cry."

"What a-—" *Jerk* was too kind.

"I know." Frank held up one hand. "I let him have it with everything but my fists. No man makes my wife cry and gets away with it."

A steely gleam burned in Frank's eyes. Jake didn't see that look often, but when it surfaced, his father was a force to be reckoned with. Jake hated the thought of Bill hurting his parents, especially his mom. "I wish I'd been there."

"It was probably best you weren't. He's gets pretty hot under the collar when it comes to the camp."

"Maybe. But I'd still like to sit down with him and talk this out."

"That's not too likely." Frank glanced at the pile of split wood. "Any news from Mia?"

"Not yet."

"I sure would hate to see her leave." Frank watched him, a faint smile on his lips.

"Yeah, me too." The memory of the kiss rocketed through him. Not just the force of desire, but how vulnerable she'd felt in his arms.

Frank clapped him on the shoulder. "That's what I thought. It's good to see you smiling, son. You haven't been your old self since you came home from Denver."

Jake glanced at the pile of wood. Until Mia stepped into his life, he'd been dead inside. He didn't realize just how dead until she boarded that plane for Dallas. He missed her terribly. "Mia's pretty special."

"Yes, she is." A wistful gleam hardened his father's eyes. "I know better than most men what a difference the right woman can make."

"A big one."

"You bet," Frank replied. "Fight for her, son. And don't let her down."

"I won't." Coming from his dad, those words carried a lot of weight. Jake pulled the ax from the block and let it hang from one hand. "I better get back to—" His phone cut him off. He snatched the device out of his pocket and checked the ID. "It's Mia."

"Tell her we're pulling for her." Still grinning, Frank ambled away.

Jake tossed the ax on the ground, accepted the call, and started to pace. "So how did it go?"

"I'm speechless." Her sweet laughter rippled past his hearing aid. "I hardly know where to start."

"How about the middle?" In Jake's experience, that was where most stories switched gears.

"All right. But you won't believe this. I need to learn to sky-dive."

"Uh—" Jake stopped dead in his tracks. *Mia jumping out of a plane?* "Over my dead body."

"Don't worry. Skydiving is a deal-breaker for me, but if I make it to the team-building challenge, I'm in for something I've never done before. It could be anything from stock car racing to extreme camping, like *Survivor.* Or it could be something easy. Mostly it's a surprise."

"That's a little crazy." Jake didn't like the idea of Mia taking chances at all.

"Yes, but it serves a purpose." She told him about her conversation with Sheryl. "I'm nervous about it. You know me—I like to be prepared. And I've never been camping a day in my life."

"We can fix that."

"You'll help me?"

"Of course." He'd do anything for her, especially something that would ensure her safety. But as he spoke, his chest tightened. Helping Mia advance with Mission Medical could mean losing her in January. On the other hand, how could he not root for her? His father's words played through his mind. *Fight for her, son. And don't let her down.*

Jake made his voice matter-of-fact. "I'll teach you whatever you want to know."

"How to pitch a tent?"

"It's easy."

"How to light a fire without a match?"

She sounded so serious, he couldn't stop himself from teasing her. "Anything at all. We'll even dig up bugs and eat them."

"Ewww!"

Jake grinned from ear to ear. Teasing Mia was just plain fun. "We can skip the bugs if you'd like."

"Yes, definitely!"

They shared a laugh, then Jake asked the question that had plagued him all day. "So how did the interview go?"

"Just fine. In fact, one of the doctors—his name's John Benton—wants me on his team."

Jake hoped the man was a hundred years old and walked with a cane, because he didn't like the idea of Dr. Anyone wanting Mia for his team. "That sounds promising."

"The whole interview went well, but Dr. Benton was especially encouraging. He's a plastic surgeon specializing in the repair of facial abnormalities. I really admire him."

Jake had too much class to be jealous, and too much honesty to pretend he wasn't. On the other hand, Mia had called *him*. "Impressive."

"It is. But . . . I don't know how to say this."

"What?"

"I probably don't even need to say it."

It had to be about the kiss. Jake didn't want to have this conversation over the phone. "Whatever *it* is, let's talk about it when you get home. I'll see you at the airport."

"Okay." She paused. "No. I can't wait. I have to say it. I miss you."

Take that, Dr. Benton. "I miss you too."

Silence settled in the way of a freshly laundered bed sheet floating down to a mattress. Slowly. Lightly. Jake took a breath. So did Mia.

Her voice, normal again, came over the phone. "So how are things in Echo Falls?"

"Good." *But get ready, Mia. Lucy's going all out on your party.*

"Any news on Camp Connie?"

"No, but Hatcher made a scene with my parents." He told her about the encounter at the café.

Mia sympathized with him and asked about Claire. They chatted a few more minutes, then she said she needed to call Lucy.

Jake didn't want to hang up, and judging by Mia's long sigh, neither did she. He felt bad not mentioning her birthday, but he had promised Lucy he wouldn't breathe a word.

She's too smart, Lucy had told him. *Don't even wish her happy birthday, because she'll know I told you. I want her to be completely surprised.*

Jake wasn't sure a surprise party was a good idea, but he'd do his part and deliver Mia from the airport to Castro's Cocina. "I'll see you tomorrow."

"I'll text when I land."

"Perfect." They said a final good-bye and hung up at the same time.

Jake picked up the ax and went back to splitting wood. Only instead of wondering about the interview, he thought about

taking Mia camping. An overnight trip crossed the line he drew for himself regarding dating, but they could take a day hike to his favorite place in the world, perfect for team building—the kind that involved just Mia and himself, learning to trust, and the perfect spot for a kiss.

chapter 17

Mia walked into the Colorado Springs airport's baggage claim, spotted Jake, and waved. When he saw her, a grin lit up his face, and he strode toward her without Pirate at his side. She'd been gone less than seventy-two hours, but it felt like seventy-two days.

They hugged hard and fast, he kissed her temple, and they stepped apart with Mia wondering if he'd wish her a happy birthday. She hadn't told him or even dropped a hint, but this morning Lucy had texted. *Happy birthday, sis! I know you don't like b-days—esp this one!—but I have a little present for you. See you tonite at the house?*

She had texted back *yes*, then spent the flight wondering if Lucy had something up her sleeve. Mia hoped not. Between the excitement in Dallas and the stress of air travel, including a seat next to Captain Chatter, she wanted to go home and crash. Or even better, sit with Jake on the porch swing, watch the sunset, and forget she was turning thirty and facing a crossroads.

He aimed his chin at the baggage carousel. "Did you check anything?"

"This is it." She patted her carry-on. "Where's Pirate?"

"I gave him the day off."

Mia wondered why, but the decision made sense. Jake mostly used Pirate for hearing issues when he was alone.

He put his arm around her waist and guided her to the parking lot. In five minutes they were on the road home, and he still hadn't wished her a happy birthday. Maybe he didn't know. It would have been like Lucy to blab, but between her pregnancy and looking out for Claire, Lucy had a lot on her plate.

Jake reached across the cab and rubbed her shoulder. "Air travel stinks. You must be exhausted."

"I *am* tired."

"Close your eyes, if you'd like."

Still no acknowledgement of her big day. Even the TSA agent had wished her a happy birthday when he saw her driver's license. Mia tried closing her eyes, but a jaunty version of the birthday song played in her head. She let out a sigh, sat up, and blurted it out. "Today's my birthday."

"Really?"

"Yeah," she said, sounding grim. "I'm turning thirty."

"Well, happy birthday." He kept his eyes on the highway. "That's a milestone."

"A big one." She waited for more, but he stayed quiet. Maybe he couldn't hear well with the window cracked an inch. "I'm coming to the house for dinner tonight."

"That explains it."

"What?"

"Lucy asked me to pick up dinner at Castro's." He gave her an apologetic look. "Sorry, Mia. I didn't know."

"That's all right."

"I'll make it up to you."

She waited for more, but he steered the conversation to the weather. *The weather? Really?* She was turning thirty, her future was in limbo, and he was prattling about thunderstorms and the Echo River running high. The dull conversation grated on her even worse than the small talk from Captain Chatter on the plane.

By the time they reached the town of Echo Falls, she just wanted to go home. "Would you drop me off? I'll drive myself to the house."

"Sure," he said. "But let's stop at Castro's first."

"I'm beat. My house is only a couple blocks out of the way. Would you mind?"

Instead of answering, he reached for her hand and squeezed. Still silent, he steered the truck into an empty spot in front of the restaurant. Considering the street was packed with cars, the spot was a lucky find. Or was it? "Jake—"

He looked her square in the eye. "Humor me, okay?"

"What's going on?"

"Come with me to pick up the food."

"But why?"

"Because I'm asking you to."

He grazed her cheek with a kiss, climbed out of the truck, and circled to her side. When Mia pushed open her door, he offered his hand, and they walked into the restaurant. She tried to stop at the register to pick up their order, but Jake steered her past it and down an aisle.

Mia dug in her heels. "Jake, what's going on? Please tell me."

Stopping abruptly, he faced her. "You're going to have to trust me. That's all I can say."

"Trust you?"

"Yes."

Mia didn't trust easily, but she trusted Jake. She also spotted a "Happy Birthday" balloon bouquet bouncing near the ceiling in the back room. The pieces snapped together. Jake hadn't forgotten her birthday after all. He was part of one of Lucy's plots. The scoundrel!

Feigning irritation when she really wanted to hug him, Mia huffed air through her nose. "You lied to me!"

"About what?"

"My birthday."

"Yeah, I did." His eyes twinkled as bright as the Mylar balloons. "This assignment was undercover. Sorry to fib about it, but the ruse was necessary."

She laughed, but pleasure was only one of the emotions roiling through her. "Do you have any idea how much I hate surprises?"

"I do. That's why we're standing here now." He gave her hand a gentle squeeze. "Are you ready?"

Gazing into Jake's sparkling eyes, she basked in the knowledge that he knew her like no one else did, and wondered if maybe—just maybe—falling in love was worth the risk of another broken heart. But then the Mission Medical posters flashed through her mind, and she recalled Dr. Benton encouraging her and Dr. Winkler's sun-damaged skin, a badge of honor in Mia's eyes. Her commitment to Mission Medical called to her heart, but so did the love spilling out of the back room. Echo Falls needed her too.

Emotionally off balance, she rested a hand on Jake's arm. When he covered her cold fingers with his warm ones, she took a breath and steadied herself. "Don't worry. I'll act surprised."

"You better, or Lucy will kill me." He gave her the lead, and she walked the final steps to the back room.

When Mia stepped over the threshold, the crowd shouted, "Surprise!" and broke into applause. The force of it nearly blew her hair back.

Lucy ran up and hugged her. "Happy birthday!"

"I'm—I'm stunned." Mia held on tight. "You did this, didn't you?"

"And Jake." Lucy gave him a mile-wide grin. "It was his

job to get you here without spilling the beans. Were you surprised?"

"Completely!"

Laughter rippled all around them. Claire and Frank approached, Claire holding tight to Frank's hand. She looked both confused and animated, as if she remembered what a party was but not why she was at this one, or who all the people were.

Mia hugged her. "Hi, Claire."

"Hello, Mia." She stepped back and smiled. "It's your birthday."

"That's right."

"Lucy planned it."

"She's pretty special." Mia gave Lucy another hug, then noticed Sam at her side. "Hey, little brother!" She hugged him too.

Mia's heart swelled to bursting. For the first time in her life, she felt as if she had a family. While Sam and Lucy were linked to her by blood and vows, Jake and his parents were linked to her by choice. No matter what the future held, she would treasure these bonds.

Lucy, her tummy bulging under a camouflage T-shirt that said "Soldier Under Construction," went to the table with the balloon bouquet and clapped her hands for attention.

As the crowd silenced, Mia savored the sweet lump in her throat. Maybe not all surprises were bad.

Lucy raised both arms in a victory sign. "We did it, folks! We surprised a woman who's never surprised by anything."

Applause and whoops filled Mia's ears. Jake, standing next to her, rested his hand on her waist. She stood a little taller, enjoying the light touch.

Lucy's voice carried above the clatter of dishes and restaurant noise. "Before we get started, I want to tell you a little about my big sister. Most of you don't know that she raised me from the time I was ten years old. She made a lot of sacrifices so we could stay together, and tonight I want to pay her back with something she gave me but never had for herself. A real birthday party."

She paused while people clapped. "You've all heard of an over-the-hill party, right?"

Frank shouted, "Mia's too young for that!"

"Oh, definitely!" Lucy raised her hands to ward off boos. "This is the opposite. We're going back to being kids, so I'm calling this an 'upside-down' party. We have games like pin the tail on the donkey, a piñata, and pinball machines, thanks to Tanner Vending." She pointed to a row of old-school machines in the back, including a claw-machine game.

The crowd applauded again. Lucy waited until the noise died down, then focused on Mia. "I hope you're not expecting a pile of presents, because we did something different."

Mia couldn't imagine what Lucy might have cooked up. "I don't need gifts. Just having everyone here—"

"Is only the beginning," Lucy broke in. "Instead of buying gifts, we passed the hat and collected money for Mission Medical."

"Lucy, that's—that's perfect. Thank you." Choking up, Mia turned to the crowd. "Thank you all."

A woman she knew from church handed Lucy a note. "We're at $872 right now. Let's aim for a $1,000, okay?"

Fresh applause broke out, and several people dug into their pockets. The generosity warmed Mia to her toes.

Lucy spoke up again. "Let's get the party started. Games first, then we'll eat dinner and cut the cake. But first—" She looked at Mia. "I just want to say that I have the best sister in the world, and Echo Falls now has the best nurse to ever walk the planet."

Sam called out, "My wife never exaggerates."

"Never!" Lucy joked back. "Okay, someone put on music, and let's have fun."

Mia couldn't stop smiling through the sheen of happy tears. Everywhere she looked, she saw friends and family. When Jenny from the Brownie Emporium came up to her, Jake excused himself with the promise of returning with her usual soda water.

Jenny hugged her tight. "Happy birthday, honey."

While they chatted, a line formed. Mia hugged and thanked everyone, including Dr. Collins and his wife, who had stopped in town between RV excursions.

Kelsey, last in line, hugged her harder than anyone. "I'm so glad you were gone Thursday and Friday. I was terrified I'd slip and ruin the surprise."

"You did great," Mia said. "I didn't suspect a thing." *Until Jake let the surprise slip a little on purpose.*

"Excellent." Kelsey grinned. "So how did the interview go?"

"Good. Actually, great."

"You must be so excited!"

"I am." *Or I was.* How did she choose between the town she now loved and serving God with Mission Medical? During the flight, she had stared down at the geometric patterns of crops and fallow ground, praying and wishing for that kind of definition in her life. Instead she had landed in a party spinning like a kaleidoscope made of family and friends.

Jake arrived with her soda water, handed it to her, and greeted Kelsey with a bland hello, his tone cool but still friendly.

Poor Kelsey blushed a pretty pink. Grinning, she punched Jake in the arm. "We did it. We surprised Mia."

Jake let the *we* hang in the air, then glanced at Mia to include her. "So were you surprised?"

"Very." *But not too surprised, thanks to you.* She couldn't seem to pull her eyes away from his. She felt the sparkle to her toes, but then her skin prickled with the awareness of Kelsey watching them. Self-conscious, Mia turned to her.

Kelsey wilted in front of her eyes. Mia knew how it felt to

love a man who didn't want you. Some of the party joy went out of her, like air leaking from a balloon.

To her relief, Kelsey put on a smile and suggested they play pinball. "I hear Jake's an expert."

"I am," he said, "but no pinball for me. Consider me a retired champion."

"Show me," Kelsey said, trying yet again.

Jake started to shake his head, but when Mia saw Kevin Romano and his buddies at one of the machines, she saw an opportunity to distract Kelsey. "Let's all play."

The three of them crossed the noisy room to the machines. When Kevin saw them, he strode forward with a mischievous grin. "It's the birthday girl!"

Before Mia could react, he kissed her on the mouth. She wasn't naïve about over-the-top flirting. That was all the kiss was, but it annoyed her, and she pulled back fast, fighting to stifle a grimace.

Jake shot to her side, hooked his arm around her waist, and tugged her close. "Watch your manners, Romano."

"Whoa!" Kevin raised both hands and backpedaled. "Sorry, Jake. I didn't mean anything by it."

"It's all right," Jake replied. "Just don't do it again."

Mia's heart did a back flip. No man had ever been so ready to fight for her. When she looked up at Jake, protectiveness glinted in his green eyes. If they'd been alone, she would have turned fully into his arms and kissed him. Instead they traded a long look, one full of questions. Easing away from his side, she started to make a joke to erase the tension. But then she saw the crushed looked on Kelsey's face and couldn't think of a thing to say.

Mumbling something, Kelsey pivoted and hurried away, shattered the way Mia had been when she walked in on her college fiancé with her roommate. The circumstances weren't at all equivalent, but the feelings matched exactly. Hurt. Disappointment. And most brutal of all, the knowledge you weren't enough.

Mia felt sick inside. Unable to stand still and do nothing, she started to follow Kelsey.

Jake stopped her with a touch to her arm. "Let her go. There's nothing you can say right now."

"I could try—"

"Mia, don't." He whispered into her ear. "She's been doing this for months. Maybe this is for the best."

"She's my friend." And her office manager. Monday morning would be horrible if Mia didn't make peace now. On the other hand, wounds needed time to heal.

Inwardly sagging, she kept her feet in place, but her mind followed Kelsey out the door. Was love worth the risk of that kind of pain? With Jake's arm around her, she wanted to sing out, *Yes! Yes! Yes!* But life didn't come with guarantees. And on top of everything, she had made a commitment to God to serve with Mission Medical—if they asked. Confusion crashed down on her like stars falling from the sky.

She barely heard Kevin's offhand challenge to Jake for a game of pinball. Another firefighter joined them and suggested an impromptu contest. Jake and Mia both bowed out, but Kevin prodded Jake until he gave in.

Lucy came up and looped her arm around Mia's elbow. "You're the birthday girl. You need to take the first crack at the piñata."

Mia made eye contact with Jake to excuse herself, then went with Lucy. Together they made the rounds from the piñata to the musical chair game, and finally to the cartoon donkey pinned to the wall with a dozen tails everywhere but where they belonged. Mia still felt bad about Kelsey, but for Lucy's sake she laughed and joked. After twenty minutes or so, the buffet opened for dinner.

Jake came up to them. “Let’s eat before Kevin and the crew clean out the tacos.”

“Don’t forget Sam,” Mia said. “He eats enough for the entire US Army.”

Mia and Jake went through the buffet line, then found seats with his parents and Sam.

Lucy followed Mia, sat next to her with a loaded plate, and reached for the bottle of ketchup she’d asked for earlier. “Beanie Baby loves this stuff. You’d be surprised how good it is on guacamole.”

Everyone at the table groaned, especially Sam. When the joking died down, Mia whispered to her sister, “Have you seen Kelsey?”

Lucy’s eyes darted up and down the tables. “Her mother’s sitting with her own friends, but I don’t see Kelsey. She did a ton of stuff for the party. She should sit with us.”

“I don’t think so.”

“Uh-oh.” Lucy lowered her voice even more. “This involves Jake, doesn’t it?”

“Unfortunately, yes. I have to find her.” Mia pushed her chair back. If Kelsey’s mom was here, there was a chance Kelsey hadn’t left the restaurant.

Lucy clasped her arm. “You can’t leave now.”

“But—”

“You have to cut the cake.”

Nodding, Mia settled back in her chair but couldn’t eat another bite.

“I think it’s time to light the candles.” Lucy signaled Sam, and they went to the front table where a sheet cake was on display. Sam pulled out a book of matches, and they went to work lighting the wicks.

After a pause, Jake glanced at Mia’s half-full plate. “Are you feeling all right?”

"I'm fine."

Lifting one brow, he studied her face in a way that made her feel as transparent as glass. "Now who's lying?"

"Good work, detective." She tried to smile but grimaced instead. "It's Kelsey. I'm worried sick—"

Before she could finish, Lucy motioned for her to come up front. Mia pushed out of her chair and walked forward to a chorus of "Happy Birthday."

She really did feel like a child tonight, but not in the good way Lucy hoped. With the candles burning bright, Mia ached like the little girl whose father never came home; the teenager who knew too much about chemo. And finally, with thirty candles blazing in the shape of a heart, the virgin with five years left to her best-by date.

A male voice, maybe Hank Jeffries, an older man at church who liked to tease her, hooted in the back. "Good thing the fire department is here! That's a five-alarm blaze if I ever saw one."

"Get the pumper truck!" someone else shouted.

Some people laughed while others good-naturedly booed. Smiling at the jokes and in spite of them, Mia blew out the candles and gave a fist pump. "To the big 3–0!"

Lucy leaned in and handed her a knife. "After you cut the first piece, I want this back."

"Why?"

"I'm going use it to give Hank a brain transplant."

Mia couldn't help but smile. "Don't bother. I'd have to stitch him up."

Lucy hugged her hard. "I love you, Mia."

"I love you too." No matter how Mia felt about Kelsey and the age jokes, she wouldn't let anything ruin this night for Lucy. "Thank you for my party. I'll never forget it."

They broke the hug, and Mia sliced the cake. A line formed, and she served up square pieces while Lucy scooped ice cream.

The smiling faces blurred in her mind until she handed a paper plate to Jake.

She saw him with utter clarity—the set of his jaw, the gleam in his eyes, one dark brow arched slightly higher than the other. Her heart melted and froze all at once. If he took her home, they would have to talk about the incident with Kevin, the kiss after the fire, and everything those moments implied. Something more than friendship. A future together . . . or not.

As badly as Mia wanted clarity, she wouldn't find it tonight—not after seeing her own worst fears so plainly in Kelsey. Mia needed time to think and consider her choices, and if at all possible, she wanted to see Kelsey tonight and repair their friendship. Avoiding Jake was an added bonus.

His husky voice filtered to her ears. "We can head out of here anytime you'd like."

She set down the knife. "I was just thinking about that. I really do need to speak to Kelsey. She's here somewhere. It might be best if I caught a ride home with Sam and Lucy."

chapter 18

Jake didn't like what he was hearing at all. Kelsey? Was Mia serious? Or was she using Kelsey as an excuse to avoid him? Something was wrong, and he wasn't about to let her leave without probing deeper. No one was driving her home except him. For one thing, her birthday present was in the center console of his truck. For another, he was fired up after that little incident with Kevin and ready to say a few things.

He rammed his hands in his pockets. "I feel sorry for Kelsey too, but you can't fix it tonight. Let me take you home."

Mia's eyes darted around the room. Jake glanced with her. People were leaving now, including Kelsey's mom, who was walking out of the room with her friends.

Mia shook her head. "I should at least call her. Kelsey is—"

"An excuse."

"No."

"Are you sure? Because from where I'm standing, we went from hot to cold in about five seconds. I don't get it, Mia."

"I'm sorry, Jake." She hung her head to the side, then looked up with a weariness born of carrying the world on her shoulders. "I know I'm sending mixed messages here. You deserve better."

At least she acknowledged the mix. He could live with that. "You're confused."

"Yes."

"I'm not." He pitched his voice low, the words just for her and rich with promise. Instead of the radiant glow he hoped to see on her face, she lowered her eyes.

"I can't do this tonight. I'm sorry, Jake, but I'm exhausted from the flight, the party. Everything."

"Then it's smart to put off talking to Kelsey."

"Maybe. Or maybe not. I don't know." She wiped frosting off the cake knife with a sticky paper towel. "I don't know anything right now, except that I'm a decade older, my office manager hates me, and I can't think straight."

The last few words quavered to the point of cracking. He didn't want to make Mia cry on her birthday, but no way would he abandon her now. Reaching across the table, he took the knife from her hand and set it by the cake. "Let me take you home. We don't have to talk about anything."

"Really?" Relief darkened her eyes into two blue pools.

"Really."

"All right, then." She put on a brave smile and came around the table. They said their good-byes, and Jake hurried her out of the restaurant. The instant they climbed into his truck, she dropped the smile, pressed her head back against the seat, and let out a breath. They drove to her house in silence until the tires crunched on her gravel driveway. Mia reached for the door handle, but when Jake opened the center console, she stopped and watched.

"Just one thing." He lifted out a shiny gold bag stuffed with glittery curls of silver, gold, and bright pink ribbon. "Happy birthday, Mia."

"Oh—" She touched the side of the bag, looked into his eyes, and took a deep breath, the kind she used to steady herself. "This is sweet of you. I can't open it here. Come on in."

He came around to her side of the truck, lifted her carry-on out of the back seat, and walked with her to the front door. Mia worked the lock, and they stepped into her living room brightly lit by a lamp on a timer, a security measure he'd set up before she left for Dallas.

She crossed the room and turned the lamp on low, then set the gift bag on the coffee table. Still on her feet, she watched him like a nervous sparrow.

Hands in his pockets, Jake aimed his chin at the gift bag. "Are you going to open it?"

Her eyes latched on to his. "It's really nice of you."

"We're friends," he reminded her. "And it's your birthday."

"Just don't remind me that I turned thirty today."

"I won't, but I will tell you this." If he moved too fast, she'd dodge him. But if he didn't move at all, he'd regret not taking a chance. Keeping a safe distance, he lowered his voice and deepened it at the same time. "You're an exceptional person, Mia. Kind. Intelligent. Generous. And beautiful too. When I look at you, I see—"

"Jake, don't."

"I see a woman I care about."

Looking down, she took a shuddering breath. Jake crossed the room and gripped her hands, but she pulled back. Not the response he wanted, but he knew how her mind worked. They had known each other for over two months now. They went to church together and shared the details of their lives. Mia thought before she spoke, prayed before she made a decision, and waited until she was sure of herself.

That control made her strong and steady, but tonight it exasperated him because it hid the vulnerable side of her personality. That was the side of her that loved with everything she had to give. That was the part of her he needed to reach. But how? A kiss? Patience? The gift on the table?

She eased away from him, circled behind the couch, and dropped down on the far side of it. "This just might be the worst day of my life."

"That's quite a statement." Especially considering his confession of caring. Her reaction stung, but only until she looked up at him.

"I'm so confused. About us. Mission Medical. Where I belong. Everything."

So his feelings for her hadn't ruined her night. It was her own she couldn't handle. And that, he decided, was a very good sign. "You're in limbo."

"Totally." Hunching forward, she rubbed circles on her temples with fingers as white as bone. "I'm sorry, Jake. It's not fair to you, I know that. But I'm falling apart here. I can't stand being unsure of myself. Undecided. Not knowing what to do. What's right or best. Or—"

He dropped down next to her. "Mia, stop."

"And then there's Kelsey crying her eyes out just like I did over Brad and that guy in college."

"Mia."

"And I'm thirty." She gave a dry laugh. "Hank was right about the cake. It looked like a five-alarm fire."

"It was beautiful," he insisted. "Every candle stood for a year that made you the woman you are now."

"And who exactly is that?" Anger rolled off her tongue. "A woman who's been engaged twice and dumped twice. It hurts! Especially with Lucy and Sam so happy and with a baby on the way."

Her hollow gaze shifted to the mantel. Jake turned his head and took in a row of wedding photographs, including one of himself and Mia posed with Sam and Lucy. All four of them wore radiant smiles.

Mia concentrated on the picture in the middle, the one of

Sam and Lucy in profile, his finger tipping up her chin, her lips ripe for a kiss. "They're so happy. And I'm happy for them. It's just . . ."

"You want to be happy for you too."

"Yes." The word hissed from her lips. "It's not fair. I did everything right. I followed the rules, and for what? Two broken hearts because I wouldn't—" She stopped midsentence.

Jake didn't understand. "Wouldn't what?"

"You know."

No, he didn't. Or wait. Maybe he did.

He had no idea what his face looked like, but Mia rolled her eyes at him. "Good work, detective. You figured it out."

"You're—"

"Waiting for marriage." Defiance, maybe bitterness, tinged her voice. "I'm still waiting. But sometimes I wonder if I'm crazy, or stupid, or just—" She pressed her hands to her cheeks. "Would you *please* leave? This is humiliating."

"Humiliating? No way."

"It is!"

The implications of her confession rocketed through him. Mia was a virgin. How many Christians successfully waged that battle for purity? Jake didn't know, but he knew a lot of people who had given in, including Sam. Mia was even stronger than he realized—and far more wounded by those broken engagements. Rejection stung. It especially stung when someone tossed a precious gift back in your face.

Studying Mia's expression now, her eyes blazing and her hair loose, with her lips pinched tight against her vulnerability, Jake yearned to be the first and only man to make love to her.

He knew exactly what that desire meant. Marriage. Forever. Good times and hard ones. A fight for honesty, goodness, and daily healing. Love for Mia pounded in his chest, his belly, his taut muscles. He longed to haul her into his arms, but she was hunched over now, her face buried in her hands.

He stayed on his side of the couch but rubbed between her shoulder blades. "Don't you dare be embarrassed by your choices."

A sigh whispered from her lips, but she didn't look at him. "I feel so foolish reacting like this. I'm not exactly sorry or embarrassed, but it's unusual."

He answered by rubbing her back some more.

"And it's not easy either," she finished.

"No, it isn't."

She finally raised her head. Whether she meant to or not, she gave him a look that nearly set his hair on fire. That look revealed just how tempted she was. When it came to Mia choosing her future, Mother Nature had given him a powerful ally. But what about Mission Medical? She glowed when she talked about making a difference. If he really loved her, and he was sure that he did, he needed to put her desires before his own.

More than anything, he wanted Mia to be content, and to feel safe and respected for her choices, so he backed way down. "I know you don't want to talk about us, but I'd like to say one more thing."

"I owe you at least that much."

"Something good is happening here. We both feel it." The truth needed to be told. "I want to be more than a friend to you, Mia. But there's no rush. Let's take things a step at a time. No decisions. For now, you hang in there with Mission Medical, and I'll support you all the way. If you get the job, we'll deal with it then."

The creases around her mouth softened into a smile. "No one has ever backed me up like that."

"Then it's about time."

The gold bag sparkled in the light. It held three gifts, each a reflection of how he saw her. Leaning forward, he picked up the bag and set it next to her. "Now, let's open your birthday present. Want to guess before you dig in?"

Relief shone in her eyes. They were both glad to slide into friendly banter. Mia lifted the bag. "It's heavy. Hmmm . . . I'm guessing Skittles."

"Good guess." But they weren't ordinary Skittles. Jake had ordered them from a custom candy company.

Mia lifted out the clear plastic bag, saw only red ones, and smiled. "That's really sweet—literally. I'll share with you."

He nudged the gift bag. "Keep going. There's more in there."

She reached inside, pulled out a wad of bubble wrap taped around the second part of the gift, and laughed like a little girl. "I love bubble wrap!" She popped a few bubbles, then peeled back the tape and held up the Leatherman tool to the light. "I have no idea what this is."

"It's a Swiss Army knife on steroids." Not a romantic choice, but he thought Mia would like it. "If that team-building exercise involves race cars or camping, you'll be prepared. I'll show you a few tricks with it."

"Jake, it's perfect. Thank you." Her eyes shone even brighter than before. "Living alone like I do, I've come to appreciate tools."

"I'm glad you like it, but there's something else in the bag."

Suddenly shy, she leaned over and kissed his cheek. "This is already the best birthday gift ever."

He hoped she liked the last item just as much. It was about as far from Skittles and a Leatherman tool as a man could get.

Mia pulled out a jewelry-size box, rectangular and wrapped in pink foil paper. She tried to break the ribbon, but it refused to give.

Jake picked up the Leatherman and showed her the mini scissors. "Here. Use this."

"I love this thing already!" She snipped the ribbon, peeled back the paper, and opened the lid. When she saw the necklace he'd bought from a local artisan, her face lit up. It was made of antique gold and stones from the Echo River in variegated shades of amber, beige, and brown.

"Jake, it's beautiful." She angled it to catch the light, causing the stones to sparkle and wink. Bending forward, she draped the necklace around her neck, worked the clasp, and touched the smooth gold with her fingers. "Thank you. I love it."

"I'm glad." He hoped she would wear the necklace for years to come and remember this night when she did. Knowing she was exhausted from both travel and the party, he pushed to his feet. "I'll get out of here so you can get some rest."

Mia followed him to the door. When he opened it, she stopped him with a hand on his arm. "Thank you for everything. The airport run, the party, my present. But especially thank you for understanding that I need time."

Her hands slid to his chest, resting lightly while she stood on her toes and kissed his lips.

He put his hands over hers and squeezed. "Take all the time you need, Mia. I'm not going anywhere." *At least not without you.*

"One more thing." Stepping back, she fingered one of the stones in the necklace. "When can we start those outdoor survival lessons?"

"Anytime."

"It has to be on a weekend because of my office schedule."

Jake opened the calendar on his phone. "Next week is out. I'm giving a fundraising speech at a Rotary Club breakfast in Denver, and then another one in Castle Rock two weeks after that."

"Labor Day?" she asked.

"That won't work for what I have in mind." The hiking trails would be full of tourists, and he wanted to be alone with her. "How about the third Saturday in September?"

"That's perfect. Where are we going?"

He had the perfect spot in mind, but he wasn't about to share it with her. "I can't tell you."

"Why not?"

"When you head out with Mission Medical, you'll be flying blind."

"Unfortunately, yes."

"So fly blind with me. This is a team-building exercise, right?"

"Yes, it is."

"So if you need help, I'm there for you. And if I need help—"

"I'm there for you." She seemed pleased. "I'll be in charge of the first aid kit."

In Jake's opinion, hiking together showed trust at its most basic—two people working together and respecting each other. When he and Mia returned from the trail he had in mind, she would know she could trust him.

After another lingering look, he strode to his truck. Mia closed the front door, but she peeked between the curtains as he backed out of the driveway. She had plenty to think about tonight, and so did he.

chapter 19

When Mia walked into the office on Monday morning, she went straight to Kelsey. Before Mia could even open her mouth, Kelsey was on her feet and apologizing.

"I'm sorry, Mia. The way I left—"

"Kelsey, it's okay. That incident with Kevin and Jake was awkward, but what you saw . . ." Mia let the words hang. "What you saw between Jake and me, it might be the start of something."

"I hope it is." Kelsey smiled bravely. "I want him to be happy. And you too. You're more than my boss, Mia. You're my friend."

Weak with relief, Mia hugged Kelsey hard. "I feel the same way about you."

They broke apart and traded awkward smiles until Kelsey sat down at the check-in window. A beleaguered sigh whispered from her lips. "I made a fool of myself with Jake, didn't I?"

"Honestly?"

"Yes. Please." Kelsey pulled her face into a wince and held it. "How bad was it?"

"Not that bad." Mia meant it. "If it makes you feel any better, in college, when I caught my ex-fiancé kissing my roommate, I did one of the stupidest things I've ever done."

"Really? What?"

Mia rolled her eyes. "You know the good girl who can't stand conflict and never rocks the boat?"

"That's you, isn't it?"

"Very much so. I still can't believe what I did when I caught them together. Of all the stupid things to say, I apologized for interrupting them. Can you believe it? I stood there and said, 'Oh! I'm sorry.' Then I closed the door, ran down five flights of stairs, and cried for three hours. I should have thrown the engagement ring at him and tossed her things out the window."

Kelsey's eyes twinkled. "But you're too nice."

And too in control. "It's just how I am. Think first, react later."

"I hope Jake doesn't hate me."

"He doesn't." Mia admired his kindness to Kelsey and how he tried hard to protect her dignity. "He considers you a friend."

"That's a relief. But, Mia?"

"Yes?"

"There's something I've been wondering. I thought you were moving to Dallas and traveling overseas?"

"I am. Or I was. I just don't know." She paused, grimacing. "Sometimes I hope Mission Medical will turn me down so I won't have to decide. But when I think of the good work they do, I'm ready to hop on a plane." And when she thought of Jake, she didn't know whether to throw her whole heart into loving him or to run away as fast as she could.

Kelsey started to say something, but the phone rang. While she handled the call, Mia retreated to her office and skimmed the day's schedule on her tablet. Thirty-two patients, including four new ones and three emergency adds? Was Kelsey crazy? Mia blew out a breath that lifted a wisp of her hair. Normally she embraced a day like this one, but she was expecting a call about today's ultrasound from Lucy late this morning.

Kelsey peeked around the corner. "Sorry about the schedule, and it just got worse. I squeezed in another emergency at 11:45."

"That's the way it goes." As long as she ate a quick lunch, she'd be fine. "Who's the emergency?"

"Bill Hatcher."

Mia's brows lifted. "That's a surprise."

"He's having back spasms again and can't drive to the Springs."

"I'm glad he's willing to come in." Mia wouldn't breathe a word about Camp Connie to him, and she hoped he'd return the consideration.

The day began. She performed blood pressure checks, looked at sore throats, washed her hands a thousand times, and laughed at Mr. McDougall's doctor joke, the same one he'd told her at his first visit two weeks ago.

The morning flew by. Shortly before eleven, Mia was only twenty minutes behind schedule, which wasn't too bad, considering the emergencies. She paused in the front office. In spite of the glass window, she heard Bill Hatcher's gravelly voice. When she peeked into the waiting room, she saw him talking to Betty Downing.

"We'll have more crime up here than we do now," he said in a voice loud enough to carry throughout the room.

"And we have too much as it is!" Betty replied. "After that break-in at the pharmacy, I'm nervous to park in the back lot."

"It's no wonder." Bill let out a snort. "If people knew how you and I felt, they'd be on our side."

Mia considered the waiting room a private place akin to her living room. Bill was a guest here, but if she asked him to refrain from politicking, he might storm out, angrier than ever and still in physical pain. She settled for eavesdropping while she e-prescribed for the patient checking out.

Mr. Hatcher's voice rose a notch. "If Jake Tanner has his way, we'll have a lot more of that kind of trouble. I guarantee it." He shifted awkwardly on the soft chair and winced.

"Yes, we will." Poor Betty coughed up half a lung.

Hatcher didn't seem to notice. "If that kennel fire didn't open his eyes to the risk, nothing will."

"Poor Frank and Claire," Betty remarked. "I hear she started it by accident."

"If Tanner can't watch out for his mother, why should we trust him to watch out for those kids?"

Spitting mad, Mia somehow schooled her features, sent the e-script, and told the patient, Mrs. Conway, to call in a week if she didn't feel better. Tight-lipped, Mia skimmed her schedule. There were three patients ahead of Hatcher. The sooner she saw them, the sooner she could finish with him and he would leave.

His voice pressed through the glass. Even muted, she could hear every word he said to Art Conway, who stood as his wife approached.

"So, Art," Bill said, "what do you say?"

"About what?"

"This youth camp nonsense."

"No opinion." Art sold insurance for a living and was everybody's friend. Mia wondered if he had a real opinion on anything other than the Denver Broncos.

Bill hunkered forward, wincing again. "You can't think it's a good thing. Wait until all those vandalism claims roll in."

Art shrugged. "Bad things happen. It's life."

"But we don't have to throw open our doors and invite trouble inside," Hatcher countered.

"Hear! Hear!" The remark came from a mom with two young children. "We moved up here to get away from bad influences."

Mia barely restrained herself from speaking up. The woman was naïve if she thought she could escape drugs, crime, and teen pregnancy by moving to a small town. Mia had been in Echo Falls for close to two months, and she'd seen all that and more.

Another man joined in the fray, then an elderly woman shouted over him.

Mia turned to Kelsey. "I'm going to break a rule and take Mr. Hatcher back now. We'll call it triage." The most urgent problem first, and Bill Hatcher was a problem.

Just as Mia reached for the doorknob, her phone signaled a text. Thinking of Lucy, she stole a glance.

Call me. Help! BED REST.

"Oh no." Not good. Not good at all. But she couldn't call Lucy with the quarrel in the waiting room. Breathing a prayer, she called Mr. Hatcher back to the exam room.

He glared at her but didn't say a word about Jake or the camp. Mia deflected the hostility with a low-key greeting, took his vital signs, and asked him about his problem.

"Back spasms." He grimaced at a jolt of pain. "Collins used to prescribe muscle relaxants."

Mia skimmed his record, saw the medicine, and did the same. "I'll send the script now. Do you still use Blackstone Apothecary?"

Hatcher smirked. "I sure do. It's the place with the busted window."

Somehow she kept her mouth shut. Stone-faced, she e-prescribed the medication, faced Mr. Hatcher, and told him to call in three days if he didn't feel better.

He grumbled a thank-you and walked out of the exam room, his cane thumping on the linoleum floor.

Mia put Hatcher out of her mind, saw the last few patients, and hurried to her office to call Lucy.

Her sister picked up on the first ring, her voice shaky with tears. "Mia?"

"Hi, honey. What's up?"

"I can't believe it. The doctor put me on bed rest. Well, sort of. He called it 'restricted activity,' but it's the same thing, isn't it? I don't want a C-section. I really don't. I'm just so—"

"Lucy, wait. Please."

"I'm just so scared. I didn't expect this."

"Is Sam with you?"

Lucy sniffed. "He's right next to me. We're sitting in the car."

"Good." Mia stayed at her desk. Lucy was her sister, not a patient, but her professionalism kicked in with full force. "Put me on speaker, okay?"

After a pause, Sam's voice reached her ears. "Hi, Mia."

"Hello, Sam. Let's see if we can sort this out together. First, aside from restricted activity, what did the doctor say about the placenta previa?"

"It's partial," Sam answered. "He said there's still time for the placenta to move up, but that Lucy should stay off her feet as much as possible."

"Did he limit her to one shower a day and trips to the bathroom?"

"No," Sam replied.

"That's good." Mia breathed a little easier. "It sounds like he's just being cautious. I like that."

"Really?" Lucy's voice cracked.

"Yes, I do. As long as you can rest and stay off your feet, there's no reason not to do it."

Sam broke in. "I asked him about being an hour from a hospital—if we should move down to the Springs. He said it was up to us. What do you think?"

"I've thought about it too. The pros are that Lucy has good family support in Echo Falls. I'm five minutes away, and Frank and Jake are in and out of the house. As long as Claire isn't too demanding, I think the pros outweigh the biggest con of moving to the Springs, which is being alone all day while you're in school. Bed rest sounds like a vacation, but it's a lot tougher than people realize."

"Mia?" Lucy sounded stronger.

"Yes, honey?"

"I can handle Claire. She mostly colors at the kitchen table or watches old sitcoms. Or she coaxes Peggy McFuzz into her lap and gives her treats."

"They're friends?"

"The best. Claire's the one who talked her out from behind the couch. They're inseparable now." While Mia smiled at the picture of Claire spoiling Miss McFuzz, Lucy let out a sigh. "I hate the idea of being alone all day, but even before the doctor visit, we talked about moving down here because of the commute. It's hard for Sam."

"I told you, Lucy." Impatience leaked into his voice. "I can handle the drive."

Mia admired his determination, but he put in long days between his classes and ROTC. In good weather, the roundtrip commute was over two hours. She worried about his endurance as much as she worried about Lucy. "That's between you two. You know I'll support you any way I can."

Sam broke in. "We're staying in Echo Falls. It's best for Lucy and the baby. I'm glad you're there, Mia."

She heard murmuring, then Lucy came back over the phone. Her voice came out lighter, even happy. "Mia, you're the best sister ever."

Mia grinned. "No, you are."

"No, you—Oh!" Lucy gasped. "I almost forget the other big news!"

So had Mia. "Pink or blue?"

"Pink. We're having a girl!"

Tears rushed into Mia's eyes. No matter what her own future held, she planned to spoil her niece rotten with frilly dresses, stuffed bears, and every Fisher-Price toy on the market.

Sam's easy chuckle reached her ears. "A daughter. I can't believe it. I have no idea what to do with a little girl."

"You'll figure it out." Mia offered the advice she gave dads-to-be in Dr. Moore's office. "You love Lucy, right?"

"You know I do."

"You'll love a daughter just as much. Before you know it, she'll have you wrapped around her little finger."

"She already does," Sam replied.

"I'm kind of relieved," Lucy admitted. "I wouldn't know what to do with a boy."

Mia grinned again, this time with a hint of envy. "You'd love him to pieces. That's all it takes."

"I would." Lucy's voice wobbled a little. "But right now, I just want a safe delivery."

"Hang in there," Mia told her. "You won't be pregnant forever, though I hear it feels that way. Let's hope the placenta moves up. It can still happen. In fact, the odds are in your favor."

She glanced at the clock. It was almost time for the first patient of the afternoon. If she didn't use the bathroom, she'd spring a leak. "Anything else before I get back to work?"

"Just one thing. I need a favor."

"What is it?"

"Claire's with Barb. We were supposed to pick her up by four o'clock, but Sam's CO called. He wants to meet with Sam at three, and Jake and Frank are installing machines at a big hotel today. I was wondering if you could pick up Claire and stay with her until Jake and Frank get back?"

Mia glanced at the schedule on her tablet and saw three cancellations. "It'll be tight, but I can do it." Seeing Jake was an added bonus.

"Perfect. I'll call Barb. If you could fix dinner for Claire, that would be nice. Her new favorite is grilled cheese on sourdough. And check Peggy McFuzz's water, okay? Claire either fills it a hundred times or she completely forgets."

"Got it."

"Thank you, Mia." A new lightness rang in Lucy's voice. "Sam and I have a couple of hours to kill, so we're going to grab lunch. Beanie Girl's craving a chili cheese dog with extra onions."

Mia chuckled. "You're going to get the worst case of heartburn ever!"

"Maybe. But if I'm going to be housebound, I might as well live it up now."

The sentiment was just like Lucy. Seize the moment! Worry about the consequences later. Mia envied her that freedom but not the heartburn.

Her tablet flashed to show her first patient had checked in a little early. "My one o'clock is here. I need to eat lunch and get busy."

"Bye!"

"Bye," Mia replied, but Lucy was already gone.

A bittersweet smile lifted Mia's lips. She would miss holding her niece in her arms if she took the job with Mission Medical, but maybe that was for the best. Lucy didn't really need her anymore. That had been the goal, and they'd always be just a phone or Skype call apart. And Mia would always be the big sister, not the younger one calling for help.

Who did Mia call when she needed that kind of support? No one, really. Not even Jake. Dr. Moore was a friend but not a substitute mother. Mia enjoyed other friendships in Denver, but she was the advice giver, not the recipient. Mostly she prayed and asked God to guide her. She would have enjoyed talking to Claire, but Claire's wisdom was lost forever.

Pushing a burst of melancholy aside, Mia gobbled her lunch and went to work. She finished with patients early, went home to change clothes, and picked up Claire from Barb's house. Claire was confused by Mia's presence and a different car, but Mia guided her with a hug and they drove to the Tanner ranch.

Claire went straight to the living room to watch television. No Netflix or Hulu in this room, but so far Claire could manage the still familiar remote to the old DVD player. When she was comfortable in her chair with Peggy McFuzz in her lap and Mary Tyler Moore on the TV screen, Mia refilled the dog's water bowl and fixed Claire a grilled cheese sandwich. She brought it to her on a paper plate, and they settled into the monotony that was Alzheimer's disease.

They talked a little, mostly about Mary's clothes and that funny man with the white hair. Claire didn't understand the more cerebral jokes, but she laughed whenever Mary pulled a funny face.

Mia ached for her, and a little for herself. There was so much she wanted to ask Claire about life and marriage, Jake's childhood, what he was like as a boy. Instead they watched Mary toss her hat in the air as if she didn't have a care in the world. Maybe she didn't, but where would Mary be in another twenty years? Would she regret any of her choices?

Claire sat entranced by the show, lost in the 1970s or maybe at home there. Aching for them both, Mia watched the sitcom until Frank's work truck chugged into the driveway. Peggy McFuzz leaped off Claire's lap and barked like a maniac, defending both her new turf and Claire.

"Frank's home," Mia said.

Honest surprise flashed on Claire's face, as if she hadn't seen Frank in a million years. She picked up the remote, muted the sound, and looked expectantly at the door.

When Frank walked in, the dog danced on her hind legs until he gave her a scratch. Straightening, he greeted Mia, then kissed Claire on the cheek. "How's my beautiful wife?"

Claire beamed at him. "I'm just fine. Sit. We're watching television." She pointed at Frank's recliner. He patted her shoulder and turned to Mia, remaining on his feet.

"Thanks for covering for us. Sam texted Jake, so I heard their news."

"A little girl." Mia smiled with a hint of wistfulness.

"We're thrilled for them," he said, including Claire, but then he lowered his voice and spoke only to Mia. "Jake and I discussed the bed rest angle. We don't want Lucy to overdo it with Claire. If we need to make other arrangements, we will."

"That's nice of you, Frank."

"Lucy's a sweet kid." He patted Claire's shoulder to include her again. "Isn't she, honey?"

"Who?"

"Lucy," he repeated. "She lives with us."

"Oh, yes." But Claire's eyes glazed with confusion. Suddenly lost, she focused hard on the television, nestled back in her recliner, and aimed the remote at the television, presumably to unmute it.

Mia braced for a volume blast. That happened when Claire mixed up the buttons. Instead Claire pressed the power button, and the screen faded to black.

"Oh no! I broke it."

"No, you didn't." Frank indicated the remote clenched in her hand. "You pushed the green button by accident. Push it again, and the show will come back on."

Claire stared at the remote as if it were a block of wood, her fingers tight and her brows pinched in concentration. As hard as she tried, she couldn't make the connection.

Gently, as if she were a toddler clutching a toy, Frank pried her fingers from the remote. "Let's see if I can fix it."

"Fix it?"

"Yes. Like this." He aimed the remote and clicked.

Mary Tyler Moore returned to the screen, and Frank set the remote on the end table. Claire had so little control in her life that letting her keep the remote seemed like a nice thing to do, but she snatched it up and somehow turned off the DVD player. A commercial for diabetes products played on the screen.

Claire shrugged and hit the power button. "I guess the show's over."

Heaving a tired sigh, Frank offered Claire his hand. "Come on, sweetheart. Let's go for a walk."

Technology evolved and people declined, but the mountains remained the same. Claire stared at him for several seconds, then blinked, her expression softening as the stiffness of Alzheimer's gave way to the softer lines of a tired, aging woman. But then a panicked look crossed her face. "The dogs—what time is it? They need to be fed."

The dogs had been picked up a month ago. Mia opened her mouth to remind Claire, a knee-jerk reaction from her own healthy brain, but Frank signaled her to remain quiet.

"The dogs are fine," he said to Claire.

"Oh, good." She looked at the blank television screen, shrugged, and pushed the recliner upright. But as Frank took her hand, the confusion returned. "The dogs. They need to be fed—"

"They're fine," he repeated. "Let's sit outside."

"The dogs—"

"They're fine, honey." Frank sounded weary to the bone, but he slipped his arm around Claire, then spoke just to Mia. "If you want to say hello to Jake, he's out in the barn."

"Thanks. I'll go right now."

"He'll like that." Frank's eyes twinkled a bit, maybe with the memory of being young and on the threshold of love. Or maybe with the history of being old and committed to the same woman his entire life.

Mia couldn't ask Claire about marriage or the glue that kept a man and woman together for a lifetime, but she saw the depth of Frank's commitment in everything he did. And in Claire, even agitated and confused, Mia saw a deep and abiding trust in her husband. Her heart swelled with admiration for these two older people, both strong individuals but partners for life.

She returned Frank's twinkle with one of her own. "You love her very much."

"With all my heart."

Mia gave Frank a hug, then hugged Claire—extra hard because Claire adored that kind of affection. Satisfied, she hurried to the barn to find Jake. She wasn't ready to make a big decision about her future, but she was very confident in the small one she wanted to make tonight. She had skipped the grilled cheese and was hungry. Dinner together, just the two of them, sounded perfect.

As she approached the barn, the interior light went out, and Jake emerged from the doorway, a shadow defined by the pearlescent moon. She couldn't see his features, only the planes of his cheeks and his square jaw.

"Hi," she called to him. "I'm glad you're back."

"Thanks for helping out. It's not easy being with my mom." They met in the middle of the yard. "How many episodes of *Mary Tyler Moore* did you watch?"

"Only three."

"And every time Mary made a funny face, my mom laughed."

"She didn't miss a beat." Mia kept her voice light, not in humor but in defiance of the dark.

When Jake smiled in the same way, Mia touched his arm. "You look exhausted."

"I am, but it's good to see you." He reached for her hand, nothing more. But when he squeezed, she felt his desire to be with her down to her toes. Every instinct told her to ease into his arms and kiss him, but she needed to be careful of their feelings. *One step at a time.*

"Are you hungry?"

"I'm starved."

"How about dinner together?"

Jake raised a brow, then stepped back as if he were surprised. "Did you just ask me out on a date?"

"Yes, I did." She grinned. "A spur-of-the-moment, let's-just-enjoy-the-evening kind of date."

"I'm in. Give me fifteen minutes to clean up. How does Andy's Barbecue Shack sound?"

Mia knew the spot. Andy's wasn't a shack at all. Located about ten miles away on the Echo River itself, it offered great food, a quiet atmosphere, and cozy booths. As an official first date, it was the perfect choice.

Mia waited in the yard, enjoying the night air until Jake came out of the house, freshly showered and in dark slacks, a blue button-down, and a lightweight jacket. She drove her car to her house with Jake following, jumped in his truck, and they headed to the restaurant. A quick dinner turned into a three-hour date complete with holding hands while strolling along the paved riverwalk.

When they were out of sight of the restaurant windows, he drew her into his arms. Moonlight filtered through the trees, casting shadows across his face and all around them. The river flowed at a lazy pace, and when Jake matched his mouth to hers, they kissed in the same lazy rhythm until she melted into a mindless puddle.

But then her fears intruded and she sobered. "Jake, I . . ." She couldn't look him in the eye. She wasn't ready for this much intensity, the longing to be only his, to love him fully and forever.

He whispered sweet assurances into her ear. "We're taking things slow, remember? That was just a kiss. There's no rush."

Maybe not for him, but Mia felt like a child trapped on a spinning seesaw—up and down, around and around, over and over until she was dizzy. When a shaky sigh escaped from her lips, Jake held her tighter.

Unspoken words lingered between them, but those words cried out in Mia's mind. She cared deeply for Jake. She admired his steady presence, his patience, his kindness and intelligence.

And she cared deeply for his family. Frank and Claire proved to her that love could last and some men could be trusted to keep their promises.

Trembling in Jake's arms, Mia faced a frightening truth. Against her better judgment, she was on the verge of listening to her heart instead of her head and falling head over heels in love with Jake Tanner.

chapter 20

The next four weeks flew by for everyone except Lucy. At least that was how it felt as she lay stretched on the couch, watching *The Mary Tyler Moore Show* with Claire late on a Wednesday afternoon. Jake was working in his office, and Frank was in town picking up carry-out Chinese since Lucy's cooking lessons were over. If she spent more than five minutes on her feet, someone told her to go lie down as if she were Peggy McFuzz.

Sam was the worst of all when it came to bossing her around. If she spent an extra ten seconds in the shower, he practically ordered her to hurry it up.

The only person who understood how she felt was Mia. She came to the house every day, but Lucy didn't think for two seconds Mia was coming to see *her.* Not a chance. Mia refused to admit it, but she glowed around Jake the way Lucy used to glow around Sam. And still did. Most of the time.

Sam was due home from school any minute, and in spite of feeling like a lowly private in his army, Lucy could hardly wait to enjoy a quiet evening, just the two of them in their room. No television or even conversation. She was happy just to watch him study.

Shortly before dusk, his car rumbled into the driveway. Peggy

McFuzz yapped and ran to the door. Lucy glanced at Claire, saw she was still asleep, and stood, her whole body aching for a hug. But then she sat down. He'd scold her if he caught her on her feet. She waited as patiently as she could, but it seemed to take forever for him to walk through the front door.

When he finally strode into the den, he was on his phone, saying, "Yes, sir" repeatedly to someone yelling at him. He sounded more downcast every time. "Yes, sir. I understand, sir."

Concerned, Lucy leapt to her feet. Sam jabbed a finger at her, then at the couch, a silent order to sit down. Lucy propped her hands on her hips and glared at him. She wasn't a child. She was his wife, and she was worried.

"Yes, sir," Sam said again. "Tomorrow at five a.m."

When the yelling stopped, Sam flung the phone down on the couch and muttered a four-letter word. That language wasn't like him at all.

Lucy's hands dropped from her hips and she reached for him. "Oh, Sammy! Are you all right? What happened?"

Ignoring both her questions, he stepped back. "You shouldn't be standing up."

"I'm fine."

"Lucy, I worry—"

"I worry about you too!" She kept her voice low, but it scraped at them both.

Sam glanced at Claire, still asleep. Lucy breathed a sigh of relief. She needed to talk to her husband without Claire saying it was time to feed the dogs, or thinking Lucy was her sister, or turning the TV on full volume.

She indicated the living room. "Let's go in there. We'll hear if Claire wakes up."

Sam dragged his hand through his buzz-cut hair, then followed her to the bigger room. They could still hear the television blasting out canned laughter, but at least they were alone.

Lucy sat on the couch and patted the spot next to her, but Sam walked to the big window and stood, hands on his hips and his back to her.

His voice drifted to her ears. "I'd give a year of my life for a decent night's sleep."

"You work hard."

"Yeah. But not hard enough."

"Sam, I—"

He didn't seem to hear her. "My CO just called for a *five a.m.* inspection."

"Oh no." Between studying and preparing for the inspection, he wouldn't get any sleep at all.

He turned and faced her, his body in silhouette. "I also have an exam tomorrow in system dynamics, a big one, and I'm not ready for it. Do you know what all this means?"

She started to answer, but he answered himself.

"It means I'm going to be up until two again, and I need to leave here no later than three thirty for the stupid inspection."

"Sam, that's awful. Why did your CO do that? It's just . . . it's mean!"

"Mean?" He gaped at her. "Lucy, it's the army. He's doing it because I've been late twice in three weeks. If I'm late again"—he made a slash across his throat—"he'll bust me down in rank."

"It's just not fair!"

"Fairness has nothing to do with it."

"Maybe it should!" Sam tried so hard. Lucy made sacrifices too. Like right now. All she wanted to do tonight was relax with her husband. Instead they were fighting. She banged her fist on the sofa cushion. "I *hate* your CO!"

"That's ridiculous."

"I don't think it's ridiculous at all!"

"It is," Sam insisted. "I'm the one dropping the ball here. It's not his fault. It's mine. Everything—this whole situation—" He sealed his lips and turned away, but not before regret cast dark shadows across his face.

Lucy yearned to be a good wife, a strong person like Mia. She didn't want to cry or yell, but all she could think was that Sam was sorry he had married her, sorry about the baby. Her breath snagged in her chest, maybe on the first crack of a broken heart.

Don't cry, she told herself. But she couldn't stop the knife-like pain. "I—I don't want to fight."

"Me neither," he said, facing her. "I've been thinking about something. You're not going to like it."

"What is it?"

"The drive is eating almost three hours a day. Brady offered me a place on his couch. I'll come home on weekends and during the week when I can. But like today—"

"Oh, Sam. No!" Not seeing him at night? He was her oasis, her rock.

"Do you think *I* like it?"

"No, but—"

"Lucy, you married a soldier. What happens when I'm deployed?"

The coming days stretched in her mind like a long, dark tunnel. Hours of Claire repeating herself. Lucy alone at night and worrying about the pregnancy, checking for spotting, wondering if every twinge was the start of something horrible. "But, Sam, I'm pregnant—"

"I know that. But I can't keep doing what I'm doing!"

"But I'm so bored." She didn't mean that exactly, but that was the word that came out.

"Bored?" Sam flung his hands into the air. "You're *bored* while I'm working *all the time.* And you're complaining about it?"

"Yes. Bored. And scared and—" Lucy didn't bother to battle her tears. They were just too strong.

Sam gaped at her, then turned and planted one fist on the knotty pine wall, not hitting it hard, but she knew he wanted to do exactly that. Shoulders slumped and head down, he took a shuddering breath before facing her again, his face red but under control.

"This is bad for both of us, Lucy. *And* the baby."

"I know," she mumbled. "It's just that I can't—I can't—" *I can't be the wife you deserve. I can't believe in God enough. I can't*— She broke out sobbing.

"Ah, Pudge." Sam's voice carried from across the room, but in a blink he was next to her, holding her tight and kissing her lips, but only sweetly. There was no point in stirring up hormones and emotions that were already churning. Lucy missed making love; so did Sam. That connection had healed rifts she couldn't see, and it joined them in ways she couldn't describe.

For the sake of the baby, she could put up with anything. Boredom. Yearning. Loneliness. She just couldn't imagine facing the day without the promise of her husband at night. New tears trickled out of her eyes. "This is nothing like I imagined."

"I know what you mean." Bitterness hardened his words, making them cold and pelting.

Doubts screamed through her mind, each one more frightening than the last. *Are you sorry you married me? Do you want out? Do you still love me?* She'd been so sure Sam would never let her down. She had put all her faith in him in spite of Mia's warnings about trusting people instead of God, and leaning on others instead of standing on her own.

Now she wondered if she'd made a mistake, if by leaning on Sam she was causing him to topple. In her mind she pictured a ponderosa pine falling sideways into a bigger, healthier tree. If the strong tree could bear the weight, the trees stayed in place. But what if the strong tree fell under the weight of the weaker one?

Sam pushed off the couch. "I hate to do this, Lucy, but I can't stay tonight. And if I don't leave now, I'll pass out right here on the couch."

He kissed her lightly, but her hormones were crazy anyway, so she stood, wrapped her arms around his neck, and kissed him for all she was worth. After several seconds, they broke apart with a mutual groan.

"Cold shower time," he muttered.

Lucy couldn't help herself. "Are you *sure* you can't stay a little while? We could go out for dinner—"

"Lucy, no! We just had that talk. And why are you standing up?" He clasped her elbow and tried to guide her down to the couch. "Sit. Now!"

She couldn't stand an order when she needed to feel loved. "Don't you dare order me around like that! I am not a dog!"

"I know that," he said through clenched teeth. "But sometimes you don't think—"

"Yes, I do!"

"Then do what's smart and sit down."

She couldn't believe they were fighting again, but she was sick to death of being bossed around. "I'm not an idiot, Sam. I'm doing everything I can for the baby, but it's not easy for me either. I'm stuck here all day with a woman who repeats herself six times an hour. I love Claire, but it's hard. You're my anchor, Sam. And now you're going to be gone at night."

No tears came now, only anger. At herself, the circumstances, and especially at Sam, because he had promised to be her knight in shining armor, and he couldn't keep his promise.

"Go!" She let her voice rise. "Go have fun at school. Hang out with your soldier buddies."

"Fine! I will." He stormed out of the living room, leaving her alone on the couch, fighting a sob that broke out with the force of a punch.

Five minutes later, when he came back through the living room with his duffel in hand, she was still crying.

He walked up to the couch, cupped her chin, and looked into her watery eyes. "You know I love you."

"I love you too."

"And I love the baby." Sam squeezed her shoulder so hard it almost hurt. "You know that."

"I do."

"You can do this," he insisted. "You're strong. And God is even stronger." After a lingering look, he kissed her lips and walked out the door.

She watched it shut behind him, as soft as a kiss but more final. Sam was wrong. She wasn't strong at all, and she still didn't see how God could love her. But who else did she have to call for help? If she called Mia, her sister would give her a pep talk. She'd lost touch with her friends from high school, even her bestie. They didn't have anything in common anymore.

With only one place to turn, Lucy folded her hands and bowed her head. *God? Are you listening? It's me again.*

She spilled her heart out. Maybe He was listening, or maybe not. Maybe He was busy with earthquakes and hungry children. Why would God have time or even an interest in her?

Her hope faded, but then Beanie Girl kicked hard enough to make her gasp. Fresh tears flooded Lucy's eyes. God seemed very far away, but her baby was inside her, alive and growing. A little girl . . . a miracle of creation, a gift, a joy, and a huge responsibility. Lucy would never be a perfect person, but it seemed that God loved her enough to trust her with this child.

Determined to do her very best, she rose from the couch and went to watch *Mary Tyler Moore* with Claire. Later she'd text Sam that everything was all right. She just hoped her tiny bit of faith would be enough to keep her strong for her husband and baby.

●●●

Jake was coming out of the pinball barn when Sam burst out of the house with his duffel slung across his shoulder. The kid's jaw was as tight as a bear trap. With Pirate following, Jake headed Sam off at his car. "What's up? You just got home."

Pirate dropped down at Jake's feet, alert and ready.

Sam flung the duffel into his trunk and slammed the lid. "I'm going back right now. My CO called an inspection for oh-five-hundred. If I'm late, I'm busted."

"Man, that stinks."

"Yeah. Lucy thinks so too. I can't do this, Jake. I just can't."

"Do what?"

"Everything. School. The drive. ROTC. Worrying about Lucy. I need to make a change or my grades will drop. I hope it's okay with you and Frank, but I told Lucy I'm going to spend some weeknights on Brady's couch."

Jake had been expecting something like this. "That sounds like a good idea."

"Yeah, well, Lucy doesn't think so. She's crying her eyes out. We're both trying, but this whole situation is miserable."

"She's bored."

"And emotional." Sam rolled his eyes. "I've got to keep it together for both of us, but it's rough, Jake. Rougher than I ever imagined."

"Hang in there."

"I will. But sometimes women are just plain confusing."

"You won't get an argument from me." Jake's mind flashed to Mia, her own mixed feelings, and how different she was from her sister. Lucy let everything out; Mia held everything in. Lucy exploded into tears, while Mia simmered on a low boil until the pot ran dry. One way wasn't better than the other, but Jake appreciated Mia's more thoughtful demeanor—except when she thought too much.

Sam looked back at the house. "I'd stay if I thought it was best in the long run, but my grades will determine a big chunk of our future. Lucy has to understand that."

"Deep down, I think she does."

"I hope so."

Jake clapped Sam on the arm. "Stay strong. This won't last forever."

"That's what scares me." Sam's voice went up a notch. "What if this is the easy part? In a few months, I'm going to have a kid to support. She'll need diapers. Baby formula. All sorts of stuff. You can't just put kibble in a bowl and set it on the floor."

Jake hid a smile. "Did you learn that in Parenting 101?"

It took a few seconds, but the tension eased out of Sam's face. "I figured that one out on my own."

"Well, good."

Sam propped his hips on the trunk. "I really miss my mom these days. She'd understand."

"She'd be proud of you."

"I hope so, but sometimes I wonder."

"I'm sure of it." Jake thought back to being twenty-one, fresh out of college, wasting time and money until he decided to become a cop. "I was just a little older than you when I joined the department. Your mom kicked my butt back then."

"Yeah." Sam crossed his arms over his chest. "She'd probably kick mine right now for complaining."

"I don't think so."

"No?"

"I think she'd tell you to take a night off and relax with your wife. Not tonight. But plan it for the weekend."

Sam looked like a man grabbing at a life preserver. "Lucy would like that. So would I."

Jake almost suggested doubling up with Mia, but the younger couple needed time alone. "Take her to Andy's Barbecue Shack. It's got a nice view of the river."

Worry danced across Sam's face. "She's supposed to stay off her feet."

"She does," Jake assured him. "Check with her doctor, but from what Lucy tells us, a quiet dinner out won't be a problem."

"I've been pretty crazy about restricted activity. Maybe I should lighten up, huh?"

"Maybe." *Definitely.* Jake didn't give advice, but Sam was asking. "Most women don't take well to being ordered around."

"Is that what I do?"

To make the point, Jake spoke to his dog. "Pirate?"

The dog jumped to his feet.

"Pirate, sit!" Pirate sat, his tail wagging in the dust. Jake gave him a training treat, then held up another one and looked at Sam. "Sam—"

"No—"

"Sit!"

"Oh, crud." A slow groan crawled out of his throat. "Am I that bad?"

"Ask Lucy."

"I know what she'd say, but I'm just so stressed out," Sam said again. "You know what comes after diapers? Braces. Dance lessons. Prom dresses."

"College tuition."

Sam groaned a second time. "Stop cheering me up."

"A wedding—"

"Oh, man. No."

"To a guy with a barbed wire tattoo around his neck."

"No!

"And a prison record."

Throwing back his head, Sam howled at the sky. *"Nooooo!"*

Jake gloated at getting the last word, but someday he hoped to have Sam's problems. A wife. Kids. Dedication to a cause and a career through the camp that still needed an official name.

When Sam surrendered with a grin, Jake punched his arm. "Get out of here."

"You'll watch out for Lucy, right?"

"Always." Jake took out his phone. "In fact, I'll call Mia now. We can all watch a movie."

"Oh, man." Sam rolled his eyes. "You're outnumbered two to one. Lucy's going to want to see *Frozen* again."

"I'll live." He might even enjoy it, except for that earworm of a song about letting go.

When Sam drove off, Jake started to call Mia, but his father pulled into the driveway with Chinese food and a load of groceries. Jake helped carry in the bags, they all ate dinner, and then he asked Lucy about inviting Mia to the house for a movie.

"No, thanks," she said. "I'm too tired."

The poor girl's eyes were still puffy from crying, so Jake decided not to push. When his parents retired to the den later than expected, he didn't call Mia after all. She'd already been to the house around lunchtime, and he didn't want to pressure her. Instead he took Pirate and went out to his office to rough out daily schedules for the camp on a dry erase board. Hiking on Tuesday. Working on cars on Thursday. Pinball at night. Relaxed and enjoying the process, he jotted his notes in different colors of ink.

It was almost ten when he finished, the perfect time for a quick good-night to Mia, so he called her. One ring. Two rings. The call went to voice mail. Even if she was asleep, she would have awoken at the ring. He sent a quick text instead. Typically she answered a text in five minutes or less. That was just her habit.

Are you up?

Eight minutes later, she still hadn't replied. Call him paranoid, but his gut told him something was wrong. No way could Jake stand around and do nothing. He snatched his keys off the desk, loaded Pirate in his truck, and sped toward Mia's house.

chapter 21

Halfway down Main Street, Jake spotted a sheriff's patrol car parked in front of Mia's office, its light bar cutting into the night like the aurora borealis. He sped up, whipped into the parking lot, and saw her car in the farthest corner, its usual spot to leave room for patients.

Had she been here all day? All evening? He jammed on the brakes, threw his truck into park, and flung the door open for Pirate. The dog leapt out, and together they jogged up the steps. Jake quickly took in the open front door, a broken window, and light spilling onto the deck. Red spray paint dripped a macabre happy face down the yellow siding.

He strode through the door without touching anything. "Mia!"

"We're back here," she called, her voice steadier than his.

Safe . . . Mia was safe. Some of the tension eased out of his muscles, but not all of it. Tonight's vandalism would also impact Camp Connie. No matter who was responsible—locals or visitors—the crime would stir up even more hostility.

The deputy—Jake recognized Brian Ross's voice—spoke in a tired drawl. "Come on back, Jake. Just don't touch anything."

"I know the drill."

He passed through the waiting area, taking in the tipped-over chairs and more red paint on the walls. The glass window to the reception area was intact, but a ficus tree lay on its side in a cracked ceramic pot, black dirt fanning across the carpet.

A familiar detachment settled into Jake's bones, but when he saw Mia at the ravaged supply closet, riffling through the samples of medicine scattered on the floor, the detachment morphed into fury at anyone who would harm her. He suppressed it like the pro he'd been, but Pirate still nosed his leg.

"It's okay, partner." Jake rubbed the dog's head. "I'm angry, that's all."

Jake strode down the hall, and Mia pushed to her feet. Judging by her scowl, she was even angrier than he was. Her wet hair dragged on the shoulders of a T-shirt with a teddy bear on it, the sleeping kind that went to the knees of her gray sweat pants. Fluffy pink slippers covered her feet. The little-girl look surprised him, but only for a moment. This was the vulnerable side of herself that Mia kept hidden—the fragile part of her that sometimes needed to cry and be comforted. The part she pushed aside while being strong for others.

Defiant and fierce, she put her hands on her hips. "I'd like to punch whoever did this."

"Me too," Jake said. "Whoever it was had a good time. I'm just glad you weren't here when it went down."

"I wish I had been. I would have—"

"You would have given them what they wanted and stayed safe." No way did he want Mia doing battle with anyone. That was his job. "Or better yet, you would have walked out the back door and called 911."

Frowning, she nudged the little boxes with her slipper. "You're right. But I hate what happened here."

"So do I." With his mouth tight, he turned to Brian. "What do we know?"

"Not much. I spotted the broken window about thirty minutes ago and called Mia. No witnesses. It looks like a smash-and-grab, maybe drug seekers."

Jake scanned the samples on the floor. The names were alphabet soup to him, but drugs of any kind might appeal to an addict. "What about a tie to the break-in at the pharmacy?"

"Very possible," Brian replied. "But that happened on a Friday night, and this is Wednesday. The kids who broke into Blackstone's were here for the weekend. Even so, I'll check everything out."

"There's another difference." Mia nudged the mess on the floor. "The pharmacy stocks controlled substances. I don't keep samples of anything in that classification. An experienced drug seeker would know that."

"But a kid might not." Brian made a note on his pad.

"That's true," Jake agreed. "Is anything else missing? Computer tablets? Petty cash?"

"We were about to check the safe when you arrived." Mia made a beeline for her office, shot past her desk, and crouched in front of a square wood credenza in the corner. Jake guessed it housed a safe.

She opened the wooden door first. "I'm embarrassed to admit this, but the lock's broken." She opened it without working the combination, peeked inside, and groaned. "It's gone. All of it. The petty cash and this week's receipts. We had about six hundred dollars in here."

Jake and Brian traded a look before Brian spoke up. "It looks to me like kids broke in, vandalized the place for fun, and stole the cash."

Jake hooked his thumbs on his belt and rocked back on his heels. "Maybe. Or maybe not. We need solid information before the whole town starts speculating. I don't want Hatcher making up stories."

"Neither do I." Brian tapped the shaft of his pencil on his notepad. "This town hasn't been the same since you two started fighting."

Jake shook his head. "I feel bad about that. I want peace, but Hatcher doesn't."

"That's between you two," Brian replied. "For now, I suggest you stay out of his way and let me do my job, all right?"

Jake nodded, but he didn't appreciate being chastised like an inexperienced rookie.

The deputy turned back to Mia. "You haven't been in town very long."

"That's right."

"Have you made any enemies? Maybe a patient who wasn't happy?"

She thought for a minute. "I saw a young woman a couple days ago. She claimed to have splashed drain cleaner in her eye and wanted Percocet. A couple things made me suspicious."

"Such as?" Brian asked.

"Her age. Her driver's license said she was twenty-one, but she looked much younger. The ID could have been fake. On top of that, there were small blisters around her right eye, but I didn't see any tearing or redness in the eye itself. When I referred her to an ophthalmologist in the Springs, she begged me for a prescription just to get her through the day. I think she closed her eyes and splashed herself on purpose to get painkillers."

"A drug seeker," Jake remarked. "But why would she bother with the graffiti?"

"I don't know." Mia glanced down the hall to the mess in the lobby. "Maybe someone helped her break in, and that person wanted to make trouble, or was high, or . . . I don't know."

Brian wrote another note on his pad. "I'll need her name, anything you have."

"Just a minute." Mia took her tablet off her desk and pulled up the patient's file. "You know about the HIPAA laws, right? Since she's a suspect, I can give you her demographics and injury details but nothing else."

She held out the tablet for Brian to see, deliberately excluding Jake in order to comply with HIPAA, and maybe to keep him from becoming too involved. He didn't like it, but he appreciated her ethics.

"Anything else?" Jake asked when Mia set down the tablet. "Any run-ins with Hatcher or the Stop the Camp group?"

A guilty look crossed her face. She was hiding something. Jake was sure of it.

"What is it?"

"It was nothing, really." She flicked her gaze between the two men. "Mr. Hatcher was in the office about a month ago. He made a scene in the waiting room."

"How bad?" Jake asked her.

"Nothing I couldn't handle."

"You should have told me." No way would he allow Hatcher or anyone else to bully Mia. "He has no business disrupting your office."

"Like I said, I handled it." She stood a little taller. Even wearing fluffy slippers and with her hair crooked, Mia could be commanding.

Jake admired that trait until she aimed that feisty glare at him. He answered with a firm look of his own. "I know you can handle difficult people. You're a pro. Even so, I don't want Hatcher or anyone else hassling you."

Brian broke in, his tone impatient now. "Hold on, Jake. Don't go blowing things out of proportion. Hatcher has opinions. So do you. We don't know what happened tonight. I'll do some checking—starting with the kids who broke into Blackstone's. I'll let you both know what I find."

Mia smiled her appreciation. "Thanks, Brian."

"I'll be in touch." The deputy faced Jake. "I know I don't have to say this, but—"

"So don't say it." Jake knew what was coming.

"Don't get involved," Brian finished. "You have skills and experience, I know that, but you're too close to the situation. Stay out of it."

Brian said good-night and left. As soon as the front door closed, Jake turned to Mia. In a blink she was in his arms, holding him tight with her head pressed against his chest.

"What a night," she mumbled. "I was almost asleep when Brian called—Oh!" She leaned back but didn't break the embrace. "How did you hear about the break-in?"

"I didn't." He told her about calling to say good-night. "When you didn't answer the text, I decided to check on you."

"That was sweet of you." She nestled back in his arms. "I forgot my phone in the rush. I'm glad you're here."

"So am I."

They stood quietly, each breathing deep until a mutual calm wrapped around them. Jake thought back to his original plan for the night and told her about Sam and Lucy, emphasizing that Lucy seemed okay when he left.

Mia sighed. "Before she married Sam, I would have run to her rescue. But she's married now. They'll have to work it out."

"And they will."

Mia, always practical, eased out of his arms. "This place is a mess, but if I clean up, I can see patients tomorrow."

"I'll help."

They walked together to the waiting room, where the graffiti looked like dripping blood. Jake took out his phone and snapped pictures to document the damage for the insurance company, and then they swept up the glass and dirt from the potted plant, straightened the chairs, and hung sheets to hide the slashes of red paint and ugly words. He finished by duct-taping cardboard over the broken window.

"It'll do for now," Mia said. "I hate to cancel the hike on Saturday, but if I can't find a contractor, I'll have to paint on the weekend."

"But the team building is coming up, right?"

"In three weeks."

"Let's do this," he offered. "We'll paint together at night and still take that hike on Saturday."

Mia flashed a smile. "I'd like that a lot."

So would Jake, though he hoped she felt the same way when she saw the challenge he had in mind.

chapter 22

Hot and sweaty, with a blister forming in spite of two pairs of socks, Mia stood at the bottom of the thundering water spilling from a mossy cliff high above them. Jake slipped an arm round her waist, and they stood side by side, gazing up at the lower portion of the double-decker waterfall. The river tumbled at least fifty feet down a rock face full of ledges, cracks, and crevices. If there was a path to the top, Mia didn't see it.

"What do you think?" Jake shouted over the roar of the water. "Was it worth the hike?"

"Every step of it," she shouted back.

Her calves ached from the three-mile trek, all of it uphill. She had kept up with Jake's long strides, and though her shoulders ached from carrying a knapsack stuffed with food, water, extra socks, a first aid kit, and the Leatherman tool, she was proud of herself for making the hike. She and Jake had climbed over boulders, waded in the shallow rush of the river, and done it all without saying very much. He was wearing his hearing aids, but they amplified the river noise as well as her voice.

Teamwork. They'd fallen into a pattern as natural as breathing in unison. Mia rested her head on his shoulder. "Not all surprises are bad, are they?"

He tightened his grip on her waist, kissed her tenderly, then kissed her again more deeply. When they broke apart, she thought of the surprise for him in her knapsack. "How about lunch? I brought brownies from the Emporium."

"We'll dig in when we reach the top."

"Uh . . ." Mia glanced up at the rock wall. "Did you say 'the top'?"

He dropped his backpack on the ground. "It's not as steep as it looks, but I brought ropes and a harness. You'll need the equipment for the last few feet."

She opened her mouth to say something, but nothing came out except stammering.

"Teamwork, remember?" Jake looked far too pleased with himself.

Mia propped her hands on her hips, feigning courage she didn't feel. "Just when I thought not all surprises were bad! Jake, are you serious?" She pointed at what looked like the side of a moss-covered medieval fortress. "That's beyond me."

"Not me. I've climbed it at least twenty times."

She stared at the wall, then at Jake. This was why they were here—so she could gain confidence. Somehow it hadn't occurred to her until now that *her* confidence and ability wasn't the issue in Jake's eyes. He was teaching her about trust. She couldn't climb that mountain without him. And to do it with him, she needed to rely on his judgment, skill, and possibly his physical strength.

He must have seen her gawking at the cliff, but he didn't say a word. No encouragement. No cajoling. No reassurances. She appreciated that he didn't baby her. The decision to go up or to go back was hers.

Her pulse thrummed in tune with the river, tumbling and rumbling until she mustered her courage. "Let's go for it."

A grin stretched across Jake's face, and he pointed at the

damp, shady rocks. "Do you see how the boulders fan away from the water? We're going to make an arc around them and take the wall at an angle. You can't see it from here, but there's a three-foot ledge that will take us almost to the top."

"*Almost* to the top?"

"That's right." Crouching, he opened his backpack and took out a yellow Kevlar rope with a harness attached. Shielding his eyes with his hand, he looked up into her face. "Did you bring gloves?"

"No. I didn't think—"

"Here you go, partner." He handed her a brand-new pair of women's gloves made of thin leather. "These will help you grip the rock."

"If I'd known I needed them—"

"You would have brought them. Team building, remember? We fill in the gaps for each other."

"If you get hurt, I'll sew you up. But I hope that doesn't happen."

"Me too." There was no fear in his voice, only delight at the challenge ahead of them.

He pulled on his own gloves, then indicated her knapsack. "Let's see what you brought. I'll carry what you really need, and we'll leave the rest here."

Crouching next to him, Mia sorted through her things. She wanted to take it all, even the extra socks and bug repellent. *Decide, Mia. What's most important?* But it was all important to her. On the other hand, her basic needs were simple. "I don't really need any of it, except the water. And the lunch. We can eat it at the top."

Jake put the food in his pack, including the brownies, then handed her a high-protein energy bar. "You'll need fuel for the climb."

While he munched an apple, she forced down the energy bar

and downed a bottle of water. Strength returned to her legs, but butterflies still danced in her stomach. "Why do I feel like we're preparing to scale Mount Everest?"

"A mountain is a mountain. No matter how high it is, the first step is the hardest. Once you're committed, the battle is half over."

"I'm committed," Mia said with more confidence than she felt. "But am I crazy for doing this?"

"Yes, but in a good way," he assured her. "You can be crazy and careful at the same time."

"How?"

"You'll see."

●●●

Jake stood and offered his hand. He was completely confident in his ability to lead Mia up the mountain, but he was equally certain the final twenty feet would test her trust in him to the max. Jake could scale the slanted wall on his own, but Mia would need help.

When she stood, he handed her a helmet, and she put it on. Determination glinted in her eyes, a little like a six-year-old about to ride her first bicycle. Jake put on a helmet too, though he didn't usually bother, then looped the rope over his shoulder and indicated Mia should follow him.

A dirt path circled the edge of the basin below the waterfall, then veered to a staircase made of boulders. A giant could have climbed it with long strides, but he and Mia would need to move from boulder to boulder, sometimes jumping a short distance, at other times crawling around or between them. He didn't tell her, but they only needed to go up the staircase. There was an easier way down.

When they reached the first rocks, Jake leapt easily from one slab of rock to the next. After a few jumps, he turned to check on Mia. Her eyes were on the rocks, her face knotted as she planned her next move.

Her hesitation worried him. Rock climbing required courage, skill, and intuition. Mia had plenty of courage, and he could coach her on the skill. But intuition was a kind of trust, a God-given sense of things a person couldn't see or know. Overthinking would only feed her fear.

"How are you doing?" he called out.

She gave him a thumbs-up, jumped to the next rock, and caught up to him. "So far, so good."

He indicated the next dozen or so boulders, some flat and others sloped to make jagged *V*s. "Just follow me and you'll be fine."

They climbed as a team, with Jake offering his hand even before she needed it, and Mia gaining confidence. They climbed higher and higher, pausing occasionally to look back at the river cascading down the mountain.

The waterfall was slightly behind them now, but the mountain that formed it rose in front of them. Jake led Mia up the last couple of boulders, until they reached the three-foot ledge that butted against a jagged rock wall about twenty feet high. Old and eroded, the granite wall slanted at a steep angle and offered excellent hand- and toeholds.

He indicated a flat rock where she could rest. "Have a seat."

"Gladly. My legs feel like overcooked spaghetti." She glanced suspiciously at the last several feet of the climb. "What's next?"

"This." He slid the rope and climbing harness off his shoulder.

Mia cast a nervous glance at the top of the wall. "I take it we're going straight up?"

"It's not as steep as it looks."

"Even so—" She muttered something to herself. "It's so high."

"Are you afraid of heights?"

"Not if I'm in a plane or on a balcony with a rail, but this is different." She eyed the wall again. "Really different."

"It's worth it." He sized up her expression and coloring. While he wanted her to rest her legs, he didn't want to give her time to feed her anxiety. "Are you ready?"

She gulped. "Maybe."

"I'll take that as a yes." He helped her into the harness, narrated every step as he checked the buckles, then laid a hand on her shoulder. "I'm going up first. I'll secure the belaying line, call down to you, and give the rope a tug. You'll see it move, but I won't pull hard enough for you to feel it. It's just a signal. When you're ready, call up to me."

"Will you hear me?"

"Easily. We're between the two waterfalls. Listen for yourself. What do you hear?"

She paused, then gave a nervous laugh. "It's quiet. All I hear is my own heart pounding."

"You'll do great." He gave her harness a final check.

"The view better be worth it," she said, grumbling to work up some fight.

Good. She's thinking ahead, not looking back. Before she could point out that maybe *he* needed a safety rope, he climbed the first five feet. "Can you see what I'm doing?"

"It's like climbing a ladder."

"Exactly. Take it one step at a time." He scaled the rest of the slanted wall like a billy goat and hauled himself over the edge. Twenty yards away, the top half of Echo Falls, wider and gentler than the lower falls, spewed from a mossy cliff. To his left, a calm blue pool reflected the sky and clouds, and to his right a trail wound back through a shady forest. Captivated as always, he paused to drink in the beauty.

"Jake!"

"I'm here."

"Are you all right?"

"I'm fine. I'm at the top now. How are you?"

"Okay, but . . ." She paused. "I just want to get this over with. Waiting is awful."

"That's part of the challenge," he called down to her. "Give me another minute."

He secured the safety rope to a piton mounted permanently in the rock. This was a popular hike in the summer, another reason he'd chosen it. It offered just the right amount of challenge for someone new to the experience. If Mia needed his help at all, it would be at the top of the climb.

"Mia?" He gave the rope a tug to signal her. "Are you ready?"

No! This is insane. I want to go home right now.

What if Jake fell? How would she get him down? Would her phone work? How long would it take for a helicopter to arrive and lift them off the mountain?

She stared intently at the niches and clefts scattered twenty feet above her head. *Don't look down.* But she did. Her body swayed and her stomach rebelled. She couldn't imagine climbing higher—with nothing at her back.

The rope attached to her harness jiggled. Knowing she wouldn't fall more than a few feet should have reassured her, but what if the piton or pin—whatever it was—gave way? The waterfall tumbled to her left, the roar distant and terrifying.

She could still go back; Jake would understand. But if she quit now, how could she face the mystery challenge from Mission Medical? It wasn't in Mia's nature to retreat from a challenge, and she refused to start now. She took a deep breath, blew it out, then placed her hand on the exact hold Jake had used. Next she used her toe to find a niche. With her body slanted, she pulled herself up and felt almost secure.

The first step is the hardest. She made the second step, and the third.

"Hey, Mia," Jake called down, his voice as calm as if they were in the Tanner kitchen. "How's it going?"

That calm tone! Instead of soothing her, his ease rankled her. "Easy as pie—not!" In a burst of anger, she made three more moves, but she stepped too fast and her left foot slipped.

"*Jake!*"

"Take it slow, Mia. I've got you."

Did he really? Could she trust Jake, the rope, the pins and hooks and things she didn't even know the names of? No. She couldn't. He was human. Accidents happened.

But where else could she go but up? Forcing air into her lungs, she dug her gloved fingers into the next cleft in the rock. *Cleft . . . rock*. The old Fanny Crosby hymn played through her mind, the part about God hiding her soul in the cleft of a rock. Mia couldn't fully trust Jake or anyone else, but she could trust God.

Clearing her mind of everything except the rock and her body, she climbed steadily, calling out her progress to Jake until she reached a ledge about ten feet below the lip of the canyon. The wall was almost vertical here.

She pictured Jake scaling the wall. Taller and stronger, he had climbed the last stretch and hauled himself over the edge by brute strength. No way could Mia leverage herself over the top the way he had. She would need to find hand- and footholds of her own.

She placed one foot in a niche, fixed her hands as best as she could, and started the most treacherous part of the climb. One move. Two moves. Her muscles strained against her own weight, but the wall was less vertical than it first appeared, enabling her to keep her weight forward.

Just a few more moves. But then the rock crumbled and her right foot slipped. Her left leg buckled, leaving her hanging by her hands. In front of her eyes, the rope remained slack, offering a silent promise that she wouldn't fall far, but also a warning that she would still fall.

"Jake!"

"You can do this, Mia."

"I lost my footing. I'm stuck—"

"Stay calm and search for a fresh hold."

Don't think. Just do it. She crawled another six inches. Then three. Panting now, she paused to catch her breath but couldn't. If she wasn't careful, she'd hyperventilate. Every muscle in her body trembled, and the top was still two feet away. She didn't have the strength to make another move. Terrified of sliding, she opened her mouth to call for help.

Before the words scraped over her dry lips, the rope tightened. The next thing she knew, she was being lifted. When her hands found purchase on the edge of the cliff, she pulled herself over the rim. Oddly weightless, she sprawled face first in the dirt. Her panicked lungs gulped for air. Dust dried her nostrils and throat, and when she dared to open her eyes, she saw a single, trampled blade of grass defiantly reaching for the sky.

Turning her head, she saw Jake's boots inches from her nose, heels up to indicate he was in a crouch.

He laid a hand on her back between the harness straps and rubbed gently. "Mia?"

The warmth of his touch seeped through her shirt and all the way to her heart. She couldn't seem to find her voice, even air. She was alive. Blessedly alive!

"Mia." The word was a command, his tone the same one Mia used to pull patients out of a drugged sleep. "Mia. Are you all right?"

"I'm—I'm—" *Fine.* Unbridled laughter billowed from her belly to her chest and out of her mouth. Rolling to her back, she raised both fists to the sky and let out a rebel yell. "I did it!"

She yelled again, just because she could.

Grinning, Jake stood and offered his hand. She took it, and he pulled her upright and into a hug so tight she thought her ribs would crack. Or she would crack his.

She buried her face in the crook of his neck. "We did it." *We.* The word tumbled and spun in her mind.

Jake loosened his arms. "I want to show you something." Keeping her close, he turned her around to face the postcard view of the river spilling down the canyon. Dark water splashed around jutting boulders, and from this angle she saw the silvery white plume of the lower falls glistening in the sun like a thousand tumbling stars.

Tears of joy rushed to her eyes. This was God's handiwork, His magnificent creation. The work of the Father who gave His Son for the redemption of all mankind. Love burned in her chest, both for the Creator and the creation. "It's stunning."

"Now turn around." Keeping her close, he guided her in a half circle.

Her gaze skimmed the calm pool rimmed by coarse sand, then the foamy water directly below the second falls, and finally the crystalline curtain spilling from a lip of rock about ten feet wide. Where the bottom waterfall crashed and roared, the upper one splashed like rain. The music of it calmed her even as she took in the mossy wall of rock.

Confident, she turned to Jake and pointed at it. "Are we going up that one too?"

"No. We're done climbing." He moved to face her and unhooked the harness.

Mia covered his hands with hers to stop him. "What about the trip down? Won't I need it?"

"We'll take the long way back."

The long way? "You mean we didn't need to climb the wall to get here?"

"No, but we needed to climb the wall." He went back to working the harness buckles. "Now you're ready for skydiving or car racing—whatever Mission Medical throws at you."

"I guess I am," she admitted as she stepped out of the harness. "But I'm very glad I don't have to climb back down. That last part was terrifying."

Jake dropped the harness on the ground and gripped both her hands. "But you did it, Mia."

"*We* did it."

"That was the point." His eyes bored into hers. "Trust, remember?"

"I'll never forget it. Jake, I—" *I love you.* But the words froze on her tongue.

Confused, she stared down at the ground. If she could trust Jake with her physical safety, surely she could trust him with her heart. But once she said those three words, there would be no going back. What about Mission Medical? She believed with her whole heart that God had opened that door. How could she go back on the promise she had made to Him?

Jake waited, patient as always, until she found the right words.

"Something deep inside me changed today. I don't know what the future holds, but I'm seeing my life in a new light."

"New possibilities?"

"Yes." The word whispered over her lips, a confession that could change everything between them. "I'm having second thoughts about Mission Medical."

One corner of his mouth lifted, but he schooled it into a gentle line. "I won't lie, Mia. I want you to stay in Echo Falls, but more than anything, I want you to live the life God made just for you."

"Thank you."

"I know you, and you don't like loose ends."

She laughed. "Very true."

"So you need to finish what you started with the job application. If they turn you down, the decision is made."

"And if they don't?"

"Maybe you could go on a one-time mission trip instead," he suggested. "Live your dream."

"Maybe." But was Mission Medical really her dream? Or was she using it to fill the gap left by Brad? God had opened the door—at least so far—but He had also opened doors here in Echo Falls. Mia shook her head. "It's too much to think about right now."

"We'll cross that bridge if we come to it." He paused. "Or you will. That's a decision only you can make."

Her heart ached and soared at the same time. No one understood her the way Jake did. But even better, they understood each other.

"Now"—he flashed a grin—"I have one more surprise for you."

"A good one?"

"The best one yet."

Mia walked at his side toward the waterfall, trusting him every step of the way. When they reached the bottom, she saw a gap between two vertical rocks. Jake led her between them, angling his wide shoulders to fit in the narrow space.

A gloomy darkness enveloped them until they stepped into a cave hidden by the waterfall. Sunlight gleamed through the tumbling water, turning it into dancing ribbons of silver and white. The damp air rushed into her lungs. Supercharged with oxygen, that first breath heightened her senses to an exquisite tingle. She smelled the earthy rock, the pure mountain water, and finally Jake's skin as he cupped her face in his hands.

He brought his mouth down to hers in a kiss that burned away whatever doubts remained about trusting him. How could she not love this strong, generous man who put the needs of others before his own? Was it too much to say that he loved her like God did? Maybe. After all, he was human. But at that moment, with the water tumbling and washing away her hurt, she decided Jake was right about surprises. Some of them were good. But others, like falling in love with the right man, were spectacular.

chapter 23

Jake considered the hike to Echo Falls a huge success. A week later, when he drove Mia to the airport for her flight to Dallas, she glowed with confidence. Even better was the hint that she couldn't wait to get home.

"It's just a week," he said to her at the security gate, "but I'll miss you."

"I'll miss you too." She glanced at the x-ray machines, saw only a few people in line, and turned back to him. "I really hate to skip out on the zoning meeting. I can't even call to find out what happened."

Nor could Jake call *her* to be sure she wasn't half-drowned in a river. As part of the team-building exercise, Mia was under what Mission Medical called radio silence. No cell phones. No computers. Her only link to the outside world was a phone number Jake, Lucy, or Kelsey could call in case of an emergency.

Mia glanced again at the empty security area. "You'll keep an eye on Lucy, won't you?"

"Of course."

"If anything at all happens—"

"I'll call the emergency line. I promise."

"Jake, I just don't know—"

"So go," he said. "Go and find your answers."

When her eyes misted, he gripped the handle of her carry-on and walked her to the guide ropes for the security check. "You'll do great, Mia. Call as soon as you can, okay?"

"I will."

After a final kiss, he watched until she passed through the checkpoint and disappeared from his sight.

With Mia out of his life for the next week, Jake gave his dad extra help with the vending business to keep from missing her so much. He was checking the candy inventory on Tuesday afternoon when his cell phone rang and he saw the caller ID from the local sheriff's office.

Deputy Brian Ross offered a friendly hello, then got down to business. "About the vandalism at Mia's clinic—I know she's gone, so I'm calling you."

"Any progress?" Jake hoped so, because he was tired of the rumors. He couldn't go anywhere without someone bringing up the vandalism—either to support him or to warn him.

"We have a suspect," Brian said, "and a confession. The girl Mia suspected of drug seeking turned out to be the seventeen-year-old girlfriend of one of the boys who broke into the pharmacy. The kids live in the Springs, but the boy's family owns a weekend place here in Echo Falls."

"So they drove up and made trouble."

"Unfortunately, yes. When a detective paid the girl a call, she got scared and spilled the whole story. She and her boyfriend broke into Mia's office in search of narcotics, took the cash instead, and he tore the place up for the fun of it."

Inwardly Jake cringed. This was exactly the kind of crime Hatcher would exploit. He held in a sigh. "I'm glad it's resolved."

"Me too." Brian paused. "Jake? One more thing."

"Yes?"

"I can't publicly take sides, but I admire what you're doing. Good luck tomorrow."

"Thank you."

Brian ended the call, leaving Jake encouraged that the camp had more silent support than it seemed.

That hopeful feeling lingered until Wednesday afternoon, when he walked into the county meeting room, an auditorium bursting with a mob of people in orange T-shirts. Surveying the crowd, he gave silent thanks that Mia wasn't with him. No way did he want her in the middle of his fight.

Today Pirate was his sole ally. Claire was struggling with a bad cold, and his dad was home with her so Lucy could stay off her feet. Sam had offered to come, but Jake told him not to miss class, especially with Lucy's next ultrasound scheduled for tomorrow. The young couple had kissed and made up after their big fight, but time was still precious to them.

Kelsey didn't show up at the meeting either. Much to Jake's relief, she was dating Kevin Romano now. As for Jake's supporters in the business community, people liked the idea of the camp, but they weren't committed enough to give up an afternoon.

If he won today's five-person vote for the zoning change, it would be on the merits of the camp. And if he lost, he didn't know what he would do with his life. Tanner Vending paid the bills, but it didn't give him a purpose, something noble to fight for and believe in.

He took a seat in the front row to give Pirate room to lie down. There wouldn't be a lot of talk today. Speakers were limited to five per side, with a five-minute limit.

At exactly two o'clock, the commissioners entered the room and took their seats around a horseshoe-shaped table. Jake had visited each commissioner personally, and two of them nodded at him. A good sign, but he needed three votes to win.

The chairwoman called the meeting to order, the crowd

settled down, and the commissioners voted quickly on other business. When the motion for Camp Connie was moved and seconded, the chairwoman cautioned the crowd to be respectful, then invited Jake to speak.

He stepped to the microphone, cleared his throat, and kept his remarks short. "I've met with each of you individually. There's no need to repeat myself now. I urge you to vote yes on the zoning change."

The crowd remained quiet until Jake sat and the chairwoman invited Hatcher to the microphone. He approached with four people flanking him, including Charles Blackstone, who took the mic first. The pharmacist made a strong case against the camp, citing the vandalism against his store. Jake was grateful Charles hadn't heard about the connection to Mia's office yet, or he would have used it to press his point.

Two more locals spoke against the camp, then a tall, silver-haired woman Jake didn't recognize took the microphone. She identified herself as a retired social worker, called Jake's plan naïve, and flamboyantly diagnosed him with a bad case of survivor's guilt. He nearly came out of his seat at that last remark. Pirate sat up but stayed at Jake's feet instead of climbing into his lap.

Bill Hatcher spoke last. As he told his story, Jake watched the commissioners and saw the sympathy he expected. No one with an ounce of compassion could hear about the arson, see Bill leaning on his cane, and not be horrified. Whether Hatcher believed Jake or not, Jake understood how he felt. They had both survived a senseless act of violence, and ironically, they both wanted to protect others. They just didn't agree on how to do it.

When Bill sat down, the commissioner who represented Echo Falls spoke into the microphone. "Madame Chairman, I call for the vote."

Jake offered a silent prayer, then faced the commissioners with the stoicism of a man who knew God sometimes said no.

The chairwoman went around the table, asking for individual votes. When she finished the roll call, the vote was 2–2.

"It's up to me," she said to the audience. "Ladies and gentlemen, Mr. Tanner, and Mr. Hatcher, I assure you that I studied this issue thoroughly. I am well aware of the controversy in your lovely community, but the circumstances force us to ask a question. If we don't do something for our youth, who will? And if not in Echo Falls, then where?

"There's a quote made famous by President John F. Kennedy. Some attribute the original to Edmund Burke, but the original source isn't clear. Nonetheless, the words are true and worth repeating now. 'The only thing necessary for the triumph of evil is for good men to do nothing.' In that spirit, I'm voting in favor of the zoning change for a youth camp in honor of fallen police officer Constance Waters."

Pandemonium broke out in the meeting room. Jake slumped forward as if he'd been shot. The fight was over. He'd won. *This is for you, Connie. For you and Sam.* Pinching the bridge of his nose, he waited for a burst of joy, but all he could hear were boos amplified to a roar.

Pirate tried to crawl into his lap. Sobering, Jake rubbed the dog's big head until Pirate slid to his haunches.

The chairwoman tried to quell the noise with her gavel, but the crowd broke into its trademark chant.

"Stop. The. Camp."

"Stop. The. Camp."

Jake's nerves tightened into piano wires, the first sign of the panic that had haunted him for months after the bomb blast. He couldn't tolerate having his back to an angry crowd, so he craned his neck to see over his shoulder. An old man from church glowered at him. A young mother hunched protectively over her baby, and just about everyone at the meeting shot daggers at him with their eyes.

Defeated by the noise, the chairwoman called for a ten-minute recess and motioned for the deputy to clear the room. Jake headed for the door but stopped at the sight of Hatcher five feet away, his back to Jake while supporters surrounded him and called him a hero in spite of the defeat. Bill Hatcher didn't see Jake, but Jake saw him—his stooped shoulders, his ill-fitting suit, the cane wobbling as he leaned on it more heavily than usual.

Something akin to shame crawled up Jake's spine. Was this really the victory he had worked so hard to attain? He felt more like a bully than a hero, yet he agreed completely with the JFK quote about good and evil. Jake's cause qualified as good, though he couldn't say Hatcher's opposition was anywhere close to evil.

He waited with Pirate for a break in the crowd, contemplating what to do next. If he had lost, he would have shaken Bill's hand and buried the hatchet. That was how politics worked—the loser conceded to the victor. On the other hand, Jake wanted to be gracious in victory and respectful to a man who had battled to the death.

Breaking protocol, he approached Hatcher and extended his hand. "You fought a good fight, Bill. I hope we can put this behind us."

Hatcher glanced at Jake's hand, then looked up with a scowl. "You won, Tanner. But don't expect me to kiss and make up."

Jake lowered his hand. "Understood."

"You can rot for all I care!"

"Bill, look—"

"Get out of my sight!" He pounded the rubber tip of his cane on the floor, swayed, but caught his balance. "You won. I get it. What else do you want? A pat on the back?"

"No. I want peace."

"So do I," Bill mumbled. "More than you know."

But I do know. For three years Jake had wrestled with his guilt over Connie's death, the need to somehow redeem a tragedy that could have been avoided if only he'd— *Stop it.* There was no point digging up the past he had worked so hard to lay to a peaceful rest.

Before Jake could find the right words, Hatcher headed for the door with supporters flanking him. Jake gave them a head start, then followed several steps behind with Pirate. When Bill hobbled into the lobby, Jake heard fresh chanting.

"We. Love. Bill."

"We. Love. Bill."

Jake stopped in his tracks. Somehow his private search for peace had turned Echo Falls into a war zone and Bill Hatcher into a *Braveheart*-worthy hero, but with a limp instead of blue war paint.

Jake waited out of view until the crowd cleared, then went to his truck to make phone calls. His dad, Sam, and Lucy were waiting for news, but Jake called Mia first—or more accurately, he called her voice mail. "Mia, I have news. You won't hear this for two more days, but we won. The camp is a go." He paused. "It wasn't a pretty win. In fact, I—I don't know what to think right now. Hurry back, okay? I miss you."

He ended the call, left messages for his dad and Sam, and headed home. Like he'd told Bill, he wanted peace. He just wished he could find it.

●●●

Mia strode into the Colorado Springs airport baggage claim with a bounce in her step, her carry-on rolling behind her, and a mile-wide grin beaming off her face. She could hardly wait to see Jake. They had spoken last night when Mission Medical returned her phone. She knew all about the zoning meeting, but she had refused to share anything about her own adventure. Some stories needed to be told in person, and this was one of them.

When she saw Jake and Pirate come through the door, she waved. Behind them she spotted Lucy, waving back frantically, Sam at her side.

"Lucy!" Mia hurried toward her. When the carry-on tipped over, she dropped the handle, ran the last ten steps to her sister, and hugged her, tummy and all. "What are you doing here?"

"I'm off bed rest." Lucy eased back from the hug. "Everything's fine. It's just like you said—the placenta moved up. No more spotting."

"I'm so glad for you!" Mia hugged her again. With the surprise fading, her thoughts returned to Jake. She heard him moving behind her, holding Pirate's leash while he retrieved her abandoned carry-on.

She eased away from Lucy and turned to him. Their gazes locked, and they both grinned. Suddenly shy, Mia couldn't seem to find her tongue. She had thought a lot about her decision but was afraid of making the wrong choice and paying for it somehow. She hoped Jake could be patient a little longer, though she knew she was asking a lot of him.

He set the carry-on upright, held Pirate's leash with one hand, and gave her a light hug. "It's good to see you."

"It's good to be home." *Home*. Did she mean that? Inhaling deeply, she breathed in the scent of his aftershave and couldn't imagine being anywhere else.

When she stepped back, Sam punched her on the arm. "So tell us everything. Did you jump out of a plane?"

Mia gave them a smug little smile. "Not even close."

"River rafting?" Lucy asked.

Jake took a shot at it. "Extreme hiking?"

"Nope." Mia raised her left hand and showed off her bruised thumb. "We remodeled a house from top to bottom. Not as risky as some things, but I missed with the hammer."

"Are you kidding?" Lucy plopped her hands on her hips and jutted one leg, sticking out her tummy. "All that worry, and you didn't do anything dangerous?"

"It was dangerous to my thumb! We rehabbed the house of a woman raising her four grandkids by herself. I had a blast." Mia would never forget the generous people she had worked with, or the moment they surprised the family with the keys. Everyone had traded high fives and hugged hard, especially Mia. Having grown up in a crackerbox apartment, where every month her mom struggled to pay the rent, she knew the value of a secure home.

Jake took her hand and pretended to inspect her purple thumb. "Hammers are dangerous things. Any power tool action?"

"Just a belt sander."

"No table saws?"

Mia knew he was joking, but his voice didn't reveal it. "I still have all my fingers." She held up her other hand and waggled it. "See? All there."

He gripped that hand too. "Maybe we should have practiced with power tools instead of taking that hike to Echo Falls."

"I wouldn't trade that hike for anything." She yearned to say more but couldn't here. She hoped he didn't have to rush home, because she wanted to have that conversation before they returned to Echo Falls.

Jake turned to Sam and Lucy. "Who's hungry? Sam, I know you are. How about lunch?"

Sam glanced at Lucy, but she shook her head. "We're going apartment hunting. Now that I'm mobile, Sam and I have a plan. We're going to rent our own place in December, take our time moving in, and be settled before the baby arrives in January."

"That's great." Mia breathed a sigh of relief. "I was worried about you being so far from the hospital. What about Claire? Has Westridge opened up?"

"No," Jake answered. "But they're next on the waiting list. It won't be long."

"So everything is coming together." *Except for me.* In Dallas she had prayed every night for God to show her where she belonged, but the seesaw in her mind just went up and down.

"We better go," Sam said. "Knowing Lucy, we'll have to stop at every store with a baby department."

Lucy counted on her fingers. "Walmart. Target. Babies'R'Us." When Sam groaned, she elbowed him. "Man up, Soldier Boy. This is my first time to shop in eight weeks. We're going *everywhere*."

Mia grinned for them both. "Don't forget—I have dibs on buying the crib. The bedding too."

Lucy patted her baby bulge. *Bump* no longer described her tummy. "I can hardly wait for Beanie Girl to arrive."

"Have you decided on a name?" Mia liked several of the choices in the running.

"Yes," Sam answered. "But we're not telling anyone until she's born."

"Just don't overdo it, okay?" Mia laid a protective hand on the baby. At twenty-eight weeks, Beanie Girl was past the "way too early" mark and firmly in the "too early but the NICU is amazing" stage.

"I'll watch out for her." Sam slipped an arm around Lucy's back. "By the way, we're staying in town for a couple nights. Kind of a delayed honeymoon."

When Sam waggled his brows at his wife, Lucy gazed at her husband with a pretty blush on her cheeks. Mia's heart swelled, but with the sweetness came a familiar trickle of doubt. Sometimes love lasted; sometimes it didn't. Only God loved perfectly, and she'd promised to serve Him with Mission Medical—if she got the job.

The four of them headed for the exit. Mia hugged Lucy and Sam good-bye, then turned to Jake. "Do you have to rush back?"

"Not at all."

"Then let's go somewhere quiet."

"Just the two of us?"

"Exactly."

On the way to his truck, they decided to stop at Caribou Coffee and then take Pirate to the Wolf Creek Dog Park. A nip chilled the autumn air, but they had coats, and Jake kept a blanket in the crew cab. When they were settled on a wooden bench, he took off Pirate's vest and told the dog to have a good time. Mia picked up her latte, Jake spread the blanket across their laps, and she handed him his large black coffee.

They sat in silence until he pressed his thigh against hers. "Let's see your thumb again."

Mia held it out so he could inspect it. "It hurt like crazy at the time."

"I bet." He kissed the bruise, then lowered her hand. "So tell me about your trip."

"It was . . . surprising." In more ways than she had anticipated. "Sheryl met me at the airport, and we drove straight to a house in a poor section of Dallas. That's where we stayed, and where Dr. Winkler told us we were remodeling a different house for a needy family. The trick here was speed. We needed to finish in five days, which meant we had to pull together and go without sleep."

"So nothing dangerous?"

"Not physically. This turned out to be a psychological challenge. Dr. Winkler's a clever man. He put together a bunch of type A personalities who all wanted to be in charge. There was lots of negotiation, and tempers flared a couple of times, but we got the job done."

"How many people on the team?"

"Thirteen total. Seven men, five women, and the contractor overseeing the remodel."

Jake stared across the field, his eyes on Pirate, until he swung his attention back to her. "Any sign of Dr. Benton?"

Mia laughed. "Don't tell me you're jealous."

"Nah." He pressed his leg even tighter against hers. "I just want to punch him, that's all."

"Well, there's no need." She made her voice light. "He wasn't there. And even if he had been, I'd feel the same way I do now."

He raised a brow at her. "Which is . . . ?"

"Happy to be here with you." Leaning against his side, she bent her neck and soaked in the warmth of him. She trusted Jake completely, but love? Emotions were fickle things. When a chill dripped down her spine, she straightened. "I'm very glad to be home, but I have to honest with you. I'm still not sure about giving up Mission Medical."

"So let's talk." He raised her hand, their fingers entwined. "Tell me what you're thinking."

"I have a couple of options. The first is to continue to pursue the full-time job. The second is to switch gears and apply to go overseas for just a year."

"A year, huh?"

"Yes."

A dog barked on the other end of the park. Another joined in, and a third added a howl. Mia had more to say, but she stopped when Jake trailed a finger down her cheek.

"I think you know how I feel about you, Mia. I don't like the idea of you leaving at all. But more than anything, I want you to be at peace—both with yourself and with God. If you need to go, then do it. Just be prepared to Skype with me every night."

His support warmed her to her toes. "Thank you, but I've ruled out leaving for just a year."

"I'm glad to hear it. But why?"

"The whole point of the career charge was to put down new roots, to grow as a person, and to serve God. There's no doubt I'd grow and serve God with a one-year commitment, but what about the roots? That wouldn't happen."

"I see what you mean."

"There's more." The most important aspect to Mia. "Going overseas for a year would add time to the application process. I checked with Sheryl. When I got back, I'd be . . . older."

"Not *that* old!" Grinning, he rose slightly from the bench and pretended to inspect the crown of her head. "I don't see a single gray hair." Next he studied her neck and face. "No wrinkles either. And no chicken neck—"

"Jake!" Mia broke out laughing. "I'm being serious here."

"I know you are. So am I."

"Good, but you're forgetting that I worked in women's health. I know what happens when women wait until their late thirties, even their forties, to have kids. Some women have no trouble at all, but others do. I've seen the hormone treatments, the in vitro, and the disappointment when science fails to trump nature. I'm not pushing a panic button or anything. I *am* only thirty. But a woman can't put off having a family for as long she wants without some risk to her fertility."

"No," Jake agreed. "I can see that. But where does God come into this?"

"At the beginning," she said firmly. "His will. Not my will. Which is the main reason I'm trying so hard to make the right decision here. When I make a promise, I keep it. And I made a promise to God to serve Him in a new way."

Jake looked toward Pirate, took a long sip of coffee, and remained silent for several seconds. When he turned back to her, she saw a calm light in his eyes. "You need to be sure, Mia. It's who you are."

"It is." She couldn't stand loose ends of any kind, especially when she felt responsible for tying them up. "That's why this is all so upsetting to me. After Brad, I prayed hard. When I was at my lowest, God opened this door. And now—" *I'm in love with you, and that scares me to death.*

Mia couldn't look Jake in the eye, or even too closely at her own heart. Had God truly called her to serve Him through Mission Medical? Or was she using the job to avoid the risks that came with falling in love? She didn't know, and she desperately needed to be confident in her decision.

When Jake didn't speak, she finished with a sigh. "I just don't know what to do."

She started to ease to the side, but he stopped her with a hand on her knee. "I love you, Mia."

"Oh, Jake." She longed to say the words too, but she couldn't push them past the lump in her throat.

He studied her face, waited, then matched his mouth to hers in a kiss so searing she trembled.

Easing back, she looked into his eyes. "I can't say it back—not yet. But I want to. I think you know I feel."

"Do I?"

"Yes," she admitted. "But I have to be certain about Mission Medical before I say the words. If they take me, how can I back out if God opened that door? And if they don't, I don't want you to feel like a consolation prize. That wouldn't be right, or even accurate. It's just—" Mia rolled her eyes. "I'm babbling again."

"If it helps, babble away."

"I don't know if it helps or confuses me more. Or if it sends mixed messages and confuses *you.*"

"Me?" He huffed through tight lips. "I'm not the least bit confused. I know exactly what I want—you and me, a couple of kids, just a normal life. It shouldn't be this hard."

"No. But it is for me."

He looked away, took a long drag of coffee, then spoke without meeting her gaze. "Being a cop taught me not to rush into situations I don't fully understand. I'm not this patient by nature. But I love you, Mia. I won't say another word about us until you're certain about your future."

Say it. Tell him you love him! But the only words to stumble off her tongue were a faint "Thank you."

Jake raised his cup in a toast. "To certainty."

"To certainty," she toasted back. They both took long swallows. The hot milk and caffeine cleared her mind, enabling her to focus on Jake's news about the camp. "Enough about me right now. I want to hear more about Camp Connie. Have you picked an official name?"

"Not yet." When he stared back across the dog park, she followed his gaze to the stream, where Pirate was nose to—never mind—with another dog.

Mia laughed. "I'm sure glad people shake hands."

Instead of smiling, Jake sighed. "They don't always. At least not Hatcher. I told you we won the zoning change, but I didn't tell you what happened later."

"I take it Bill was upset."

"It's more than that." He drummed his fingers on his paper cup. "Camp Connie is a good idea. So why do I feel like a jerk? Kids need what it will offer. I'm sure of it. But people I've known all my life, good people like Charles Blackstone, are sincerely unhappy about it."

"That's true."

"Was I right to push it through?"

She had asked herself the same question. When did a righteous cause become a hair shirt or an albatross? How did a person judge God's will for their lives? The chilly air pricked against her cheeks. "To be honest, I've been worried about the entire situation. On the other hand, you won fair and square. That's a pretty significant go-ahead."

"But it came at a cost."

Mia loved Jake too much to be less than completely honest. "I'm all for fighting for a cause, but I can understand why people are upset. Echo Falls is their home, and they want to feel safe. Right or wrong, they see the camp as a threat. I'm not at all worried about kids making trouble. But how well can Camp Connie function if there's such hostility?"

"I'm worried about that too."

"You'll be a target. So will the kids you want to help. With the current atmosphere, they're going to be watched. Your motives are the best, but I have to wonder what Connie would say."

"I don't know. I just want to do something to honor her. I want her life to count for something."

"And yours," she said carefully.

"Mine?"

"Camp Connie gives you a purpose. That's good. Human beings need that, but maybe you could do something else. Have you thought about that?"

"Now and then." He glanced again at Pirate, now barking and chasing after a big black dog of some kind. I'd have to go back to school for a year, but I could teach."

"You'd be great. High school?"

"Definitely. Maybe history."

"It's ironic, isn't it?" Mia waved her arm to indicate the grass and sky, the row of trees, the faraway mountains. "We're sitting together in this beautiful place God created, wrestling with our dreams, and thinking about giving them up—not for each other, but because they don't fit anymore. Like old shoes."

"Maybe your dream doesn't fit. Frankly, I hope it doesn't. But mine fits me perfectly."

Mia said nothing.

"I'm still committed to the camp. I just hope the Stop the Camp group mellows out."

"Maybe they will." Though Mia doubted it. "Any news on the vandalism? Did they check out that girl who came to my office?"

Jake huffed. "I forgot to mention it to you on the phone. Brian called last Tuesday while you were gone. You were right about the fake ID." He gave her the details. "The story hit the newspaper yesterday, so you can imagine the talk."

"Unfortunately, yes." Mia felt terrible for him. "With the zoning meeting over, maybe things will calm down."

"I hope so, but people are still wearing those orange T-shirts. I tried to talk to Hatcher again yesterday, but it was another bust."

A breeze stirred the aspen leaves into shimmering gold and brought a sharper chill to the air. Jake pulled the blanket higher on her legs. When she snuggled closer, he reached into his other pocket, took something out, and slipped it to her. "Here."

Mia knew the bag by feel. "Skittles!"

She tore open the bag, and they shared the candy, playfully fighting over the red ones. Mia watched the sunshine on the dancing leaves, wondering whether her dreams were worthy or selfish, a call from God or an escape hatch. No matter what happened, she knew one thing with certainty. There was nothing sweeter than sitting on a park bench and sharing Skittles with the man she loved and trusted, even if she couldn't say the words.

chapter 24

On the Wednesday before Thanksgiving, Mia finished seeing patients early and drove to the Tanner house. Frank and Jake were stocking vending machines, leaving Claire, Lucy, and Mia to work on Thanksgiving dinner.

Mia trotted up the front steps and let herself in. Following the warble of laughter to the kitchen, she walked in on Lucy and Claire dressed in matching aprons decorated with quilted turkeys. An apple peeler was clamped to the counter, a bowl of Pippins awaited their fate as pie filling, and Claire was using the rolling pin on the crust while Lucy made car sounds. They didn't hear Mia, so she sneaked up behind them and honked like a car horn.

Claire and Lucy both hugged her, laughing at her lame joke as if she were the real Mary Tyler Moore, until Mia pointed to the aprons. "Those are adorable."

"Here." Lucy handed her one. "This is the official uniform for Team Turkey. I found them at Walmart."

Mia slipped her turkey apron over her head, tied the strings in a bow, and thought of the first time she had clapped eyes on Jake in that Las Vegas coffee shop. In less than six months, her life had come full circle, in part thanks to the voice mail she received late this morning from Mission Medical. She had been with her last patient of the day and missed the call. Alone in her office, she played the congratulatory message from Sally Richmond and felt no excitement at all—only a stabbing pain at the thought of leaving Jake and Echo Falls.

Surely God would have given her peace if she was meant to take the job? She had squirmed even more when she read Sally's follow-up email containing the formal employment offer. In the absence of that deep inner peace only God could give, Mia had murmured a prayer and decided to say no. She was still restless inside, but she planned to tell Jake about her decision tonight and compose a reply to Sally's email over the long weekend.

She straightened the apron with a quick tug. Mission Medical could wait awhile. Right now, she wanted to enjoy the preparations for her first Thanksgiving dinner with home-cooked food and a happy family around a big table.

"So what should I do?" she asked.

Lucy indicated a deep bottom drawer labeled *Cookbooks*. "We need Claire's apple pie recipe. It's probably in her recipe box."

Mia found the metal card file, set it on the counter, and spoke to Claire. "I love apple pie."

Rolling pin forgotten, Claire beamed. "So does Randy."

"Who's Randy?" The question was out of Mia's mouth before she caught Lucy shaking her head.

"Randy is . . ." Claire's brows clamped down, carving deep furrows on her forehead.

"Randy's your brother," Lucy explained to Claire.

"Oh, that's right." Relieved, Claire opened the recipe box and fingered through the cards.

With Claire occupied, Lucy whispered to Mia. "She probably means Jake. She calls him Randy now. She doesn't remember, but Randy died last year."

"That's sad."

"It is, but don't tell her. It'll be news to her, and she'll grieve all over again. There's no reason to put her through that."

"Thanks for the advice." Mia was learning a lot from Lucy—both about Alzheimer's disease and choosing to be kind rather than right. "Does Jake look like Randy?"

"Yes. Quite a bit." Sadness washed over Lucy's face. "At least she recognizes Jake as someone she cares about. The other day she didn't know Frank at all. He walked in from work, and she threatened to call the police. It freaked them both out—especially him."

"Poor Frank."

"As much as it hurts, he's great with her. He gets impatient with her, of course, we all do. But even when it's awful, I can see how much he loves her. I can't imagine what this is like for him."

Neither could Mia. Frank's commitment to his wife both inspired her and left her aching inside. She stole a glance at Claire leafing through the recipe box, not seeing the cards but somehow knowing she needed something.

"Do you need help?" Mia asked.

"No, dear. I'm fine."

Mia and Lucy traded a look, then watched as Claire removed the recipe cards one at a time, setting them down without really seeing them. When the box was empty, she held it upside down, shook it hard, and looked back inside.

"Are you looking for the apple pie recipe?" Lucy asked as a reminder.

Relief washed over Claire's face. "Yes. The recipe. Mama has it memorized, but I don't."

She said *Mama* as if her mother were in the next room and not deceased for twenty years.

While Mia fought a lump in her throat, Lucy stepped to Claire's side. "Let's look together, all right?"

Picking up the cards one at time, she read the recipe names out loud, with Claire occasionally announcing, "Oh, I remember that one!"

The poignancy stole Mia's breath. Memories were such fleeting things, yet the human brain stored them like food for the winter of old age. Claire wouldn't remember this day, but Mia would—her first Thanksgiving with Jake. The first of many to come, she hoped.

Lucy set the last recipe card aside. "It's not here. We'll find a recipe in a cookbook."

"Cookbook!" Amazement flashed across Claire's face. "Mama's cookbook!"

Lucy started to speak, but Claire raced out of the kitchen and toward the stairs, mumbling "cookbook" over and over, maybe so she wouldn't forget.

Mia took one look at Lucy's pregnant belly and told her to sit. "Take a break. I'll go with Claire."

"Don't mind if I do." Lucy blew out a breath that lifted her bangs. "Cooking a turkey dinner is a lot of work."

"But worth it." *Oh, so worth it!*

Mia followed in Claire's wake, trotting up the stairs to the second floor. She passed Jake's sister's room, then came to another open door. She paused to glance inside, saw one of Jake's shirts draped on a chair, and realized this was his bedroom.

Pausing, she stole a glimpse into the everyday life she hoped to share. The queen-size bed boasted a navy comforter and was neatly made. No clothes littered the floor, and only a few odds and ends sat on the dresser. His well-thumbed Bible lay on the nightstand along with a bestselling crime novel. Inhaling, she breathed in a faint trace of his aftershave.

They were a lot alike—neat but not too neat. They both read at night, but she escaped into lighter stories. Did he snore? She had no idea and didn't care. Softly aglow, she broke her gaze from Jake's pillow and headed for the bedroom at the end of the hall.

Stepping inside, Mia saw Claire on the far side of the room, seated on a small couch. In front of her stood a table stacked a foot high with boxes, magazines, and photo albums.

Where Jake's room was neat and orderly, this one bore the signs of Claire's contorted mind. The bed was made, but sloppily. Clothing languished in laundry baskets. Everywhere Mia looked, she saw labels with words like *Frank's underwear* and *Claire's socks*. Even the closet was labeled. So was the door to the bathroom, with the word *Toilet* in big letters and an arrow. Mia could only imagine the trauma behind that mix-up. An overwhelming gloom flooded through her, but at the same time, she wanted to cheer for Frank and his fight to preserve his wife's dignity.

With her heart aching, Mia focused on Claire. Still mumbling, "Cookbook, cookbook," she shuffled through the clutter on the table.

Mia sat next to her, sadly aware that Claire couldn't answer even the simplest questions. *What color is the cookbook? When did you see it last?* On her own, Mia went through a stack of photo albums until she discovered a true treasure—Frank and Claire's wedding album, the old-fashioned kind with hinged pages and mounted photographs.

Mia shoved the other albums aside and placed the book on the table between herself and Claire. "This must be your wedding album."

Something vaguely troubled flashed in Claire's eyes, but she nodded and turned to the first photograph, a stunning portrait of twenty-something Claire wearing an off-the-shoulder wedding gown and a ring of daisies in her hair. Her smile beamed off the page.

"You're beautiful!" Mia exclaimed.

"Was I?" Claire mumbled as she turned the page.

"Yes, you were. And you still are."

The next photograph showed Claire and her six bridesmaids; the one opposite showed a serious young Frank with his groomsmen.

Claire turned the pages slowly, taking them through the ceremony, the first dance, all the traditions, and finally to a shot of Frank and Claire waving good-bye from inside a limousine, confetti flying all around them.

Mia's heart swelled to the size of a balloon. "What a glorious day you had." *And a glorious marriage.*

Claire stared at the last picture. "That's Frank."

"And you."

"Oh my—" Her voice cracked. "I don't remember." Her gaze lingered on the photograph, then shifted to an envelope taped to the back cover. Claire's name was printed on the front in a strong masculine hand.

A love letter from her husband? Mia sighed at the romance of it. "Would you like to hear the letter?" Nosy or not, Mia was dying to read it.

Claire blinked fast and hard. "Oh, Frank—"

Mia took her answer for *yes*, slipped a handwritten letter from the envelope, and started to read aloud. "My dearest Claire: Forgive me. I beg you. I never meant to—" *Hurt you the way I did.*

Mia's stomach dropped to the floor. Frank hurting Claire? How? What had he done that deserved to be immortalized in a letter taped in a wedding album? Mia glanced down and saw a date in the late 1990s. Her innate sense of privacy urged her to stop reading, but she couldn't pull her eyes from the words.

I will never forgive myself for leaving you the way I did. There are no excuses. None. Believe me, I've tried to find them, but every time I point a finger at you, three are aimed back at me.

People joke about a man having a midlife crisis, but there's nothing funny about a man taking stock of his life and being bitterly disappointed. His dreams are dead. His hope is gone. And maybe worst of all, he feels too old to fight.

That's how I felt when I told you I needed to make a change. Vending and pinball machines are going the way of the dinosaurs. Our children don't need me. And you, Claire . . . you didn't seem to need me either. For two people who were hot to trot for twenty years, we sure fizzled out.

"I have no business reading this," Mia mumbled to herself, but she couldn't seem to put down the letter. Claire stared at the envelope, mumbling, "Frank, Frank," over and over while she traced her name on its front, her index finger trembling.

Mia skimmed quickly to the end.

You asked me when I left if there was another woman. I told you no, and that was the truth. You asked me if I still loved you. I told you no, and that turned out to be a lie. I don't know why I thought leaving you and the kids would make me happy, but I was dead wrong.

I don't expect you to forgive me overnight, or because of this one letter. But I am asking you to give the two of us a second chance. I've gone back to church, Claire. Not in Echo Falls but here in the Springs. I'll go to counseling like you wanted. I'll do anything to save our family.

But know this too. If your answer is no—if I've hurt you too deeply to regain your trust—I will let you go with all the grace I can muster. Your happiness means more to me than my own. I just wish I'd realized that four months ago.

Love, Frank

Mia's heart hammered against her ribs. Frank Tanner, the most faithful, loyal man she had ever met, had walked out on his family. Why? Simply because he wasn't happy; because his wife and children weren't enough for him. He had sacrificed his marriage on the altar of "Me" and wreaked havoc with his wife's emotions, and his children's lives as well.

Yet Frank and Claire had survived as a couple. Surely their recovery counted for more than the trauma? *Be logical,* Mia ordered herself. *Look at the facts.*

But as Mia fought to suffocate her own fury and fear, Claire clutched her wrist with cold, bony fingers. Staring hard at the letter, she mewled like a crying baby.

"Frank! Oh no. Oh no. *Frank—*"

Mia dropped the letter against the back cover, closed the book to remove the pages from Claire's sight, and restacked the photo albums. Later she'd sneak up and put the letter back in the envelope, but right now, Claire needed a friend.

Mia pulled the distraught woman into her arms. "It's okay. It's over."

A silent prayer whispered in her mind. *Lord, are you telling me something here?* She didn't think Frank's letter was a sign from God like Gideon's fleeces, but it flapped in her mind like a yellow caution flag. Marriage to any man would bring challenges. Love in any form came with risks. Was she willing to put her heart in the care of another human being, when even a man as sincere, loyal, and faithful as Frank could fail?

Jake was human. And like all men, the son of Adam. Fallen. Sinful. Imperfect. Christian men stumbled all the time, even strong ones. Mia knew better than to expect, demand, or even need perfection. But in this one area, she desperately needed to feel secure.

She stared at the wedding album while Claire wept herself into a silent shudder. Together in a dark place, where the past became the present and the future threatened to repeat the past, Mia plummeted into the shadowy recesses of confusion. She was sick of being unsure, undecided, and unsettled, but she couldn't stop being the little girl whose daddy didn't come home, or the heartbroken woman who had thrown herself at God's feet, begged for a new purpose, and experienced the elation of seeing that prayer answered with an open door.

Who was Mia to slam the door on Mission Medical? After reading Frank's letter, she couldn't do it. She needed to go home. Now. To pray. To think and decide.

Claire, still shaky but no longer sobbing, blew her nose on a tissue. With the cookbook forgotten, Mia stood and offered her hand. "Let's go downstairs."

When they returned to the kitchen, Lucy was at the counter peeling apples. As if nothing had happened, Claire went to the sink and washed her hands.

"That took forever," Lucy remarked as she put a fresh apple on the corer. "Did you find the recipe?"

"No." Mia slipped out of her Team Turkey apron and draped it neatly over a chair. "I'm sorry, but I have to go."

"Oh no." Lucy frowned. "Is it work? An emergency?"

"No. Well, yes." To Mia, the pressure to decide felt like an emergency.

"Are you coming back?"

"Not tonight. Sorry," she said again. She lifted her purse from a chair and moved toward the door.

Lucy approached from behind and spoke quietly over Mia's shoulder. "Did something happen with Claire?"

"No."

"Then what's the emergency?"

Mia was a lousy liar, so she offered a bit of truth. "I heard from Mission Medical."

"Really?" Lucy lit up. "But you're staying here, right?"

"I don't know. I thought so, but now—" She shook her head for what felt like the millionth time. "I just don't know."

Lucy gawked at her. "Mia, that's crazy. You belong here. You know that."

"What I know"—she dragged out the word—"is that God answered my prayers when I was at my lowest after Brad, and He did it in such a personal way. How can I walk away from that?"

"It's easy!" Lucy flung her arms out to the side. "You follow your heart! God opened *this* door too. Mia, you can't leave."

Claire, still at the sink, watched them without a word, her eyes as dull as tarnished spoons.

Mia couldn't bear to look at her. Why did a man leave his wife after twenty years of marriage? How had Claire come to trust her husband again? Looking at the older woman now, Mia couldn't help but wonder if love and surprises, good and bad, were really worth the risk.

The question ballooned in her mind until it crowded her faith into a corner. No way did she want to see Jake now. He'd take one look at her face, see right through her, and dig for answers in that gentle way that tugged her up mountains. Head down, she dashed out the front door, down the steps, and plowed smack into his flannel-covered chest.

"Whoa, there." Grinning, he steadied her. "What's the rush?"

"I—uh—I—" Mia never stammered, except when her heart and mind locked up. "I have to go home."

His fingers tightened around her arm, holding her upright and trapping her at the same time. "Something's wrong."

A high-pitched laugh spilled from her throat. An inappropriate laugh like the one in Mia's favorite *Mary Tyler Moore* episode, where Mary couldn't hold back hysterical laughter at the funeral for Chuckles the Clown.

Jake studied her face. "I'm missing something here."

"Yes, you are." With nowhere to hide, she clung to her constant life preserver—her career. "I heard from Mission Medical today. I got the job."

His eyes lit up in her favorite way. "And?"

"I don't know yet."

The brightness drained from his irises, changing the color from the green of dewy grass to the dullness of weathered bronze. A lifeless expression she hadn't seen in months rolled across his face, and his arms slid to his sides. "I'm surprised. I thought—"

"I know. I'm sorry." Her tongue twisted and sparked like a downed power line. "I thought I knew what I wanted, but now—now I just don't know. I'm surprised I feel the way I do. But I have to be certain."

"Yes. You do." He clipped each word. "But something's not right here. You're not being honest with me."

"How—What—" *Good work, detective.* "Yes, I am!"

He lifted a brow—telling her he didn't believe a word she said.

Mia bolted for her car, climbed in, and slammed the door. Speeding away, she saw Jake in the rearview mirror, hands on his hips as he let her drive away. But only for the moment. Mia knew how Jake thought. The fight wasn't over, but she hoped he'd give her at least a night to pull herself together.

chapter 25

The instant Mia's car vanished from sight, Jake strode into the house. Maybe Lucy knew what in the world had happened, because Jake sure didn't. Mia hadn't told him outright that she loved him, but she had sure acted like it.

He made a beeline to the kitchen, his temper flaring. He took in the piecrust and peeled apples, Lucy at the counter in a turkey apron, and his mom in a matching apron seated at the table, a ball of pie dough and a cookie sheet in front of her. A third apron was neatly folded over the back of a chair.

Lucy dropped her spoon in a saucepan of melted butter and rounded on him, her hands fisted on her hips and her tummy poking out. "Did you and my sister have a fight?"

"No!"

"Then why did she just leave like a crazy person?"

"I don't know. We saw each other last night. Everything was fine." More than fine, considering they'd kissed for an hour on her couch.

"I don't understand it. I thought she loved it here—with us." Lucy glanced at the apron on the chair and frowned. "It's not like Mia to be so wishy-washy."

Or so scared. Going into cop mode, he sized up the evidence.

There were two witnesses—Lucy and his mom. He glanced at Claire making cookies with the dough. Make that one witness.

Sighing, he turned to Lucy. "Tell me everything."

She pointed to the peeled apples starting to brown. "We were looking for Claire's apple pie recipe. When I said 'cookbook,' Claire went upstairs to look for it. Mia followed her."

"And then?"

"I don't know. They were gone about fifteen minutes. When they came down, Mia told me there was an emergency and she had to leave."

"What kind of emergency?"

"She didn't say, but it wasn't for work. When I asked again, she blurted that she got the job with Mission Medical."

"How did she seem?"

"Rattled. Upset." Lucy paused. "You know that fake smile she puts on when she's scared?"

"Yes, I do."

"That's how she looked."

So the event that upset Mia had occurred upstairs. Claire, memory-impaired or not, was the only witness. Jake pulled up a chair and sat next to her. "Hey, Mom."

Claire looked up from the ball of dough in her hand. "Randy!"

He didn't bother to correct her. "I hear you're making an apple pie."

"Yes, we are." She seemed surprised he knew.

"Did you find the cookbook?"

"Oh—" She looked up from the dough. "Mama's cookbook! I know where it is."

She pushed up from the chair and headed for the door, mumbling "cookbook" over and over so she wouldn't forget. Jake followed her upstairs, staying a few steps behind to avoid distracting her. When they reached the master bedroom, she went to the couch and sat.

Jake dropped down next to her, taking in the mess on the table. "Do you see the cookbook?"

She scanned the clutter, then picked up a magazine, opened it, and showed him a picture of a bulldog wearing a Sherlock Holmes hat.

Stifling a groan, Jake refocused on the table and tried to think like Mia. What would she see and pick up? The photo albums, probably. And his parents' wedding album, definitely. He slid it out from under the stack, opened to the first page, and saw his mother's radiant smile. Joy shone in her eyes, a sharp contrast to the vacant stare of Alzheimer's disease.

Had Mia opened the album, witnessed Claire's decline, and been worried Jake would go down the same road? Was she running from the disease? Jake doubted it. Mia ran *to* hurting people, not away from them.

Or did the wedding pictures evoke the memory of her broken engagements and stir up old fears? That possibility seemed more likely, but not by much. Surely she knew she could trust him.

He flipped through the next few pages, pausing only to take in a shot of the wedding party that included his Uncle Randy. No wonder his mom mixed them up. Randy, roughly Jake's age in the photograph, could have been his twin.

He hurried through the photographs until he reached the back cover. There he saw a letter and an empty envelope. He picked up the pages, saw his father's printing and the date, and knew he was holding the smoking gun behind Mia's departure.

His mother clutched his wrist. "Frank. Oh, Frank. No. No."

Desperate to protect his mom, he slipped a magazine into her lap. "Let's look for a dog."

She glanced down at the old copy of *Dog World*, then back at Jake, then to the album again.

"Let's find a dog like Pirate. Or how about a white one like Peggy McFuzz?"

She ignored him. "The letter—"

"I know, Mom." He would have given anything to erase the memory of that awful time, but all he could do was distract her. He turned the dog magazine to a new page and pointed. "Look. It's a collie. They're your favorite."

A faint smile lifted her lips, and she turned the next page on her own.

Relieved, Jake skimmed the letter and returned it to the envelope. He'd been twelve when his dad moved out, and that summer had been pure misery. At first he'd been furious with his father, disappointed, resentful, and protective of his mother. But then his father had come home, and slowly the Tanner family had healed.

For Jake, the past was just that—the past. He now admired his dad tremendously—not in spite of his failings, but because Frank owned his mistakes. Willing to sacrifice everything to save his family, he had won back his wife's trust.

Surely Mia could see the healing; or maybe she had reacted like a kicked dog. Either way, he needed to talk to her now—and in person.

He slipped the dog magazine out of Claire's hand. "Come on, Mom. Let's go downstairs."

He helped her to her feet, guided her back to the kitchen, and told Lucy he was going to Mia's house. Lucy gave him a big thumbs-up and an even bigger hug.

Jake needed to tell his father he was leaving, so he headed for the barn. As he walked into the business office, Frank hung up the phone. "Jake. Good. Do you have a minute?"

"Not really."

"What's wrong?"

"Mia." He didn't want to go into the details. "It's a long story. But I can take a few minutes. What's up?"

"Westridge just called. A two-bedroom apartment opened up starting December first."

"That's great news." They would all breathe easier with professional 24-7 care for his mother.

Frank leaned back in the old office chair until it squeaked. "I figure we'll start to pack but stay here through Christmas. That'll be less confusing for your mom."

"It's a good plan." And a painful one. Once Claire and Frank moved to Westridge, she would never come back to the house again. Counselors advised against it, because a visit would only confuse and upset her.

Right now, Mia was confused and upset too. The one person who might have helped her understand was Claire, but Claire's reasoning ability was long gone. On the other hand, maybe Frank had insights for Jake. "Dad, can I ask you something?"

"Of course."

He told his father about Mia reading the letter and how confused she was about her future. "When she came here, she'd given up on dating and was a hundred percent committed to Mission Medical. But things changed for her—for us."

Frank glanced at a framed photograph on his desk. It was of Claire, a formal portrait taken on her fiftieth birthday, before she started forgetting words and putting her keys in the cookie jar. Frank nudged the frame a quarter-inch to the left, then turned to Jake. "We're happy about you and Mia. I mean, I know your mom would be happy too."

The *we* was an old habit, the kind of habit Jake wanted to form with Mia. "I wish I could tell you she's staying in Echo Falls, but she's having second thoughts."

"Because of the letter?"

"I think so."

Frank slipped a wooden toothpick out of his pocket and started to chew. "That's the problem when a man makes a stupid mistake. God forgives and we heal, but the consequences don't disappear."

"I think she put you on a pedestal because of how you cope with Mom and the Alzheimer's. You just got knocked off it."

"Well, good. I don't belong up there, and neither do you. No man does."

"So what do I do?" Jake asked. "How do I convince her to trust in what we have?"

"You don't."

Jake loved his dad, but the cryptic answer made him grit his teeth. "But you did something, because here we are."

"By the grace of God, yes." Frank tossed the toothpick in the trash. "But it wasn't my doing. All I could do was pray."

"I remember that time, Dad. You did a lot more than pray. You and Mom went to counseling, and you stayed in church, even though you didn't like it sometimes."

"You picked up on that, huh?" Frank gave a dry chuckle. "Sorry, but the pastor at that time didn't help me at all. That's not saying he wasn't spot on for others, but I needed to hear more about Jesus and less about those potluck dinners your mother used to love. I thank God every day for preachers on the radio."

"You still listen to them."

"All the time. I'm a blessed man, Jake. And the biggest blessing of all is my family."

Amen to that. "I'm glad you and Mom worked things out."

"Me too, but don't give me the credit. I'm the one who walked out. The decision to reconcile belonged solely to your mother. In the middle of it all, when I thought we didn't have a chance, I promised to respect her choice, whatever it was. No pressure. That kind of love puts the other person first."

Jake knew exactly what his father meant. Christ had bled that kind of love on the cross. As a cop and a man, Jake understood sacrifice in his marrow. But when it came to waiting for Mia's decision, he wished she'd make up her ever-lovin' mind.

"You want my advice, son?"

"That's why I'm here."

"Do what's hard, and you'll know you're not cheaping out on God, yourself, or the people you love."

Talk about tough love. But that kind of love was tough on a man's own desires, not the people he cared about. Jake didn't need to hear anymore. Knowing what he needed to say to Mia, he turned toward the door. "Thanks, Dad. I'm headed to Mia's place now."

"I'll be praying, son. Stay strong and fight hard."

Jake intended to do exactly that. This was Mia's fight, but she didn't have to battle the doubts alone.

He never made it to her house. Instead, when he spotted her car at Echo Falls Primary Care, he parked next to it, trotted up the office steps, and rapped on the door.

chapter 26

Only Jake knocked on a door like a cop ready to kick it down. Seated at her desk, Mia peered through the window at his truck in the parking lot. The dark blue paint glinted in the setting sun, a reminder of Las Vegas and the first time she rode with him, but nothing else was the same. Instead of blistering heat, the air carried a chill. And instead of being almost strangers, they were in love.

Mia had been expecting him, but she still didn't know what to say. Just when she had made up her mind to turn down the offer, she received a personal email from Dr. Benton welcoming her to his team. *This position will change your life. Even better, it will change the lives of hundreds of kids. We worship a mighty God, don't we?*

Jake knocked again. She wasn't ready to speak with him, but she couldn't avoid him either. Knowing how he thought, she was certain he'd sit on the porch until she gave up and let him inside.

Frustrated, she went to the door and opened it. "I'm sorry, Jake. But this isn't a good time—"

"You read my dad's letter."

"Yes. I did. I'm sorry." She felt like an eavesdropper. "How did you find out?"

"My mom led me to it. I wish she could tell you her side, but she can't. So I will. My parents went through a hard time. My dad messed up. My mom forgave him. They worked it out. End of story."

He paused, giving her time to reply or to fall into his arms, but Mia couldn't just forget her fears and melt like Lucy did. Giving in to the inevitable, she opened the door wider. "Come on in."

Jake crossed the threshold but stopped to survey the walls they had painted after the vandalism. He indicated the room with a wave of his hand. "Why come here? I thought you'd go home."

"In some ways, this *is* home." She led the way down the dark hall to her office. The room wasn't set up for visitors, so Jake dragged a chair in from an exam room, while Mia sat in the big chair behind the desk that fit Dr. Collins's personality far better than it fit hers. Maybe the same was true of Echo Falls.

Jake draped a boot over his knee, leaned back, and glanced at the computer screen, where her reply stopped at *Dear Dr. Winkler*. "So you're still deciding."

"I guess so." She went to the window, intending to close the plantation blinds. Instead she peered through the slats at the setting sun. Peach and lavender clouds streaked the sky, while the fading light turned tall trees into silhouettes, hiding the intricacies of their branches. From a distance, the trees appeared flat and black, much like her decision.

"That letter did something to me," she said to Jake without facing him. "When I read it, all I could think about was being hurt again. I know that's childish, but it's how I felt."

"And still feel."

"Yes."

Determined to be both brave and wise, she faced him. "When Brad dumped me, I begged God to give me a new purpose. Mission Medical seemed like the perfect answer. I was happy again, even thrilled. When I read Frank's letter, it threw me back to how I felt before God opened that door. Those broken engagements were awful."

Jake's jaw hardened. "I can see why the letter upset you, but what I feel for you isn't going to change. I'm not Brad or that other idiot or even my father. I love you, Mia. You can trust me. You have to believe that."

"Yes. I do, but . . ." She couldn't find the words.

"But what?"

"I just don't know what to do!" Moaning, she pressed her hands against the top of her head. *Think, Mia! Stay calm. Look for the logic.* But where? Churning inside, she turned to the computer, pulled up the Mission Medical website, and clicked to the photographs taken of children before and after their surgeries. With her hand shaking, she turned the screen toward Jake. "How do I say no to this?"

He studied the children so long, she wondered if he'd turned into a block of ice. But then he let out a slow breath. "Maybe you can't."

"Can't what?"

"Say no."

"Are you telling me to say yes? But, Jake, I—" *I love you.*

He cut her off by rising from the chair and clasping her arms. Then he bent forward, matched his lips to hers, and kissed her into silence. When he pulled back, he spoke in a voice far steadier than hers. "Let me say something before I change my mind."

"All right." Mia gave a rueful smile. "I double-think enough for both of us."

Stepping back, he gripped her left hand and paused. Was he

going to drop to one knee and ask her to marry him? Her right hand went to her chest, and she waited in silence, hoping yet full of dread and terribly afraid of another blast of confusion.

He grazed her ring finger with the pad of his thumb. "My dad has a saying. 'When in doubt, do what's hard.' That way we know we're not denying God the chance to do something better than we could ever imagine." He raised her hands an inch, taking the weight of them in his own. "So I'm going to take his advice and do what's hard."

His Adam's apple jumped, then sank back into place. "I love you, Mia. I want you to live the life God designed just for you. If—*if*—that life is in Dallas and overseas, you need to grab it with both hands. But if that life is here, I want to grab it with you. We can't do that if you're swinging back and forth."

"Oh, Jake."

"Mia . . ." Her name whispered past his lips. "I want us to be together—always."

She finally raised her head. "Always? Is there such a thing?" She yearned to believe in forever, like a little girl reading a fairy tale, but her experience mocked her hope.

"I believe there is," Jake answered. "But I'd be a fool to stand here and say things you don't have the faith to believe." He paused, then let out a slow breath. "I'm human, Mia. With God as my witness, I'll never stop loving you. If that means being just a friend, I'll do it. But if it means the two of us becoming something more—husband and wife—you have my solemn vow that I'll love you forever. But we both know my dad said the same thing to my mom."

"Yes," she murmured. "That's the crux of it."

"You have to trust God here. Not me—Him."

"I do trust Him. I *do*." She wanted to stomp her feet and scream like a toddler. "That's the problem. He opened the door for me at Mission Medical. He swung it so wide I'm amazed.

But then I met you, and another door opened. How do I choose? And don't say, 'Do what's hard,' because both choices are hard, just in different ways."

Jake remained still, neither affirming her claim nor denying it, maybe because both choices were equally valid. But Mia needed to choose. Stepping back, she swept her arm to indicate her diplomas, the medical books, and her neat desk. "Look at me. I travel light. I'm single. I'm highly trained. It makes sense for me to use those gifts, doesn't it?"

"Of course it does. The question isn't *should* you use your gifts. It's *where*."

"Oh, Jake. I can't stand being like this—"

"Like what?"

"Confused. Upset." Close to tears, even if they didn't show. "Uncertain." She rolled her eyes. "I'm about ready to flip a coin. Heads, I go. Tails, I stay."

He reached into his pocket, dug around, and handed her a quarter. "You can flip it if you want, but deep down, I think you know what you want."

"Do I?"

When he didn't answer, she stared at George Washington's grim face.

Jake took her hand and folded her fingers over the quarter. "I'm leaving now. If you're really going to flip it, do it when I'm gone."

He stared into her eyes, then hauled her against his chest, lowered his lips to hers, and reminded her with a kiss of what only a man could give to a woman. How could she walk away from such powerful feelings? Why would she even consider it? Yet even as she lost herself in the kiss and in Jake, she couldn't escape the fear that she was somehow breaking her promise to God.

With her heart stuttering, she eased out of his arms. He

stepped back, studied her face for a full ten seconds, then left with a nod that bordered on curt. A moment later his truck rumbled out of the parking lot.

Mia buried her face in her hands and prayed as hard as she could. "Please, God. *Please.* I need you to *show me* what you want me to do." She waited, prayed some more, begged and wrestled with herself—both the frightened little girl she hid from the world and the responsible adult who never let anyone down.

When an answer didn't come, she composed an email saying she was thrilled to join the Mission Medical team and would attend the Christmas party in Dallas on December 12. Then she composed a second email saying she was grateful for the opportunity but her plans had changed.

Fed up with herself, Mia decided to stop thinking and just *do*. To stop being so overly responsible and be more like Lucy, who embraced life as it came. Taking a breath, she snatched Jake's quarter off the desk and flipped it high into the air. "Heads, I go. Tails, I stay."

It landed three feet away on the worn carpet. Bending down, she saw George Washington staring into the future. Before she could second-guess herself for the millionth time, she sent the email saying yes.

●●●

Jake headed home, checked in with his dad, and headed out to the pinball barn with Pirate. He turned on the game called Pop & Go and played for a solid hour. The pings and clangs rattled through him, but even more jarring was the vibration of his phone in his pocket and Pirate nosing him.

Jake let the silver pinball slide off the paddles, lifted his phone, and saw a text with a photograph of a quarter lying heads up on Mia's office carpet. Sinking inside, he read the words below it. *Flipped the coin. I'm saying yes to MM. Don't know what else to say. Just . . . thank you.*

He spat a word he almost never used. The coin toss had been a ploy. In his experience, when a person resorted to flipping a coin, they knew what they wanted but couldn't admit it. If that was true for Mia, maybe she really did belong overseas with Mission Medical.

He shoved his phone back in his pocket. *Do what's hard*. He couldn't think of anything harder than letting Mia go. He loved her and wanted to marry her. But Mia needed to be secure in her choices, strong in her faith, and bold enough to love him in spite of her fears.

He pressed his back against the wall, slid to the floor, and draped his arms over his knees. Pirate nudged him with his cold nose, then dropped down next to him. Head bowed, Jake prayed with all his might for God to give Mia the peace, courage, and clarity she craved. A chill settled deep in his chest. *Do what's hard*. Even with the love and grace of a Savior, sometimes that advice really stank.

chapter 27

On the morning of the Mission Medical Christmas party, Mia drove herself to the Colorado Springs airport, left her car in long-term parking, and took off for Dallas despite blowing snow and the promise of more bad weather to come. Peering out the window at the clouds below, she wondered again if she'd made the right choice. Lucy didn't think so. On Thanksgiving Day, she had threatened to lock Mia in a room with Jake until she came to her senses. Jake, on the other hand, had avoided her entirely for the past two weeks.

Twice she tried to compose an email to Dr. Winkler saying she had changed her mind, but she felt too guilty to go back on her word. She'd dug a hole for herself, and she didn't know how to get out. On the other hand, the hole wasn't a bad place to be. In fact, her commitment was noble and good—

"Shut up," she muttered to herself as the plane descended.

With her doubts still whispering, she rented a car and drove to Mission Medical headquarters, a campus-style facility located three hours from the city. The weekend trip was more than a Christmas gathering. As the new clinic coordinator, she was scheduled to move to Dallas by January 15, train for a month on the campus, then travel to Africa with Dr. Benton and his team. Tonight she was having dinner with her future coworkers at one of the cottages used to house staff members.

Dressed in black slacks and a sparkly white sweater, Mia walked into a lively gathering. Excited conversations filled the air along with Christmas carols celebrating the birth of Jesus and the reason they were all here. She fit right in and almost relaxed, but after the turbulent flight and long drive, she felt as if she were still in motion.

"Hey, everyone," Dr. Benton called over the chatter, "grab a seat in the living room. We're going to take care of some business."

Mia sat on the couch next to Donna Burke. A nurse in her late fifties, Donna was making her third trip overseas. The man on Donna's left was a retired anesthesiologist who could hardly wait to get on the plane with his wife, the nurse seated next to him.

The other team members included a young married couple, both pediatricians, and Dr. Benton's brother, the program administrator and a permanent employee like herself. Dr. Benton, wearing a Hawaiian shirt with a surfing Santa Claus on it, bantered with everyone, though Mia wondered why he was holding a medium-sized wicker basket.

He raised a hand to signal for attention. "Good evening, folks. Glad you could all make it."

One of the internists, the husband, piped up. "Wouldn't miss it for the world, John."

"Me neither," Donna replied.

Everyone murmured approval, even Mia, though she felt like an imposter. Did anyone else have doubts like hers? It didn't seem like it.

"Some of you are veterans," Dr. Benton continued, "and some of you are rookies. I thought we'd play a little 'getting to know you' game. Would you each take out your phone?"

Mia stifled a groan. *Great. A surprise.* But maybe this would be a good one. She took her phone out of her pocket and waited for instructions.

A mischievous grin stretched across Dr. Benton's face. "Now pull up the last picture you took."

No. Just no. The last picture she took zoomed in on the quarter on her carpet. How would she explain it? She gave serious thought to scrolling past it, but Dr. Benton was watching her.

"No cheating." He winked at her. "I don't care if it's the worst selfie in the world."

Mia faked a laugh, left the picture of the coin on the screen, and hoped this game wasn't going where she thought it was.

Dr. Benton walked around with the basket. "Drop your phones inside. I'm going to hold them up one at time, and you're going to guess whose phone it is."

When the basket came Mia's way, she added her phone, then laughed and groaned with everyone else about being caught unaware.

The first phone Dr. Benton chose sported a lavender case and showed a picture of two adorable little boys with Donna.

"Too easy!" said the anesthesiologist. "Donna's in the picture."

"My two grandsons," she replied.

"Won't you miss them?" the female pediatrician asked.

"Terribly," she admitted. "But right now, I'm where I belong."

Everyone murmured in agreement, including Mia, though her face felt stiffer with every breath.

Dr. Benton selected the next phone, glanced at the picture, and grinned as he held out the device. "Looks like we have another proud grandparent."

"That's mine." The anesthesiologist's wife beamed.

The anesthesiologist's phone showed the same little girl, and the phones belonging to the pediatricians showed pictures of each other.

There were three phones left. As Mia expected, Dr. Benton lifted hers from the basket and studied the screen for what felt like a long time. When he held it up, no one said a word.

"Looks like heads won," he said.

Mia played it cool. "Yes, it did."

"What were you deciding?" Donna asked, all smiles.

An embarrassed blush erupted on Mia's cheeks and burned hot. No way did she want to reveal her indecision. *Stay calm. Laugh it off*. But she couldn't control the trembling deep in her bones. "This will sound silly."

"Go for it." Dr. Benton handed her the phone. "Why the coin toss? Or better yet, why take a picture of it?"

Where did she start? How did she sum up the past six months? Falling in love and being scared; her desperate need to be responsible, keep her word, and never let anyone down, especially God; her need to never depend on anyone. The only person Mia could truly trust was herself, but here she was—trembling, red-faced, and so lost she wanted to cry.

She needed words but couldn't find them. *Where are you, Lord?*

Seven people stared at her, waiting for her story. She tried to smile, but her mouth refused to bend. With nothing left but the truth, she surrendered to it. "I met someone. He's wonderful. But back in April, when my ex-fiancé broke our engagement, I begged God to give me a new purpose. And He did. So here I am."

No one nodded, not even Dr. Benton.

"It seemed wrong to change my mind, especially when God opened the door. But Jake is amazing. He's strong and caring, gentle, kind, and funny too. He's . . . he's the best man I've ever known. When I had to choose between Jake and Mission Medical, I couldn't do it. So I flipped a coin."

Dr. Benton studied her as if she were one of the damaged children he repaired. "Mia, you don't have to be here."

She stared at him, incredulous. "But I made a promise. I gave my word."

"Maybe the promise was a mistake." He paused, letting the words fall like a gentle rain. "We all make them. It happens."

"But I try so hard—" The inner trembling conquered every nerve in her body. Was the path to peace really that simple? All she had to do was change her mind? Admit to a mistake?

So why was it so hard to let go and receive the gift of Jake's love—a gift that came from God as surely as the opportunity with Mission Medical? *Think, Mia! Think!* But instead of finding words, she saw herself as a frightened little girl at Jesus' feet, her head in His lap and tears streaming down her cheeks. Maybe if she was good enough, bad things wouldn't happen. Somehow, in the pursuit of that perfection, that little girl had failed—but God hadn't. He was with her right now in the hearts and minds of these seven people who saw her more clearly than she saw herself.

Mia broke down and sobbed. Donna put her arms around her, and the others stood and crowded in, laying their hands on her back and shoulders. Someone started to pray. Others joined in, and though Mia barely heard the words, the love soaked into her soul and met a need she didn't know she had.

The need to be cared for by others.

The need to set down the load she carried.

The need to trust like a child, and to belong the way God intended when He put the lonely in families.

The lump in her throat popped like a balloon, and her sobbing throttled up into laughter. Joy welled up in her chest, flooded through her, and wiped away every doubt about where she belonged—in Echo Falls with Jake.

When the prayers faded to silence, Dr. Benton gave a hearty "Amen."

Mia leapt to her feet. "I'm going home." *Home to Jake.*

Donna hugged her hard. So did everyone else, except Dr. Benton, who held out his hand. "Safe travels, Mia. Do you need a ride back to Dallas?"

"No, I rented a car." *Thank you, God!* Both for the rental car and her 4Runner waiting in long-term parking back in the Springs. The thought of surprising Jake with an early return thrilled her, but she had one loose end before she left. "Dr. Benton?"

"Yes?"

"I'm sorry I wasted your time."

"You didn't. In fact, we're honored God used us to help you find your way home."

Home. She choked up again. "Me too."

Dr. Benton just smiled. "Live your life, Mia. Raise a family. Serve your local community—it's all love, and it's all good."

"Thank you." She teared up again, delighted in another round of hugs, and left for Dallas with her heart certain and her joy complete.

When she arrived in the city, it was too late to catch a flight to Colorado Springs, so she settled for a seat on the first flight in the morning. After booking her ticket, she checked the weather app on her phone, specifically the radar map for Echo Falls. Swirls of green, yellow, and orange painted an ominous picture, but she refused to think about snow, blizzards, and flight delays. Instead she prayed for travel mercies and checked into a hotel.

She didn't sleep well at all. While she was certain Jake would forgive her for a mistake, she was equally sure she had hurt him. The irony suddenly struck her as crazy. She had been as random as a pinball because she was afraid to trust Jake; in the process, she had made it hard for him to trust her.

chapter 28

Packing tape," Lucy muttered to herself as she perused the boxes scattered around the bedroom. "Where did it go?"

Yesterday Jake had given her three rolls of it, plus a handy dispenser that wasn't nearly as handy as he thought. Nonetheless, with Sam taking finals this week—his last one was today—and out of her way, she had packed up most of their bedroom. Everything except the gifts from the baby shower last Saturday. Fleecy blankets, adorable onesies, baby equipment, and boxes of Pampers were stacked in a mountain by the dresser.

With Beanie Girl due in three weeks, the timing for the move to their apartment in the Springs was perfect. No way did Lucy want to be an hour from the hospital when she went into labor. She was nervous enough without adding a long drive and winter weather to the mix. Maybe, if she could be strong through the delivery, she could believe she was grown up enough to be a good wife to Sam—and a good mother to Beanie Girl.

The baby kicked in her belly. Lucy and Sam had picked a name, but they were keeping it a secret.

"So far, so good," she said to her daughter. The last ultrasound had showed Beanie Girl head down and the placenta in the correct position, but Lucy was still scared.

Pausing to rub her back, she peered through the snowflakes sticking to the windowpane. After five days of sleet and snow, the yard glistened under a blanket of pure white, except for the muddy ruts left by car and truck tires. It was beautiful outside, the perfect day for hot chocolate and snuggling with Sam.

With Frank and Claire visiting Westridge today, and Jake picking up groceries in town, Lucy's thoughts slipped into a silent conversation with Mia, where she lectured her perfect big sister about being OCD and a control freak. As noble as working for Mission Medical seemed, Lucy thought Mia was making the biggest mistake of her life.

"Oh—" A twinge in her back circled around to her belly button. Lucy had been having Braxton-Hicks contractions for a few weeks now. The pre-labor spasms prepared her body for giving birth and were usually painless, but this morning they had been annoying.

The sharp pang frightened her enough to pray. "God, are you there?" She placed her hand on her belly. "It's me again—Lucy. You already know this. I'm scared about everything."

How would she know she was in labor? What if she missed the signs? Would it hurt a lot? And the birth itself—she chomped down on her lower lip. She shouldn't have watched all those YouTube videos. Forget breathing techniques, she wanted a hospital and an epidural. But more than anything, she wanted Sam to be proud of her.

"Help me through this, Lord," she prayed again. "No more drama, okay? Just a smooth, easy—"

Liquid gushed down her leg.

Her mouth agape, Lucy stared at her wet yoga pants, the puddle at her feet, then at her tummy.

"Oh no. No! Oh, Beanie Girl—" Lucy cradled her belly as if

she could hold the baby in place. "It's too soon, honey. Not a lot too soon, but we're here, and your daddy isn't. And—And—" A contraction stole her breath.

Hunched over, she gripped the windowsill and panted until it passed. "Oh, Lord. Help me."

First babies took a long time to come, didn't they? There had to be time to get to the hospital. She just needed to call Jake, and he'd drive her to Colorado Springs. Easy as pie. Sam could meet them at the hospital, Lucy would have the baby, and her daughter would have the full benefits of doctors, nurses, and a NICU if she needed one.

"No problem," Lucy said. "Lord, we can do this."

Speaking out loud helped, in part because she imagined Mia's calm voice in her head. She wanted that voice in her ear too, so she called her sister's cell.

One ring. Two rings. Then Mia's recorded voice telling her to leave a message.

She didn't want Mia to worry, so she took a breath to steady her words. "Call me as soon as you can, all right?" *I'm in labor and scared to death!* Hysteria danced on her tongue, but she managed a quick "Bye!"

She started to call Sam but glanced at the clock and stopped. He was in the middle of a tough engineering exam, and there was no reason to rattle him this minute. First babies didn't just pop out. That was what everyone said, and Sam needed to finish that exam without any added pressure. It wouldn't hurt to wait a little longer to call him.

"We can do this," she said again to herself and God.

Calmer now, she called Jake. He picked up on the first ring and answered with a smile in his voice. "Let me guess. Beanie Girl wants guacamole and ketchup."

"Uh—" Another contraction stole her breath.

"Lucy?"

She panted into the phone. "I'm—I'm—" A groan crawled out of her throat.

"Lucy!" Jake shouted in her ear. "What's wrong? What's happening?"

The pain twisted from her back to her belly. When it eased, she burst into tears. "My water broke. I'm in labor!"

●●●

"I'm on my way."

Jake abandoned the half-full grocery cart in the middle of the aisle, hurried with Pirate to the truck, and sped home. He knew a little about childbirth from his police department training but not enough to play Dr. Jake in real life. With Mia gone and Sam in Colorado Springs, the best plan by far was to get Lucy to the hospital.

But there wasn't much time—both because of her labor and because of the hazardous road conditions. Back in November, heavy rains had softened the hillsides, and now a rain-snow mix was falling for the fifth day in a row. Two rockslides had already occurred north of town, and there was serious talk about closing the main road as a precaution.

He sped down the driveway and hurried into the house with Pirate behind him. "Lucy? Where are you?"

"Back here!"

He found her bent over the bed, her hands braced on the mattress while she panted through a contraction. Pale and grimacing, she let out a moan that clawed at his heart. Lucy tended to be dramatic, but that moan was as genuine as the little suitcase she was trying to pack.

When the spasm eased, she turned to him. "I should have packed sooner, but I didn't think it would happen like this. I can't believe it. It's too soon, and—and—" She sniffed back tears. "Jake, I'm scared."

"You'll be fine. So will Beanie Girl." No way would he let anything happen to Connie Waters's granddaughter.

His training kicked in. Rule Number One: Stay calm. Easier said than done for a man with a soul-deep terror of failing to protect people in his care. Pirate sat at Jake's feet, alert and ready for an order. Jake didn't need him right now, so he dismissed the dog with a few words.

Rule Number Two: Assess the situation. The bed was covered with packing boxes, so he pulled up the chair from Sam's desk and helped Lucy sit down. Her color was better now, her breathing even and steady.

He gripped her wrist and took her pulse. "How far apart are the contractions?"

"I don't know."

"Since you called me, how many have you had?"

"Just one."

So one contraction in ten minutes, plus a first baby. Everyone knew first babies took their time. Her pulse thrummed a strong and steady beat, just a little fast, as he would have expected. "We have some time here."

"Uh—" She clamped down on her lip, either from pain or trying not to cry.

"What is it?"

"I think maybe I've been in labor since this morning. I thought I was just having more Braxton-Hicks, but when my water broke, I started to think. The contractions started right after Sam left for school, and they've been happening regularly. I'm so stupid, Jake. I didn't realize—"

"You are not stupid, Lucy." The poor kid. He gave her shoulder a squeeze. "You're human, and this is new to you. But forget packing a bag. We're leaving right now."

He hooked an arm around her waist, and they headed through the house. He snatched her coat from the hook, helped her into it, and glanced at her shoes. Snow boots. Good. She'd need them for the short walk to his truck.

With his arm around her, he opened the front door. Snow and sleet pelted his face, stinging his cheeks like needles. His gaze narrowed to the stairs, ice covered and far too dangerous for a woman in Lucy's condition. "It's too slick. I'll throw down some cat litter."

Lucy nodded. "Yes. Please."

Jake opened the closet by the front door, took out the bag of clay litter his family kept for just this reason, and spread the dusty grit on the deck and steps.

When he finished, he went back inside and glanced at his watch. She'd have another contraction any minute, so he decided to wait before tackling the walk to the truck. Instead he reached for his phone. "I'm going to check on the road."

"The road? Why?"

"Possible rockslides."

Lucy clutched the coat around her belly. "That won't happen. It just can't."

But Jake knew otherwise. Bombs went off, houses burned down, and human beings broke each other's hearts. And sometimes babies came too soon. Churning inside, he called the road info line.

Instead of the usual bland recording, a gruff male voice rumbled into his ear. "This is an emergency alert—repeat, an emergency alert for Highway 924, in and out of Echo Falls. The road is closed in both directions due to active rockslides. I repeat. The road is closed."

Jake knew Echo Falls inside and out, every road and trail. There was no other way out. A fear as cold as the snow settled into his bones.

Lucy stared at him, wide-eyed, her hand on her belly as she waited for a report.

Jake gave it to her straight. "The road's closed."

"Closed? It can't be. The baby . . . she's early. Jake—Oh." Her eyes flared and she started to pant. Another contraction. A strong one.

Jake gripped her arms, taking her weight when her knees buckled. "Hang on, Luce."

"I am—" *Pant. Pant.* "I have—to be—strong." More panting.

"You're doing great."

"Am I?" She sounded small, like a little girl.

"Yes. You are."

When the contraction eased, Jake guided her to the couch. "Just sit and rest. All right?"

"But—"

"I'm going to get you out of here."

"How?"

"I'm working on that part." Jake had failed Connie once, but he refused—*refused*—to fail her twice. Stay here or try for the hospital? With Lucy's contractions still ten minutes apart, the hospital was still the best choice. If the road was blocked more by snow than rocks, he could possibly push through the mess in four-wheel drive. Brian Ross would know, so Jake called the deputy's personal cell phone.

Brian answered on the second ring. "Jake, I'm glad you called. We need help—"

"So do I." He told Brian about Lucy. "Where exactly is the rockslide?"

"About two miles outside of town."

"How bad is it?"

"I'm looking at a lot of rock and at least three feet of snow. It's deep, and the mountain isn't stable."

Jake dragged his hand through his hair. "Can I power through it in my truck?" Even as he asked, he knew the answer.

"Not a chance."

"I have to get Lucy out of here." He kept eye contact with her, watching as she nodded fast and hard. "We need a clear road to the Springs right now."

"I can't do it. The county road crew is tied up somewhere else. We have to wait our turn."

"Or do it ourselves. If I can get Hatcher out there with some heavy equipment—"

"You? He hates you."

"He hates what I'm doing." Underneath all that rage, there was a decent man who had inspired a crowd to shout, *We love Bill*. Jake knew exactly what he needed to do, wanted to do, and what would honor Connie Waters far more than a camp that never had a name.

"I'm calling him now," he told Brian. "I'll get back to you."

Praying Hatcher would answer the office phone, Jake scrolled to his number. One ring. Two rings. *Please, God. No voice mail.*

"Hatcher here."

"Bill, it's Jake Tanner. Don't hang up."

Silence shouted at him.

"The road out of here is closed."

"I heard."

"Sam's wife is in labor and needs to get to the hospital. If you'll clear the road, I'll pull the plug on the camp. You have my word."

A stunned silence pulsed in Jake's ear. One beat of his heart. Two beats. He took a deep breath and held it. Finally Bill's voice came out strong. "Do you mean that?"

"Every word."

"Then consider it done. When I get a look at the slide, I'll call you with an estimate of how long it'll take."

"Thanks, Bill."

The instant Jake ended the call, a weight lifted from his shoulders. He'd done everything he could for Lucy and the baby. The rest was up to God.

He turned to Lucy and silently gauged her condition. Aside from the trembling line of her mouth, she was remarkably composed. "How are you feeling?"

"Scared." Her eyes took on a misty shine. "And grateful. I know what Camp Connie means to you—or meant to you."

"You, Sam, and the baby mean a lot more."

"And Mia." Her brows slammed together. "My sister's an idiot." Jake opened his mouth to argue, but Lucy stopped him by raising her hand. "Don't tell me otherwise. You're the best thing that's ever happened to her, and she runs away—oh!"

Another contraction. Jake went to her side, watching the clock and counting the seconds as the spasm peaked. This contraction seemed longer than the last one, but he wasn't sure.

"Have you called Sam?" he asked.

"Not yet. I was going to wait until he finished his final, then tell him to meet us at the hospital. I'll call him right now."

Jake walked into the kitchen, both to give Lucy privacy and to make a call of his own, one he didn't want her to overhear. For all his outward confidence and the hope that Hatcher would clear the road fast, Jake knew full well he might have to deliver Lucy's baby. The thought scared him to death.

He had two lives in his hands, and the best person to help him was Mia. If he had to text her a 911 message to call home, he'd do it. But he hoped she would answer—preferably on the first ring.

●●●

Mia never answered her phone while driving, but she was at a dead stop because of a rockslide blocking the road into Echo Falls. Yellow tape marked off the hazard area, and a sheriff's car was parked in the opposite lane, its light bar flashing a warning. Five cars idled ahead of her, and about a dozen sat behind her, all waiting while a deputy in cold weather gear organized the tangle of cars trying to turn around.

When she saw Jake's caller ID, she debated whether or not to answer. She loved the idea of surprising him—in a good way, for a change. On the other hand, she tingled all over at the thought of hearing his voice.

She picked up on the third ring. "Hey, there."

"Mia, thank God you answered."

That tone—and the prayer. Her spine snapped into an iron rod. "What's wrong? Is it Lucy?"

"She's in labor."

"Labor?" Mia pressed her hand to her forehead. "Are you sure?"

"Positive. Her water broke."

"Well, that settles that." *Thank you, God, for sending me home in time.* "Which hospital? I'll turn around now."

"Turn around? What do you mean?"

"I'm here. In Echo Falls. Well, almost. There's a rockslide."

"You mean you're *two miles* away? You're not in Dallas? What—How—"

"I'll explain later." She could barely speak over the lump in her throat, but her hand remained steady as she gripped the gear shift, ready to ease into a U-turn. "Tell me which hospital. I'll meet you there."

"No hospital."

"Then where—oh no." Mia's hand froze with the 4Runner still in park.

"That's right. We're at the house. Her water broke less than an hour ago. The contractions are ten minutes apart, but they're pretty intense."

"When did they start?"

"Early this morning, but she didn't realize what was happening. I called you for a crash course in Childbirth 101. But if you're here, that changes everything."

She opened the car door and stood on the frame to get a better look at the snow and rock blocking the road. It was deep, cold, and no doubt treacherous. But if she could scale Echo Falls, she could trust God to get her through the debris. "I'm on my way, but I'll have to go through the slide area on foot."

"Mia, no! The mountain isn't stable. There's help coming to clear the road, plus we have some time, right?"

"Probably." She looked at her watch. "I want you to time the contractions."

"I'm doing it now. They're about ten minutes apart—"

A sharp cry pierced Mia's ear through the phone, followed by Lucy calling Jake's name.

"Make that nine minutes."

Mia swallowed hard. "Where is she now?"

"On the couch."

"Get her bed ready. Put down clean sheets and gather some towels. Birth is messy. If you can, check the baby gifts for an infant care kit. When Beanie Girl comes, use a suction ball to clear her nose and mouth."

"Oh man—" His voice wavered, but just a little. "Lucy's calmer than I am."

Mia pictured him dragging his hand through his hair and smiled. Even strong men like Jake sometimes turned to jelly. "You've got this, Jake. I know you do. Birth is a natural process. If I don't get there in time, just let it happen. Don't pull or push. Just watch and be ready to catch the baby."

He hesitated. "Like a football, right?"

"A very slippery football. Now get to work, and don't forget to wash your hands up to your elbows."

"Got it, doc. Anything else?"

"No." *Just that I love you.* "Actually, a lot, but it has to wait. Let me talk to Lucy, okay?"

When he handed over the phone, Mia closed her eyes, picturing Lucy as the little girl she used to be and the brave woman she was now. Snow whipped and churned around the 4Runner, wrapping Mia in a white cocoon until Lucy's shaky voice came over the phone.

"Mia? Are you really here?"

"I sure am, so let's bring Beanie Girl into the world. Tell me about the contractions."

"They suck." Not one of Lucy's usual words.

"On a scale of one to ten, with ten being the worst pain ever, what are they?"

"Eight? The last one was horrible."

"I'd like to know how dilated you are, but we'll hold off on that." Modesty would fly out the window soon enough, and the information wouldn't change Mia's instructions to Jake. "Have you talked to Sam?"

"Yes. He finished the exam early and was already on his way home. I told him about the rockslide, but he said he'd find a way. He's great, Mia. I love him so much."

Frank. Jake. Sam. Three good men with the faith to move mountains for the women they loved. "Hang in there, honey."

"I-I'm trying."

"Babies don't just pop out. We have some time." Mia glanced out the snowy windshield. When she saw a blob of bright yellow on the other side of the slide area, she started the wipers. It was a bulldozer. Another one pulled up next to it. "They're clearing the road now. It won't be much longer."

"How long?"

"I don't know, but they're working on it."

"I'm just so scared—" The words cut to a squeak. "Mia? Why is this happening?"

"Well, your body decided—"

"That's not what I mean. Do you think God is punishing me? Or that He's mad at me because I can't do everything right like you do?"

"Oh, Lucy. No. You are so wrong." Both about God punishing her and about Mia doing everything right. "For one thing, God loves us just as we are. He knows about our mistakes, and He's strong when we're not."

"Like now," Lucy whispered. "He's helping me."

"And He helped me in Dallas." *Grace. God's kindness when I was stubborn and scared*. Mia swallowed a lump. "Look at the mess I made with Jake. I hurt him. I know I did."

"I'm so glad you're back. Tell me you're staying."

"I am. But more on that later. Right now you're the focus. You and Beanie Girl."

"I can't believe I'm doing this. And Sam's not here." She sniffed back tears. "It's me and God."

"And Jake."

"Yes—ooooh!" Another contraction.

Mia talked her through it while looking at the second hand on her watch. The spasm lasted close to a minute and had come eight minutes after the last one. Lucy's labor was picking up steam. They didn't have several hours like Mia hoped, but she'd save that information for Jake. When the contraction ended, she encouraged Lucy to rest and save her strength.

Angry shouting erupted outside her car. Mia turned her head and saw Sam going nose-to-nose with the deputy organizing the vehicles jockeying to turn around. She turned off the engine of her car, flung the door wide, and spoke to Lucy at the same time. "I see Sam. I'll call you right back."

"Yes—tell him I love him. Bye!"

"Bye!" Mia jammed her phone in her pocket and hurried over to the deputy.

Sam saw her and cried out, "Mia! I can't believe it. Lucy's having the baby. Right now! At home. I have to get to her, and Deputy Dimwit—"

"Sam, stop it." Mia used the stern tone she reserved for hysterical fathers-to-be. They were usually the strong ones, men like Sam who were used to being in charge. "Pull yourself together. Now."

His jaw dropped, but he composed himself.

Mia glanced at the deputy's name tag. "Officer Haywood, please forgive my brother-in-law. I'm Nurse Practitioner Mia Robinson. My sister—Sam's wife—is in Echo Falls. She's in labor, and it's progressing fast. We need to get to her as soon as possible, even if it means going through the slide area on foot."

"Sorry, Ms. Robinson, but that's not safe."

"Not safe?" Sam flung his arms up to the sky. "I don't care about *safe*. My *wife* is having a *baby*!"

Rocking back, the deputy gave Sam a firm but patient look. "Son, keep calm. That's the best way to help her."

"But—I—We—" Red-faced, Sam spun away, hunched over, and sucked in lungfuls of air. The poor kid was a wreck.

The deputy turned to Mia. "Let's check the progress with the backhoes."

He signaled Sam, and the three of them ducked under the yellow tape to get away from the cars turning around. About a hundred feet away, the backhoes worked in tandem, scooping debris and pushing it into the river.

Mia sighed. At this rate, it would take hours to clear the road enough for even a single car to pass through. On the other hand, she and Sam could tackle the slide area on foot. Never mind the danger. Lucy needed her, and so did Jake. Mia spoke in a low voice just for Sam. "I'm willing to risk it if you are."

"You bet I am."

Deputy Haywood must have heard, because he turned to her with a raised eyebrow. "I can't let you do that, Ms. Robinson. It's just not safe."

Mia laced her next words with authority. "Deputy Haywood,

I have never willfully disobeyed a law in my life, but with all due respect, Sam and I are crossing this slide."

"If you break a leg, you'll have an even bigger problem."

"We're willing to risk it," Sam said.

The deputy glanced between them. "I understand the need. But I also see the danger. Let's check the status with the plows." He bent his neck and spoke into the mic on his collar. "Haywood here. We have an emergency involving a pregnant woman in Echo Falls. How long to clear a path for medical personnel to hike through?"

Deputy Brian Ross identified himself. "Roger that. Checking now."

Sam spoke under his breath. "We're going no matter what, right?"

"Yes, we are."

Mia was ready to make a break for it when the radio crackled. "The backhoe operator says it'll take about thirty minutes."

"What do you think?" Sam asked Mia.

She glanced at the half-buried boulders and the dirt and snow that would come up to their thighs. More rocks were no doubt hidden beneath the debris, making the crossing slow and doubly treacherous. "I hate to wait, but I think it's smart."

"Me too." Sam's expression turned battle-hard. "But just thirty minutes. That's all."

Mia agreed. "Let's see how Lucy is doing."

She lifted her phone and called Jake. At the same time, Sam tried to call Lucy. Neither of them answered, a sure sign Beanie Girl was demanding their attention.

"Stay calm," Mia said, as much to herself as to Sam. "Jake can handle this. He was a cop. He has some training."

Sam stared at his phone and muttered, "Please, God" about a dozen times.

Together they watched the backhoe clear a narrow path one

slow, heavy shovelful at a time. When he broke through to their side, Mia recognized Bill Hatcher.

To her surprise, he gave her a salute and shouted, "Good luck to your sister!"

Shoving aside her questions, Mia waved her gratitude. With Sam in the lead, they walked as fast as they dared, slipping and sliding on compacted snow and ice until they broke through to the other side. Out of breath, they jumped into Officer Ross's patrol car and rode with the siren blaring.

They both tried to call again. Still no answer.

chapter 29

Jake heard Mia's ringtone, but he'd left his phone in the other room when he half-carried Lucy to the bed. He couldn't leave to answer it now, while she was whimpering through another contraction. They were coming fast, one on top of the other. Leave it to Lucy to break every rule in the pregnancy book, especially the one about first babies taking a long time to make their way into the world. Beanie Girl was crowning—meaning Jake could see the top of her head.

"You're doing great," he said to Lucy.

"I am?" The poor girl was dripping with sweat. Her fingers clenched at the sheets, and between contractions, she gulped in deep breaths and blew them out.

"Yes, you are. So is Beanie Girl." As for himself, he wasn't so sure. As calm as he seemed on the outside, his pulse was as rapid as Lucy's. If Pirate had been allowed in the room, he would have crawled into Jake's lap.

For the tenth time, Jake ran through his training in his head. There was one basic rule: Don't interfere with the natural process. That was fine, as long as the process was natural, but Lucy had run into trouble with the placenta previa. The baby was early but not too early. On the plus side, the last ultrasound had showed Beanie Girl in the proper head-down position.

"I'm trying to be brave, but I want Sam." Lucy wiped the tears off her cheeks with a corner of the bed sheet.

"He'll be here soon."

"And Mia—oh crud!" Lucy let loose a moan that turned to a shriek. "Jake, help me! Oh, God, please. Please—"

Her cries nearly destroyed him. What if she started to bleed? What if the umbilical cord was wrapped around the baby's neck? What if Beanie Girl didn't breathe on her own? Jake had never seen a woman so helpless, except Connie lying in that bombed-out building. He could live with that memory, but he couldn't live with something awful happening to Beanie Girl or Lucy.

Please, God. Help us.

The next contraction showed even more of the baby's head. Lucy pushed and bore down. More of Beanie Girl's head emerged. Lucy shrieked again. Red-faced, her hair in a tangle, she clutched the sheets and pushed with all her might.

"You're doing it, Lucy!"

"Aaaaach!" She clenched her teeth, squeezed her eyes tight, and bore down again.

Jake could only watch and wait and be ready with towels and that green bulb to suction Beanie Girl's mouth. The old training video played in his mind. *The baby will be slippery. Don't drop it.* Not a chance. Not Connie's granddaughter.

"Oh! Oh!" Lucy pushed again.

"Hang in there, honey! She's almost here. I see her face!"

Another push. Then another.

"The shoulders are out."

Lucy pushed one more time, and the wet, bloody, slippery baby shot into Jake's waiting hands. Using the green bulb, he cleared Beanie Girl's nose and mouth. Air filled her lungs, and life flowed through her tiny body—and into Jake's hands. He felt her first breath as plainly as he had witnessed Connie's last.

When the baby started to cry, so did Jake. He didn't even try to hold in the tears as he wiped Beanie Girl off with a soft towel. Lucy was sobbing and reaching for her, so Jake placed the baby on her stomach with the cord still attached. The afterbirth needed to be delivered, but the thump of the front door hitting the wall in the living room distracted him.

"Lucy!" Sam rounded into the room, saw his wife and daughter, and totally lost it. The poor kid was blubbering more than Jake.

Mia raced over the threshold while shoving out of her damp coat. Her gaze shot to Lucy and the baby first, then the birth mess, and finally to Jake. He drank in the sight of her face, the relief, and especially the way she schooled her features into a professional calm. Later she would laugh and cry, he knew, but right now she was the picture of poise.

She rested her chilled fingers on his arm. "You did great."

He couldn't stop staring at her. To make sure she was real, he brushed his fingers down the sleeve of her red sweater. "I can't believe you're here."

Her voice dropped to a whisper. "There's so much I need to tell you."

But what was it? If she was still undecided about their future, he didn't think he could stand it. He sealed his lips, unsure of what to say or do.

Mia broke in. "I'll finish here. Why don't you clean up?"

"Thanks, I'll do that."

Mia turned to Lucy, and Jake lumbered up the stairs to his room. A hot shower cleared his head but did nothing to ease his uncertainty about Mia's surprise arrival. Surely it was a good sign. But she had waffled on him before.

When he returned to Lucy's room, the sheets were fresh, and the new mother was propped up on pillows with her daughter in her arms. Beanie Girl, wearing a knit cap and swaddled in a blanket, resembled a pink burrito. Sam sat in a chair next to the bed, while Mia stood opposite him. When Jake knocked on the doorframe, Lucy looked up.

"Jake! You're the best. I can't thank you enough."

Sam stood and hugged him hard. "My mom would be grateful. So am I." They traded at least six back slaps before they broke apart.

Lucy blinked away happy tears. "Jake, you were great."

"No," he said, "you were. You and Beanie Girl did all the work. I just played catcher."

Mia smiled in that Mona Lisa way of hers. "You did more than that. You ushered a new life into the world."

Lucy gave a fist pump. "Teamwork! With Mia coming in for the last five minutes of the game. Touchdown!"

Jake and Sam traded high fives, and Lucy crooned to the baby, telling her she already had her mommy and daddy wrapped around her little finger.

Mia smoothed the blanket over Lucy's legs. "Mother and baby are doing just fine. Beanie Girl is on the small side, but her color is excellent. No problems with the afterbirth either. With the history of placenta previa, I checked carefully."

"So we don't need the hospital?" Sam asked Mia.

"I don't think so.

Jake was glad to hear it. "That's good. The road won't be cleared for a while."

Mia turned to him with a sheen in her eyes. "Congratulations on your first delivery, Dr. Tanner."

He shared a poignant look with her, then flashed a smile at Lucy and Sam. "I'm honored to have been here. But for the record, I hope I never have to do it again."

"Same here!" Lucy kissed the baby's head. "Well, at least not at home."

Mia kept her attention on Jake. "But it was glorious too. Wasn't it?"

"Yes. Very much so." From Connie's death to Beanie Girl's birth, Jake had come full circle and found peace. But that circle would be a hollow place to live without Mia in the center of it. He aimed his chin at the door, raising his brows to ask if she was ready to talk.

She nodded, then spoke to Lucy and Sam. "Jake and I are going to leave the three of you alone, but before we go, I want to know my niece's name."

Lucy held the baby out to present her. "Mia, Jake, meet your brand-new niece—Merri Constance Waters. That's 'Merri' spelled M-e-r-r-i, because it's cute and it fits her."

Mia caressed Merri's pink cheek with her knuckle. "It's perfect."

Jake couldn't have agreed more. There was no doubt in his mind—Connie was smiling in heaven.

Mia kissed Lucy on the cheek, patted Sam on the arm, blew a kiss to Merri, then headed for the door. Jake congratulated Sam again and followed her.

●●●

Lucy gazed at her daughter's scrunched little face, then glanced up at her husband. "She has your nose."

Sam craned his neck for a better look. "Sorry, Pudge, but if you ask me, she looks like a little old man."

"Sam! You're supposed to say she's as beautiful as her mother."

"She is. And right now, you're the most beautiful woman in the world. And the bravest. I can't believe this happened. I should have been here for you."

"I missed you terribly," Lucy admitted. "When my water broke, I didn't think I could do this. But God saw me through it."

"He helped us both."

A weight floated off her shoulders. "I've been worried about being a good wife to you."

"Are you serious? Lucy, you're the best person I know. You're funny and kind. Generous too. And so full of life. You're sexy and—and you're mine. I love you."

"I love you too. But until now, that didn't seem like enough."

"*Not enough?* Lucy—"

"Wait. I need to finish." She snuggled Merri even closer. "Someday you'll deploy, and I hate the thought of being alone. I'm not strong like you are. But today, when I needed you and you weren't here, I had to lean on God for myself. I might always be a little afraid, and not very good at folding your socks or remembering things, but I'm sure of this—God loves me and He won't leave me."

"No. He won't." Sam swallowed hard. "I will always try my best, Luce. But I'm human. In case you hadn't noticed, I tend to bark orders now and then."

Lucy laughed. "Just now and then?"

"Maybe a *little* more than that." He kissed her tenderly on the lips. "I'm not perfect, Luce. But God is. He loves us even more than we love each other. And that's a lot."

"Yes."

"I love you, Pudge."

Lucy wrinkled her nose. "Give me a few months, and I won't be pudgy anymore. You'll have to find a new nickname."

"Forget it. I'm sticking with Pudge."

She rolled her eyes. "I love you, Soldier Boy."

"I love you too," he said again.

Cheek to cheek, they took in their daughter's round face and the fringe of dark hair under her pink cap.

Naked and needy, Merri Constance gave a hungry cry—a need Lucy was uniquely equipped to meet as surely as God was able to meet the needs of her own human heart. With love for her family overflowing, she offered her breast to her baby the way Mia had showed her earlier. Merri searched blindly, her mouth opening and closing like a baby bird, until Lucy stroked her cheek to guide her and she latched on. Grateful and at peace, Lucy nursed her daughter for the first time.

●●●

The minute Mia was alone with Jake in the hall, she turned to him. She yearned to declare that she loved him, but the break he'd taken upstairs seemed to have hardened his emotions. The stony set of his jaw knocked her off balance, but she was utterly certain of her decision to come home.

"Did I surprise you?" she asked.

"Completely." Instead of looping his arm around her waist, he shoved his hands in his pockets. "Let's talk in the living room."

She led the way to the sofa and sat. Pirate, snoozing on the far end, jumped down and went to Jake, nosing his leg until Jake gave him a scratch. Content, the dog returned to the couch and curled up next to Mia. The big room was chilly to the point of being cold, and gloomy because of the pewter sky. Jake lit the kindling already laid in the hearth. The newspaper erupted into flames, and the scrap lumber sizzled with it.

Mia watched his every move, stroking Pirate as Jake added a split of pine, then poked at the fire. Finally he stood tall and faced her. In spite of the magnet-like pull in her belly, she remained on the couch.

He cleared his throat. "You're back early."

"I am."

He didn't move a muscle, not even a twitch. "Why? What happened?"

You . . . Us . . . The explanation she had prepared on the flight home fizzled on her tongue. "I don't know where to start, except to say I was an idiot for leaving in the first place." *Tell me I'm not an idiot for coming back.*

Jake rubbed the back of his neck. "Yeah, that coin toss was kind of brutal."

"And stupid. But it worked in a backwards sort of way."

"How?"

She told him about Dr. Benton and the phone game. "When I tried to explain the picture of the quarter, I couldn't stop talking about you. Every person in that room saw how I felt—and knew where I belonged. But I have to be honest, Jake. Even then, I hesitated."

"I'm not surprised. You were pretty ambivalent about the whole decision—about us."

"Not exactly."

His eyes narrowed, maybe with suspicion or doubt. "I don't understand."

"I've never been confused about my feelings for you. But I was terribly confused about what it means to trust God. Somehow I got it in my head that if I did everything right, bad things wouldn't happen. But that's not trusting Him, is it?"

"No." His voice whispered over the crackle of the fire.

"Life will always have good times and hard ones. Birth and death. Laughter and tears. Trust means something different to me now. It's not about avoiding the hard times. It's about going through them with God's grace and the help of other people." *With a husband like you.*

He merely nodded. "I understand what you're saying. Life takes some sharp turns."

"Camp Connie?"

"And the death of it."

Mia's brows shot up. She had forgotten about Bill Hatcher and the backhoe. "Something happened, didn't it?"

His face softened into an ironic smile. "When Lucy went into labor, Plan A was to get her to the hospital. But I couldn't—not without help. So I made a deal with Bill. If he'd clear the road, I'd pull the plug on Camp Connie."

Mia searched his face, her heart breaking for him. "You worked so hard. The camp was your dream."

"Not anymore." He shifted his weight from one foot to the other but stayed by the fire, either to warm himself or to avoid her. "Frankly, I'm more relieved than disappointed. Being the bad guy didn't sit well with me."

"No. It wouldn't." Not at all. Jake had the heart of a hero. He loved her with that same unselfish courage, and she had treated him badly. "I'm so sorry for leaving like I did. I shouldn't have—"

"Mia, wait." He held up one hand, either pushing her away or absolving her of guilt. "Camp Connie wasn't meant to be. I can see that now, and I'm at peace. You're not the only person who chased a good dream and gave it up for something better. We're a lot alike in that way."

"Yes, we are."

She had made this mess, and it was up to her to scale the last few feet of the wall between them. Determined to go forward and not back—to look up to God and not down at her fears—she crossed the room in confident strides. Jake turned to face her, putting the heat of the fire on one side of their bodies and the cool air on the other. Mia rested her hands on his chest. The fire burned hot and bright, filling the room with air as warm as breath.

When she spoke, the words came out with utter certainty. "You asked earlier what changed my mind. It wasn't just what happened in Dallas."

"No?"

"*You* changed my mind—the strong, good man that you are. I love you, Jake. And I don't need to toss a coin to know that I belong here—with you."

His pupils flared, but he didn't say a thing.

Her fingers, still resting on his chest, curled into her palms so tightly that her nails dug into her flesh. Doubts assailed her, but she raised her chin. "I'm yours, Jake. Only yours. That is, if you still want me."

At last he cupped her face, his palms warm against her cheeks, then stared into her eyes so long that time seemed to stop. "I want you, Mia. Don't doubt it for an instant. I want every part of you—the bossy part and the funny part. The woman who's always prepared, and the one who's afraid to be late. I want the woman God made you to be."

"Oh, Jake. I love you so much."

"I love you too," he murmured. "But I have one more question to ask."

"Anything . . . Anything at all."

"Don't say *yes* unless you're certain, because this is the most important question a man can ask a woman."

He paused, giving her time to think.

When she realized—hoped—what the question would be, she didn't need even a second to know her mind. "Ask me," she whispered, trembling now. "Please."

Stepping back, he lowered his hands to his sides. The fire crackled and snapped. A log hissed in a languid sigh. Snow fluttered against the tall windows, painting a lace curtain as private and exquisite as their love. Jake took her hand in his and waited just long enough for Mia to etch his face in her mind—the glint in his green eyes, his lean cheeks and straight nose, the set of his jaw as he dropped to one knee.

"I love you, Mia. To the best of my ability, I promise to honor, respect, and treasure you forever. Will you marry me?"

"Yes!" She had never been more sure of anything in her life. "Yes! Yes! Yes!" She couldn't say it enough. "Yes!"

Some surprises were good, and some were spectacular. Others were blessed, even sacred. With tears of joy spilling down her cheeks, Mia swayed fully into Jake's arms and raised her face to his. Slowly, with his eyes burning bright, he brought his mouth down to hers. Time stopped. All her questions ceased to matter. She couldn't think at all as Jake's kiss smoldered and burned, crackled and popped, and melted her into a very happy puddle.

Epilogue

Nine Years Later . . .

In keeping with the tradition started by Lucy, the Tanner family celebrated milestone birthdays with an upside-down party and a surprise of some kind. Frank was turning eighty, and Jake and Mia were determined to give him the best party ever. Streamers, piñatas, and party games filled the old pinball barn, along with family and friends, including Jake's siblings and their kids.

Best of all, in Jake's opinion, he and Mia had a big surprise for Grandpa Frank. Mia was pregnant again. No one else knew, not even Lucy.

The party had been going strong for a couple hours. The games had been played and prizes awarded to the winners; the food was eaten; and now it was time for Frank to open the gifts stacked on a table.

Jake and Mia approached the pile of bags and boxes with Gracie, his new hearing dog, trotting at his side. Pirate had crossed the rainbow bridge a few years ago, with Jake holding his friend's head in his lap. No dog could ever replace Pirate, but Gracie was sweet and terrific with the kids.

Frank, seated in the recliner Jake and Sam had carried out from the house, was telling knock-knock jokes to his grandkids while he stroked Peggy McFuzz. At the age of fourteen, she was an old lady and Frank's best friend.

Everyone missed Claire, of course. Three years after moving to Westridge, she had passed away peacefully in her sleep. In spite of Jake and Mia begging Frank to live with them, he had decided to stay at Westridge in the independent living section. He liked being close to restaurants and doctors, and he had made friends there, older folks who shared his interests.

Jake admired his dad tremendously. As a father himself now, he had a new perspective on balancing family and career. When Frank sold the vending business, Jake had gone back to college for a teaching credential. Now he taught history and government at the Echo Falls high school, and he often told the story of Camp Connie. It always made for a good debate. He loved his work, mostly because teaching gave him a chance to encourage hundreds of kids instead of just a few.

He and Mia also owned Echo Falls Primary Care, where she worked part-time. Another nurse practitioner shared the load, and Kelsey—now married—still managed the front office.

Life was good, and it was about to get even better.

Jake slipped an arm around Mia's waist. "Are you ready for this?" She was only ten weeks along, but her middle already felt thicker to him.

"More than ready." She squeezed him back. "Though I have to wonder if Dad will be as surprised as you were."

"Not even close." The memory of Mia coming out of the bathroom, her mouth hanging open and the pregnancy test stick in hand, still made him grin. "You shocked the daylights out of me that morning."

She gave him that sexy smile he loved, then stole a kiss. They'd been perfectly happy with their two sons. Caleb was eight and the spitting image of Jake. Justin was six, and so named because Jake had gotten Mia to the hospital "just in time" for the birth.

Grinning, he skimmed the crowd. His brother and sister and their spouses were enjoying a stack of photo albums. Next Jake spotted Merri Constance bossing around her three siblings. Merri, Sam Jr., Poppi, and Elsa were stair-step kids, each one a little smaller than the older sibling. The family had just returned from the US Army base in Wiesbaden, Germany, and were enjoying six weeks' leave.

Jake and Mia took turns handing gifts to Frank, saving theirs for last. He opened all sorts of fun things before Jake picked up the box from Mia, the boys, and himself. "It's the last one, Dad. Any guesses?"

Playing to the crowd, Frank tapped a finger on his chin. "Hmmm. Is it bowling ball?"

Three-year-old Elsa laughed and clapped her hands.

"I know," Caleb called out. "It's a basketball!"

"It is not!" Justin argued. "It's a—a truck!"

Jake and Mia traded an eye-roll. Sibling rivalry ran strong between the boys.

When Frank gave Jake a wise smile, Jake handed him the box. Showing off again, Frank shook it, raised it to his ear and listened, weighed it in both hands, and hemmed and hawed until Merri bounced to her feet like her mother. "Open it, Grandpa!"

Mia stepped to Jake's side and looped an arm around his waist. Frank popped the ribbons with his pocketknife, reached inside, and lifted out a stuffed hen like the one Jake had given Mia in Las Vegas.

"It's a chicken." Frank held it high, then examined the hand-lettered tag around the hen's neck. "It's named Mia. We used to put these in those claw machine games. But wait—there's more."

He pulled out a rooster with a tag that said *Jake*, then two smaller roosters named Caleb and Justin, and finally a tiny yellow chick sporting a frilly tag with the words *Baby No. 3.*

A wide grin stretched across Frank's wrinkled face. "I'm going to be a grandpa again!"

Applause and shouts erupted from the crowd, and Frank, Jake, and Mia all hugged. Mia whispered to Frank that if the baby was a girl, they wanted to name her Claire.

Jake broke away to trade high fives with his sons, who for once agreed they wanted a brother and not a bratty little sister. When Caleb and Justin scrambled away, Sam shook Jake's hand and razzed him about having a daughter for a change. While friends and family clapped him on the back, he sought Mia's gaze and found her hugging Lucy hard, the way they always did.

When the women eased back, Jake walked over to Mia. She stepped into his arms and hugged him even harder than she had hugged her sister. "Do you know how much I love you?"

"A lot?" he said, teasing her.

"Good work, detective."

He kissed her then, lightly but with the promise of all the years to come. Thankfulness flooded through him. *Lord, who am I to deserve this joy?* Jake was no one special—an average man who worked hard to make the world a better place. A father who tried his best. A husband with a wife far better than he deserved. And yet here he was—blessed beyond all human logic.

With Mia in his arms and their sons doing battle at the Clown Car game, he rejoiced in the greatest blessings in his life—the love of God, the promise of heaven, and the family he would always call his own.

Dear Readers,

As I write this letter, my father-in-law is in the end stages of Alzheimer's disease. Al Scheibel has been in my life for thirty-six years now. I remember him before the ravages of Alzheimer's, when he loved to sail to Catalina Island, smoke cigars, and tell stories like the "Foot-Foot" joke. When I see him now, I almost don't recognize him. And yet he's still Grandpa Al to my kids; Dad to my husband, me, and his daughters; and simply Al to his wife of many years.

Alzheimer's is a wretched disease. There's no cure. No letup from the pressure of it. No escaping the inevitable. At the same time, it has brought out a depth of love in our family that is remarkable. That great love inspired the character of Claire in *The Two of Us*.

My sisters-in-law are both inspirations. Peggy, a former preschool administrator, went back to school to become an RN specializing in dementia and geriatric care. When Dad was in the middle stages of the disease, she pulled on her preschool experience to create activities for him. The birdhouses Lucy and Mia make with Claire were inspired by one of Peggy's crafts for Dad. Coloring, photo albums, and labeling things were all based on real experience.

My sister-in-law Patti gets a gold medal for taking Dad on outings, bringing him treats, hugging him, protecting him, and loving him no matter what. Her patience is epic. So is her good humor. Embarrassing things happen when a person has

Alzheimer's. Some people would pull away, but Patti just moves closer and loves him more.

Kathy Neal is a close family friend and a technowizard. When Big Al messed up the remote and TV like Claire does, Kathy was the go-to person to fix it. Trust me, that happened a lot. She's part of the family and heard all of Big Al's jokes at least ninety times—Foot-Foot, the dog story, too many to name here.

My husband, Mike, is the prayer warrior in the group. Even if Dad doesn't understand the words, he feels the love in those prayers. He hears the Bible verses Mike reads to him, and he nods. YouTube is a great resource for old hymns for an old man. It's also great for videos of airplanes taking off and sailboats skimming the Pacific, both things my father-in-law loved. He spent his career as an engineer at Lockheed, designing aircraft and being part of the Lockheed Sailing Club. When he sees those videos, he smiles.

But he smiles most for Dorothy, his wife of close to sixty years, my mother-in-law, and a woman I greatly admire. Love shines in his eyes when she visits him, and I have to believe that somehow, somewhere deep in the recesses of the human soul, love trumps this awful disease.

If someone in your life is battling Alzheimer's, I pray you find peace. It's a rough road, but let's not forgot the main thing. We have the promise of eternity where there's no disease, no memory loss, no suffering. Like the old hymn says, "When we all get to heaven, what a day of rejoicing it will be."

Until then, let's love like we're loved by God—unconditionally, with mercy and unending grace.

All the best,
Victoria Bylin

RIP Alan F. Scheibel, August 18,1928—September 2, 2016

Victoria Bylin is a romance writer known for her realistic and relatable characters. Her books have been finalists in multiple contests, including the Carol Awards, the RITAs, and *RT Magazine*'s Reviewers' Choice Award. A native of California, she and her husband now make their home in Lexington, Kentucky, where their family and their crazy Jack Russell terrier keep them on the go. Learn more at her website: www.victoriabylin.com.

Sign Up for Victoria's Newsletter!

Keep up to date with news on Victoria's upcoming book releases and events by signing up for her email list at victoriabylin.com.

More from Victoria Bylin

When a wedding-planning gig brings single mom Julia Dare to the Caliente Springs resort, she learns that her college sweetheart, Zeke Monroe, is the manager. As they work together on the event, Zeke and Julia are pushed to their limits both personally and professionally.

Someone Like You

You May Also Like . . .

Genealogist Nora Bradford has decided that focusing on her work is far safer than romance. But when a former Navy Seal hires her to find his birth mother, their connection is undeniable. The trouble is that they seem to have met the right person at the worst possible time.

True to You by Becky Wade
A Bradford Sisters Romance
beckywade.com

On a visit home to Maple Valley, Iowa, political speechwriter Logan Walker meets intriguing reporter Amelia Bentley. She wants his help on a story, and he wants to get to know her better. Their attraction is mutual, but what will happen when he tells her the real reason he's returned?

Like Never Before by Melissa Tagg
melissatagg.com

Love isn't always a fairy tale, and it doesn't always go as planned. Sometimes the best stories, though, are the ones that are the most unexpected. This novella collection includes stories that celebrate the power of love to triumph . . . even when circumstances go awry!

With This Ring? A Novella Collection of Proposals Gone Awry by Karen Witemeyer, Mary Connealy, Regina Jennings, and Melissa Jagears